COVENANT

Also by Brandon Massey

Novels
Thunderland
Dark Corner
Within the Shadows
The Other Brother
Vicious
Don't Ever Tell
Cornered

Collections
Twisted Tales

Anthologies
Dark Dreams
Voices from the Other Side: Dark Dreams II
Whispers in the Night: Dark Dreams III
The Ancestors (with Tananarive Due and L.A. Banks)

COVENANT

BRANDON MASSEY

Dark Corner Publishing
Atlanta, Georgia

"A life is not worth living until you have something to die for."

-- Dr. Martin Luther King, Jr.

The crack of a hunter's rifle echoed across the lake, distant and brief.

Untroubled by the sound, a familiar noise in these parts, Anthony Thorne tilted his face to the clear Georgia sky and let the morning sunrays caress his skin. Beneath him, their aluminum bass boat bobbed on the tranquil silver waters of Lake Allatoona. It was June, a week after school had let out for summer vacation, and there was no better place to be in the whole world than out fishing with his father.

Seated across from him, his father sipped coffee from a steel thermos. He was a slender man with a mocha complexion, salt-and-pepper mustache, and wire rim glasses, dressed that morning in a Georgia Tech baseball cap, checkered shirt, and khakis. A silver Seiko sports watch encircled his wrist, band glinting in the sunshine.

His father's gaze rested on the tip of his rod suspended above the water, but his eyes were unfocused, as if he were deep in thought.

It puzzled Anthony. During the drive there, his father had been quiet, too. Dad had never been especially talkative, but this brooding silence, broken only by the occasional terse comment or grunt, was weird even for him.

High above, a falcon silhouetted against the sky circled the lake. A flock of ducks cruised the waters, oblivious to the watching predator.

Anthony adjusted his fishing rod, the handle of which rested inside a slot alongside the boat. A tackle box sat in a side compartment, full of lures and fresh bait. He and his dad had been fishing together regularly since Anthony was ten, and the feel of the boat, and the sights, sounds, and smells of the lake, had become as familiar to him as his own neighborhood.

The only thing that wasn't normal was his Dad's mood.

"Nice out here today," Anthony said, to break the silence.

Dad glanced at him, gaze muddy. "What was that, Junior?"

"I said, it's nice out here today. A good day for fishing."

Dad grunted. "We haven't caught anything yet."

"I'm gonna catch me a big bass. How much you wanna bet?"

Dad didn't respond. He had retreated into that strange silence again.

Anthony wondered if Dad was upset with him over something, though that didn't really seem likely. His report card had been excellent—he'd wrapped up his sophomore year with a 3.4 GPA, and had lettered in three sports. Unlike some of his friends, he hadn't gotten into any kind of trouble, and he'd been doing all of his household chores, without being nagged by either of his folks.

Anyway, on those rare times when Dad had an issue with something he'd done, he came right out and presented the problem up front with Anthony, expressed his thoughts in clear terms, and then moved on. He didn't hold it in like he was holding in this thing, whatever it was.

Maybe he'd gotten into a big argument with Mom. But on second thought, that seemed just as unlikely. His parents got along pretty well—Anthony couldn't remember the last time he'd heard them raise their voices at each another, and when they went out in public together, as a family, his parents always held hands, like a couple of infatuated teenagers.

Something with his younger sister? Again, not likely. His sister spent all her time on the phone with her giggly girlfriends, and besides, she was a true Daddy's girl, practically broke into tears if Dad so much as gave her a stern look.

The last possibility he could figure was Dad's job. He was a sports writer for a big Atlanta newspaper, loved his work for all Anthony knew, and why not? Thanks to Dad, he'd met several of his favorite pro basketball and football players and had a roomful of autographed jerseys, trading cards, and balls. He loved writing and had actually decided that he wanted to be a sports journalist, too, and often fantasized about working side-by-side with his father in the newsroom, or maybe writing a column together.

Job problems didn't make much sense, so Anthony had decided to go ahead and ask Dad what was on his mind, get it right out in the open the way Dad liked to do with him—when suddenly the falcon circling overhead banked, dipped, and swooped to the lake's surface. The ducks took flight with a frenzy of squawking and batting wings, but the falcon easily overtook one of them, seizing the unlucky bird in its powerful talons and spiriting it away into the treetops.

Anthony glanced at his father. Dad had followed the falcon's hunt, too.

"Better than watching *Wild Kingdom*, huh, Junior?" Dad smiled for the first time all morning.

Anthony felt a loosening in his chest, like a stone rolling away from his heart. "Yeah. I wouldn't want to be that duck."

"I wouldn't mind being that falcon. Duck tastes pretty good if you cook it right."

"You've eaten duck?"

Dad nodded. "Duck, rabbit, squirrel, squid, snake."

"Snake? Dad, that's gross."

"I had it in China when I was there covering a story on their national basketball team. A buddy of mine dared me to try it, so you know I had to take him up on it."

"What'd it taste like?"

"Like chicken. A little beefier, though."

"Nasty." Anthony laughed. "You have more guts than I do. I wouldn't have touched that stuff."

"If someone had dared you, you would have. You're like me. You've got that I'll Show You gene."

"What's the I'll Show You gene?" Anthony asked.

"If someone says you won't or can't do something, then you have to prove them wrong. Remember when Coach Tripp said you weren't good enough to start?"

Anthony remembered. Basketball squad, freshman year. Coach Tripp had put Anthony on second string, and when Anthony had asked why, the coach had flatly stated he wasn't good enough to start. Determined to prove him wrong, Anthony had put in long, grueling extra hours of practice, and by the third game of the season, the coach had promoted him to a starting spot at forward.

Anthony shrugged. "I guess I like challenges."

"Your entire life, Junior, people are going to challenge you." A shadow passed over his father's eyes, and for the moment, that sense of his dad being submerged in troubling thoughts was back, though he continued to talk: "They'll draw a line in front of you and warn you not to cross it. They'll threaten you with dire consequences if you do. Most of the time, they're hollow threats. Other times, though, they're serious about keeping their promise to make things tough for you if you cross the line."

"So do you cross it anyway?"

Dad stared at him. His gaze was so intense, so *furious*, that Anthony felt something inside him shrink, and he abruptly decided that he didn't want to know what could make his father that angry.

"If the line is worth crossing—yes," Dad said, iron in his voice. "You've gotta have the good sense to know the difference between doing it for pride, and doing it because it's the right thing to do."

13

"Always do the right thing," Anthony said automatically. It was one of his dad's favorite sayings.

"Good to know you've been listening during these father-son chats of ours." Dad smiled, eyes brightening once more. He nodded toward Anthony's rod. "Hey, check it out. I think you got something there."

A fish tugged at the line. The lake was full of cod, perch, and bass, some of them quite large, and this one was pulling so forcefully that it might be a big one.

Grabbing hold of the spinning reel, Anthony stood. He lifted the tip of the rod, turned the handle of his reel.

The fish jerked at the bait, yanking him forward. Anthony nearly lost his balance, but his father placed a steadying hand on his arm.

"Easy now, son. Draw it in, nice and slow."

"I think it's a huge one."

"You can handle it." His father prepared the landing net, as if Anthony catching the fish was a foregone conclusion.

Heart knocking, Anthony wound the reel. The fish fought him with each turn, but Anthony dug his feet in, and kept spinning.

"There you go, Junior. You've got it, keep it coming."

With a triumphant yell, Anthony tore the fish out of the water. The fish flailed on the line, a gorgeous largemouth bass, gleaming like quicksilver in the sunshine.

"Whoa!" Anthony shouted. "Look at him!"

"Hell, looks like it might be a ten-pounder." Dad rubbed his hands together. "Bring him home."

Anthony swung the rod around and lowered his catch into the awaiting net. Dad looked up from the flopping fish, grinned.

"Guess what we'll be eating tonight?"

"Not snake," Anthony said.

Laughing, Dad slapped him five. He bent to the net to attend to the fish.

The crack of a rifle shattered the morning, much louder than the distant gunfire he'd heard a few minutes ago.

Although he and his father didn't hunt, Anthony had heard rifles discharge many times during their fishing trips, had seen the hunters in their blaze orange vests and hats entering the woods to stalk deer and quail. Hunters were supposed to keep to the northern side of the lake, but this shot sounded as if it had come from nearby, behind them.

Turning, Anthony looked to the shore.

14

A couple of hundred yards away, a figure raced away from the banks and into the forest. The person didn't wear the orange vest of a licensed hunter. He wore dark clothing and moved like a fleeting shadow through the pine trees.

Knowing instinctively there was something wrong about what he was seeing, Anthony felt his insides seize up with cold dread.

Dad gasped. "Junior . . ."

Anthony spun. Dad had dropped into his seat. Bright blood soaked the front of his shirt.

Anthony couldn't breathe. Couldn't move. Couldn't think.

His father's eyes rolled. He clutched at his chest, where there was so much blood, oh God, more blood than Anthony had ever seen in his life.

Although his father's glasses hung askew on his face, his gaze fastened firmly on Anthony, lips quivering.

"I love you . . . and . . . your sister, your mom . . . . tell them . . . . I'm sorry . . . ."

He spilled forward and hit the floor of the boat, body as lifeless as the fish in the net.

Soon after, a boy's scream echoed across the lake.

Part One

The Ghosts of the Past

1

Fifteen years later

Anthony was running late. He was supposed to meet his wife for lunch at noon, and as usual, Atlanta traffic was uncooperative. It was five minutes to twelve, and though he was only a mile away from the restaurant in Midtown, traffic looked as if it would turn the rest of his drive into a frustrating, half-hour ordeal.

He brought his Chevy Tahoe to a stop at a red light. The day was far from over, but it had already proven to be as awful as he'd expected.

The anniversary of his dad's death always was.

The searing June sunshine bounced off the windshields of oncoming cars, boring like laser rays into his brain and intensifying the dull headache that had dogged him all day. He slid on a pair of sunglasses, but the headache remained.

Located between downtown on the south and Buckhead on the north, Midtown was a bustling district of high-rise condos, trendy restaurants and boutiques, corporate headquarters, art venues, and lately, it seemed, endless construction projects. Ahead, Peachtree Street narrowed to one miserable northbound lane, while construction crews on break gabbed on cell phones and gawked at women strolling past in short skirts.

He was looking forward to lunch with Lisa, but he wondered if he should have stayed in and saved himself some aggravation. Although moping around at home, chest tight with emotion he couldn't eradicate, probably wouldn't have been much better. Lisa, well aware of how he tended to brood around this time of year, had lured him out of the house to try to cheer him up—but what she failed to accept was that nothing would truly cheer him up on that day.

The light switched to green. He inched through the intersection, saw a side street ahead, and swung a sharp left at the corner. The road was empty of traffic and intersected West Peachtree, which paralleled Peachtree Street for a good distance, far enough to carry him to his destination.

Problem solved.

Five minutes past noon, he pulled into an asphalt parking lot across the street from the restaurant. He hurried inside, smoothing down his rumpled button-down shirt and cargo shorts, absently twisting the band of his father's silver Seiko.

Gordon Biersch was a brewpub that created micro-brews on the premises. It had a sort of Industrial décor: high ceilings, hardwood floors, leather booths, and a large, polished wood bar. The beer was brewed in giant steel tanks partly visible through windows near the back of the building.

The place was packed with the business lunch crowd: fresh-faced college grads in Polo shirts and khakis or bright blouses and skirts, Blackberries clipped to their waists and company-issued ID badges dangling around their necks from lanyards. The youngish wait staff, attired in black, moved about with calm efficiency, balancing pints of beer on trays.

Anthony spotted Lisa waving at him from a booth on the far side of the dining room. She rose to meet him and clutched him in a tight embrace.

"Sorry I'm a little late." He kissed her on the cheek. "The usual traffic issues."

"Gotta love the ATL, baby."

Lisa wore a tan, double-breasted pantsuit, and black pumps. Elegant diamond studs twinkled in her ears, and a small gold cross dangled around her neck. Her dark brown hair was styled in a cute bob that framed her fine-boned sienna face and accentuated her cinnamon eyes.

Whenever Anthony looked at his wife, his heart rate kicked up a notch. Of course, she was fine—with her tight dancer's body, baby-smooth complexion, soft full lips, and big eyes a man could lose himself in, she demanded attention wherever she went. When their paths had crossed four years ago at a Memorial Day cookout hosted by a mutual friend, he had to admit that his initial, intoxicating attraction to her had been purely physical. Within five minutes of talking to her, however, he realized she was much, much more than just a pretty face and knockout figure.

He'd been doing his own thing, recently discharged from the Marine Corps, high on a lucrative book deal and planning to enjoy his status as an eligible bachelor, but meeting Lisa changed everything. A year and a half after they met, they married. Three years into matrimony, he could honestly say, much to the chagrin of his single buddies, that every moment he spent with her was the best part of his day.

Especially on a day such as that one.

Lisa sipped her iced tea. "How're things going?"

"I haven't written a word all morning, I forgot to shave, and I've got a killer headache. But I'm glad to see you."

She reached across the table and took his hand. Her touch was warm.

"If you want, I can leave the office early," she said. Her voice lowered, and a seductive glint came into her eyes. "Keep you company . . . and make wild, passionate love to you."

"Now that's a tempting offer."

"But?"

"After lunch I was planning to visit the gravesite."

"Of course." She squeezed his hand. "Want me to come with?"

"You don't want to come, Lisa. I'll be in an even worse mood than I'm in now."

The waiter stopped by the table. He was a tall twenty-something with reddish hair and wrists as thin as bamboo sticks. Anthony knew instantly from the man's effeminate demeanor that he had a dash of sugar in his tank, as his mother would have called it; Midtown was known for its large population of gays and lesbians.

Anthony ordered a pint of dunkles, one of the house lagers. Lisa regarded him with a cocked eyebrow.

He shrugged. "What the hell, I'm off the clock for the rest of the day."

"You've still got plenty of time to finish the book. It's due when? November?"

"End of October."

"I'm looking forward to reading it."

He grunted. "I'm looking forward to finishing it."

His work-in-progress was his fifth novel, the latest installment in a crime series. He had been writing crime stories since he was fifteen, and with the exception of poems, reports, and essays for high school English classes, had never written anything else. Although he'd once entertained fantasies of becoming a sports writer like his dad, the prospect of chronicling athletes paid outrageous sums of money to play games was about as appealing to him as working as a clown in a traveling circus.

Crime writing was different. Although fiction, it was relevant to him in a way that sports journalism would never be, more relevant to him than his readers—and there were, surprisingly, legions of them—would ever realize.

The waiter delivered his beer. Anthony took a sip of the light, smooth brew and requested a minute to skim the menu.

"Have you talked to Danielle today?" Lisa asked.

"I called her cell and left a message. She hasn't called me back. Big surprise."

"Right." Lisa rolled her eyes. "Are you going to visit the site without her then?"

"Looks like it." He dropped the menu on the table. "Anyway, let's talk about something else. How's your day been doing?"

"My day's been great so far. I could tell you about the intellectual property rights contract I drew up on this morning, but that would bore you to tears."

Lisa worked as general counsel at a technology consulting company in Buckhead, writing contracts and handling other legal matters. When she'd graduated from Emory law school several years ago, she'd joined one of Atlanta's top firms as an associate, but had tired of seventy-hour work weeks and the all-consuming need to generate billable hours. Being general counsel position offered her a chance to work an eight-hour-day, without the stresses of a pressure-cooker law firm environment.

"But I've got some good news," she said.

"I could use some of that. They're giving you a raise?"

"Nope. Lauren's pregnant!"

Lisa was the eldest of three sisters. Lauren was the middle girl. She and her husband had been trying to start a family for a while.

He knew where this conversation was headed, but he said only, "Really? Wow, that's great news. You're going to be an auntie. Congrats."

"It's exciting." She folded her arms on the table, leaned in closer. "Being an auntie will be fun, but I'd love to be a mother."

22

"I'd love to order lunch." He made an exaggerated display of studying the menu. "I think I'm going to order a burger. How about you?"

"Ha, ha, you're such a comedian. I didn't know I'd married Eddie Murphy."

"You didn't. Eddie Murphy has kids—lots of them. I don't want any kids."

"Come on, you would make such beautiful babies. I bet they'd have your eyes, your honey-brown complexion, your cute dimples."

"My brooding demeanor."

"You aren't a brooder. You talk to me."

"My cynicism."

She smiled a little. "Well . . . ."

The waiter returned. Anthony asked for the mushroom Swiss burger and garlic fries, and Lisa ordered a chicken Caesar salad.

After the server departed, Lisa turned a questioning look on him. Inwardly, he groaned. She wasn't ready to let this go yet.

He said, "All right, listen, when we first started dating, what did I say when you asked me if I wanted to have kids? Didn't I say I don't want kids?"

"That was four years ago, Tony, and we weren't married then."

"I'm supposed to have changed my mind since we've been married?"

"You should consider it."

"You're something else." He shook his head. "Why do women always think they can change a man?"

"Because men hardly ever know what they want. You need a woman to clarify things."

She was smiling, and she was so lovely that he had to smile, too. They'd probably had this same conversation a thousand times, with neither of them giving in, and though they always kept the tone humorous, he knew she was absolutely determined to change his mind.

What she needed to accept was that he had inherited his dad's I'll Show You gene—in this case, showing her that she could not, and would not, change his stance, and if that he some day decided he wanted to be a father, it would be because *he* had reached that decision on his own, not because she had worn him down.

But when Lisa wanted something, she could be like a force of Nature, and there was nothing she wanted more than children. In her mind, that was what couples did: they met, married, had children, and lived happily ever after. She was the product of a two-parent household, one of those families so harmonious it seemed surreal, and though her ignorance of what a dysfunctional family was like sometimes frustrated him, he knew that the stable home from which she came was part of what had drawn him to her. She helped him remember how things had used to be in his own life.

"I've learned to never say never," he said. "But honestly, what's the rush? We should just enjoy each other, do some more traveling. I'm only thirty, you're only thirty-two."

"Only thirty-two? My eggs have an expiration date on them, baby, and it's not too far off."

"I read a story on the Web the other day about a sixty-year-old woman who gave birth—to triplets."

"Please. I don't want to be carrying a child at sixty, and you sure as hell don't want to be a first-time father at fifty-eight."

He laughed. "With my back? I know that's right."

"All jokes aside, we need to think about it, Tony."

"Can we have this conversation some other time?"

"Okay, but we *will* have it."

And I'll say the same thing, he thought.

For the rest of lunch, they talked about office gossip, publishing industry rumors, family drama, and possible weekend plans. After he paid the bill, he walked her to her car, a white BMW 5-series sedan.

"I'll see you this evening, sweet stuff." She slipped into his arms and brazenly palmed his butt. "We've got married folks' business to attend to tonight."

"Wouldn't miss it for the world." He kissed the tip of her nose.

She swatted his rear end. "Call me if you need anything. I love you."

"Love you, too."

They kissed, and she got in her car and pulled out of the parking lot.

In her absence, he once again became aware of his headache. It had retreated during lunch, but as he stood there alone it came back in a furious rush, pounding behind his eyes.

He unlocked the door to the Tahoe. Pent-up waves of heat steamed out. He stepped back to allow the air to escape, and stopped when he noticed the steering wheel.

Someone had affixed an envelope to the center. The envelope was white, business size. His first and last name was typed on the front in black text.

What was this? Had someone been inside his car?

He looked around, saw no one suspicious, and leaned inside the truck. He peeled the envelope off the wheel. A dime-size wad of a gum had been used to apply it to the surface.

The envelope was sealed. He tore it open and found a tri-folded sheet of ordinary white copy paper.

The message had been typed:

> *Do you want to know what happened to your father?*
>
> *Read Psalm 37:32.*
>
> *To learn the truth, be online today @ 18:00.*
>
> *Until then,*
>
> *A Friend*
>
> *P.S. You must keep this secret. They are everywhere.*

2

Outside the SUV, the air around Anthony had turned as thick as syrup. It jelled in his lungs, made it difficult to breathe. He examined the letter again. Who had left this for him? Was this for real?

He looked back and forth across the parking lot, and to the street beyond, and saw nothing of interest. People were going about their business. No one paid attention to him.

And how had the letter-writer gotten into his truck? He always locked the doors.

He looked inside the truck again. An object dangled from the short beam that supported the rearview mirror: a canary-yellow fishing lure, crafted in the shape of a minnow.

It was the exact same kind that he and his father had used on their last fishing trip.

His knees turned rubbery. He slumped onto the driver's seat, dragged the door shut.

The heat inside was smothering. He inserted the key in the ignition—his hand trembled so badly it took four tries to fit it into the slot—and twisted. The engine rumbled, the air conditioner blasting into life.

He fumbled open the glove box and withdrew the Beretta M9 stored inside, and a magazine of ammo. He slammed the magazine into the pistol—it took an uncharacteristic two taps to get it into the well—racked the slide, and gripped the gun in his lap with both hands.

Better, that was better.

Angling the muzzle toward the floor, he surveyed the parking lot again. But again, no one was watching him. The messenger, whoever it was, was gone.

His galloping heartbeat finally slowed. He placed the gun in close reach on the passenger seat.

In his haste to arm himself, the letter had slid onto the floor. He picked it up.

Read Psalm 37:32.

Up until the time he was fifteen, his family had used to attend church every Sunday. He hadn't cracked open a Bible since those days, so not surprisingly, didn't have one on hand. But he had his iPhone. He unclipped the handheld from his belt holster and keyed in commands with his thumbs to access the Web browser.

He found a Web site that housed the entire text of the Old and New Testaments. He pulled up the book of Psalm, thirty-seventh chapter, and read the thirty-second verse on the small color display.

The wicked watcheth the righteous, and seeketh to slay him.

Something that felt like an electrical charge leaped through his heart.

"What the hell is this?" he said.

The wicked watcheth the righteous . . .

According to the cops, the high-velocity bullet that had torn into his father's heart, killing him in less than a minute, had been due to a hunting accident. Some Einstein stalking deer or quail had erroneously loosed a shot across the lake that happened to smack into his father's chest. No one had ever stepped forward to claim responsibility, and the case was summarily closed.

Anthony thought the hunting accident story was about as plausible as the idea that Tupac Shakur was still alive.

He remembered what he had seen: the shadowy figure running through the trees, like someone fleeing the scene of a crime. It hadn't been a hunter.

It had been a sniper.

Old grief surfaced in his throat like stomach acid, stung the back of his mouth. He swallowed thickly, wiped cold sweat away from his brow.

The police had dismissed his eyewitness account as the overheated imaginings of a shell-shocked kid; his testimony wasn't even included in the official record of the case. The investigation was concluded so quickly it was as if someone behind the scenes with a helluva lot of pull had engineered a swift resolution.

The wicked watcheth . . .

As farfetched as it seemed when remembering the ordinary, family-oriented man his father had been, Anthony believed that his dad was murdered because of something he knew, or had done. His dad had acted so damn strangely that morning, had been ruminating on some troubling matter that he wouldn't talk about, and Anthony clearly recalled his father's puzzling statement that, *"they're serious about keeping their promise to make things tough for you if you cross the line . . ."*

Who had Dad been talking about? What line had he crossed?

Questioning his mom about what Dad might have meant hadn't helped at all. Blitzed with grief, she'd forever refused to talk about Dad's death.

He read the note again. As much as he wanted to believe that this person could lead him to the truth, experience suggested that this letter could be a hoax.

That past March, Anthony had been featured in a piece in *The New York Times* about bestselling crime novelists. The writer of the article had dug into Anthony's background, learned of his father's death, and asked him about it. Anthony had unloaded on him, frankly expressing his doubts in the hunting accident story and declaring that, some day, he would see to it that the guilty party would be brought to justice.

In the days after the story ran, he was deluged him with dozens of e-mails from people claiming to have knowledge of the case. A couple of crackpots even confessed to the killing and begged for his forgiveness.

On the advice of his attorney, he forwarded the messages to a private investigator. The investigator conducted research, and discovered that none of the claims and tips was valid. Not one.

This letter might be just another waste of time. The initial flood of messages had stopped a week or so after the news story's publication, but every now and then, some nut case stumbled across the article online and sent him a rambling, ridiculous message.

But two things about this one were different. For one, none of the bogus people had ever been bold enough to break into his car and leave a letter.

He plucked the fishing lure off the rearview mirror.

28

And how could they know about the lure? How could they have known this was the same kind they'd been using that morning when he'd landed that prize bass? That detail wasn't in the news stories that reported the "accident," wasn't in the official police records.

"Just another crackpot, Tony," he said, in a shaky voice.

Hope was dangerous. Hope led to disillusionment, crushed dreams. He had a great life with Lisa, an island of quiet happiness they'd built for themselves, and if he started nurturing hope on this thing, he was setting himself up for heartache, he was going to reopen some painful old wounds, and he didn't know if he could handle any more.

He weighed the letter and the lure in his hands. There was a trash can on the other side of the parking lot.

On impulse, he got out of the truck and marched to the garbage can. Poised at the edge of the basket, he hesitated. Read the letter again.

To learn the truth, be online today @ 18:00.

It was as if the messenger realized the depths of his cynicism and doubt, and understood the only way to reel him in deeper was to tempt him with another clue.

In spite of himself, it was working.

"Man, you're a sucker, you know that?" he muttered.

He turned away from the trash and got in his truck.

He was probably going to regret falling for what was almost certainly a cruel prank. But the thing about hope was that it never quite faded away.

3

Anthony's younger sister sometimes went with him on his visits to their parents' gravesites. Unable to reach her on her cell and not getting an answer on the house's landline, he dropped by the family home in Decatur.

In spite of the cryptic message, he had every intention to pay his respects at his parents' graves. Nothing mattered more than duty to family. Yet as he drove, he continuously scanned the rearview mirror, alert for a tail, finding none.

Maybe the messenger had decided to leave him be until that evening's online meeting.

The family house was a brick Colonial with red and beige trim, framed by live oaks and sugar maples. The neighborhood was solidly middle-class, which meant the streets were quiet at two o'clock on a Friday afternoon, excerpt for clusters of loitering teenagers on summer vacation.

As he pulled into the driveway, he frowned. Since his last visit a few weeks ago, the grass had grown almost knee-high, and the gardenia bushes along the front needed to be trimmed. Trash spilled out of the garbage bin beside the garage. Soggy newspapers cluttered the walkway leading to the door like a trail of breadcrumbs.

When Mom had died of heart failure five years ago, she'd left the house to him and Danielle. Long before their mother had passed, though, Danielle had been living there with her son, Reuben, so they simply stayed. The agreement was that Anthony would pay the basic utilities and annual property tax bills, and his sister would take care of the maintenance.

He wasn't surprised to discover that she was failing to hold up her end of the deal.

Danielle usually parked her car—a Ford Explorer he had purchased for her last year—in front of the attached garage. The vehicle was gone, but that didn't mean anything. She could have handed the keys to one of her boyfriends, which she often did, in spite of his disapproval.

He went inside. He took the Beretta with him, wearing it concealed in his in-the-waistband holster. Perhaps he was being a little paranoid, but until he knew what was going on he didn't want to be separated from his piece again.

The front door was unlocked.

"Hey!" he said. "Anybody here?"

No answer. But he heard hip hop music thumping from upstairs. Reuben was home.

Rather than heading immediately to the second floor, he wandered down the carpeted hallway, navigating around the clutter— empty bags from fast food restaurants, old shoes, pieces of junk mail. The stink of cigarettes hung in the stale air, mingled with the faint scent of marijuana, the ghost of his sister's countless highs.

He had to resist the compulsion to tidy up the place. He hadn't come there to do house cleaning.

A chain of photographs lined the hallway wall. Baby photos of Anthony and Danielle. Pictures of Anthony and his dad at Anthony's Little League baseball games. A portrait of his dad, somber in a gray suit. A shot of his mother, a beautiful auburn-haired woman with a gentle smile. Photographs of the entire family together, everyone grinning.

All of the photos on the wall had been taken before his dad's murder, as if the entire family had died with him on the lake.

Near the end of the hallway, there was a door on the left. It was closed, as usual.

He opened it, and entered his father's study.

The room had been largely undisturbed since his dad's death. Mom had been unable to commit to clearing it out, and neither he nor Danielle had been up to the grim task.

It was furnished with an oak desk, a swivel chair, an oak bookcase stuffed with his dad's beloved history books and sports bios. An upholstered reading chair and a floor lamp. A filing cabinet full of ancient, irrelevant documents. Autographed photos of his father posing with pro athletes crowding the walls, interspersed among framed copies of various sports stories he had written and the numerous award plaques he had won for his journalism.

Dust covered everything, and fragile spider webs hung from the corners and between pieces of furniture. Although his mother hadn't removed any of the items from the room, she had used to clean it regularly, as if keeping it tidy for his dad's eventual return. Since her death, no one had touched it.

Holding back a sneeze, he sat at the desk.

A black Underwood typewriter with faded keys occupied the desktop, accompanied by a Mason jar full of dull lead pencils and dried-out ink pens. Three photographs crowded the edge of the desk: Mom and Dad together on a Caribbean cruise ship; Danielle and Dad dressed to the nines for a church-sponsored father-daughter dance; Anthony and Dad on a fishing trip, holding up their catches for the camera.

He picked up the fishing trip photo. He traced his finger across his father's face.

They said that time healed all wounds, but that was bullshit. Some wounds, time allowed to fester and spread, until they had consumed body, mind, and soul. Those wounds had taken down his mother in her prime, sent his sister plummeting down a long, bleak chasm of addiction . . . and him . . . well, he woke up every morning wondering if that would be the day he would finally die of a violent crime.

As he often did, he imagined that he could speak to his dad through the old picture.

What were you involved in, Dad? Why did someone want to hurt you?

He looked around the study again. Over the years, he had turned the room upside down and inside out, in a fruitless hunt for clues. Nothing would be gained from another search. The revelation promised by the messenger, fraudulent as it might be, was the only lead he had, and he wanted it to be genuine with a desire so intense that his heart clutched.

The wicked watcheth the righteous, and seeketh to slay him.

He stared at his dad's eyes, suspended forever in a better time.

Who had been watching you, Dad?

Sometimes, he awoke from nightmares of reliving the morning on the lake, woke convinced that he had his father's blood on his hands, blood that had drenched his palms when he'd held his dad to his chest and screamed until his vocal cords gave out. He would stumble into the bathroom and submerge his hands under scalding hot water, though they were clean, but he had to wash the dream blood away, had to wash away the memory of the wetness, the cloying coppery odor. Lisa had entered the restroom late one night when he was scrubbing at the ghost blood, her eyes alarmed, and when he'd muttered, "the blood, I have to get the blood off," she'd come to him, turned off the water, gently dried his hands with a towel, led him back to bed, and held him to her bosom until he drifted back to sleep.

He didn't want any more of those ghost blood dreams. He didn't want any more days like today, when he awoke with a grinding headache, as if nursing a bad hangover.

What he wanted was what he'd always wanted: justice.

And he vowed that no matter what, one way or another, he was going to get it. And soon.

4

The condemned man lived in the north metro suburb of Alpharetta, in a four-bedroom, three-bath home with stucco exterior. Entering the gourmet kitchen, Noah Cutty helped himself to the contents of the double-door refrigerator.

The wide shelves contained bottled water, orange juice, eggs, margarine, condiments, a cardboard box of left-over pizza, a container of milk past the expiration date, and a twelve-pack of Bud Lite missing half the bottles. Stored in the freezer were an array of Hungry Man frozen dinners, and a half-gallon tub of butter pecan ice cream.

Cutty removed the pizza, milk, frozen dinners, and ice cream and dumped them in the trash. He twisted the cap off each beer bottle and poured the amber fluid down the sink drain, lips curling as the corrupting stench reached his nostrils.

The body was a temple, and fatty foods and over-processed meals defiled it. Alcoholic beverages of any kind—with the exception of the Eucharist—were a lure of the devil, and had no place in a proper home.

The large kitchen island had a gleaming wood top. On it, there was a crystal bowl of fresh fruit: green apples, bananas, oranges.

He selected an apple and took a tiny bite. Taking small bites and chewing thoroughly before swallowing promoted proper digestion and kept the temple in peak condition.

Nibbling on the apple, he left the kitchen for the hallway.

The target was a divorcee with an adult son in college in Alabama. He lived alone, and until his arrival, Cutty was free to peruse the house at his leisure, as he often did before executing orders. He liked to become acquainted with his targets, to learn of their lives and, especially, of their sins, of which there were always so many.

In the hallway, afternoon sunshine slanted through the arched window at the far end of the two-story foyer and imparted a lustrous shine to the travertine floor. Framed photographs of landscapes—a desert at twilight, a snowy mountain summit at sunrise, a sunny beach with powder-white sand—hung on the walls.

According to the backgrounder Cutty had read on the man, the mark fancied himself an amateur photographer, and had presumably snapped these pictures. Cutty approved of the photos. God had created the earth, and his handiwork was worthy of admiration.

A room off the hall served as a library. As Cutty headed toward it, he passed by an oval, gold-edged mirror.

He paused, as he often did lately, to appraise his reflection.

He wore his division's standard daytime uniform of white tracksuit and low-cut white sneakers. His pale skin contrasted only slightly with his snow-white raiment. His hair, too, was so blonde it was almost white, and was precisely trimmed in a buzz cut.

His eyes, however, were the luminous blue of a summer lightning strike. People often felt anxiety when subjected to his direct gaze.

His muscular, ripped physique was an instrument of power, too. He could bench press four hundred pounds for ten repetitions, squat with seven hundred for eight. His strength more than adequately compensated for his height: he was five feet two inches tall.

Legendary men were often short in stature. Napoleon Bonaparte. Alexander the Great. Joseph Stalin. Strength of character, not height, not even physical prowess, was the truest measure of a man.

He picked a piece of lint out of his hair, and entered the library.

It featured tall, built-in mahogany bookshelves packed with volumes. Two wing chairs fashioned of buttery burgundy leather. Mahogany end tables. A fine Persian rug.

He stepped to the bookshelves and studied the titles. There was a plentitude of Christian books, including volumes by C.S. Lewis and other approved writers.

Between the shelves, a gigantic, leather-bound Bible lay open atop a polished bronze pedestal. The edition looked worth a small fortune.

First placing the apple on an end table, Cutty lifted the Bible off the pedestal. The book was open to the first chapter in Job: *There was a man in the land of Uz, whose name was Job; and that man was perfect and upright, and one that feared God, and eschewed evil.*

He carefully turned the delicate, crisp pages to Joshua, another book of the Old Testament. He loved the Old Testament. Throughout numerous ancient accounts, and especially in Joshua, God was revealed as a ruthless deity who would not hesitate to command his faithful to carry out bloody conquests to further the kingdom's agenda. Violence, when performed in the name of and for the glory of God, was not only righteous—it was *expected.*

Compare that to the New Testament. Love your neighbor. Turn the other cheek. Withhold judgment, lest you be judged. Those were wonderful lessons, to be sure, but what if you were facing an unrepentant sinner who deserved eternal torment in the lake of fire?

He read a few favorite verses about the valiant Joshua laying siege to the city of Jericho and slaying all the heathens within, and then he returned the book to the display stand.

On another shelf, he found a set of books that also appeared to be collector's editions. They were bound in expensive leather, and each bore the title: *The Lord of the Rings.* It appeared to be a three-volume set.

He had never read the books, but he didn't have to in order to comprehend that they were pagan works. He would discuss this matter with their quarry when he arrived.

He picked up his apple and crossed the hall to enter the great room—and before entering, slipped in front of the mirror for a moment to check his hair again. Okay.

In the great room, Maria Valdez, the underlying reason for his fussy concern over his appearance, sat cross-legged on the plush carpet. She also wore the uniform of white tracksuit and sneakers, but her skin was as rich and golden as his was pale. Her thick, dark hair was knotted in a ponytail that hung to the middle of her slender back.

Her eyes were closed in meditation. She drew slow, deep breaths.

A new member in their esteemed ranks, Valdez had been his partner for only a week. She was quiet, but that was fine with him. It was a pleasure to simply look at her.

In her late-twenties or early thirties, Valdez was a total bombshell. She had that silky black hair. Those ripe lips. Those dark, enchanting eyes. That figure—although her tracksuit fell loosely around her shape, the material occasionally clung to her curves when she moved quickly, and hinted toward a breathtaking form.

Valdez wasn't married or otherwise attached. Marriage and dating were not allowed for servants in their position. Neither were children.

Beyond her presumed marital status, he knew nothing whatsoever about Valdez's background, and he didn't particularly care. His superiors had assigned her to be his partner, and he assumed they had made a wise decision, as usual. As it read in Hebrews 13:17: *Obey them that have the rule over you, and submit yourselves . . .*

Typically, women were restricted from serving in their division. Exceptions were occasionally made if a female servant possessed valued talents. Although he had yet to see Valdez do anything out of the ordinary, he was confident that she would prove her worth in due course.

The sound of a vehicle entering the garage drew his attention.

Valdez opened her eyes. They were the brown of late autumn leaves.

"He is here," she said, in thick, Spanish-accented English.

"Indeed, he is." He finished the apple and disposed of it in a wastebasket. "Take your position, please."

Valdez rose to follow him. She was five-six, four inches taller than he. Somehow, the height advantage she enjoyed made her more attractive.

He moved to the right of the hallway that led to the door for the attached garage. Valdez took up position on the left.

From his shoulder holster, he withdrew a Glock semi-automatic outfitted with a sound suppressor. Valdez gripped a .38 revolver, the standard-issue rookie's gun.

The door at the end of the hall opened, and their quarry entered, feet thumping across the stone tile. Cutty glanced at Valdez, and nodded. He would handle this.

When the mark reached the end of the hallway and turned to go toward the kitchen, he saw Cutty. He yelped in surprise.

"Who the hell are you?" he said, voice crackling with shock and indignation.

The mark was in his late forties, about six-two, with thinning brown hair and bronzed skin that could have only been gained from hours on a tanning bed. He wore golfing gear: white shirt and khaki shorts. According to the dispatcher, he had returned home from a trip to the local country club.

His name was David Wright. Cutty had never met him before or heard of him until he'd been given the mission that morning, but it didn't matter.

"Good afternoon, Mr. Wright," Cutty said. "You've spread lies about us."

"What the—"

Cutty shot Wright in both knees. The gun, muffled by the sound suppressor, made soft pops.

Wright screamed, collapsed to the floor.

"It is written," Cutty said, " 'Touch not mine anointed.' Do you understand what you've done?"

Curled up in fetal position, Wright moaned in agony. Blood pooled around him, staining the travertine.

Valdez watched quietly, her perfect face expressionless.

"Bring me a chair from the kitchen," Cutty said to her.

She looked at him, gaze muddled.

"A *chair*," Cutty said. He traced the shape of the desired object with his hands. "El chairo?"

He knew only two words of Spanish, the proper term for "chair" not being one of them. But Valdez said, "*Si*," and hurried to the kitchen.

Their organization operated throughout the world, and servants hailed from every nationality and spoke dozens of languages. Still, Cutty wondered why he had been paired with a woman who had a weak grasp of English. It sometimes seemed like his superior was playing a joke on him.

She brought a ladder-back chair. Cutty swung it around so he could face Wright, and sat. Valdez hovered behind him.

Face shiny with sweat, Wright said, "Who the fuck are you people?"

"Please, Mr. Wright," Cutty said. "Is that proper language for an allegedly Christian man?"

"Give me a fucking break . . ."

Cutty shot the man in the shoulder. Another muffled pop. Wright howled, rocked against the floor.

"No more of that obscene language," Cutty said. "It offends me."

Tears streaming from his eyes, words coming in quick gasps, Wright said, "Please . . . tell me . . . what's this about? You . . . want money? You-you here to rob me? There's a . . . safe in the bedroom . . . closet . . ."

"I have no interest in your material possessions, you filthy, drunken heretic," Cutty said. "I'm storing my treasures in heaven, where thieves do not break in and moths and rust do not destroy."

Although considerable agony wracked Wright's body, he managed to look bewildered. "I don't understand—"

"You publish a well-circulated magazine that claims to report on matters of relevance to God-fearing people," Cutty said. "For the past several issues, you've run a vicious smear campaign against our organization, reserving your worst venom for our anointed leader."

Wright's gaze clarified. "But . . . freedom . . . of speech . . . my rights . . ."

"There are no such inalienable rights. Not any more. Freedom to express opinion exists only within the strict regulations of the God-focused society that we are bringing to fruition."

"Right . . . you're right." Chest heaving, Wright bobbed his head in acceptance. But it was much too late for that.

"You were warned to cease your blasphemy, Mr. Wright. Twice, in fact. You've been boldly unrepentant in your sins, and need I remind you how God deals with unrepentant sinners?"

"I'm . . . sorry," Wright said, babbling now. "Forgive me . . . please. The devil . . . the devil made me do it . . ."

"We are taught to resist temptation," Cutty said. "Personally, I think the reason for your demise lies in your selection of reading material. I saw a rather pricey collection of volumes in your library. *The Lord of the Rings?* I've not read them, but I can tell from the titles that they are pagan works. Surely you know the commandment not to worship false gods."

"But they're . . . only stories, books—"

Cutty laughed harshly. "Only books, eh? Kingdoms have been built and destroyed based on books. Do not trivialize the power of the written word—you, of all people, should know better."

"Please." Wright sniffled. "I'm begging . . . begging . . . you to forgive me . . ."

"It is not in my power to forgive sin. You should know that, too. Or have those books about pagan gods and rings muddled your grasp of the fundamentals?"

"No, I—"

Cutty shot the man in the head, placing the hollow-point bullet precisely between the eyebrows. Wright's skull knocked against the floor, and he twitched in death throes.

Cutty rose off the chair and fired another round into the man's throat. He lowered the muzzle, and pumped a third round into his heart.

Wright's death spasms ceased. His dead eyes gazed blindly at the ceiling.

Valdez approached the body and tested the pulse on his wrist. Bowing her head, she made the sign of the cross over her chest.

Cutty holstered the Glock in a shoulder rig underneath his jacket. "Don't mourn for him, Valdez. The unrepentant sinner got what he deserved. As you sow, so shall you reap."

Admiration glimmered in her dark eyes. "You are a wise man."

He smiled. "Thank you, but I'm only a humble servant, doing the work I've been called to do by the Lord."

He removed a cell phone from his pocket and made a call on the encrypted line.

A male voice answered: "Yes?"

He had never met the dispatcher, though the man worked out of their campus headquarters in metro Atlanta. Likewise, he doubted the dispatcher could identify him on sight. For their important duties, secrecy was crucial.

"The work is done," Cutty said.

"Excellent. We value your service."

Upon placement of the call notifying the dispatcher of the successful completion of his mission, a crew waiting on standby would be sent to the mark's residence to dispose of the body. Wright's house might be torched and burned to the ground, his remains incinerated. His cadaver might be weighed with stones and dropped into the Atlantic. His corpse might be ground to mulch and buried in a landfill—from dust you came, to dust you shall return.

"Our work is our joy," Cutty said. "We are faithful servants."

"There is more work for you. An especially sensitive assignment of utmost importance."

Cutty's heart rate quickened. A special mission? It sounded like a task that could boost his standing in the ranks.

"We are ready to serve," he said.

"There is a meeting tonight in the Armory. It commences at twenty hundred hours. Bring your partner, of course."

A key reason why servants in their division were not allowed to marry was because of the work schedule. It was not a nine-to-five job. Servants of their kind were always on call and expected to render service at a moment's notice.

"We will be there."

5

Upstairs, Reuben had moved into Anthony's former bedroom at the end of the hall. The door was closed, and a large black and white sign posted on the door warned: RESTRICTED AREA - NO HATERS ALLOWED. Hip hop rumbled inside, vibrating the door, the walls, the floor.

Anthony knocked. No answer. With the music cranked that loud Reuben wouldn't have heard a space shuttle launch in the driveway.

He knocked again, harder. "Hey, Reuben! Open up, man, it's your uncle!"

The music's volume dropped. The door opened a crack.

Anthony stood an even six feet, but his nephew had gained a couple of inches on him. Every time he saw the kid, it looked as if he had grown taller.

Reuben regarded him with languid grey eyes. "Hey, Unc."

"Can I come in, or do you have a girl in here?"

"Man, I wish." Reuben smiled, exposing teeth bracketed with braces. He pulled the door open wider. "I'm just hangin' out, you know."

Although Reuben was tall, he still looked and dressed like the teenager he was. He wore a long white t-shirt and baggy denims that hung loosely on his gangly frame. Acne was scattered across his café au lait complexion, and he was struggling to cultivate a goatee.

Entering the room, Anthony looked around to see how Reuben had further desecrated it since his last visit. In his youth, Anthony had used to keep the room neat, but Reuben had little inclination for tidiness. Wrinkled clothes covered the bed. Boxes of sneakers were scattered across the floor. Empty bags of fried pork rinds and cans of Red Bull were everywhere.

The walls were plastered with so many posters they might have been a new form of wallpaper. Glossy pictures of tricked-out Bentleys, Lamborghinis, Range Rovers. Magazine spreads of voluptuous, nearly naked women in provocative poses. A full-length shot of the hot rap star of the moment, the guy snarling at the camera, clad in a wife beater t-shirt to best display his prison tattoos, platinum chain, and air-brushed muscles.

The only organized area was the computer desk. A desktop PC, a large, flat screen display, and a laser printer occupied the smooth plane of cherry wood.

"Have a seat," Reuben said. He slapped a bag of pork rinds off a nearby chair, clearing the cushion, and settled into his swivel chair in front of the desk, long legs sprawled in front of him.

Anthony took the seat. "I called here a short while ago, but no one answered."

"My bad, man, guess I didn't hear the phone ring. Been listening to my music." He bobbed his head in sync with the muted beat.

"Where's your mom? I've been trying to reach her for hours."

Reuben shrugged. "Probably hangin' with some dude, you know."

Anthony knew. Danielle often disappeared for days on end, leaving Reuben at home to fend for himself. Occasionally, the kid would stay with Anthony and Lisa when Danielle was out of pocket, but if Danielle found out she took offense, ranting that she could raise her kid on her own and didn't need his help.

She needed help from someone, because Reuben was headed down a troubling path. He was an intensely bright kid, a quick study, but his grades were marginal, and he'd been suspended numerous times for tardiness, or ditching class altogether. He had no interest in athletics, extracurricular activities, or working a summer job. His friends, if you could call them that, were similarly apathetic, concerned only with impressing girls and appearing cool.

In Anthony's view, the root of most of the issues was Reuben's lacking a father figure. Reuben had never met his biological father—some loser who had vanished before Reuben was born and had never resurfaced—and Danielle had yet to marry or form a lasting significant relationship, and if her track record of choosing worthless men was any indicator, she never would.

Anthony tried to do his part to be there for the kid, as a positive male influence. They sometimes went to Hawks games, played hoops at the local park, and went head-to-head on X-Box. But as Reuben had gotten older, he'd grown less interested in hanging out with Anthony, as if being in the presence of an adult branded him as completely uncool.

Anthony didn't know what to do about the boy, or if he could do anything at all that would help. Hell, every day he wrestled with his own emotional issues. How was he fit to be Reuben's surrogate dad and keep him on the straight and narrow?

And Lisa wondered why he didn't want children.

"I was stopping by to see if she wanted to go to the cemetery with me," Anthony said. "Did she say anything to you about that earlier?"

"Nah, man."

Figures. "Do you know what today is?"

Reuben scratched his head. "Friday the twelfth, right?"

Anthony stared at him. Was he serious?

"It's the anniversary of your grandfather's death, Reuben."

"Oh, snap." Reuben cupped his hand over his mouth. "Sorry, Unc."

"I'm going to visit his grave, and your grandmother's grave, too. You're welcome to come along if you'd like."

"Nah, that's all right. I'm kinda busy here, you know."

What in the hell can be more important than paying your respects to your grandparents? Anthony wanted to shout at him.

But he kept his mouth shut. The kid didn't know any better.

Reuben swiveled to the computer. His fingers danced across the keyboard.

He was a whiz with computers. Anthony had bought the machine for him last Christmas, an upgrade over the PC he had acquired for him a few years ago. He wanted to encourage his nephew's talents in a useful direction.

Last year, Reuben had created a program for him to track his book royalty statements. It worked far better than the Excel spreadsheet Anthony had been using for that purpose, and Anthony had actually considered licensing it to sell to other writers. He was convinced that Reuben had a great future ahead of him as a software developer, but the boy had to *want* to do it.

"How's that program coming along that I asked you about creating, for the press release promo?" Anthony asked.

"Ah, man. I started on that but ain't finished it. I been busy, you know. When you need it by?"

A month ago, Anthony had asked Reuben to create a program that would send press releases to media outlets worldwide, based on specific, user-defined criteria. The idea was that when Anthony released a new book, he could use the software to zip a press message about the novel to the thousands of newspapers, magazines, television networks, radio stations, and blogs across the Internet. Although numerous press-release distribution software packages and services already existed that Anthony could have purchased, he wanted Reuben to create the program for him, to further develop his talents—and hopefully, his motivation.

"As soon as you can get to it," Anthony said. "I know you're a busy guy, with school out and everything."

Reuben chuckled. "You know how it is, Unc."

The sarcasm had sailed right over his head.

"Has your mom said anything to you about cutting the grass?" Anthony said.

"Man, she let some dude borrow the lawnmower like two weeks ago."

"She did what? Who?"

"I don't know, one of her boyfriends, I guess. Some dude."

Anthony knotted his hands and counted to ten.

"There're a bunch of newspapers scattered across the sidewalk, too," Anthony said. "You ever think about picking them up, throwing them away?"

"Mom ain't never said nothing 'bout that."

"I know she didn't, so that's why I am. You need to do your part to keep the house clean, Reuben. You're fifteen, man, old enough to start paying attention to those kinds of things."

Reuben glanced at him. "Sure, whatever."

"The garbage pickup comes every Tuesday, too. You need to roll that bin down to the curb and let them empty it. Right now, it's practically spilling out of the can."

"Okay, whatever." Reuben was typing.

"Hey, look at me."

Reuben turned, frowning. "What?"

"Nothing in life is free. I gave you that computer for Christmas with the expectation that you'll start fulfilling certain responsibilities in school and around the house."

"Okay, yeah, whatever."

"Don't 'whatever' me. You know I can't stand that."

Reuben saluted him mockingly. "Yes, sir. That better, Uncle Tony, sir?"

"Don't be a smart-ass. I'm not asking you for that for much. A few basic responsibilities. Remember our agreement."

"Aye, aye, sir."

It was impossible to know if he was getting through to the kid. He probably wasn't. Most likely, Reuben viewed him as a big pain in the ass, and would agree to anything to get him out of his face.

"When you talk to your mom, tell her I came by." Anthony started for the door. "And hey, we should hang out sometime soon. Maybe we can go fishing."

Reuben blinked. "Fishing?"

Why had he suggested fishing? He hadn't been fishing in fifteen years.

"Fishing, or ah, something else," he said. "We'll see. I'll give you a call."

Reuben spun back to the computer, and hit a button. The music blasted out of the speakers again at full volume.

Anthony had been dismissed.

6

After his visit to the cemetery, Anthony went home.

They lived in an eighty-year-old, Queen Anne Victorian in Grant Park, a historic Atlanta neighborhood of Victorians, Craftsman bungalows, quaint red brick sidewalks, and stately elms, maples, and oaks. The public park, the oldest in the city, was home to Zoo Atlanta and the Cyclorama, a popular Civil War exhibition. Their house was located on a wooded, one-acre parcel around the corner from the park.

They'd moved into the place six months into their marriage, and they'd done extensive renovations to the exterior and interior. The new fiberglass siding was hunter-green, with black trim. A new spear point, wrought-iron fence enclosed the property. They'd re-sodded the yard with Bermuda grass and installed mulch and flower beds, too; the impatiens Lisa had planted last month were looking good.

He pressed a remote control affixed to the sun visor. The gate to the driveway swung inward.

The plan to purchase an old house and renovate it originally had been Lisa's idea, but Anthony had quickly warmed to the possibilities. He wasn't a fan of the housing subdivisions that consumed Atlanta's suburbs, with their tyrannical homeowners associations and cookie cutter floor plans. They'd spent a bundle on the house and all the work, but he'd discovered an unexpected pleasure in restoring something from the past, in putting a shiny new gloss on history.

He parked in the three-car garage, another addition. He flipped down the sun visor and unclipped the envelope.

The note had said to be online at eighteen hundred hours. Less than two hours away. He took the envelope inside with him.

The interior was an elegant blend of Victorian era charm and contemporary style. Rich hardwood floors. Traditional pocket windows, so long you could step out of them and onto the wrap-around veranda. Vaulted ceilings. Hand-carved crown molding, wainscoting, and intricate woodwork. Comfortable modern furniture in soft tones, with gentle lines. State-of-the art appliances, and wiring throughout the house for the stereo system.

He took the staircase off the main hallway to the basement. The finished basement was comprised of a media room that contained their home theater set-up, an entertainment area with a billiards table and mini-bar, a fitness room full of free weights and a treadmill, storage space, and his office.

His office was almost pure Spartan: a large, windowless room with white walls and beige carpeting. A simple desk stood in the center, and held his laptop computer and a laser-jet printer/scanner/fax machine. A bookcase contained his most-frequently used reference texts, and a mini-refrigerator full of bottled water and snacks occupied a niche underneath the desk.

The only photographs were Lisa's bridal portrait, and a photo of his father at work in the newsroom. The pictures stood on opposite corners of the desk.

Many of his author colleagues adorned their work spaces with framed posters of their published books. Anthony didn't have any such posters. In fact, the novels he'd written were mixed in with other volumes held in the library upstairs.

There were two doors at the far end of the room. One led to the half-bath, and hung partly open. The other door was closed and secured with an electronic keypad lock, accessible via a code known only to him and Lisa.

Settling into the desk chair, he powered on the computer. The machine was connected to the Internet via a wireless modem, but he rarely took the laptop out of the office.

He checked his primary e-mail account, an AOL address he'd maintained for several years and which was listed on the "Contact Me" page of his author Web site. In his inbox, he found a handful of complimentary remarks from readers about his novels, a few pieces of spam advertising penis enlargements and drugs for erectile dysfunction, and that was all. Nothing from the mysterious messenger.

So how was this guy going to get in touch with him online? Should he expect an e-mail? A tweet on the Twitter account he rarely used? A Facebook friend request?

He wasn't sure, but it was only fifteen minutes to five o'clock, a little over an hour to go until the meeting. He signed onto all of his social networking accounts and kept his e-mail inbox open. Meanwhile, time crawled at an excruciatingly slow pace.

He grabbed a bottle of water from the mini-frig, opened Microsoft Word, and brought up the file of his novel-in-progress, tentatively titled, *The Darkness in the Ghost.*

The book, as did the others in the series, chronicled the exploits of an urban mercenary known only as "Ghost." Ghost was a Marine veteran who had come home from work one evening to find his wife brutally raped and murdered. The police apprehended a suspect, a serial rapist who confessed to the crime, but when the case reached trial, the killer wound up getting released on a technicality.

Disgusted and furious, Ghost tracked down the killer and held a trial of his own—the kind that ended not with the bang of a judge's gavel, but with the lethal discharge of a 9mm pistol.

Thus, Ghost's bloody vendetta against a corrupt society and inept legal system was born. Ghost typically was moved to help those who had lost loved ones in terrible crimes and found no help from the law, and his style of street justice—basically blowing a hole through anyone who dared to stop him from finding the perpetrator and ultimately leaving the guilty party with a bullet in the head—had gained him a fanatical following amongst those readers who liked to read about their justice served straight, no chaser.

There must have been many such readers, as each new entry in the Ghost series hit bestseller lists in a dozen countries. The surprising success was a blessing, but Anthony would have gone on writing the stories whether or not they had even been published. He had been writing about Ghost, in various incarnations, for fifteen years.

So far, he'd completed over two hundred pages of the new novel, but as he hunched over the keyboard, he found it impossible to concentrate. For once, real life had become more intriguing than fiction.

Nevertheless, he toyed with the manuscript, changing a word here, rearranging a sentence there, just to pass the time. Fortunately, a call on his cell saved him from a prolonged bout of writer's block.

"Yo, AT, what's up, man?"

It was Mike Alfaro. Although he and Mike usually chatted about once a week, Mike never would have let that particular day pass without giving him a ring.

"I'm working," Anthony said. Although he and Mike went way back, he didn't consider telling him about the message he'd received. Before he shared it with anyone he needed to prove that it was genuine.

"Working, huh?" Mike laughed. "Better you than me. I rolled out of bed like an hour ago."

"You're a lazy slob."

"I was tired, man. Had a lady friend over, she kept me up all night. Girl wore me out as bad as our DI used to."

Both of them had served in the Marine Corps, had done boot together on Parris Island in South Carolina. The hard-hat DI who'd led their platoon had been such a hard-driving maniac that he'd found his way into recruits' nightmares.

"You know I don't believe that," Anthony said.

"True words."

"Where'd you meet this one?"

"On Jarhead. She liked my photo, sent me a private message."

Jarhead was a Web site devoted to Marine Corps veterans. It offered a message board open to anyone, private e-mail, and news of interest to vets. Although it wasn't meant for dating per se, some of Anthony's old Marine buddies had used it as a means of hooking up with members of the fairer sex, many of them groupies obsessed with bedding a devil dog.

"She a Marine?" Anthony asked. "Or just a groupie?"

"A real Marine. Discharged last year. She told me she scored a perfect 300 on the PFT—the men's one."

The PFT was a Physical Fitness Test that challenged you with pull-ups, sit-ups, and a three-mile run. Female recruits were subjected to a less-intense version, and for a woman to notch a perfect score on the men's exam was impressive indeed—only three guys from their platoon had pulled it off during boot, including him and Mike.

"You gonna see her again?" Anthony asked.

"Doubt it. She lives in San Diego, she was only in ATL on business."

"You can try the long distance thing."

"Do I need to break this down to you, AT? It was strictly a booty call."

"Oh, right." Anthony chuckled. "I forgot about those."

"Since you've been locked down—excuse me, *married*—you're totally out of touch with the bachelor life, huh?"

"I experience it vicariously through you," Anthony said. "What I wonder is when you plan to hang up the spurs?"

"When I meet a woman who can tame me. Ain't met her yet."

"She's out there somewhere. Speaking from experience here."

"Don't hold your breath." Mike hesitated, and when he spoke again, his voice was subdued. "So. Everything okay today?"

Anthony paused, and thought: *This is so sad.* On such a significant day in his life, he received a concerned call from his friend, while his own sister avoided him and his nephew didn't even understand why the date was relevant.

It was partly why he'd enlisted in the Marines straight out of high school. With a broken family at home and little interest in college, he'd sought fellowship in a group with a purpose to which he could devote himself, and found the Marine discipline, ethos, and camaraderie to his liking. He'd earned a reputation for being totally squared away, a hard-core grunt who'd *eagerly* fought on the front lines in the infantry, and in spite of the numerous combat missions in which he'd participated, he'd never sustained more than minor flesh wounds and trivial bruises, something that, in hindsight, was a bit of a miracle.

If his first novel had not found a publisher and sold for a healthy six-figure sum, he probably would have re-enlisted. As it happened, he found himself plunged into a writing career, met and married Lisa, and spent his days spinning stories about a character who embodied more than a little wish fulfillment—and taking calls from war buddies who cared more about him than his own blood relatives.

A hard lump of emotion formed in his throat.

"You there?" Mike asked.

A familiar beep sounded from the computer. Anthony bolted upright in his chair.

A message had appeared in his e-mail inbox. It was from "truthgiver15@hushmail.com," an address Anthony had never seen before.

The subject line of the e-mail stated:

Click this link, but only if you're ready

It was precisely six o'clock. Anthony found the stranger's punctuality encouraging.

He opened the message. It contained no text, just a link, a long web address with a string of seemingly random characters—letters, numbers, and punctuation symbols—evidence of powerful encryption at work.

Heart booming, Anthony said, "Sorry, Mike, gotta run. I'll holler at you later."

7

When Anthony clicked the link, a new browser window opened, filling his screen. Quickly, the browser rendered a page comprised of a large dialogue box with a light, grayish background.

It was a chat room, but it was hosted on a web site with an indecipherable web address. A secure site, presumably, though Anthony had no clue exactly who might be interested in this chat.

TRUTHGIVER15 was already in the room. Anthony's own chat room handle was already selected for him: GHOSTWRITER79.

"Funny," Anthony said.

Staring at the screen, he bent forward in the chair. He typed a message, fingers tingling.

> GHOSTWRITER79: WHO R U?
> TRUTHGIVER15: DID YOU READ PSALM 37:32?
> GHOSTWRITER79: YES. WHO R U?
> TRUTHGIVER15: A FRIEND WHO KNOWS THE TRUTH.

"We'll see about that," Anthony said under his breath. "The jury's still out."

> GHOSTWRITER79: HOW DO I KNOW THIS ISN'T A JOKE?
> TRUTHGIVER15: DID YOU FIND THE LURE?
> GHOSTWRITER79: HOW DID U KNOW ABOUT THAT?
> TRUTHGIVER15: I WAS THERE WHEN THEY FOUND YOUR FATHER'S BODY.

Anthony rocked backward in the chair. He felt as if someone had kicked him in the stomach.

Old memories flooded his mind. Staring at his father's lifeless body on the floor of the boat. Pulling his dad into his arms, blood drenching his clothes, his hands. Screaming, screaming, screaming . . . Somehow managing to start the motor and steer the boat across the lake and back to the docks, gaze straight ahead, refusing to look at his dad for he knew if he did he would lose it . . .

That was where his mind hit a wall. He couldn't remember what had happened after he reached the docks, as if the part of his brain that stored events in memory had simply switched off like an overloaded circuit. All he could remember happening afterward was sitting on a hard plastic chair in the local police station, waiting for his mom and sister to arrive.

If this guy was saying he'd been there when they'd found Dad's body ashore, maybe he was telling the truth.

Anthony blotted his damp palms on his lap, and typed again:

GHOSTWRITER79: PROVE 2 ME U WERE THERE.
TRUTHGIVER15: YOUR DAD WAS WEARING A GEORGIA TECH CAP. THERE WAS A STEEL THERMOS OF COFFEE IN THE BOAT. HE WORE A SILVER SPORTS WATCH, THE SAME WATCH YOU WEAR TODAY.

As the words filled the screen, Anthony was twisting the watch around his wrist. Jesus. Only someone who had been there would know these details. None of these things had ever been printed in the newspaper, weren't included even in the official police report. Anthony had read the documents himself, using his relative celebrity to convince the cops to let him take a peek at the case file.

Whoever TRUTHGIVER15 was, *he had been there*.

TRUTHGIVER15: NOT AN ACCIDENT, ANTHONY. IT WAS A COVER UP.

"Of course it was," Anthony whispered. "Don't you think I know that?"

He pounded the keys:

GHOSTWRITER79: WHO DID IT?
TRUTHGIVER15: I'M SORRY YOU HAD TO SEE THAT HAPPEN. YOU WERE ONLY A KID. IT WAS A TERRIBLE THING.
GHOSTWRITER79: TELL ME WHO DID IT!

54

TRUTHGIVER15: NOT ON HERE. NOT SAFE.
GHOSTWRITER15: WERE U INVOLVED?

Anthony waited. The messenger did not respond—and his silence was an answer in itself.

"*Sonofabitch,*" Anthony said.

He shot out of the chair, paced around the desk. Hands clenched into fists. He had a strong and entirely irrational urge to smash his hand through the screen, as if he could grab the so-called "friend" by the throat on the other side of the Web connection and strangle a confession out of him.

The computer beeped.

TRUTHGIVER15: I WANT TO HELP YOU FIND OUT THE TRUTH.

"Now you want to do the right thing, asshole?" Anthony said. "Fifteen fucking years later?"

He sat down hard and hammered the keyboard:

GHOSTWRITER79: WHY DO U CARE?   THAT WAS 15 YEARS AGO!

TRUTHGIVER15: JUSTICE NEEDS TO BE DONE.

GHOSTWRITER79: U COULD HAVE DONE JUSTICE THEN. TELL ME THE TRUTH!!!!

TRUTHGIVER15: NOT ON HERE. NOT SAFE.

GHOSTWRITER79: NOT SAFE FROM WHO?

TRUTHGIVER15: VERY POWERFUL ORGANIZATION.

GHOSTWRITER79: GIVE ME A NAME.

TRUTHGIVER15:   TOO DANGEROUS. THEY MONITOR THE WEB.

It made no sense at all. Why would an organization as powerful as this person was suggesting mastermind his dad's murder? His father had written about sports, for God's sake. He hadn't been some investigative political reporter, digging up explosive stories that would topple the White House. He'd just been Dad, devoted husband, great father, an all-around ordinary guy.

All that was true, but he'd always suspected there was someone big behind Dad's murder, hadn't he? A conspiracy. The question was: why?

The computer beeped again.

TRUTHGIVER15: READ MATTHEW 7:15.

Anthony ripped open a drawer, grabbed a steno pad and pen, and jotted down the scripture.

GHOSTWRITER79: MORE BIBLE VERSES? WHAT ARE YOU, A PRIEST?
TRUTHGIVER15: FAR FROM IT. WE MUST MEET.
GHOSTWRITER79: NAME A TIME AND PLACE.
TRUTHGIVER15: GO WHERE YOUR FATHER WOULD TAKE YOU AFTER GT BALL GAMES. 22:00 TONIGHT.

How could this guy know about that place? Anthony hadn't visited it in well over a decade.

GHOSTWRITER79: I'LL BE THERE. HOW WILL I KNOW U?
TRUTHGIVER15: I KNOW YOU.
GHOSTWRITER79: YOU'VE BEEN WATCHING ME. THAT'S HOW U GOT THE LETTER IN MY TRUCK. WHO THE HELL ARE U? GIVE ME A NAME, SOMETHING.
TRUTHGIVER15: CALL ME BOB.

Bob? Hi, and I'm John Doe, nice to meet you.

GHOSTWRITER79: LAST NAME?
TRUTHGIVER15: BARKER.

Anthony laughed out loud. Bob Barker. Sure, man.

TRUTHGIVER15: KEEP THIS SECRET, ANTHONY. THEY ARE EVERYWHERE. SEE YOU @ 22:00.

TRUTHGIVER15 left the chat. The chat room vanished, the browser window closing, as if the guy's exit triggered a session deactivation.

His tongue felt like a board. He grabbed the bottle of water and chugged the rest of it in a few big gulps.

Glancing at the notepad, he found a Web site that contained the full text of the Bible. He pulled up Matthew 7:15.

Beware of false prophets, which come to you in sheep's clothing, but inwardly they are ravening wolves.

What the hell was that supposed to mean?

The security system chirped, signaling that a door or window had been opened somewhere in the house. He heard feather-light footsteps traveling across the floor upstairs.

Rising, he flipped up the edge of his shirt and grasped the Beretta. He stepped into the hallway outside the office and edged toward the staircase.

"Lisa? That you up there?"

"The one and only!" she said.

He slid his hand off the gun.

8

He met Lisa in their bedroom on the second floor. She'd gone to a Pilates studio after work for her twice-weekly workout session and was near their king-size sleigh bed, peeling out of her white spandex leggings and top. The shower ran in the bathroom behind her.

She cut a lovely sight in the form-fitting clothes, and on any other day he might have drawn her to him and held her firm, warm body close, but he greeted her with only a brief kiss on the lips.

"We need to talk," he said.

"Is everything okay?" Her eyes searched his face. "You look like you've seen a ghost."

"Go ahead and shower first. That'll give me time to make us a stiff drink."

As she gave him a puzzled look, he went downstairs to the butler's pantry off the kitchen. At the wet bar, he grabbed two shot glasses, and with a shaky hand, added a splash of cognac to each. He took the shots and the cognac to the breakfast room table.

About five minutes later, Lisa entered. She'd changed into an oversized t-shirt that featured a character from *The Boondocks* cartoon, baggy shorts, and flip flops.

"Okay, talk to me," she said, sitting cater-corner from him. "When you say we need to talk in a tone like that, I get nervous."

He passed her a drink. She wrinkled her nose.

"Is this Hennessey?" she said. "You know I don't do hard liquor."

"You'll want it for this."

He showed her the letter from Bob, and the lure. He told her everything they had discussed in the chat room.

When he finished, both of their glasses had been drained.

He poured new shots, his hold a bit steadier around the bottle. Although Bob had warned him to keep their communications secret, there was no way he could have kept it hidden from Lisa, and unloading with her had calmed his nerves.

Lisa was shaking her head. "Wow. I know you've never believed it was a hunting accident, and I've had my doubts, too, but this might finally be the break you've been looking for."

"This guy, Bob, was *there*. He told me what my dad had been wearing, the steel thermos he always used to keep his coffee in, the watch." He tapped the lure he'd placed in the center of the table. "And don't forget this."

She picked up the lure between thumb and forefinger and examined it like a crime scene tech scrutinizing evidence.

"Assuming that this Bob was involved, why tell the truth now?" she said. "It's been fifteen years, Tony."

"I intend to find out when I speak to him."

"What do you make of this all-knowing organization he claims can monitor your chats on the Internet?"

Anthony shrugged. "I would assume a political group of some kind, maybe some rogue government agency. He wouldn't give me the specifics, just those Bible verses."

"That's another odd thing. The biblical quotes. Is this Sunday school?"

"Could be it's the safest way for him to communicate certain things. Like a code, you know? I guess it'll all make sense later."

"Why would some clandestine group want to kill your father?"

He sighed. "I have no idea, Lisa. I'm assuming he'll tell me when we meet."

She nodded. "Of course he will. He's given you just enough tantalizing clues to entice you. You know, the more I think about it, the more this sounds like the plots of your novels."

Anthony had been about to raise the shot glass to his lips; he stopped. "Hold on, you lost me. What're you talking about?"

"You won't want to hear this." She set the lure on the table, pushed aside her glass. "But how can you be sure that Bob isn't setting you up for a scam?"

"A scam? He hasn't said anything about wanting money for his info."

"Not yet."

"Are you kidding me? I thought I was the cynic in this marriage."

She touched his hand. He didn't see cynicism in her eyes. He saw worry.

"You desperately want to believe this is going to lead you to the truth," she said. "You've waited so long to get closure, justice. Now, you're seeing a glimmer of hope."

"I wouldn't call it that. I'd call it healthy curiosity."

"Hope," she said with a squeeze of his hand. "I know you, Tony. I wouldn't be doing my duty as your wife if I didn't ask you to take a step back and view this situation from another perspective. This Bob might be a con artist."

Count on Lisa to think of something he'd never considered. It reminded him of why he'd married her. She was beautiful, she was kind-hearted, she was funny, but most of all, she was smart.

She folded her arms on the table, watching him.

"You make a good point, but I think this is legit," he said.

"Based on a handful of details."

"Not just any details. He told me stuff no one else would know, things that hadn't been reported. He must've been there."

"Maybe he *was* there—as an innocent bystander. Or, he might know someone who'd been present, and they fed him the details. You know how nosy people can be, snooping around murder scenes, gawking at traffic accidents."

"That seems pretty far-fetched," he said.

"But it's possible."

"How about the place he scheduled for our meeting tonight? How would he know that my dad used to take us there after Tech games?"

"A little research," she said. "All he'd have to do is get his hands on your dad's obituary. Your dad was a sports writer, so the paper he worked for ran his obituary, correct?"

He nodded reluctantly.

"Do they have archives of the paper stored somewhere?" she asked.

"Probably online."

"And does the obituary say anything about how your dad would take you on fishing trips, and to Tech games?"

"It does."

"And anyone who's been to a Tech game knows where folks like to go eat on game days."

60

"Yeah." He absently twisted the wrist watch a few times. "Now that I think about it, I may have even mentioned it during an interview or two."

"There you go." Lisa smacked the table. "I rest my case."

"But why wait fifteen years to contact me? There must have been a good reason for him to wait so long."

"That was one of my first questions. Why wait fifteen years— unless there's something to be gained from sharing the alleged truth with you? And why contact you on the *anniversary of your father's death*, when you're guaranteed to be at an emotional low, heartsick and vulnerable?"

He tossed back his second shot. The cognac's slow burn couldn't match the tension boiling in his chest.

"You're making a lot of sense, and it bugs the hell out of me," he said.

"Think about it, Tony. We don't advertise our wealth, and I know money doesn't matter much to you, but the publishing industry mags have reported some of your recent book deals, haven't they?"

"They have."

"This Bob character could easily find all of that information online, too."

He gazed at his empty glass. Although he'd earned a substantial income from his books over the past five years or so, his self-image wasn't based on the number of zeroes on his bank account statement. The money was there, he was thankful for it, and that was that. He knew as well as anyone the pitfalls in materialism—like a loved one, it could all be taken away in an instant.

But could this be a set-up? An elaborate, cold-blooded con?

I was there when they found your father's body . . . I want to help you find out the truth . . . justice needs to be done . . . .

He slowly shook his head. "We'll have to agree to disagree on this one. This is real. I feel it in my gut."

She threw up her hands. "God, you can be so stubborn sometimes."

"Blame my dad. Got it from him."

"I don't want to see you hurt. You've suffered so much already, more than anyone ever should in a lifetime."

"I have to see this through, Lisa. I don't know what else to tell you."

"Maybe we should call the cops."

"No way. No cops. Until we know who's behind this, we should keep it secret, like Bob said. As far as we know, the cops have something to do with it."

"Now you're sounding paranoid."

"Am I? Sorry, but I can't forget how quick the cops were to label my father's murder a hunting accident and close the case."

"I don't know." She ran her fingers through her hair. "I've never been one for conspiracy theories, secret cabals controlling the world, that sort of thing."

"And I've never been one for trusting the system."

She sighed with exasperation. "All right, you win—on one condition."

"Which is?"

"If this guy says anything, no matter how subtly worded, about a payoff—"

"Then I'll break his face," Anthony said.

"I was thinking that we involve the police and nail him for extortion."

"After I break his face."

"Sure, break his face, fine. Do we have a deal?"

"Deal."

She pushed away from the table, grabbed the bottle of cognac, and screwed the cap on.

"Where are you going with that?" he asked.

"If you're determined to meet this Bob character tonight, you'll need to have a clear head. You need to be in a state of mind to ask him some pointed questions."

"I suppose you're going to help me brainstorm some of these pointed questions."

"You know me well." She stored the bottle on the kitchen counter. "Grab a pen and a pad, Tony, and let's hash this out together."

9

A gigantic drive-in that had been a city landmark for decades, The Varsity was located on North Avenue, across the way from Georgia Tech and in the shadow of Atlanta's skyscrapers. Their distinctive red neon sign, a giant "V," blazed in the summer night, summoning drivers roaring along nearby Interstate 75/85, the Downtown Connector.

Anthony parked on the top level of the two-tiered parking deck. As Bob had likely counted on, the restaurant was jumping with customers who pulled up to the drive-in bays, and others who headed inside the building to grab their Friday night grub. For one worried about being conspicuous, there was anonymity in numbers.

A platoon of security guards patrolled the parking lot, maintaining order and ensuring that no vehicles remained parked beyond the allotted one-hour limit. Exceed an hour, the posted signs warned, and you would return to find a boot attached to your wheel.

He read his watch. A quarter to ten. He waited behind the wheel, drawing deep breaths, as if he could exhale away the heavy emotions that weighed on his heart.

His dad had used to bring him, Danielle, and Mom to The Varsity after they attended football and basketball games at Georgia Tech, his dad's alma mater. Eating chili dogs, burgers, and fries amid the raucous crowd, talking to each other about whatever game they had just watched, people-watching, laughing and joking among themselves . . . those were some of his most vivid, cherished memories of his family before the walls had caved in on their lives.

He hadn't visited the restaurant in fifteen years, but would feel a stab of anguish every time he drove past, a knife twisting in an open wound. Consequently, he tried to avoid driving past.

He should have suggested that they meet somewhere else. He didn't feel as if he had a good hold on himself there. He felt, literally, tears hanging behind his eyes, ready to spill out.

Toughen up. You can do this.

To refocus, he did a quick inventory of his gear.

Although the night was warm, he wore a light windbreaker. He'd slipped a miniature digital voice recorder inside the breast pocket, a device he used when conducting interviews with experts for book research. He checked it to make sure it was functional, and decided to leave it in Record mode from that moment forward.

Underneath his jacket, he also had the Beretta in his waistband holster. He double-checked that it was loaded. It might be a violation of the concealed-carry law for him to take the gun inside this place, but that was a risk he was willing to take.

Blowing out a final, lung-clearing breath, he got out of the truck and walked to the stairs that descended to the ground level of the parking lot. The air was dense with aromas: hot dogs, hamburgers, grilled onions, fries. Music throbbed from cars, and laughter and conversation was everywhere, Atlantans out on a beautiful June night.

As he walked, he scanned back and forth. No one took special note of him. He was just another guy dropping in for chow.

Bob had not told him whether to wait outside, or to go in. He hung outside the entrance until his watch struck ten. After looking around again and seeing no one out of the ordinary, he went inside.

The huge lobby was packed, over a dozen queues of customers streaming to the long, gleaming counter. He waited in an area that featured glass-fronted cases of Varsity memorabilia, trinkets for the tourists who'd made the drive-in one of their Atlanta must-sees. When no one approached him after a couple of minutes, he moved to stand in line, thinking he might buy a Coke, to pass the time.

Someone bumped him from behind.

He started to spin around, but a hand gripped his bicep and a man's voice whispered close to his ear:

"It's Bob—don't turn around. Buy something to eat and go to the counter with a view of the parking lot. I'll be the one reading the Bible."

Bob released him, and sidled away. Anthony watched him in his peripheral vision: Bob was about six-two, lean, with gray hair. He wore a blue jacket, wrinkled white-washed jeans, and loafers, no socks.

From the rear, he looked like an absent-minded college professor, not an oily scam artist or a demented, doomsday conspiracy theorist.

Anthony hadn't eaten anything since lunch, and his stomach was clenched so tight it had killed his appetite. Nevertheless, he ordered a chili dog, fries, and a Coke, the same meal he'd get during visits with his family.

Carrying his meal on a plastic tray, he wandered into the crowded dining area. Bob was huddled at the long counter near the window. He sipped a cola and held a small Bible in one hand, idly turning pages.

With his ruddy, weathered complexion and thinning gray hair, he might have been in his late-fifties or early sixties. He wore black, horn-rimmed glasses, and a pocket protector bristling with pens was clipped to his white, button-down shirt. If he weren't a rumpled college professor, he certainly affected the appearance of one.

Anthony made a show of looking around, as if searching for a seat, and casually moved to the counter, leaving a few feet between himself and the stranger. There were only a handful of other diners at the counter, and they were several feet away, engaged in their own conversations.

Without turning to look at Anthony, keeping his gaze on the window, Bob spoke. He had a faint Georgia accent probably leavened by spending time outside the South, much like Anthony had lost his accent when he went abroad with the Marines.

"Thanks for coming, Anthony, but we don't have much time. I think they've followed me here—and if they have, your life is now in danger, too."

10

According to their intelligence, the target of their mission had gone to an Atlanta dining establishment called The Varsity. Cutty exited the interstate and cruised eastward along North Avenue. The restaurant was ahead, a neon palace in the night.

Cutty drove a late-model, black Chevy Suburban with tinted, bullet-proof glass, a supercharged engine, and reinforced steel panels. He could have selected any vehicle from their extensive fleet, but he'd chosen the Suburban because it was the largest available.

He liked big things: big trucks, big guns, big buildings. Not because he was short in stature and attempting to over-compensate. Great size reminded him of the Almighty.

God was bigger than everything, a hugeness that was impossible for the human mind to comprehend. To surround yourself with large items served as a reminder of God's vastness, how you were so insignificant in comparison to the Divine.

At the debriefing earlier that evening in the Armory, his superior had handed him a big mission, too. Their mark was a high-ranking member of their organization, a past leader in their division, but he was a Judas who sought to betray them in the worst possible way. Cutty's superior had confided that this was such a crucial task that only one of Cutty's caliber was worthy of the job.

Cutty would not fail. Throughout his eight years of service, his mission completion rate was one hundred percent, a division record. When you were fulfilling your life's true purpose, God blessed the work of your hands.

Quiet as usual, Valdez sat in the passenger seat, watching the night-dimmed city pass by through the window. Like him, she wore nocturnal gear: black tracksuit, black sneakers. Her hair was so thick and dark it blended nearly perfectly with her clothing.

Lately, he'd been entranced with her hair. He wanted to run his fingers through it and see if it felt as silky as it looked. He imagined snipping a tiny lock of it when she wasn't looking, and keeping it on his person, to privately touch whenever the mood took him.

She glanced at him, suddenly aware of his attention.

"Is okay?" she asked.

"Yes, everything's fine. Here's our turn."

He turned into the diner's crowded parking lot. He had never eaten there, and he immediately decided that he never would. The cloying aromas of the artery-clogging junk food almost invoked a gag reflex.

Growing up, he hadn't been allowed to consume fast food of any kind. His family had lived on a communal farm in south Georgia. They had cultivated their own fruits, vegetables, and grains, raised chickens, and fished in a nearby lake. As a teenager, he'd once eaten a McDonald's hamburger, and had suffered an upset stomach for two days.

"Look at these heathens, Valdez, defiling their temples," Cutty said. "Doesn't it disgust you?"

"*Si*," Valdez said, scowling with displeasure.

"Burgers, fries, hot dogs, shakes. All crap that destroys the temple. And they're allowing their children to eat this garbage, too. No wonder our nation's kids are fatter than ever."

She bobbed her lovely head in agreement. He raked his gaze across her body, which was concealed, frustratingly, by her loose-fitting clothing.

"Do you ever allow crap like that into your temple?" he asked.

"Ah, no," she said, and made a gagging sound.

He smiled. "I bet you don't. I bet your temple is in fantastic condition."

She only looked at him.

"Do you like my temple?" he asked. "I work out six days a week, perform lots of weightlifting and cardio, and I eat well, too, only wholesome organic food, no garbage like they serve here."

She appeared bewildered. Somewhere, he'd lost her.

"Never mind," he said. "Let's find somewhere to park in this grease pit."

After a minute of cruising, he found a spot on the ground level of the double-deck parking structure, in a corner not far from an exit.

Intelligence had indicated that the Judas was due to rendezvous with an individual who might be assisting him in his treachery. Cutty's first priority was to identify the man's accomplice. Then, to detain the Judas for questioning, by force, if necessary.

Cutty secretly hoped that the use of force *would* be necessary. He had not asked his superior about the nature of the Judas' betrayal, hadn't inquired how the man schemed to damage their organization. The details were irrelevant. Unrepentant disobedience to God's authority was a sin, and harsh punishment was an appropriate response.

The wages of sin is death. That was Romans, chapter six, verse twenty-three. Sin was not a game. God meant business.

He retrieved a large duffel bag from the back seat. Among other things, it contained a lightweight gray jacket, baseball cap, and tinted eyeglasses, elements of a rudimentary disguise.

There was little possibility that the Judas would identify him. The traitor had left their division prior to Cutty's recruitment, and as agent in the most covert unit, Cutty's identity was known only to his superior and the few others who had served alongside him. To all others, he was only a voice on the telephone, a username on the network.

But he had advanced as far as he had because he believed in taking extra precautions. He found the zipper along the seam of the black tracksuit pants, yanked it down, and snatched the bottoms away to reveal the blue jeans he wore underneath. He swapped the tracksuit jacket for the gray one, and donned the cap and the eyewear.

He lifted his arms. The jacket adequately concealed the bulge of the pistol that lay holstered against his ribs.

"I'm going to check out the scene inside, see if I can locate our guy," he said. "Sit tight. I'll radio you with further instructions."

A tiny, flesh-colored earpiece was wedged in his ear, as well as in Valdez's, and miniature microphone transmitters were affixed to the collars of their shirts. The communications system enabled them to stay in contact when separated by up to a thousand yards.

He opened the door, paused. "Want me to grab a burger for you while I'm inside?"

She frowned. "Ah . . . no."

"That was a joke," he said.

"Ah! Funny, very funny." She laughed, but it was one of those obligatory laughs that people offered out of courtesy, not out of genuine amusement.

He did not understand women under most circumstances, and this Valdez was a total enigma. Perhaps, if they could enjoy a long, productive partnership, they could establish a rapport . . . and perhaps that rapport could lead to something more.

The thought gave him a warm jolt of pleasure.

On the sidewalk outside the restaurant, an elderly panhandler in a wheelchair beseeched passerby for money. He was a pathetic sight: rheumy eyes, cracked lips, wooly gray hair and beard that desperately needed trimming. He wore torn, soiled clothes that looked salvaged from a trash heap.

Although Cutty had urgent business inside, he approached the man.

"God loves you," Cutty said.

The man squinted. "Huh?"

Cutty opened his wallet, found a twenty-dollar bill, and offered it to the beggar. The man opened his mouth in a grin that showed diseased-darkened gums and rotted teeth.

"God loves you," Cutty said again, "and so do I."

"Oh, God bless you!" the man said.

"May God bless you as well, my friend." Cutty removed a card from his wallet and pressed it into the man's grime-covered fingers. "The gates of the Kingdom are open. Those are the times and locations of our Sunday services, and you may also view our programs on television or listen in on the radio."

"I'll do that, brother. I sure will."

Cutty smiled and gave the man's frail shoulder a friendly touch. One should never overlook an opportunity to minister to the downtrodden. *For he that is least among you all, the same shall be great.*

His smile fading, he headed inside.

11

I think they've followed me here—and if they have, your life is now in danger, too.

Standing beside Bob, Anthony could not resist the urge to turn and stare at him.

"You're serious about this," Anthony said. "I mean, really."

Bob did not look at him, but his thin lips were drawn into a solemn line. He either was gravely serious, or had the best poker face Anthony had ever seen.

Swiveling back to the window, Anthony picked up his chili dog and took a bite. Although he and Lisa had brainstormed questions that he'd memorized during his drive to the diner, his mind had gone blank.

"I chose this location for our meeting because the security is tight, and it's noisy enough in here to drown out our conversation," Bob said. "Keep your voice down a notch or two and keep looking out the window, and we'll be fine."

Chewing, Anthony nodded.

"Have you told anyone what I've shared with you thus far?" Bob asked.

Anthony shook his head.

In the window's reflection, Anthony saw a smile touch Bob's face. "Come now, Anthony. You're a married man, happily so, from what I've researched. You've told your wife."

Anthony swallowed, sipped his Coke. "Maybe."

"She would eventually find out, anyway. Wives have a sixth sense for knowing when their husbands are hiding something from them. I was married once, seventeen years."

"My wife thinks you're a scam artist."

"Savvy lady. What do you think?"

He stared at Anthony's reflection. Anthony stared back.

"I think you might have some useful information," Anthony said.

"Some useful information?" Bob dabbed at his lips with a napkin, smiled as if amused at a mild joke. "I do indeed have some useful information. But I offer it freely. Money can't purchase redemption, in spite of those who would like us to believe otherwise."

"Is that why you've decided to help me find out why happened to my dad? For your redemption?"

"Yes." Bob's reflected gaze didn't waver. "After doing the kind of work I've done for the past twenty years, let's just say this is my best shot at doing the right thing for a change."

"What kind of work have you done? Killing innocent people?"

"I might be wrong, but I'm thinking you could use a little redemption, too," Bob said, brushing off the questions. "Fifteen long years of blaming yourself for never getting justice, writing those violent vigilante books full of your outrage with the system . . . feeling as if you've failed your old man."

"Hey, you don't know me, all right?" Anthony struggled to keep himself from spinning around to face the guy. "You might've looked me up in Google, done your Internet research or whatever, but you don't *know* me."

"I know that you're here talking to me, in spite of what your better half advised."

"Why come to me with this today? Why not a year ago? Or, how about fifteen years ago?"

"Or how about fifteen years from today? Does my timing matter? You've come here because you want answers, and you believe I can help you find them."

"Can you?"

"How far are you willing to go to get to the truth?"

"All the way. Whatever it takes."

"If you start this journey, you can't turn back. This is the point of no return, friend. If you want to fold your cards and forget all of this, now's the time. Or you can go all in with me." He sipped his drink, studied Anthony's reflection.

Anthony looked around. He looked at the customers at the tables, eating and drinking and talking and laughing, living their happy and carefree lives, unaware that death always lurked behind you and waited until you least expected it to strike and take everything away in a heartbeat . . . . He'd not lived in their blissful world for fifteen years.

"I'm all in," Anthony said. "I've always been all in."

Bob placed his beverage on the tray beside the small Bible. He laid his long fingers across the book's cover, as if taking an oath.

"Imagine an organization, Anthony. They claim to represent the kingdom of truth and righteousness, and they've presented evidence to support their claim. They do many positive works in the community. They've given substantial amounts of money to charities. They've given hope to the hopeless, homes to the once homeless. They present a wonderful façade to the world, but deep inside, the core of this organization is as evil and bent on securing ultimate power as the worst totalitarian movement in history."

"Who are they?"

Bob continued as if he hadn't posed the question. He spoke in a soft tone, but his voice was threaded with energy and passion.

"They have members and sympathizers at every level of society, from your garbage man to university presidents, from the waiter at Waffle House to the judge in federal court, from the elementary school teacher to the news anchor you watch on television every evening. They're everywhere. Some of them are probably here right now, in fact, but they're invisible, because they look like you and me.

"They've committed every crime imaginable in the name of their cause," Bob said. "Assault. Murder. Rape. Robbery. Blackmail. Embezzlement. Fraud. They have divisions of highly trained personnel so overzealous they make the CIA, NSA, and FBI look like bleeding-heart pacifists. Unlike those agencies, which at least are supposed to obey the laws of our country, these people have no regard whatsoever for the laws of man. They claim to answer to only a higher authority."

"Is this some kind of religious group?" Anthony asked. "Like a cult?"

The question brought a bitter smile to Bob's lips. "This organization has developed a technology division so advanced they can tap into public and private databases that allow them to access and manipulate any data you can imagine—and some that you probably can't. Does that sound like a sect of fundamentalists living in log cabins in the wilderness?"

"Now that you've put it like that . . . no."

"We live in interesting times, Anthony. Technology and commercialism have taken over our society. You can communicate on Twitter in real time with a thousand social contacts via your Blackberry, find your favorite Starbucks double-latte damn near anywhere you go, meet your future spouse online, buy anything under the sun at Wal-Mart for half price, capture video of a crime on your cell phone that winds up as the lead story on the nightly news.

"In spite of all these great advancements and conveniences, folks feel more isolated than ever. Emptier. More depressed. Wondering if this, this technologically-driven, commercial marvel of a world we've created, is all there is to life. Is it?"

He looked directly at Anthony for the first time. Behind the thick lenses of his glasses, his eyes were troubled, and Anthony realized that he was asking *him* what Anthony had assumed was a rhetorical question.

"Hey, I . . . I don't know, man," Anthony said.

"An honest answer." Moving back to the window, Bob chuckled, but it was a grim sound. "I don't know, either, friend. All I have is a bit of faith, and that comforts me."

Good for you, Anthony thought, but he kept quiet.

"But these people," Bob said, "oh, *they* know, all right, and they, and those like them, have leveraged their alleged knowledge to the tune of billions of dollars in profits and unprecedented influence. They will assure you that this world around us, your iPod and fuel-efficient hybrid vehicle, your Facebook friend list and your admin job in a cubicle farm at a multinational corporation, is *not* all there is to life, oh no. There is a glorious heaven where the faithful believers go. There is an eternity in hell for that sinner who cut you off in traffic. There is a God who loves you and has a greater purpose for you. But to gain access to heaven and this loving, just God . . . there's a price."

Anthony grunted. "Isn't there always?"

"Please understand," Bob said, index finger pointed. "There are many, many sincere and noble believers and religious leaders throughout the world, and we are better for them. They're the good ones, and we need more of them, so very badly."

"But they aren't the problem."

"Our issue is the ravening wolves preying on the sheep. The false prophets. Those who are selling God—packaging God in books and DVDs and seminars and conferences, those haranguing you from their golden pulpits to send in more donations or else God will condemn you to everlasting damnation. Those who are using God as a weapon to usurp control of your bank account, your vote, your home, your family, your *soul*."

"Look, I don't keep up with religion, churches, any of that stuff," Anthony said. "Far as I'm concerned, fifteen years ago, God told me he didn't give a damn about my family. So why should I care about him?"

"We are all of us seekers on the path. You'll have to discover the answer to that question on your own. I don't know."

"And I don't *care*," Anthony said, with more anger than he intended. He took in a deep breath, steadied himself. "You haven't told me how my dad fits into any of this."

"He wanted to bring them down." Bob's voice dropped to a whisper, and his gaze searched the mirror-image of the area behind them. "Do you think they would allow someone to destroy their well-oiled machine of commerce and power? Do you think they would let anyone disrupt their plans? Do you think they would stand idly by while someone erases everything for which they've labored?"

Anthony shook his head. "I'm finding it hard to believe my dad was involved in anything like that. He was a sports writer, man, not a community activist."

"He was an activist for that which mattered most to him, as you are. Your family."

Anthony drummed the counter. "It sounds . . . crazy. But I've always thought . . . well, I knew there was something on Dad's mind that morning . . . ."

"Probably pondering the very dilemma that ended his life," Bob said.

"You said you were there at the lake."

"I know the man responsible, Anthony."

"Who is he?"

"Even if I were to give you his name, you couldn't get to him, not the way that you think you can. There's only one way to bring them down. You have to turn their machinery against them."

"Why can't you do it? What do you need me for?"

"I've gathered enough damning evidence to crush them. But we must be careful—we can't trust law enforcement. These people have too many contacts, an army of minions at every level, from federal agencies on down to the local Barney Fife. As I warned you, they're everywhere."

"Again, why me?"

"I needed someone like you to finish the job."

74

Bob's reflected eyes focused on Anthony for a beat, and then traveled toward the far end of the room.

Anthony glanced around the dining room, too, but he saw nothing of concern. "What do you mean, you needed someone like me?"

"Someone with the ability and the motivation, and I'd say you have plenty of both." He turned to Anthony. "They're on to you now, Anthony. Go home, get your wife, and stay on the move till you find the truth. Don't let your dad's death be in vain."

Bob shuffled away, head lowered. He ambled down the corridor to the lobby, and disappeared in the shifting masses of people.

With studied casualness, Anthony surveyed his surroundings. Initially, as before, no one stood out.

They're onto you now, Anthony.

Then he noticed a broad, pale-skinned man sitting at a table in the corner, near the edge of the corridor.

Eyes hidden behind tinted glasses, the guy wore a plain baseball cap and gray jacket. He sipped bottled water through a straw and slowly scanned back and forth from the lobby to the dining area as if waiting for someone to arrive with food.

Briefly, Anthony felt their gazes connect. The hairs rose at the nape of his neck.

He's one of them.

Anthony swung back to the window.

He wasn't sure at what point he had bought into Bob's story. Maybe from the very beginning, when he'd found the letter in his SUV. But he felt full-blown paranoia swelling in his chest, speeding his heart rate, as if he'd been injected with some crazy, reality-bending drug.

He noticed Bob had left behind his tray. It held a bag of cold fries, his beverage, and the small Bible he'd been reading.

Bob could have left behind the book by mistake, but Anthony doubted it.

He carefully placed his own tray on top of Bob's. He carried both trays toward the north exit, away from the pale stranger.

75

At a trash can near the doors, using his body to block anyone behind from watching, he grabbed the book and emptied the contents of both trays into the trash. Without looking behind him, he pocketed the Bible and went out through the glass double doors.

On the landing, he reached inside his pocket and clicked off the digital recorder.

Heart thundering, he took the stairs to the parking lot.

12

Cutty had been watching the Judas conversing discreetly with a tall, well-built black man when the Judas abruptly turned away and walked out. He shuffled past where Cutty sat, but he did not look at him. He didn't need to—what had happened was obvious.

Cutty had been made.

It happened sometimes. The Judas had once been a leader in their division, after all, and had been trained to recognize a tail.

It didn't particularly bother Cutty. The thick fumes of junk food had begun to nauseate him, and he was ready to get out of there, drive far away, and grab a hot shower to cleanse the stink from his pores.

The Judas navigated through the crowd and went toward the restrooms. Cutty had briefly reconnoitered the restrooms earlier, and found there was no exit that way. He would return to the Judas after he finished appraising the black man.

The man was looking around the room. For an instant, he and Cutty made eye contact.

Cutty felt a tremor in his stomach. Although he'd never before seen this man, intuition told him that there was something about this guy, something unusual and intriguing, and worth a closer look.

He watched the guy stack two plastic trays and take them to a trash can near the north exit. The guy dumped the contents of the trays and left through the doors. He didn't look back.

Cutty spoke into the radio transmitter affixed to his shirt collar.

"Valdez, there's a person of interest coming down the north stairwell. Black man, about six feet tall, in his early thirties, in a dark windbreaker, jeans, and a baseball cap. Don't stop him, but see what he's driving and get his plates."

He waited for Valdez's response, hoping that she understood his directions. After a few seconds, her voice crackled in his earpiece.

"Okay."

He would have to assume that she had comprehended his orders. He didn't have time to baby-sit her.

He dumped his bottled water in a wastebasket and left the dining area for the lobby, using his broad shoulders like a wedge to force through the knotted crowd. A couple of times he had to give guys taller than him a hard shove. They turned and looked down at him as if to say something rude, but when they saw the expression on his face they shut their mouths like meek little lambs.

You didn't have to be tall to be intimidating. It was all about presence.

He shoved open the door to the men's room. There were six urinals, but none were in use. Four toilet stalls stood along the wall. The doors to all of them hung open, except the one at the end.

He knelt to the linoleum floor, checking for a pair of legs in the stall with the closed door. He saw none.

He grabbed the metal trash can and levered it underneath the door handle. He withdrew his Glock and, angling the muzzle toward the ceiling, stalked toward the corner stall.

"I know you're in there, Judas," Cutty said. "You must answer for your betrayal."

Cutty kicked the door. The cheap dead-bolt lock broke from the impact of the kick, and the door banged open.

The stall was empty. But the toilet was full—of urine, and crap.

Apparently, he wasn't the only one who had reconnoitered. The Judas must have visited earlier, set up the locked door, and left behind the disgusting mess in the toilet, a bold thumbing of his nose at Cutty and the organization.

An ordinary man would have sworn and been overcome with rage, but Cutty was better than that: a godly man was slow to anger. He channeled his energies into his work. Years of prayer, self-denial, and stringent discipline had armored him with an unflappable composure of which he was quite proud.

Holstering his gun, he kicked aside the trashcan from the door and hastened out of the restroom. He spotted the women's restroom across the corridor, and realized at once how the Judas had fooled

78

him a few minutes ago. He'd merely entered the ladies' room, knowing that Cutty would make the natural assumption that he'd gone into the men's lavatory.

He didn't bother searching the ladies' restroom. The Judas would be out of the building by then, and they were going to lose him if they didn't act fast.

He radioed Valdez and got out of there, ramming like a tank through the crowd.

13

Hands shoved in his jacket pockets, Anthony hurried across the parking lot and to the concrete staircase that led to the upper level of the parking deck. As he ascended, he had the distinct sense that someone was watching him, a sensation like a feather lying against the back of his neck.

He glanced over his shoulder.

A stunning Latina woman was climbing the stairs, too. Dark hair pulled away from her golden, porcelain-smooth face, she wore a black tracksuit, black sneakers, and a lightweight cream-colored jacket. She held a cell phone to her ear and was speaking in rapid-fire Spanish.

She noticed his attention, and smiled.

But it was a smile that said only, *yes, I know I'm gorgeous, and I know you like what you see, and I'm acknowledging your existence because it's the polite thing to do, but sorry, I'm not really interested in you, so please keep moving.* A smile that beautiful women paid to men a dozen times a day.

But something about her bugged him. Gut instinct.

He reached the top of the stairs and went to his Tahoe. At the driver's door, he acted as though he was fumbling for his keys in his jacket, but he stealthily moved his right hand to the butt of his Beretta.

In the corner of his eye, he watched the woman stroll past. She was still on her call, gesturing excitedly, but then she looked in his direction. It was intended to be a meaningless, oh-there-he-is-again look, but he felt as if he had stuck his finger in an electrical outlet.

She's one of them, too. She followed me up here to see what car I was driving . . . maybe to check my license plates . . .

He whirled to face her. "Who are you?"

Ignoring him, the woman put away the phone and rushed back to the staircase.

"Hey!" he said.

Quickly, she descended out of sight.

Cursing, Anthony hustled behind the wheel, slammed the door. He slipped the Beretta out of the holster. The weight of the pistol calmed him, but only a little.

He took the Bible out of his jacket pocket and thumbed through it. Various passages were highlighted with multicolored pens. At the front of the book, on a page that stated, "This Bible Belongs To," a name he didn't recognize was inscribed in girlish handwriting.

He placed the book on the passenger seat, leaned toward the windshield, and scanned the parking lot below. He didn't see Bob or the short guy with the tinted glasses, and the Latina woman had vanished as if she'd been only a figment of his paranoid imaginings.

But his nerves crackled like live wires.

Setting aside the gun but keeping it within reach, he backed out of the parking space and took the ramp to the lower level. He exited the lot via a rear entrance. Hitting a side road, he fed the gas and blew through the night.

Trouble was on the way, the nature of which he didn't yet fully understand. But he had to get home, and quickly.

14

Outside The Varsity, Cutty and Valdez searched for the Judas, with no luck. The traitor had escaped.

"He is gone," Valdez said, wind tossing strands of hair across her face. "What do we do?"

"Follow me," Cutty said.

He marched across the parking lot to the Suburban. Protocol required that he contact the dispatcher and notify him that he had lost the Judas, to allow them to use their awesome resources to relocate him. But placing that call would be the equivalent of admitting failure, of telling his superior that he was not as capable as they believed him to be, and that they'd erred in giving him the task.

He had never failed, and he would not this time. God hated losers.

Ensconced in the driver's seat, he powered on the mobile data terminal, which was mounted in the console beneath the stereo. Much like the computers with which police cars were outfitted, the MDT was a customization to the truck, connected via satellite to their organization's servers. All of the vehicles in their division's fleet were similarly equipped.

A small, removable keyboard was slotted beneath the screen. He slid it out and placed it on his lap.

The greeting, *"Welcome to the Genesis Network"* filled the display, white text floating on an ocean-blue background.

"The man I asked you to follow," he said to Valdez, "you got the plates from his vehicle like I asked you to?"

"*Si.*"

"God bless you, Valdez," he said. "You rock."

She smiled. "*Gracias.*"

He returned his attention to the screen, and entered his username and password to sign on to the network.

The Genesis Network was the brains of their division, a cutting-edge system of servers and software designed and administered by techies. Gen, as it was casually known amongst them, was linked—sometimes secretly—to public and private databases across the globe. He'd once toured the underground core data center where the network was housed, and had been awed by the vast chamber of servers taller than him, the giant monitors streaming rivers of data, and the gimlet-eyed programmers who spoke in such geek-speak they were nearly incomprehensible. He was not a techie. He was a field guy who went out and got his hands dirty. But he appreciated the value of high-tech tools; we lived in an age when information was worth more than money, and Gen made his job immeasurably easier.

Ironically, he had been reared in a household that lacked a television set, radio, and even a telephone. The devil, he'd been taught as a child, was skilled at using the wonders of modern technology to deceive you, and out of concern for the spiritual health of the family, Father had banned those devices from the home. It was not until his late teen years that he learned God's most valiant warriors were using technology to wage their war against the wicked.

After entering a series of keystrokes, he arrived at a menu that offered access to the State of Georgia Department of Motor Vehicles records. A blank field requested license plates data.

"And his plates are?" he asked.

She told him in her halting English, and he typed in the combination of letters and digits. Almost immediately, Gen had a hit.

The results included the license registrant's name, vehicle make, model, and VIN, registrant's date of birth, height, weight, current street address, and a photo from his most recently issued driver's license.

It was the same man he'd witnessed talking to the Judas in the grease joint.

"Anthony Thorne, Junior," Cutty said. "Thirty years old. Resides at 522 Cherokee Avenue, in Atlanta."

At the bottom of the screen, a command allowed you to request a full background check on any given individual. It could take up to an hour or two for Gen to compile a complete personal profile, so he went ahead and requested the comprehensive report. It might prove useful later.

As were all fleet vehicles, the Suburban was equipped with a GPS navigation system. He entered Thorne's address. The estimated drive time was thirteen minutes.

"Let's go talk to this guy," he said.

15

From outside, home appeared as Anthony had left it. Soft light glowed at the windows, and the porch lamp was on, fat moths batting against the fixture.

Anthony parked in the garage, but left the door up. He'd left the driveway gate open, too. Planning ahead.

Before going inside, he looked toward the front of the house. There was nothing out of the ordinary, just sporadic traffic breezing past on a Friday night.

Driving back, he hadn't noticed a tail. But if these people had the technological resources that Bob claimed, they wouldn't have needed to trail him. A run against his license plates, which he was increasingly convinced was why the Latina woman had followed him to his truck, would give up his street address.

Gun drawn, he rushed inside. No signs of forced entry downstairs. Good.

Upstairs in the master bedroom, Lisa lay atop a blue exercise ball, mechanically burning through the set of three hundred crunches she performed each night before hitting the sack. She was something of a fitness fanatic, doing her Pilates and running on the treadmill and working out on the exercise ball, determined to beat back the inevitable pull of gravity and age.

He hoped she had some gas left in her tank, because tonight might get hairy.

He holstered his gun. "Lisa, we've gotta talk."

Fingers interlaced behind her head, she twisted around to look at him, short of breath. "Hey. Heard you come in. How'd it go?"

He hadn't called her during his drive home. He'd driven so fast that speaking on the phone might've distracted him, led to him wrapping the SUV around a tree. Besides, this was the kind of conversation they needed to have face-to-face.

He said, "I need you to do something, right this second, and we don't have time to go over lots of questions."

"Huh?" She bounced off the ball. "What're you talking about? What happened at The Varsity?"

"I need you to get dressed and pack a suitcase with enough clothes for a couple of days, stuff for the both of us. Pack only the necessities. Light clothes we can move fast in."

"*What?*"

"Bob is legit, Lisa. Some big, extremist religious organization, a cult or whatever, is at the bottom of things. I noticed two of the members there—they *saw* me, and I think they're coming here."

"Baby, please, slow down—"

"We don't have time! Don't argue with me, okay, just trust me and do what I say. I'll explain everything later, but we have to get the hell out of here."

She stared at him, as if convinced that he was playing a joke and she was waiting for the punch line. When he didn't laugh or smile, her gaze faltered.

"You aren't kidding," she said.

"No. We've gotta get moving. Now. *Please.*"

"This is nuts." But she made a beeline to the walk-in closet.

He opened the nightstand drawer on his side of the bed and dug out the Smith & Wesson .357 he kept stored inside. He swung open the cylinder; the five-shooter was already loaded with hollow-points. As Lisa came back into the bedroom dragging a piece of carry-on luggage, he handed the gun to her.

She hesitated. "Is this necessary?"

"It might be. Take it."

Reluctantly, she accepted the revolver. She knew how to handle firearms—at his insistence, she accompanied him to the firing range every month—but she'd never been a big fan of them. She seemed offended by the idea that ordinary civilians would want to keep guns in their house, and she merely tolerated his preoccupation with them.

"Keep it close while you pack," he said. "I'm going to the basement to grab a few more things."

"Okay."

He could read from her eyes and voice that she didn't believe they were in danger, that she might have even worried that he'd finally gone over the deep end. That was fine with him, so long as she did what he asked.

On the way downstairs, he looked outside a front window. The only person on the street was a neighbor of theirs who liked to walk with his German Shepherd at late-night hours.

He turned a dial beside the doorway to brighten the porch light. Anyone creeping outdoors would be caught in the glare, might be less likely to boldly approach the house.

In his office, he unplugged the laptop, wrapped the power cord around the machine, and thrust them both into a large canvas satchel that hung on the back of the door. He dropped the satchel on the floor and he went to the electronically secured door at the far end of the office.

He punched a six-digit code into the keypad. There was a beep, and the lock disengaged with a click.

The custom made oak door, reinforced with a steel core, was heavy. When he pushed it open, the familiar fumes of metal, oil, and gunpowder met his nostrils.

He switched on the overhead fluorescents. The room was about the size of the walk-in closet in the master suite. It contained a few items of clothing, but mostly it contained guns.

A stainless steel rack on the left held a collection of six rifles and shotguns: two Winchester rifles, a Mossberg twelve-gauge shotgun, a Remington, a Weatherby Athena, a Springfield tactical rifle.

On the right, six handguns hung from hooks, an assortment of revolvers and semi-autos: a Glock 19, a Walther PPK, a Beretta M9 like the one he kept in his car, a Colt .45, a Heckler & Koch 9mm, a .50 caliber Desert Eagle.

Assorted Ka-Bar knives were arrayed on a stand beneath the handguns. A large metal cabinet in the corner of the space housed ammunition for every firearm.

His Marine Corps saber, sheathed in its leather scabbard, occupied a prominent spot on the far wall.

Another metal case contained night vision binoculars, a utility flashlight, and other accessories. The pieces of clothing, dangling from hangers, included his Marine dress blues, concealable body armor, and a camouflage outfit. His olive-green duffel bag lay on the concrete floor, beside a pair of well-worn combat boots.

He'd only ever allowed Lisa and his closest friends into the room. Only those in his inner circle understood his interest—perhaps it had become his obsession—in amassing weaponry like a survivalist living in a remote mountain-top cabin and awaiting Armageddon.

Although Bob had warned him to keep moving, he could have opted to load all his weapons and turn his house into a fighting hole. But he didn't know enough about who he was dealing with, and if they were as well-equipped and ruthless as Bob had suggested, they might drop a nerve agent in the ventilation system and render him helpless, cut the power to the house and break in under cover of darkness, or flush him out with a series of hand grenades.

Going on the run was, at the moment, the only strategy that made sense.

He selected three different handguns, shoved them into the duffel, and dragged the bag to the ammo cabinet. He unlocked the doors and pulled out dozens of rounds of ammo for each firearm, dumped them in, too.

From the accessories bin, he took night vision binoculars, a flashlight, and other equipment that might come in handy. He grabbed the body armor vest off the hanger.

Lastly, at the far end of the closet, beneath his saber, he knelt to what appeared to be a large air filter grille set in the wall near the floor. The aluminum grille was actually the front of a wall safe, and opened like a hinged door when he pulled a miniature lever at the bottom edge.

He swung out the front panel, did three quick twists on the combination lock, and opened the safe.

Rubber-banded packets of cash, in denominations of twenties, fifties, and hundreds, lay stacked inside, totaling approximately twenty thousand dollars.

Every day that he left the cash in the safe, the relentless march of inflation nibbled away at its value. Keeping the money in a high-interest bearing savings account would have been the financially savvy move.

But in a desperate situation, he wouldn't have immediate access to the money. In a world where computer viruses could sucker-punch financial systems, where Category Five hurricanes could tear through cities and send hordes of people swarming to banks to fund their escapes, you couldn't count on an ATM or a financial institution to save you in a tight spot.

Paranoid? Yeah, he'd known that it was a bit crazy even as he was socking the money away. But now he was glad that he'd done it.

He removed five bundles, about five thousand dollars worth, and dropped them in the bottom of the duffel.

His watch read twenty past eleven. He'd been home for only fifteen minutes, but the seconds were advancing at hyper-speed.

After securing the closet door, he hustled across the office, grabbed the satchel off the floor, and ran upstairs.

16

In the bedroom, Lisa had dressed in a blue velour suit and running shoes, and tucked her hair underneath an Atlanta Braves cap. She was zipping shut the carry-on that lay on the bed.

"I'll take this." He grabbed the carry-on's side handle. "You just bring your purse and the gun."

"Thanks." She glanced at the duffel bag hanging from his shoulder. "I don't think I want to know what you've got in there."

"Plenty of things I hope we don't need. Let's roll. Leave the lights on, so people think we're home."

"You haven't said where we're going."

"That 'cause I haven't figured it out yet. We'll get to that."

The telephone rang. They stared at the phone as if it were a detonator on a ticking bomb.

"It's almost eleven-thirty," he said. "No friend or family would call this late, unless it's an emergency."

She read the Caller ID display. "It says unknown caller. Could it be a wrong number, you think?"

"I doubt it."

She frowned. "Come on, Tony."

"Listen, if it's someone we know and it's urgent, they can reach us on our cells."

"You think it's those people Bob warned you about?"

"It's the only thing that makes sense to me right now."

"But our number is unlisted." For the first time, a hint of true anxiety glinted in her eyes.

"That's exactly why I'm worried. Let's go."

Outside in the garage, while she waited in the truck, he stored the duffel bag and carry-on in the cargo space. As he slammed the liftgate, he heard a vehicle rumbling at the mouth of the driveway.

He spun, hand on the pistol.

A black Chevy Suburban crawled past the house. The driver might have been innocently searching for a friend's residence, but he doubted it. It moved too slowly, too deliberately. He scrambled behind the wheel.

"What's wrong?" Lisa asked.

"A black Suburban drove by, real slowly, like the driver was casing the place."

"How could they know where we live?" She looked in the side mirror.

"I think they got my plates when I was at The Varsity, ran them against a database, got our street address."

"They can do that?" Her eyes were wide, disbelieving.

"Later." He gunned the engine and strapped the seat harness across his chest. "Later, I promise, I'll tell you everything I know. But first, I need you to buckle up. This might get rough."

She muttered under her breath, but did as he asked.

He shifted into Reverse and hit the gas pedal, and they rocketed out of the garage. He spun the steering wheel, backing into the turnaround, and straightened out. Then hit the gas.

Apparently having doubled back, the Suburban rolled across the driveway, blocking their escape.

"Oh, shit," she said.

"Hang on." He kept his foot on the gas pedal.

The Suburban's driver's side window slid down. The pale, stout man from The Varsity was perched behind the wheel, though he no longer wore the tinted glasses. Surrounded by the darkness of the vehicle's cabin, his face looked as if it had been carved from ice.

He had a large pistol, and he was aiming it at them.

"I order you to stop!" he shouted.

Screaming, Lisa ducked in her seat.

"Hold on!" Anthony said.

He roared through the open gate and wrestled the wheel to the right. They tore across the front yard, divots of grass flying, narrowly avoided an oak tree, and catapulted over the curb and banged onto the street, the undercarriage crashing against the pavement.

"Jesus," Lisa was saying over and over, as she huddled on the seat. "Oh, Jesus, Jesus."

Anthony twisted the wheel, floored the accelerator. They surged down the dark street.

Behind them, gunfire erupted.

Lisa shrieked. Anthony glanced in the rearview mirror, saw that the guy had gotten out of the Suburban and was shooting at them. He wore a black tracksuit, as did his partner, the Latina woman. She was out of the vehicle, too, gun in her hands.

Sometimes, he hated when his instincts were right.

A bullet twanged off the rear bumper. Another round hit them, and something shattered. It sounded like a taillight.

"Stay down," he said to Lisa, but he hadn't needed to say it. She lay nearly flat against the seat, the harness twisted around her chest. Her eyes were squeezed shut, as if she were wishing this was all a nightmare that would soon end.

At a four-way intersection, he ran the Stop sign and swerved around the corner, tires wailing. He checked behind them.

The guy and the woman had climbed back in their truck, and were coming.

17

Lying low against the seat, half-wishing she could be absorbed like oil into the leather, Lisa braced herself for a bullet plowing into her spine, for the SUV to tip over and hurtle her through the windshield, for a car driven by an innocent to strike them head-on and crush them inside. The night, already troubling since Anthony had shared his account of his communications with the enigmatic Bob, had become more terrifying than anything she had ever imagined, a menacing new world where worst-case scenarios seemed not only plausible, but likely.

How could this be happening to them? They were ordinary people. They lived quiet lives. How had they gotten sucked into this?

Anthony handled the Tahoe with cool intensity, spinning the wheel with authority, hitting the gas and the brakes crisply, as if being shot at by maniacs was an everyday occurrence. Although he rarely spoke of it, she knew he'd completed combat missions in the Marines, had been in situations where his life was on the line and the lives of others rested in his hands, but she had never seen this side of him. The Anthony she'd fallen in love with was gentle--strong, too, yes—but mostly gentle and thoughtful, with an acute awareness of the frailty of life and a quiet commitment to making the most of each day, never taking his loved ones for granted.

But this man so weirdly calm in the face of peril was foreign to her—and she was, she had to admit, thankful that he was around.

He shifted the truck into Reverse, and the tires chewed through dirt and rocks and climbed a slight, bumpy hill. She turned her face to the windshield, and from her vantage point, saw only leafy trees against a black sky.

"Where are we?" she whispered.

"You can pop up and look."

The truck rocked to a stop. He shut off the lights and the engine.

Heart knocking so loudly it seemed to rattle the windows, she rose in the seat. They were at the terminus of a driveway crowded with weeds and shrubbery. The cracked, canted lane curved around a gigantic maple and a spray of tall weeds, and emptied into the quiet street beyond.

Behind them stood a Craftsman-style home in disrepair, shingles faded and draped in kudzu, windows boarded over with plywood. A chain-link fence festooned in vines bordered the yard, holes torn through the link fabric.

"We're only about five or six blocks away from home," he said. "I figured we could lie low here for a few minutes, till the coast is clear."

"What the hell is going on, Tony? Who were those people? Why were they shooting at us?"

"They saw me with Bob. Bob betrayed them, I think, and they probably figure that he and I are working together."

"Working together on what?"

"Bringing them down."

"Bringing down whom? Who *are* they?"

"Sorry, I don't have many answers, Lisa. Bob was vague. But this group after us—they're powerful, well-connected."

"You mentioned they might be some kind of cult?"

"That's what Bob said."

More questions stormed through her thoughts, but hard shudders suddenly wracked her, and she hugged herself. The night was warm, but she was drenched in perspiration, freezing.

Anthony took one of her hands in his. His steady strength and his warmth were what she needed.

"I feel like I'm about to fall to pieces, but you're so composed," she said. "I guess you've been in situations like this before."

He laughed softly. "Not quite like this."

"These people after us . . . you think they murdered your dad?"

"That's what I'm going to find out," he said, eyes hard as gunmetal.

"But how—"

94

He brought his finger to his lips, and she left the question unfinished. He pointed toward the street.

Through the trees and shrubbery, she glimpsed the Suburban. It lurked past the driveway like a panther sniffing for prey.

Involuntarily, she held her breath.

"There's only the one vehicle," Anthony whispered. "I'd worried that they might have dispatched a whole squad after us."

Past the driveway, the truck halted.

She let out a rush of air, swallowed. "They know we're back here."

Nodding, Anthony gripped his pistol.

"You may want to duck again," he said.

18

Cutty had commanded Valdez to stop the Suburban in the middle of the street.

"Thorne's around here somewhere, Valdez," he said. "I can feel him."

Cutty perched on the edge of the passenger seat, clasping the Glock. After their failed attempt at preventing Thorne from leaving his residence, he had ordered Valdez to drive so he could have his hands free to shoot.

En route to Thorne's residence, he had used Gen to dig up Thorne's home phone number. The number was unlisted, but the system spat it back to Cutty within seconds of his request. He'd hoped to get Thorne on the phone, to confirm his presence at home and talk to him for a few minutes—until he arrived and put a gun to Thorne's head and demand he explain his role in the Judas' treachery.

By running, Thorne gave Cutty license to kill him. Only a man guilty of sin sought to avoid God's justice, and the wages of sin is death.

Gloved fingers clenching the steering wheel, Valdez was silent, rosy lips pressed together. In the pursuit, she'd handled the big truck with considerable, unexpected finesse, and he wondered what other skills she possessed.

He opened the glove box and removed a pair of night vision binoculars.

He hadn't received the results of the background check on Thorne, but he was growing antsy to get it. Thorne wasn't behaving like the typical gutless sinner who rolled over at the first sign of violence. The guy had an unusual amount of daring.

"Make a U-turn and go by the driveway we just passed," Cutty said. "I want to get a closer look at what was in all that thick undergrowth."

"Okay."

She executed a textbook U-turn. A handful of houses stood along the street, homes that appeared to have been built decades ago, with trimmed shrubbery and well-tended lawns. The homes were in good condition except for the one on his right, a lot so overgrown with weeds, shrubs, and trees that the residence itself was almost completely concealed.

A crumbling driveway gave access to the back of the property, and that was where he wanted to inspect more closely.

He lifted the binoculars to his eyes.

Like a chariot commandeered by the devil himself, Thorne's SUV thundered out of the darkness. The high-beams flashed on, searing the interior of the Suburban.

Blinded, Cutty dropped the binoculars and fumbled for the Glock.

"He has gun!" Valdez shouted.

She slammed into Reverse, flinging Cutty forward in the seat.

Although disoriented by the sudden glare, Cutty saw it, too. Thorne had opened the driver's side door and popped around the side, and he was gripping a gun in both hands and holding a stance like he knew what he was doing.

Who was this guy?

Gunfire shattered the night. Rounds hammered the grille and windshield, and thank God, the vehicle was equipped with bulletproof glass, or else Cutty knew he would have taken one in the head.

But he thought he heard a tire blow. When he felt the truck veer hard to the right and heard Valdez's anguished cry, he knew his suspicions were correct.

They hurtled across the street, vaulted the curb, and sideswiped an elm. Valdez brought the truck to a stop before they mowed down a picket fence in someone's front yard.

The commotion alerted the neighbors. Porch lights switched on at a few residences, and a house-robed old woman with wild hair wandered onto her front porch with a phone pressed to her ear.

The prospect of nosy neighbors calling police didn't concern him. The understaffed and overworked Atlanta Police Department typically took nearly an hour to respond to emergency calls. Cutty would need only to notify his dispatcher, and the dispatcher would see to it that law enforcement's response would be further delayed. When you were doing God's work, all obstacles were removed from your path.

Ahead, Thorne climbed back into his vehicle and exploded down the street.

"Go, go, go!" Cutty said.

She mashed the gas, and the Suburban leaped forward.

Cutty opened the sun roof. He rose through it, planted his arms on the roof, and fired at the truck from a distance of about fifty yards. His first shot grazed the vehicle's rear bumper, and his second and third shots missed entirely.

The Tahoe hauled around the corner, tires screeching.

Cutty dropped back into his seat. "Stay on him, Valdez!"

"But the tire—"

"Forget the tire! Keep driving!"

"*Si*," she said, voice taut.

Rubber flapping from the ruined tire, the exposed steel rim ringing as it ground against the pavement, Valdez gave chase.

"I need more firepower," he said. He reached into the back seat and snagged his rifle, stored in a black nylon case.

Before his current assignment, he had been a member of the sniper unit, and like he was everywhere else, he'd been the best. He'd once nailed a target between the eyes from half a mile away, a record in the division that still stood.

He unzipped the case. It contained a Remington 700, the police version, a bolt-action rifle outfitted with a Leupold riflescope that gave it an effective range at night in excess of three hundred meters—the length of almost three football fields. A zippered compartment held Winchester .308 match grade ammo.

"Keep him in sight," he said. "I'll take care of the rest."

19

Anthony had hoped that blowing out one of the goon's tires would bring an end to the chase, but then he watched the vehicle career around a corner about a hundred yards behind them, slowed but still in the hunt.

"These people are relentless," he said.

Grant Park, the Cyclorama, and Zoo Atlanta were on his right, all of them dark and gated at that late hour. He steered over the curb and plowed down the wide, steep expanse of thick park grass, the bumps and valleys tossing them about in their seats.

Bouncing around, Lisa dared to peer over the dashboard. "Where are we going?"

"To the park. It's a nice night. I figured we could get out, take a stroll under the moon and stars, maybe spread out a blanket for a picnic."

"Picnic? What?"

She looked at him as if he were crazy. So much for trying to lighten the mood with a joke.

"I'm taking a shortcut," he said. "They won't be able to get their truck up to speed 'cause of the tire, so I want to try to shake them off. Sit tight."

Teeth clenched, Lisa braced her arms against the dashboard as they knocked about. He had to give it to her—she was hanging tough. He had seen grown men who pissed their pants under enemy fire, but she had kept her emotions in check.

They reached the bottom of the hill and entered a huge parking lot. The Suburban was above and behind them, racing around on the adjacent road. It would have been too risky for the maniacs to navigate a hill with a blown tire.

He drove across the parking lot, heading to the opposite side of the park, which faced Boulevard Avenue. Cloaked in darkness, a trio of teenagers was huddled surreptitiously in a circle, maybe smoking something illegal, and when they saw him rolling up they dropped their glowing contraband to the ground and took off running.

"Kids up to no good," Lisa said in a motherly tone. "Their asses need to be at home."

"Makes me wonder what Reuben is doing, at home with no supervision."

"We hope he's at home."

"I'd rather not think about it."

They reached grass again and climbed the incline, though this one was not as steep as the one they had descended. He swerved to avoid smashing a set of wooden benches and a trash can.

Behind them, the Suburban had reached the side street that intersected Boulevard, orange sparks dancing around the tire's exposed rim. They were at least three hundred yards behind.

"We're gonna lose them," Anthony said.

A rifle shot cracked the night. Bark exploded like shrapnel from an elm tree on their immediate left.

"Shit, he's got a rifle," Anthony said. "Get down!"

Lisa dropped low again, and he dipped, too. Cold sweat bathed his face. A sniper could hit a target from a mile away with the right weapon and in good conditions, and in a moving vehicle at night, this guy had barely missed them from a few hundred yards distant.

What the hell kind of religious organization did these people work for, anyway?

He wrenched the wheel to the right, to present a tougher angle to the shooter and to gain cover from a row of wide oaks. But the move offered only temporary security. The Suburban was on the prowl and the guy would be working to get in position for another shot.

They reached the top of the incline. They rolled over the sidewalk, bounced across the curb, and jumped into the four-lane street, landing amidst a thin stream of southbound traffic.

He glanced in the rearview mirror, saw the Suburban had reached the corner of the intersection. The rifle jutted out of the passenger window.

He jerked the wheel to the left and swung across the median. An oncoming car blared its horn and braked, the driver shouting obscenities.

"Sorry, my bad," Anthony said.

He turned off Boulevard and onto a downward sloping street that led into a residential area. At the next intersection, he made a left, and found himself on a house-lined road that ran parallel with Boulevard.

He ignored a Stop sign. As he passed through the intersection, he saw, a couple of blocks down on his left, the Suburban waiting at the same intersection at which he had last seen it.

"Damn," he said.

"What's wrong?" Lisa asked.

"They know I want to get to the highway."

"They seem to know a whole lot."

"I'm guessing they've done this kind of stuff before."

He sped three blocks, racing past parked cars and houses, and then he hung a hard left, climbing up the road back toward Boulevard.

At Boulevard, he cut to the right, but looked to the left, where he had last seen the Suburban.

The guy had gotten out of the vehicle. He crouched at the rear corner of the SUV, rifle at his shoulder, the scope at his eye.

Anthony stood on the accelerator.

The rear windshield shattered: the bullet flew through the interior of the truck in a smoking streak and exited through the front windshield, leaving a ragged hole.

Bent so low in the seat he could barely see over the dashboard, Anthony ran a red light—thankfully there was little traffic at that hour—and forged ahead at sixty miles an hour.

Behind them, the Suburban dwindled into darkness.

"Can I get up now?" Lisa asked.

"I think we're out of range."

"Jesus, that was close." Sitting up, she blotted perspiration from her brow with her jacket sleeve. He noticed that some of the color had drained out of her face. "God. I feel like I could vomit."

"Need to?" he said. "There're napkins in the glove compartment."

She winced, drew in deep breaths, shook her head. "I'll be okay."

"Thanks for keeping it together," he said. "I know this is a helluva lot more than you signed up for when you married me."

""Right." She laughed sourly. "I'll be fine, really."

"Do you want me to drop you off with one of your sisters, or at your parents'?"

"Drop me off?"

"Lisa, I don't know where this is going to lead. It might get much, much worse."

"But they had to have seen me back there," she said. "And keep in mind, if they found our address, they could easily find out that we're married. They'll assume I'm as involved in this as you are, and in a sense, I am."

"Good point."

She touched his knee. "I'm staying with you. There's no safer place for me to be."

"Appreciate the vote of confidence."

He took the entrance ramp for I-20 East, and they hurtled like a missile through the night.

20

In Thorne's haste to flee his residence, he had left open the driveway gate. Valdez urged the crippled Suburban inside and parked in the turnaround. That section of the drive was flanked by a dogwood with pinkish flowers that offered concealment from the front of the house.

Valdez cut the engine and let out a long, low breath that Cutty interpreted as disappointment.

"Thorne's escape is only temporary," Cutty said. "Clearly, Satan was assisting him, but we have God on our side, Valdez. God won't allow us to fail."

Valdez gave him a weary smile. "For we are faithful, si."

"Yes. We are the Lord's faithful servants. He will deliver the wicked into our hands. We must not doubt."

"Is sin."

"Yes, doubt is sin. And I never doubt—*ever*."

Leaving her with those words of wisdom, Cutty hopped outside and assessed the damage to the vehicle. Thorne's gunfire had left a couple of pebble-deep dents around the grille, as well as a scratch on the windshield, but the right front tire was ruined.

The vehicle included a full spare, but he wouldn't perform the repair himself. That was mission support's duty.

He phoned the dispatcher on his cell phone, gave his location, and requested the appropriate auto service. The operator assured him that a mechanic would be sent within an hour.

He also informed the dispatcher that area residents had likely phoned Atlanta police and reported shots fired, and might have included a description of the Suburban. The man promised to take care of that incident, too.

The dispatcher did not inquire about what had become of the Judas, and Cutty did not volunteer an update. He stated only that the mission was in progress. He was not accountable to the dispatcher; he was accountable only to those God had placed in authority above him—his division superior and their anointed leader—and the Almighty himself.

From the outside, Thorne's home was impressive. He wondered what kind of work Thorne did for a living. He found it dubious that a man so skilled with firearms and combat tactics served in an ordinary nine-to-five desk job.

Avoiding the front, where bright lights shone, they approached the back entrance. The big French doors stood locked, moonlight shimmering on the glass.

"Would you do the honors, Valdez?" he asked.

She indicated the white sticker on one of the window panes, warning that the home was secured by an alarm system.

"Go ahead and pick the lock," he said with a grin. "I've got a hunch."

She removed a lock pick gun and tension wrench from a waist pouch and knelt to work on the cylinder pins. Within fifteen seconds, she sprang the lock.

He had expected her to take longer. For a rookie fresh out of training camp, she was unusually skillful.

When they opened the doors, the security system beeped once, and then quieted.

"Ah, I was correct," Cutty said. "They were in such a rush to get out of here they didn't bother to arm the system."

Her eyes sparkled in awe at his keen instincts.

With a generous sweep of his arm, as if they were entering his own home, he beckoned her to go in ahead of him. He lightly brushed his fingers across her ponytail as she swept forward, just a quick, innocent touch, and the feel of her hair across his flesh gave him a warm, tickly sensation.

He put his fingers in his mouth for a moment, tasting her essence, and followed her inside.

They were in a large kitchen furnished with ultra-modern appliances, granite counters and island, and hardwood floors. It was meticulously clean, the cooking surfaces, sinks, and countertops spotless and gleaming.

Then he saw the bottle of alcohol on the counter.

"Look at this, Valdez." He read the label. "Hennessey? This looks like hard, vile stuff. Thorne must be an alcoholic."

He screwed the cap off the whiskey and upended the bottle over the sink drain. The pungent fumes drew tears from his eyes, but he didn't stop until he'd poured all of it out. He tossed the bottle in a wastebasket.

"Alcoholic beverages are a lure of the devil," he said. "The nectar of the damned. But of course you know that."

"*Si,*" she said. "Is very bad."

The refrigerator was a stainless steel behemoth, and actually built into the wall. He pulled open the doors.

It was stocked with temple-fortifying foods: fruit, vegetables, milk, juice, bottled water, a tub of butter, deli meats, cheese, condiments.

"Uh oh," he said. "Look what we have here."

She peered over his shoulder as he pointed out a lower shelf that held a six-pack of bottled beer, and a twelve-pack of a caffeinated cola.

"Not only is Thorne an alcoholic—witness more alcoholic drinks—he drinks caffeinated cola, too. Caffeine is another drug, Valdez. We've got a serious addict on our hands."

"Ah, si."

Clucking his tongue, he removed the beer and the soda and methodically poured the contents of each bottle and can down the sink drain. He returned to the refrigerator and opened the freezer door.

The racks were stuffed with meats, fish, more vegetables, and, disappointingly, a pint of gourmet vanilla ice cream, which he promptly trashed.

The pantry beckoned on the other side of the room, and he saw a wet bar off the kitchen that surely contained a whole storehouse of poison, but he had done enough. Continued exposure to Thorne's addictions would have only nauseated him, and he couldn't afford to be ill. He needed to keep up his energy and eat a proper meal of his own, as he had a busy night ahead of him.

"Would you mind preparing sandwiches for us, Valdez?"

A frown. "Eh?"

"Sandwiches. I prefer turkey, Swiss cheese, lettuce, and mustard. I'm sure there's fresh bread in the pantry, but be careful in there. Doubtless it's full of all manner of unwholesome things."

She hesitated, and then went to the pantry doors.

"God bless you," he said. "You know, I bet you'll make some godly man very happy one day. You've got so many wonderful, wifely qualities."

She looked at him, eyes flat and indifferent.

"That was meant as a compliment," he said.

She said nothing. Had he offended her?

He stammered. "Umm, anyway, while you do that, I'm going to look around some more and see what else I can learn about this heathen."

She turned away.

He was puzzled. Women were so mysterious it was as if they spoke a foreign tongue. Had Adam endured these same challenges with Eve?

He entered the main hallway, a long corridor illuminated with soft light from a crystal chandelier. Photographs hung on the wall, and he stopped to examine them.

Evidently, Thorne had deciphered the language of women. In one framed photo, Thorne and a striking black woman stood face to face in front of an altar, holding hands, their eyes full of love, while a pastor looked on in the background with a benevolent smile.

He thought he'd glimpsed someone in the passenger seat of Thorne's SUV. Thorne's spouse was a point against him. A husband on the run would have to consider his wife's welfare, would be burdened by her womanly needs and weaknesses and inability to defend herself, and as a result, would be more vulnerable.

If Thorne were wise, he would dump his wife off somewhere, and go about his business alone. But he didn't blame Thorne if he kept the woman around. She was a looker.

He moved to another picture. It was a black-and-white bridal portrait that showcased the wife to her full stunning effect. Clasping a bouquet, the woman gazed at the camera with her big, dreamy eyes, lips full and soft, lush cleavage tantalizingly displayed.

He ran his finger along the picture, stopping at the mound of her cleavage. Delicious heaviness spread through his groin.

He was thirty-two years old, but he'd encountered live, exposed breasts only once in his life. When he was thirteen, one of the teenage girls who'd lived on their commune, a sassy blonde named Holly, had enticed him into the loft of one of the barns. She'd lifted up her blouse and exposed her large creamy breasts and invited him to touch them, which he did, nervously at first and then with growing eagerness, and the next thing he knew she was massaging his crotch . . . and soon, he erupted in his pants.

He'd been so ashamed of his sin that he'd fled the barn. He'd never spoken of the episode to anyone, and Holly, knowing their community's strict rules, had thankfully kept it secret, too. If Father had learned of the incident, he might well have castrated him.

But . . . he wondered how the breasts of Thorne's wife would look, unfettered. How soft and warm and full they would feel in his hands. How the nipples would taste.

The sound of clattering silverware in the kitchen shattered his reverie. He glanced down the hallway. Valdez was not watching him, but his face burned.

You must not covet a man's wife. Remember the commandments.

With effort, he turned away from the photo and entered a spacious great room. The room was immaculate, as was the rest of the house he'd seen thus far, and furnished with comfortable furniture, oak tables, and leafy, live plants. A marble fireplace looked commodious enough to spit-roast a hog.

On an end table, he discovered a photo that instantly shed light on a few matters. It was a shot of a younger, yet stern-faced, clean-shaven Thorne in a United States Marine Corps dress uniform, one of those graduation-from-boot-camp portraits.

A Marine. It explained the man's facility with firearms and his gutsy maneuvers.

This mission had suddenly become a lot more interesting.

A doorway opened into another room: a library. He turned on the overhead light, an ornate brass fixture. The room had a marble floor, a couple of dark leather wing chairs, an oak cocktail table, Tiffany-style table lamps, and bookcases stocked with hundreds of hardcovers.

He ran his thumb along the spines. There were texts that pertained to American history and culture, but most of the books appeared to be fiction.

Not surprisingly, there were no Christian books, no Bibles.

A dismaying number of the fiction texts were mystery and crime stories, too, with words such as "blood," "death," and "fear," appearing frequently in the titles.

Cutty had never read any of these books, and never would. He read only the Bible and other approved works. If you weren't careful, the spirit-polluting products of secular culture would lead you off the path of righteousness.

He was about to turn away to visit another area of the house when he came across a series of books with the word "ghost" in the titles. The author of each novel was Anthony Thorne.

He plucked one of the books off the shelf. The title was *Ghost Hunter*. On the inside back flap of the dust jacket, he found a black-and-white photo of his guy.

"Well, I'll be darned," he said.

Not only was Thorne a Marine, he was a writer, apparently, a successful one.

Although doing so risked the contamination of his spirit, he read the story summary on the jacket flap. The novel concerned a character named Ghost, a Marine, who learned about the vicious murder of a young woman's husband and offered to track down the killers when the police failed to apprehend them.

"Ghost practices only one form of justice—the justice of the streets," the copy stated.

Intriguing.

Anthony Thorne was looking like the caliber of challenge that could make a career for an ambitious young soldier and a loyal servant of the Kingdom.

Part Two

The Hunted

21

Barreling through the night, they traveled east on Interstate 20, away from Atlanta. Cool air fluted through the punctured front and rear windows, as if the Tahoe had been transformed into a giant wind instrument.

Anthony didn't know exactly where they were headed, and wasn't particularly concerned about it. All he wanted to do was put distance between them and the maniacs.

He'd equipped the SUV with an after-market stereo receiver that included a USB input for MP3 players and iPods. To get Lisa up to speed on everything, he plugged the miniature digital voice recorder into the port and played back his conversation with Bob at The Varsity.

The recording was distorted by background noise, and the whistling wind added another annoyance, but when he turned the volume to the highest level, their dialogue was coherent.

Arms laced over her chest, Lisa listened intently. At several points, she nodded, or shook her head, frowning.

He remained quiet throughout the recording, scanning the road for suspicious vehicles. Hearing Bob's voice again, however, made him wonder what had become of the man. Had the fanatics caught him, or had they lost track of him at the restaurant—and honed in on Anthony as their next best option?

The conversation ended with Bob's last words: *"They're on to you now, Anthony. Go home, get your wife, and stay on the move till you find the truth. Don't let your dad's death be in vain . . ."*

Anthony turned it off. "Well?"

"Wow." She pulled her fingers through her hair. "I agree with you—this is for real. Any doubts I might've had after listening to this are nullified by the fact that these people Bob spoke of just tried to kill us."

"Being shot at tends to be pretty convincing."

"I still want to know how they found out who you are, where we live."

"They have access to databases, like Bob said. I think they ran my plates against the DMV computers and pulled up our address."

"How the hell is that possible, Tony? There are privacy laws against that kind of thing."

Fire blazed in her eyes. She'd been taught to believe that the world was an orderly place regulated by laws mostly obeyed by a sensible citizenry. He'd always found her faith in the system endearing and refreshing, if a bit too idealistic.

"They seem to be above the law," he said.

"No one is above the law."

"They were shooting at us as if they were on their own private firing range, not in the middle of a residential neighborhood, Lisa. Whoever they are, they obviously aren't worried about getting arrested."

"We should call the police."

"No way."

"Why the hell not?" She was nearly shouting.

He kept his tone calm. "Think about it. If these people are operating without fear of the cops, it's because they have influence over law enforcement, which is something Bob said, too, remember?"

"They can't control *every* cop for God's sake, as if all the officers are a bunch of mindless robots."

"Maybe not. Maybe they manipulate only the big-wig commanders who call the shots. Either way, we can't take the risk. We call them, and they could be on our asses like white on rice in a hot minute."

"You're being overly paranoid."

"No, I'm being overly realistic."

She glowered at him, sighed, looked away out the window.

"We're on our own," he said. "Thing is, baby, we've always been on our own."

"What?" She swiveled to face him.

"The system you love and trust, the laws you studied in school, this high-tech society we think is so great—they're broken, 'cause they're products of people, and *people* are broken."

"Don't be ridiculous. I'm not broken. You aren't."

"We all are, in different ways. We've all got chips and fractures in us, like pieces of old china at a garage sale. Broken."

"You have this incredibly pessimistic opinion of people, Tony, and I can't buy into that. I won't. Most people are good and want to do the right thing."

"Please. Most people are too self-absorbed to care about doing the right thing. Sure, we talk about it a lot, and every now and then we're moved to stand up for a cause bigger than ourselves, but for the most part, all we want is our own little comfortable island, and we don't give a damn about what happens beyond it. All of us are guilty of that, Lisa—we're guilty of apathy and self-absorption, and that's why the system fails us, that's why it always will."

She stared at him. "Is your name Anthony, or Ghost?"

He stopped himself—he hadn't intended to launch into a rant. Until then, he'd used his writing as a vehicle to vent his deepest emotions and beliefs about this stuff. When questioned, as he often was by readers and media, whether he actually believed in the things his characters said and did, he offered up the indifferent response, *Hey, lighten up, it's only fiction. That means I make these things up.*

As Lisa studied him as though seeing him anew, he felt too exposed.

"Anyway," he said, "no cops. Okay?"

"You're so stubborn." She shrugged. "But fine, no cops."

It was a few minutes past midnight. Highway traffic was sparse, but those on the road were roaring past at speeds in excess of eighty miles an hour, typical Atlanta drivers who drove with death wishes.

He kept to the far right lane and maintained his speed at a relatively modest seventy. With the damaged windows and a presumably shattered taillight, he didn't want to risk attracting the attention of a cop and be put in the position of explaining what had happened.

From between the front seats, Lisa picked up the Bible that Bob had left him, riffled through it. "Back to Bob. Why did he leave you this?"

"We're assuming he left it for me."

"And who the heck is Kelley Marrow?"

"Who?"

"The Bible belongs to her, according to this." She tapped the first page.

"Oh, that. I've no idea who she is. But remember, Bob enjoys giving clues through the scriptures. He's done it twice so far. I figure it has to have something useful in it."

"There're probably hundreds of passages highlighted in here." She ran her finger along some of the verses marked with the multi-colored pens. She snapped the book shut. "I'm way too frazzled to read this right now."

"We can check it out later."

"Furthermore, if he's accumulated evidence that he claims can destroy this organization and bring your dad's killer to justice, why not give it to you directly, or at least tell you where it is?"

"He might be worried about the security of the information, decided to hide it within a bunch of clues."

"Possibly." She yawned, but cut the yawn short as if angry at her body slowing down on her when she was finally getting into a groove. "Let's work from the bottom up, then. What religious organization do you think these people represent?"

"A cult, but one more mainstream than your average bunch of isolated fanatics. They've got deep resources, as we've seen, probably lots of money backing them."

"The Roman Catholic Church is the largest religious organization in the world," she said. "But I really don't think Bob was talking about them. This group sounds smaller than that."

"But big enough to pose a real threat."

"Bob said your dad tried to bring them down, and that's why they got him. That doesn't make any sense to me. Your dad was a sports writer, Tony. What could he have done?"

"Maybe he got wind of a damaging story about these people, started to dig deeper, and they found out."

"Does that sound like him?"

"Not really. He loved his job, but he wasn't obsessed about it. I can't imagine him risking his life to write some kind of expose in a subject area that wasn't even his beat."

"But it's possible."

"At this stage, anything's possible, don't you think?"

"What church did he attend?"she asked.

"Greater Hope Baptist. In Decatur. All of us went every Sunday. It was a small church, had maybe three hundred members, everyone knew each other."

"Sounds like our church," she said.

He considered the small United Methodist church of which she spoke to be hers, not his. He hadn't visited the church since their wedding ceremony three years ago. But Lisa and her family were longtime members and rarely missed a Sunday service.

"They're similar, I guess," he said.

"Small, family churches don't have teams of assassins on call, though."

"We're clearly talking about a larger group here," he said. "Aren't there a lot of big churches here in Atlanta? Megachurches, or whatever they're called?"

"There sure are. I don't even know where to start." She sifted both hands through her hair, a familiar sign that she was exhausted, and she yawned again, too. "Damn. I feel jumpy and totally wiped out at the same time. But you look as if it's only another day at the office."

"Not how I feel, though," he said. He added: "I feel like our island has been invaded."

"Our own little comfortable island, where we don't give a damn about what happens beyond it," she said, repeating a sentence from his tirade.

"It's pretty late, Lisa. Why don't you let back the seat and relax?"

"I can't relax when every time I look up, I see a bullet hole in the windshield."

"Point taken." He unclipped his iPhone from his belt. "I think it's time we find somewhere to crash for a while."

"Who're you calling?"

"The only guy I can call this late: Mike Alfaro."

22

Sitting at the round, cherry wood table in the breakfast room, Cutty and Valdez enjoyed a late-night snack of turkey-and-Swiss sandwiches on wheat, celery sticks, and ice cold milk.

Cutty sliced his two sandwiches into quarters, and halved the quarters, too. He'd also chopped the celery into quarter-inch nuggets. A bunny rabbit could have consumed larger portions, but those were the proper bite sizes for easy digestion.

"These sandwiches are excellent, Valdez," he said.

"*Gracias.*"

Her plate held only half a sandwich. She nibbled at it daintily and dabbed at her lips with a napkin after each bite, which he found adorable.

"Do you enjoy cooking?" he asked.

She glanced at him. "*Si.*"

"I approve of that. Where I grew up, the women did all of the domestic duties and light farming, while the men folk did the strenuous farm work, fishing, and hunting. Those are the roles God intended for us."

She said nothing, but her eyes sparkled.

She was so agreeable. As a woman should be. She reminded him of Mother, who had always deferred to Father in family matters, always placed his needs and the needs of their nine children above her own. What a godly woman she had been. He missed her.

Valdez chewed a miniscule bite of her sandwich. He observed the gentle undulations of her slender throat as she swallowed, and wondered how it would feel to lick her there, just once, and taste that smooth, pliant skin.

He said, "Do you want to get married someday, Valdez?"

116

"Someday. Si."

"Do you want children?"

She nodded. "Someday."

"How many children would you like?"

"Cuatro."

He smiled patiently. "Translation, please?"

She held up four fingers.

He laughed. "Four children? Really? I want four children, too!" His grin was so wide that he had to put a napkin to his mouth, as if to keep all of his excitement from spilling out of him at once. "Isn't it amazing that we got paired together? It proves the hand of God at work in our lives, wouldn't you say?"

She didn't return his smile. "We cannot marry. It is not for us."

"Of course, that's true. Marriage isn't allowed for servants in our division. But, God willing, I don't intend to serve in this capacity for the rest of my life. Do you?"

"Ah . . . no."

She lowered her gaze to the table. She had stopped eating.

He realized that he had embarrassed her. Once again, his inexperience with the fairer sex had betrayed him.

"I apologize," he said. "We hardly know each other and here I am discussing marriage and children."

She kept her gaze on the table, twisting a napkin around her finger.

"Excuse me." He picked up his food and milk. "I think I'll go back to the library to ah, check out the books Thorne wrote."

She appeared relieved that he was leaving.

Walking away, he chastised himself. He had to be careful what he said to her, or else when this mission concluded, she might request a re-assignment. If that happened, it would break his heart—because he was sure he was falling in love with her.

In the library, he placed his meal on an end table and resumed his perusal of Thorne's work. Although he had originally intended to search the entire residence, as was his habit, the books could tell him everything he needed to know about his mark, since the title character, Ghost, was obviously Thorne himself. The books were maps of the man's tormented soul.

Picking a chapter at random from *Ghost Hunter*, he found himself in the middle of a grisly, yet richly detailed interrogation: Ghost was using a pneumatic nail gun to drive carpet tacks underneath the fingernails of a murder suspect, to compel the man to admit to his role in a crime.

Each lurid sentence crackled with fervor. Thorne *believed* in what he was writing, which meant he was a profoundly evil man.

Barely able to take his eyes away from the novel, Cutty slowly chewed a sandwich morsel.

After several blood-saturated, obscenity-laced pages, the violent scene ended. He flipped forward in the book and soon found another. This one featured Ghost pummeling a police officer who was described as "corrupt."

It made Cutty laugh out loud. Corrupt? These *books* were corrupt, and were precisely why censorship of mass media was not only desirable, but necessary. A society that allowed the distribution of filth like this was destined to sink into moral turpitude.

He wanted to speak to Thorne and demand to know why he felt the need to channel unadulterated depravity into the pages of a book and offer it for popular consumption. He wanted to know why he was glorifying violence. Why he was advocating disobedience to established authority. Why he had rebelled against God's plan.

When Thorne supplied satisfactory answers to those questions, Cutty would kill him. No one who earned his living producing such degenerate tales was fit to live in God's Kingdom.

A text message arrived on his cell phone. It was from the dispatcher: the auto service had been completed. Mission support had kept their promise to complete the repair within an hour.

He ate a few more bites of the sandwiches, chased the food with the milk, and returned to the kitchen. He brought Thorne's book with him, as evidence to present to his superior.

Valdez had cleared her dishes off the table. She sat there, quietly reading her pocket Bible.

She gave him a lukewarm smile. He had fallen out of her good graces, and somehow, he would have to redeem himself.

He took his plate and glass to the sink, washed them, and placed them in the dish rack. Although he was in the home of a spiritually unclean man, he'd been raised to observe good manners at all times.

He cleared his throat. "Mission support got in touch. We're ready to go."

"Si. I see them outside just leave."

"I didn't hear them from the library. Those guys operate with *mucho* stealth, huh?"

His use of an authentic Spanish word, one he'd not realized that he knew until it came from his mouth, summoned a genuine smile to her face.

He opened the patio door.

"After you, *senorita*."

She bowed slightly, and walked out of the house. He didn't know where that Spanish word had come from either, and he interpreted it as proof that God planned for him and Valdez to be together someday. Everything was going to be fine.

At the Suburban, he tossed her the keys, and she deftly plucked them out of the air.

While she drove away, he powered up the MDT and logged on to Genesis.

The background report on Thorne had arrived.

23

Mike lived in Duluth, a suburb about thirty minutes northeast of Atlanta. The city was a case study of the rapid growth that had swept across the region a decade ago. Strip malls, restaurants, and assorted retail stores blanketed the streets where not long ago there had been only fields and forest. Signs advertising various housing communities bristled from the ground at seemingly every intersection.

The area's boom phase had ended, unfortunately. These days, many of the strip malls were full of empty stores that had gone out of business, and among the signs touting new subdivisions were nearly as many ads promising deals on foreclosed properties.

"I hope he doesn't think we're crazy," Lisa said, as Anthony turned into a residential neighborhood.

On the phone, Anthony hadn't given Mike the full scoop, only told him that they were in trouble and needed somewhere to crash for a short while. Mike had readily agreed, as Anthony had known he would.

"He'll be cool," Anthony said. "You know Mike. This'll sound like the plot of a movie to him."

"It would sound like one to me, too, if we weren't living it for real."

The neighborhood in which Mike lived was so new that many of the houses were still under construction. Several home sites were merely square plots of red clay with "Under Contract" signs sticking up from the ground. Bulldozers and backhoes lay like sleeping giants on other properties, and construction debris littered sections of the road.

Mike's home was in a cul-de-sac, a ranch with a red brick front, white fiber cement siding, bay window, and attached two-car garage. An elm sapling strained to grow in the front yard, young leaves shuddering in the night breeze, and a United States flag rippled on a pole beside the door.

Slowing in front of the driveway, Anthony tapped the horn.

He'd also told Mike that they needed to hide the Tahoe—and promised that he would know why when he got a look at the SUV.

"I can't believe we're coming to his house at one o'clock in the morning," Lisa said.

"Mike's a night owl. I bet you he was watching a movie he's seen a thousand times."

"I hope you're right. I feel bad about disturbing him."

"Don't feel bad. He won't."

The garage door rose. A late model, metallic blue Jeep Grand Cherokee was parked inside. Alongside the jeep stood a red Ducati motorcycle, sleek as a rocket on wheels.

Mike wandered outside the garage. He was in his early thirties, short but powerfully built, with dark hair trimmed in a high and tight cut. He wore a *Raiders of the Lost Ark* t-shirt, blue sweats, and sneakers.

Mike's family had emigrated from the Philippines to the United States before his birth, and had wanted him to pursue a career as a physician, an attorney, or, failing those, a nurse, a popular vocational choice in their family. Mike had shocked them when he enlisted in the Marine Corps after graduating high school. He had grown up idolizing American action movie heroes and wanted to live the dream.

He had lived the dream, all right. During his six-year active enlistment, he had logged more time in combat zones than any other grunt Anthony knew, with the exception of himself. Like Anthony, he'd suffered only minor wounds, which considering the action they'd seen, seemed downright miraculous sometimes.

Mike waved them into the garage.

Anthony parked next to the bike. He pulled the digital voice recorder out of the stereo and pocketed it.

"Let's take the Bible with us, too," he said to Lisa. "While we're here, maybe we can start reviewing it, try to make sense of things."

Nodding, she slipped the Bible in her purse—next to the .357 he'd given her.

Guns and Bibles, he thought. A strange combination if ever there was one.

"Evening, ladies and gents," Mike said. He grinned. "Don't you know I *love* having visitors in the wee hours of the morning? Usually booty calls, though."

"Hey, Mike." Lisa hugged him. "Thanks for letting us come."

"No doubt." Anthony gave Mike a handshake and a pound on the shoulder. "I really appreciate this, man. It means a lot."

Mike waved off their praise. "Hey, all I was doing was having a Hannibal Lecter marathon. *Manhunter* to *Hannibal Rising*. I'm at *The Silence of the Lambs* so far. "

Anthony winked at Lisa, and she smiled briefly.

"Yo, AT, was this damage caused by gunfire?" Mike examined the Tahoe's shattered right tail light, dents on the bumper, and the ragged hole in the rear windshield. He shuffled around the side and saw the rupture in the front window, too.

"What does your expert opinion tell you?" Anthony asked.

"My opinion?" Mike put his fists on his waist. "I think you been in a scuffle with a rifleman, AT."

"We're on the retreat from a rifleman—a whole bunch of them, we think."

"And you haven't bagged them all yet? You're slipping, dude."

"What can I say? Married life has made me soft."

"They track you here, you think?" Savage interest glinted in Mike's eyes, and he glanced out the garage at the dark street beyond.

"We don't think so," Lisa said. "Tony gave them the slip. You should've seen him in action."

Anthony shrugged. "I did what had to be done."

"Damn, I was hoping I might see some action, too." Mike punched the button beside the doorway to lower the garage door. "Let's head in. I can't wait to hear what this is all about."

24

Mike's home was decorated in a style that could have been called, "Contemporary Bachelor." There was no furniture at all in the living or formal dining rooms. In the kitchen, there was a basic, hardwood dinette table and chairs. In the family room, where Mike watched his movies, there was a black leather loveseat and armchair, beech veneer coffee table, steel side tables, stainless steel floor lamps—and the centerpiece of it all, the theater system: sixty-inch, flat-panel plasma HDTV standing on a thick wooden stand. Surround sound speakers positioned for maximum cinematic effect. Two tall, black cabinets that stored hundreds of DVDs.

Everything was squared away as if in preparation for a barracks inspection. No embellishments, no artwork, no plants. The only photographs were his recruit graduation portrait, pictures he'd taken with members of his platoon, and a few photos of his parents and older sister.

"Nice place," Lisa said. "It could use a woman's touch to soften the ultra-masculine vibe, though."

Mike grinned. "Got a girlfriend who likes to decorate?"

Anthony said, "Lisa knows only *quality* ladies, Mike, not the kind of girls you'd go for."

"Here's to you." Mike gave him the finger. "Anyway, you guys want coffee? I brewed a fresh pot."

"Coffee sounds good," Anthony said. "I need to keep my edge."

"You?" Mike asked. "I doubt it. You live on the edge."

"That was eons ago."

"Bullshit," Mike said. "You've got warrior blood, man, like me. That never goes away."

"I hate to interrupt the macho posturing here, but where's the powder room, guys?" Lisa asked. "I need to wipe the dew off the lily pad."

"You need to do what?" Mike asked.

"My wife's being a lady—I know you aren't used to those," Anthony said. "First door on the left in the hallway, sweetheart."

Lisa left the kitchen.

"Hey, I can appreciate a good woman," Mike said. He got three coffee mugs from the kitchen cabinet. "She's gotta have a little swagger in her, that's all. She needs to be ballsy enough to keep me in line."

"Your warrior princess is out there somewhere." Anthony leaned against the counter. Although the dinette chairs beckoned, he wanted to get a blast of java first, to counteract the exhaustion he knew would hit him once he got off his feet.

A key rack hung on the wall beside him. Several sets of keys dangled from the hooks, each assigned to rental property that Mike owned; printed address labels on each key ring identified the residence. After his honorable discharge, Mike had gotten into the business of purchasing foreclosed properties or those in need of renovation, buying them outright, doing whatever rehab was necessary, and then renting them out or selling them.

He had pulled back from the business about a year ago. Confessed it had become too much like work, and he was determined not to spend his life running on the career treadmill. He kept ten of the properties as rentals, used a property management company to collect rent and manage tenant issues, and lived off the rental income—which financed his desire to purchase collector's editions of his favorite movies, entertain countless women, travel, and sleep in till noon if he so wanted.

Mike passed him a coffee, black. Anthony drew a sip of the rich brew and immediately felt more awake.

"This is good stuff," Anthony said.

"Jamaican Blue Mountain," Mike said. "Expensive as hell, but well worth it. A lady I met in Negril turned me on to it."

"Figures. She turn you out, too?"

Mike winked. "On the serious tip, what kind of shit are you in? You know I wanna be involved, whatever it is."

"I don't know if you want to wade into this one. I haven't figured out yet what kind of animal we're up against, but it's something truly hairy."

"Try me."

Anthony produced the voice recorder. Switching it on, he placed it on the dinette table and turned up the volume.

As the tinny voices crackled from the small speaker, Lisa returned to the kitchen. She took coffee as well, and the three of them sat around the table.

When the recording ended, they filled Mike in on what had happened that evening, and their theories.

"If these fanatics are responsible for what happened to your dad, you *know* I'm in," Mike said, eyes burning. "Shit, I'm in anyway, just 'cause of what they've done to you guys, but if this Bob dude is right—"

"Then I'll finally get what I've wanted for fifteen years," Anthony said. "A shot at justice."

"Yeah, like a nine millimeter shot," Mike said.

Both Mike and Lisa knew what kept Anthony awake some nights: a lucid vision of the shadowy figure racing away from the lake. A dream of chasing down the killer. A fantasy of putting a pistol to his head and squeezing the trigger . . .

Lisa touched his arm. "One step at a time, guys. First, we've got to figure out who we're dealing with, and I think this may be the key to it."

She removed the Bible from her purse and slid it across the table toward Mike.

Mike picked it up. "I was raised Catholic, but I haven't been to church or read a Bible in ages." He opened the book, paused on the first page. "Who's Kelley Marrow? Sounds like someone I used to date."

"Seriously?" Lisa asked.

"Nah, not really." Mike flipped through the book. "Someone got happy with the highlighters, huh? They used all the colors of the rainbow in here."

"We think the highlighted scriptures are clues," Anthony said. "A message Bob is trying to tell us."

"A message about what?" Mike said.

"Where we can find this evidence he's gathered against the organization, I think," Anthony said. "It could be a shot in the dark, but that's what we're assuming, anyway."

"Could be." Mike returned to the front page and tapped it with his finger. "But this name's gotta be in here for a reason, bro."

"It might only be the name of whoever owned the Bible," Anthony said.

"Sometimes people plant big clues right out in the open," Mike said. "Haven't you seen that in the movies? A big fat clue will be so obvious that people ignore it, 'cause they figure something so simple can't mean anything."

"Kelley Marrow sounds like a fairly ordinary name," Lisa said.

"I'll run it through Google, see what pops up." Pushing away from the table, Mike grabbed a note pad and jotted down the name. "This Kelley chick might be someone we need to have a chat with."

"Listen, I appreciate your offer, but we didn't come by to ask you to get involved," Anthony said. "We only wanted somewhere to lie low for a little while."

"Don't insult me, AT," Mike said. "I'm involved, all right?"

Anthony glanced at Lisa. She shrugged.

"The more the merrier," she said.

"And you guys can stay here as long as you want," Mike said. "I'm gonna hop on my PC for a while. You can join me, or catch some shut-eye in the guest room, or hang out here and watch movies."

Lisa stretched her arms above her, yawned. "I'm so tired I want to cry, but I'm going to start reviewing these marked-up scriptures."

"I'll stay out here with you," Anthony said. "You got a piece, Mike?"

" 'Course I do. Who're you talking to, dude?"

"Keep one on you," Anthony said. "I don't think anyone followed us here, but . . ."

"Be prepared." Mike nodded grimly.

25

The online background report ran close to twenty-five pages. It confirmed what Cutty had already learned about Thorne—address, date of birth, vehicles registered to him, marital status, home phone number—but it also gave him much, much more.

Thorne's Social Security number. His mailing addresses for the past twenty years. The duration of his military service, pay grades he'd achieved, and where he had been stationed throughout his enlistment. The income he had reported to the IRS over the past seven years and the taxes he had paid. The purchase price of his home, and an assessment of its current value. His credit report and cumulative score from the three reporting bureaus. His estimated net worth.

Also included were details from his marriage certificate three years ago, which contained the name and birth date of his comely bride, the former Lisa Boyd, and their parents' names, too. The firearms license for which he had been approved, not the least of which were a concealed weapons permit and details of the prodigious number of weapons he had registered.

"This guy is planning to wage war, Valdez," Cutty said. He put his thick finger on the MDT display. "He's got fifteen—*yes, fifteen*—firearms on file. Is he not intending to be a soldier in Satan's army?"

"*Si,*" Valdez said. She drove aimlessly around the dark city, as he had yet to give her a destination.

"I wonder where he stores all of this weaponry. I should have searched the rest of the house."

Her eyebrows arched. "Go back?"

"No. It's irrelevant. Remember the word—no weapon formed against you shall prosper. With God on our side, it doesn't matter if Thorne has a thousand guns in his arsenal."

The report listed every account Thorne held: banking, investments, credit cards, utilities, Internet access, cellular phone providers, insurance. It included account numbers for each respective entry, and passwords, too, when applicable.

Cutty could have taken the information, and, for all practical purposes, *become* Thorne. In an information-based society, every person could be reduced to a digital dossier, with data vulnerable to tampering by those who possessed the requisite keys.

Underneath the account list, there was a menu of commands that allowed the user to monitor or freeze a target's financial assets.

He selected the MONITOR option.

From that moment forward, if Thorne withdrew money from an ATM, or made a purchase with his debit or credit cards, Genesis would record the time, location, and amount of the transaction. It had proven a successful method to trap a mark about ninety-eight percent of the time, and worked because targets had no clue their spending patterns were being observed.

But always, someone was watching, someone was recording.

If Thorne somehow managed to slip their virtual net, however, Cutty would execute a freeze. An account freeze was a riskier tactic, because the mark would quickly realize something was amiss and go on alert. But without funds, no one could run for long.

The last section of the report offered information on Thorne's known associates, a basic table containing names and addresses of about a dozen family, friends, and business colleagues. In the event that other, more precise tracking methods failed, Cutty could turn to the associates index, and start digging.

His cell phone vibrated. The incoming number belonged to division headquarters. Probably the dispatcher calling.

"Cutty speaking."

A gravelly voice rumbled: "This is the Director."

Cutty straightened so fast in the seat that the keyboard flipped out of his lap.

Valdez glanced away from the road. "Is okay?"

Cutty covered the handset. "It's the Director."

Her lips formed a startled "o," and she dropped her speed, as if concerned the Director would remotely take note of her speedy

Brandon Massey

driving and rebuke her—which wasn't all that far-fetched, as all fleet vehicles were linked to a central computer.

Cutty cleared his throat. "Uh, how are you, sir?"

"If I'm calling you at this hour, obviously I am not well," the Director said. "You lost your primary target."

He should have known they would find out about the Judas. They knew everything. The Director, in particular, had a reputation as a man who rarely slept, who constantly scanned Genesis in search of updates on the dozens of division missions in progress throughout the world at any given time. A whippet of a man in his late-sixties, with close-cropped steel-gray hair, hawk-like eyes, and a pointed chin, he'd once been a legendary Army master sniper, and had in fact recruited Cutty into the organization, trained him, and drawn him up through the ranks.

Their teacher-student relationship hadn't afforded Cutty any special privileges. The Director actually seemed to drive him harder than he did the other servants, was quick with a lacerating rebuke, and downright parsimonious with his praise.

He often reminded Cutty of Father.

"I did indeed lose the target, sir, and I apologize for not yet sharing that information with my dispatcher," Cutty said. "I've been engaged with a secondary target that I have reason to believe is significant."

"The primary target is off the grid. We've lost it, due in part to your botched efforts at containment."

Cutty pulled in a tight breath, silently suffered the tongue-lashing.

"But that target is no longer relevant," the Director said. "You are correct. Your secondary target is indeed more significant."

Cutty released a pent-up breath. "Praise God."

"Mr. Anthony Thorne poses an urgent threat," the Director said. A target's name was rarely invoked, certainly not during phone calls, though they communicated over encrypted lines. The Director's break with protocol suggested the gravity of the situation.

"I've been studying a background report on Thorne," Cutty said. "He's a Marine."

"I know that," the Director said. "That's not why he's a threat."

"It isn't?"

129

"The Prophet himself summoned me to speak of Thorne. He awakened from a *most* disturbing dream of the man, this very night. What do you say of that?"

Cutty couldn't say anything. The Prophet had dreamt of Thorne? In Cutty's eight years of service in the division, the Blessed One had never expressed a personal interest in one of his missions.

"Your silence speaks volumes," the Director said.

Cutty swallowed. "What message did the Prophet receive in his dream?"

"That's not for you to know. Suffice to say, it was most troubling."

Although the Director declined to supply more information, Cutty's vivid imagination offered only one possible answer: *assassination.* The Judas was more than a mere betrayer, and Thorne was much more than an intriguing accomplice. The two men, and whatever other co-conspirators they had engaged, were scheming to murder The Prophet.

It was such an unthinkable idea that he dared not speak it aloud.

"Eliminate Thorne, his wife, and anyone who stands in your path," the Director said. "This must be done most expeditiously. The Prophet is eagerly awaiting a report of the successful completion of your mission."

Cutty was trembling. To be charged with a mission in which the Prophet had a deeply-vested interest . . . this was the opportunity of a career.

"It will be done," Cutty said.

"The one who performs this divine service will be blessed beyond measure," the Director said. "Those were The Prophet's words. Consider the blessings in store for you, the desires of your heart, and they will be granted."

Cutty looked at Valdez, and his pulse quickened. The desires of his heart, indeed.

"I'll expect your report of completion by oh-nine hundred hours—today," the Director said, and terminated the connection.

"What did Director say?" Valdez asked.

"The Prophet—yes, *the Prophet himself*—is demanding that we eliminate Thorne and his wife," Cutty said. He read his watch. "And we've got less than eight hours to do it."

26

Anthony and Lisa had begun to work through the highlighted passages in the Bible. He had brought his laptop inside to the kitchen table, and as she read each citation aloud, he typed it into a text document, also noting the color in which each verse had been highlighted.

Lisa's theory was that once they'd transcribed all of the scriptures, they could review them as a whole and search for patterns, perhaps in the color coding or the order in which they'd been marked, and maybe a coherent narrative of some kind would emerge. He tended to agree with her idea. In light of what they knew thus far, it was the only theory that made any sense.

In the past half-hour, they had transcribed about a dozen passages from the books of Genesis through Deuteronomy. Such as:

Genesis 1:1-2, in green: *In the beginning God created the heaven and the earth. And the earth was without form, and void; and darkness was upon the face of the deep. And the Spirit of God moved upon the face of the waters.*

Genesis 34:1-2, in yellow: *And Dinah the daughter of Leah, which she bare unto Jacob, went out to see the daughters of the land. And when Shechem the son of Hamor the Hivite, prince of the country, saw her, he took her, and lay with her, and defiled her.*

Exodus 23:20, in blue: *Behold, I send an Angel before thee, to keep thee in the way, and to bring thee into the place which I have prepared.*

Numbers 20:11, in lavender: *And Moses lifted up his hand, and with his rod he smote the rock twice: and the water came out abundantly, and the congregation drank, and their beasts also.*

Deuteronomy 32:35, in orange: *To me belongeth vengeance and recompence; their foot shall slide in due time: for the day of their calamity is at hand, and the things that shall come upon them make haste.*

And on it went. They had over a hundred more left to review. It would take hours to cover them—and he could only guess how much longer it would take them to decode the overall meaning.

"Good Lord," Lisa said. She set down the book and rubbed her eyes, which had begun to show faint red veins. "And when I was a kid, I thought Sunday school was brain-numbing."

"Let's take a break." He pushed away from the table. "Want more coffee?"

"No, thanks. I already have the caffeine shakes. Look."

She held up her hand, palm facing parallel to the table. It trembled slightly.

He refreshed his own cup. "Well, so much for grabbing some shut-eye anytime soon."

She laughed bitterly and picked up the Bible again, riffled through the pages.

"I'm really not feeling Bob right now," she said. "Why couldn't he send you an e-mail with everything you need to know? He could've set up a free account for you under a fake name and no one would have been the wiser."

"He said they monitor the Internet, though."

"Right. Never mind me, I'm not thinking straight."

"We'll get through this." He sat beside her, glanced at his watch. It wasn't yet two am, but he felt as though he'd been awake for two days straight. He sipped his coffee.

She yawned into her hand. "Question for you."

"Shoot."

"What do you think of all this focus on the Good Book?"

"Meaning?"

"Do the scriptures inspire any ideas, any reflection? Or would it make no difference if we were copying passages from *The Cat in the Hat*?"

"I love Dr. Seuss. All his stories rhyme."

She gave him her please-be-serious look: eyes narrowed, lips curled.

"Okay, honestly, I haven't thought much about it," he said. "At the moment, it's just work to me. I hope it leads us to answers about my dad's murder. That's all I care about right now."

"Revenge," she said.

"Justice."

" 'To me belongeth vengeance.' We read that verse in Deuteronomy."

"A book that was written what, thousands of years ago? It's not relevant to my situation, my life."

"Do you think any part of the Bible is relevant to your life?"

"Ah, I know where this is going. Yes, I never go to church with you, I don't read the Bible, I don't pray, and all that bothers you. But it's not my thing, Lisa."

"Not until you're in your hour of need."

"I was in my hour of need fifteen years ago, and God was nowhere to be found."

"You can't blame God for that, Tony," she said softly.

"So if I can't blame God for what happened, why should I depend on God to give me justice? Face it, God doesn't give a damn, Lisa—certainly not about me and my family." He pointed at the Bible, finger shaking. "That book? It's full of fanciful stories and wishful thinking."

"A lot of people would disagree with you on that, including me."

"To each his own. Until someone's walked in my shoes they have no right to tell me how I should think or feel. I saw my dad *murdered* . . . he bled to death in my arms. Am I supposed to take comfort from some old book written by dead men? Is that going to make it all better, make me put on a happy face?"

"I'm sorry," she said, voice so hushed she was nearly inaudible. "I shouldn't have brought it up."

"No, you shouldn't have." Tears had welled up in his eyes. He wiped them away, almost angrily, but that didn't stop the flow. A thick sob was building at the base of his throat, waiting to explode out of him.

He excused himself to the bathroom. At the sink, he washed his face with cold water. He bowed his head and pulled in several deep, quavering breaths.

Don't cry, man.

Gripping the edge of the porcelain vanity with white-knuckled fingers, he stared at himself in the oval-shaped mirror. His eyes were red, glassy. He told himself no murderer had even been brought to justice by a victim's tears. That Mom, Danielle, and even he had cried often in the days and weeks after the murder—and those collective rivers of tears had changed nothing.

Self-control. Iron will. Guns. Power. Those were the tools that would deliver real justice. Not some old book. Not God. Not tears.

Toughen up, Marine.

The wave of grief receded. He snatched a tissue out of a box, blotted his eyes again, and left the bathroom.

Mike met him in the hallway. "Hey, AT. Everything okay?"

"Fine as can be," Anthony said, and went back to the kitchen.

Lisa looked up from the Bible, eyes redder than before, and probably not solely from fatigue. She offered a conciliatory smile.

"It's cool," he said. "Let's move on."

His cell phone rang.

27

He read the Caller ID display. "The number's blocked."

"Don't answer it," Lisa said.

"If it's them, maybe I can find out something that'll help us," Anthony said.

"Go for it, dude," Mike said. Reluctantly, Lisa nodded.

Anthony answered the call. "Hello?"

"Mr. Thorne." It was a man with a gentle voice. "As this may be my only opportunity to speak to you before I eliminate you, I first wanted to gain insight into the root of the evil that's corrupted your soul."

"Who is this?" Anthony asked, though he suspected it was the pale, stout man who had fired on them.

"I was especially intrigued by the books I discovered in your home library. You appear to be a successful author, in a secular sense."

These people had gotten into their home? He put his hand to his sweat-filmed forehead, trying to remember if they had activated the alarm system when they'd left. Probably not. They had been in a helluva hurry.

Besides, he wondered if a locked door, or an engaged security system, would have held these people at bay.

"Why the hell were you in our house?" Anthony asked.

They were in our house? Lisa lip-synced, outrage twisting her face.

Anthony pressed the button on the cell to activate the speakerphone feature. When the fanatic spoke again, his disconcerting choir-boy voice carried throughout the kitchen.

135

"You have a beautiful home, clean and tastefully designed, yet your work reeks of hatred," he said. "Tell me, Thorne: why have you chosen to sow discord and wickedness through your books?"

"You called our house earlier, didn't you?" Anthony asked. "How do you know all this stuff about us?"

"At the end of the age of man, that which is hidden shall be made clear."

Mike and Lisa frowned.

"What the hell does that mean?" Anthony asked.

"God delivers the wicked into the snares of the righteous. He's a mighty god, indeed, worthy to be praised."

The three of them looked at one another, and Anthony knew they were all thinking the same thing. Was this guy for real? It was like having a conversation with someone from another planet.

"Listen, who are you working for?" Anthony asked.

"The kingdom of God is at hand. Repent from your wickedness."

"Start talking, sense, dammit! Who the hell are you working for?"

"Manners, manners." The man clucked his tongue. "Please refrain from using foul language. It offends me deeply."

"You were shooting at me like a damn sniper, so don't give me your holier-than-thou bullshit."

"Mr. Thorne," the man said tightly, "in spite of your apparent intelligence and material success, you have misread the signs of your age. The kingdom is fast approaching, and sinners such as you will be cast into the darkness, where there will be weeping and gnashing of teeth."

"Who let you out of the nuthouse, man? Jesus."

"Don't you *dare* take the Lord's name in vain, you brimstone-drinking heretic."

"Sure." A laugh escaped Anthony. "I'm standing here trying to believe that people like you actually exist. Please tell me you haven't fathered any children."

"Why did you decide to do the devil's work, Thorne? How long have you been in league with the adversary?"

Anthony only shook his head.

"How long have you and the Judas been scheming to destroy us?" the man asked.

"Who the hell is the Judas?" Anthony asked, and as soon as he posed the question, realized the answer: Bob.

"I should have known that an immoral man such as you could never admit to the depths of his sin. You likely think yourself a noble man. But the devil is the great deceiver, Thorne."

"Sounds like I'm not the only one who's been deceived. Why are you working with these people? How long have you been murdering for them in God's name?"

"It's pointless to run from us, really," he said, in a bored tone. "Let's meet at a mutually agreeable location, and conclude our business in person. What do you say?"

"I say, kiss my black ass."

The man sighed. "You're determined to make this harder on yourself and your wife, aren't you? How is Lisa doing? How are her parents, Earl and Robin?"

"Leave my parents out of this, you bastard!" Lisa shouted, veins standing out on her neck.

He chuckled. "It seems I have an audience. Perhaps you, Mrs. Thorne, can convince your bull-headed husband of the futility of prolonging this tedious exercise."

"Yeah, he's bull-headed, and so am I," she said. "Far as we're both concerned, you can go to hell."

"Sadly, it appears you are equally yoked in sin."

"Who in your organization killed my father?" Anthony asked.

The caller quieted.

Anthony clutched the phone in a steel vise grip, and both Mike and Lisa appeared to be holding their breath.

But in a flat voice, like a robot programmed to recite a slogan, the man said, "We represent the truth. We shine a light in the darkness. We are subduing the earth to prepare it for the King's arrival. Dominion will be ours."

"Goddammit, tell me who killed my father!"

"God has led me to you, Thorne. It's your destiny to perish by my sword. Repent for your sinful ways now, and perhaps God will forgive you before I strike you down."

"You crazy—"

But the man hung up. Chest heaving, Anthony stared at the phone as if it had stung him.

"What a freakin' nut job," Mike said.

"That's an understatement," Lisa said.

"We've gotta get out of here," Anthony said. "We know the guy's elevator doesn't go all the way to the top, but he sounded way too confident. My gut tells me they know where we are, and they're on their way."

28

Mike crossed his thick arms over his chest. "Forget it. I'm not going anywhere. I fought the Taliban in Afghanistan and survived. No way I'm running from a bunch of Jesus freaks."

"There might be a whole squad of them this time, Mike," Anthony said. He shoved his laptop into the satchel. "They might be fanatics, but they'll be armed to the teeth."

"It's you and Lisa they want. They don't care about me."

"You're our friend, and we came to your house tonight," Lisa said. "On the basis of that, they might care a whole lot."

"Bet we could take 'em, AT," Mike said with a gleam in his eye. "We've got plenty firepower here between the two of us. What do you say, bro?"

"I don't want to fight another Iwo Jima in the middle of your subdivision," Anthony said. "Innocent people could get hurt."

"Yeah, probably a bad idea." Mike looked crestfallen. "Would've been fun, though."

"Some other time." Anthony slung his satchel over his shoulder and picked up his duffel. He glanced at Lisa, saw she was ready. "We've gotta roll."

"Where you going?" Mike asked.

"Probably a hotel."

"To hell with that." Mike went to the key rack above the kitchen counter. He plucked off a set and tossed it to Anthony.

"What're these for?" Anthony asked.

"A house of mine in Roswell. See the address label on the ring?"

Anthony nodded.

Covenant

"Go there and hide out," Mike said. "Tenants moved out last week and the utilities are still on, and the place is already furnished, too. It's a quiet, mature neighborhood—I like it so much I just put a contract on another spot a few doors away. Owner moved to Florida and gave me an offer I couldn't refuse."

"You don't have to do this for us," Anthony said.

"And take these." Mike threw another set of keys at Anthony. "To my Jeep. You can't be driving around with bullet holes in your windshields—big red flag to the cops, and you say these freaks have connections with cops."

"We can't take your car," Lisa said.

"You're going to take my car, end of story. Just bring it back with a full tank of gas, that's all I ask. Nothing worse than loaning someone your ride and they bring it back with the gas tank on E."

"Thanks for everything," Anthony said. "I'll call you as soon as I can."

"By the way, I've been Googling Kelley Marrow, the name written in the Bible? I haven't found anything conclusive yet, but I got a feeling about it. I'm gonna keep digging."

"E-mail anything you find to me on Jarhead," Anthony said. "I think my main e-mail's probably been compromised. I've never used my real name on Jarhead, so that's a good alternate address for now."

Mike nodded. "Good point. Got it."

Soon, they were settled in Mike's SUV and pulling away from the house. Like Mike's home, the vehicle was fastidiously clean, as if it had been recently driven off the showroom floor.

"He's such a sweet guy," Lisa said. "I'm worried about him."

"He's a hell of a fighter," Anthony said. "Don't let his juvenile jokes fool you. If these people screw with him they'll have a war on their hands."

"Do you really think they could've tracked us to his house?"

"They called me on my unlisted cell phone number. So yeah, I think they could've tracked us there. Matter of fact, I've been thinking my cell gives them the means to do it."

"What're you talking about?"

"These phones transmit signals to cell phone towers." He held up his phone. "I've heard of cases in which the cops were able to track down criminals because they had information on the cell phones the bad guys were using. A cell can work like a homing device, if someone has access to the data."

140

Brandon Massey

"Which these people seem to possess," she said. "If they can find out the number, why not the signals, too?"

"Plus, this gadget is GPS-enabled—I use it all the time to map out routes around the city. They might be able to tap into the GPS satellite network my cell uses and pinpoint my exact location."

"That's scary as hell, Tony."

"The glory of technology." He dropped the iPhone into the cup holder. "I've gotta ditch it somewhere."

"Okay." She dug her Blackberry out of her purse and held it up for inspection. "What about mine?"

"We'll ditch yours, too. We'll stop by a twenty-four-hour store and pick up a prepaid cell."

A drizzle had begun to fall. Rainwater glistened on the newly paved streets of the community, made the blacktop shine like licorice.

He swung out of the subdivision and made a right onto a two-lane road. The road wound through a thin layer of forest before reaching a four-way intersection that, at one forty-five in the morning, held only thin traffic.

"So where's the nearest twenty-four-hour superstore?" she asked.

"We'll follow the trail of retail."

At the intersection, he hung a left, onto a wide thoroughfare. The road was lined with chain restaurants, coffee shops, and strip malls. Suburban utopia.

Gazing out the rain-smeared window, Lisa released a melancholy sigh that he understood all too well. It was the sadness of seeing your old, normal life washing away like detritus down a rain gutter.

"I see a superstore ahead," she said softly.

"I see it, too," he said, but turned into the parking lot of a burger joint. Lights blazed inside; it was one of those locations that remained open until late into the night. Only a handful of cars sat in the lot, and none of them looked suspicious.

"Hungry?" she asked.

"Since it doesn't look like we'll be getting to sleep anytime soon, we need to eat something to keep up our energy. I could use a double cheeseburger. How about you?"

"I'm actually starving."

He pulled into the drive-through lane. An employee who sounded half-asleep took their order. Five minutes later, laden with a

141

bag full of hot food and two large colas, he nosed into a parking space at the corner of the lot, near a trash can.

They broke open the bag and ate in silence. Soft rain pattered against the windows. Although it was a tranquil setting, he vigilantly checked the rearview mirror and the street ahead for the Suburban or other questionable vehicles.

Lisa suddenly dropped her bag of French fries in her lap. "I can't do this. I want our lives back."

"We'll get them back," he said.

"Those assholes were in our *house,* Tony."

"But they haven't taken our house," he said, but he knew what she really meant. Their home, trampled and ransacked by these bizarre people, would forever be tainted.

"What if they do take it? We're starting to see what they're capable of. What if they add something to my record to get me disbarred? What if they drain our bank accounts? They can take everything away from us. Don't you see?"

"It's going to be fine, Lisa." He put his arm around her shoulder, pulled her closer, kissed her forehead. Her skin was salty with cool perspiration.

"When?" Her gaze bored into him. "When's it going to be fine?"

"As soon as we find out the truth."

"When will that be?"

"Soon."

She closed her eyes. Laid her head against his shoulder, trembled. He stroked her hair.

"That freak knows my parents' names," she whispered. "What if . . . something happens to them?"

"He was only trying to scare us, Lisa, intimidate us with the depth of their information. He's after us, and us alone. And guess what?"

"What?" She looked up at him.

"I've got something for him." He made a fist. "It's called a knuckle sandwich."

She laughed. It was weak, tired, but better than nothing.

"We stick together, we keep it together, and we'll get through this," he said.

"I'm trying."

"Give yourself some credit. You handle worse stress than this every day. Don't you deal with Atlanta rush hour traffic?"

That brought a genuine laugh.

He picked up the empty bag and shoved in their cell phones. He mashed their food wrappers and containers on top of the phones, and folded down the top of the bag.

"Say goodbye to your cell phone bill," he said.

He got out of the SUV, stuffed the bag in the nearby trash can, and returned behind the wheel.

"We're off the grid now," he said. "Unless we do something stupid, there should be no way for them to track us."

"Then I say it's time to go shopping," she said.

29

Even at two o'clock in the morning, the superstore's parking lot was a quarter full. Anthony ditched his notion of grabbing a parking spot near the door and settled on a well-lit area a couple of dozen yards away.

"We must be a nation of insomniacs," he said. "I thought this place would be empty."

"Honey, please," she said. "Shopping is a compulsion for folks. I have girlfriends who go shopping no matter what time it is—it's something to do, like eating or watching TV."

Inside the massive, brightly-lit building, bleary-eyed shoppers wandered the wide aisles like zombies cursed to browse store shelves for the rest of their existence. Clerks shuffled the floor as if dazed, yet avoided making eye contact with customers, either too tired or apathetic to care. A couple of tired-looking young women were pushing giant carts with little children in tow, the kids' heads drooping sleepily.

"There should be a law against bringing a child into a store this late," she said. "What kind of parent does that?"

"They're handing down valuable life lessons. Shop till you drop—literally."

In the electronics area, they selected a basic, prepaid cell phone and three calling cards, each with a hundred minutes.

The main benefits of the phone were that they could activate it without giving a credit card number or name to the cellular provider, and they could purchase additional minutes as they needed them. Their use of the phone should be invisible to the zealots.

As they walked to the bank of cash registers, Lisa tugged his arm.

144

"Hold on, I want to look at something," she said.

She led him into the Books department. The shelves were arrayed with popular fiction and non-fiction titles, including, he noted, several copies of his most recent novel in mass market paperback. In his current state of mind, it felt as though he were looking at a book written by someone else.

"What're you looking for?" he asked. "Something to pass the time while we're on the lam?"

"This." She pointed to a flashy floor display for a hardcover book entitled *The Keys to the Kingdom: Open the Doors to the Life You Want.* It was written by a Bishop Emmanuel Prince.

The front cover included a color photograph of the author standing in an oak-paneled office. He was a lean, fair-skinned black man perhaps in his early fifties, clean shaven, with short hair, grey eyes, and the balanced, handsome features of a Hollywood A-Lister. He was impeccably attired in a dark two-piece suit, and he had a confident smile that displayed perfect, capped teeth.

Although it was hard to gauge his height from the picture, the length of his slender torso made him appear to be very tall, well over six feet.

As Anthony studied the photo, his stomach tightened.

"Who is this guy?" he asked. "I feel as if I've seen him before."

"I'm quite sure you have. He's all over the place. Books, DVDs, TV, radio, conferences, the works."

"I never paid any attention to him, or any other preacher. Why'd you want to look at this?"

"Check out the publishing company." She fished the Bible out of her purse and turned to the copyright page. The book had been printed by New Kingdom Publishing, Inc., which had an address in Austell, Georgia, a suburb west of Atlanta.

"I noticed it a little while ago," she said. "I wasn't sure it meant anything, but thought I'd point it out to you."

He shrugged. "I've never heard of them."

"The publishing company is owned by Bishop Prince's church—New Kingdom Church International."

A chill skipped down his spine.

"Seriously?" he asked.

"It could be only a coincidence," she said. "His church might print and distribute millions of these Bibles, and Bob happened to pass this one on to you. It probably doesn't mean anything."

Anthony glanced at the bishop's photo again, and once more felt that coiled knot of tension in his gut.

"What do you know about the church?" he asked.

"They're in Austell, near Six Flags. It's a non-denominational church. And let me tell you, it's gigantic. Huge. The biggest church I've ever visited, by far."

"You've been there?"

"I went there for a wedding, maybe five years ago. The place is literally a self-contained city. One of my girlfriends is a member, and she loves it."

"But you didn't?"

"It's much too big for me. I prefer our small church, where you can actually speak to the pastor. At New Kingdom, I hear they treat Bishop Prince like a movie star."

"He sure looks like one."

He picked up the bishop's book. He traced the man's chiseled face with his finger.

Something about that face unsettled him. But he couldn't put his impression into words. It was only that, a deeply troubling feeling—like smelling something burning and being unable to determine the source.

He opened the book and skimmed the summary on the inside flap of the dust jacket.

Bishop Emmanuel Prince reaches one of the largest audiences in the U.S. and across the world—over 280,000 people attend his churches every week, and millions more tune in by television, radio, and Internet to hear his lessons of inspiration and wisdom. His fourteen books have sold over thirty million copies and are available across the world in forty-one languages.

In his new book, Bishop Prince lays out ten simple action steps that will help readers open the doors to the life they are born for . . . greater fulfillment in their finances, relationships, health, and spirituality. Incorporating key biblical fundamentals, personal testimony, and devotions in the easygoing, charming manner that has made him a beloved figure

*worldwide, Prince's message will encourage, educate,
and inspire readers from all walks of life.*

"He's sold a truckload of books," Anthony said. "Funny that
I've never heard of him until now. I need to get out more."

"He was on the cover of *Time*," she said.

"So was Osama bin Laden, if I recall."

She scratched her head. "I don't know, Tony. It's hard to
imagine that his church would be involved in murders and
conspiracies. I've seen Bishop Prince on TV—he's really charismatic,
smooth, comes across as a nice, family guy."

"Hitler was a charmer, too." Anthony put the book under his
arm. "Let's go."

"You're buying it?"

"I'm intrigued."

Before leaving the department, he plucked an Atlanta metro
map off a rack, as he'd realized that he had no idea how to reach
Mike's rental in Roswell. In the past, he would have consulted his
GPS-enabled cell for such information.

Technology made life more convenient, but it was also a
crutch.

At the cash register, he paid for their items with cash.
Although he usually used his debit card for most everything, he didn't
want to take a risk on the zealots hacking into his bank account,
finding out where and when he'd used his card, and using the
information to track him. Going forward, they had to operate on a
cash-only basis. It might have been a paranoid measure, but it made
him feel better.

"That's an awesome book," the cashier said. She was a young,
freckle-faced woman who seemed hyper-alert at that late hour. "I
love Bishop Prince. He's anointed."

"Anointed?" Anthony asked.

Her eyes shone earnestly. "God speaks through him."

"Is that so? Then I guess I better read this right away."

She grinned. "It'll be a blessing on your life."

"I could use a blessing or two."

Walking across the parking lot, Anthony said to Lisa, "The
preacher man has a lot of fans."

"In the age of the megachurch celebrity pastor, he's as big as
they come."

In the SUV, while she reclined her seat and got comfortable, he slipped the book out of the plastic bag and once again examined the bishop's handsome countenance.

She yawned. "Can we go, please? I'm starting to crash again."

He twisted the key in the ignition and pulled away from the store, his gaze straying, over and over again, to the picture.

30

Mike's property in Roswell was located in a neighborhood of modest Colonials and split-level homes on small lots, the street flanked with tall elms and oaks dripping with rain. At two-fifty in the morning, lights burned in only a couple of the residences, the glow of television sets flickering through the windows.

Anthony pulled into the asphalt driveway. Built perhaps twenty-some years ago, the house was a split-level in good condition, with white siding, dark shutters, and a detached two-bay garage. A row of holly ferns lined the front of the house, and a live oak anchored the trimmed yard.

He left the engine on and remained sitting behind the wheel, brow furrowed in thought. A classic Stevie Wonder song played at low volume on the satellite radio system: "Superstition." Which summed up his state of mind. That night, he was believing in plenty of things he didn't understand.

He'd received no revelations about the bishop's photo, and had returned the book to the bag for later consideration. Driving, he'd been alert for a tail, and had detected none, either.

But he continued to feel on edge, as if the dark sky were slowly lowering to the earth like a hydraulic press, threatening to crush him beneath its weight. That sense of impending violence had once been routine to him, but years of sedentary civilian living had reduced his threshold for extreme stress. Until that day, about the most pressing decision he'd faced on a regular basis was where he and Lisa would go out for dinner.

He had to man up. Keep it together. Be the rock that Lisa considered him to be. Get to the truth behind his father's death. This was it. No slacking off. No excuses.

149

Beside him, Lisa surfaced from a brief slumber, stretched, yawned.

"Is this the place?" she asked in a scratchy voice.

He nodded.

"Then let's go in. What're we waiting for?" She reached for the door handle.

He touched her arm. "Wait."

"Why? Is something wrong?"

"I'll be right back. Sit tight."

Brandishing the Beretta, he let himself into the house. As Mike had promised, it was furnished—Spartan furniture much like that in Mike's own home—and tidy. A flip of the light switch and a turn of the kitchen faucet confirmed that the utilities worked.

He swept around the first level. All clear. On the upper level, he checked to ensure that the three bedrooms were empty, and returned to the master bedroom.

One of the windows faced the street. He turned on the bedside lamp and moved it closer to the glass, which was veiled with plastic Venetian blinds.

Then he walked out of the house and locked the door behind him. He climbed inside the Jeep.

"All clear?" Lisa asked. "Can we go in now?"

"We're not staying here." He pointed to the bedroom window, where the lamp glowed warmly behind the blinds. "But I wanted it to look like we are."

"You're worried that those people might track us here?"

"Let's not underestimate them. They might've determined that we were staying at Mike's place in Duluth, pulled him up on their super database network or whatever they're using, and got a listing of all his properties. It's reasonable for them to assume that Mike might let us hide out at one of his rentals."

"But he has something like ten places that he rents out. How would they figure out it's this one?"

"Process of elimination." He reversed out of the driveway. "We don't know how many people they've got searching for us. They could have a team of a dozen operatives combing the city."

"You think?" She gnawed her bottom lip.

"I happen to think we're dealing mainly with the nutty guy and his female partner," he said. "But if we're going to stay ahead of them, we have to outfox them."

"Where are we going to stay then? A hotel?"

"Right here."

He swung into the driveway of a ranch with brick exterior and a "For Sale--Under Contract," sign in the yard. It was across the street and a few doors down from Mike's split-level. The place was dark, several plastic-wrapped newspapers were scattered across the sidewalk, and a lockbox was secured to the doorknob of the front door.

She was nodding. "Ah, Mike recently put a contract on this house. He mentioned something about getting a good deal on a place near the rental."

"Since he hasn't officially closed on it yet, this property shouldn't show up in the cult's super computer, either."

"I also thought he said the owner's already moved to Florida. It should be empty."

"Compliment me on my brilliance later. Meantime, scoot behind the wheel and get ready to pull into the garage when I wave you in. I'm going to go around back and open the door."

"You mean you're going to break in."

"That's such a crude way to put it."

He fished his flashlight out of his duffel and found a crowbar in the cargo area. Before heading to the back, he pulled the "For Sale" sign out of the grass. If neighbors happened to spy them inside the home and noted the sign in the yard, they might suspect a break-in and contact police.

He walked around the back of the house, feet swishing through the damp Bermuda grass. The houses on either side had tall wooden privacy fences around the perimeters of their yards, shielding him from prying eyes.

He panned the flashlight across the back of the house. Plastic lawn furniture on the concrete slab patio. Back door with a simple lockset, no deadbolt.

The crowbar was unnecessary. He used a video rental store card to disengage the lock, set the real estate sign against the doorframe, and entered into a kitchen.

The house was furnished with basic, economical pieces, was clean, and appeared to have been painted recently, in soft neutral colors. Evidently the owner had made an effort at staging the home to appeal to prospective buyers.

The utilities were still on, too.

He entered the attached garage. It was broom-clean, and empty. He hit the button to activate the garage door opener, and the sectional door slowly climbed.

Lisa nosed the SUV inside.

He pushed out a deep breath.

He dared to believe they were safe. For the time being.

31

By following the GPS signal transmitted by Thorne's cell phone, Cutty had traced him to a residence in Duluth, a home owned by Michael Alfaro, an individual whom had appeared on Thorne's known associates list. Shortly after their telephone chat—which had, frustratingly, revealed little about Thorne's iniquitous motives—Thorne had left Alfaro's and gone to a fast food establishment within two miles' proximity of his friend's house.

They canvassed for Thorne at the burger joint—and found his cell phone in a garbage can at the edge of the parking lot, along with another phone that apparently belonged to his wife.

It appeared Thorne had figured out that he could be tracked via the cell, and had ditched it, whereupon he had either gone to an undisclosed location, or returned to Alfaro's. He was proving to be a most resourceful adversary.

Using a map of the housing community that Genesis pulled from a publicly accessible database, Cutty determined the placement of Alfaro's home in relation to the rest of the neighborhood. The house stood on a cul-de-sac, fronting a parcel of dense forest that separated the various building phases of the subdivision.

He did not risk having Valdez drive past the house, for Thorne or his friend could be conducting surveillance. Instead, he instructed her to park on the other side of the woods, in the driveway of a home that was under construction. None of the surrounding homes had been completed, either. Theirs was the only vehicle on the block, conspicuous, to be sure, but there should not be any traffic through that side of the community.

They climbed out of the SUV. Valdez carried her .38. He had drawn his Glock, and had the Remington rifle slung over his shoulder, too, and the night vision binoculars dangling around his thick neck.

He led the way across a newly sodded yard, wet grass squishing beneath their sneaker soles, and they entered the woods at the rear of the property.

The cold, persistent drizzle had dampened the forest. Overhanging leaves dripped water onto their heads. Higher above, the pale moon peeked like an observing eye through a cheesecloth of clouds.

"God is watching us," he whispered to Valdez over his shoulder, and indicated the moon with a nod of his head.

She glanced from him, to the heavens. Said nothing.

"It's what the Prophet teaches," he said. "God is always watching, always judging, to see if we are fit for the kingdom or deserve to be cast into hell. The Prophet has God's ear, Valdez. More than that, he's God's *mouthpiece*—so we can rest assured that everything he teaches comes directly from the mind of the Almighty. You do believe that . . . don't you?"

"Si." She nodded vigorously.

He smiled. "Of course. I knew you would. Or else, you wouldn't be working with us, would you?"

"No."

"Sometimes I have to ask these things. It is written that those who are not with the kingdom are against the kingdom—and hell will be their reward. That goes for all of us. None is spared divine judgment."

She nodded again. The sincerity in her eyes gave him a warm feeling. She was a true believer. Their future in the coming kingdom—together as husband and wife, he prayed—was assured.

Others would not be so blessed. The unbelievers. The worshippers of false gods. The hedonists. The unrepentant sinners. Although those unfortunates would be present in the kingdom, they would not enjoy the rights to which servants were entitled. They would be outcasts—some day, literally confined in camps on the most barren edges of civilization.

He looked forward to that day. The world would be a cleaner, happier place without such people staining the earth.

They neared the edge of the forest, and stopped behind a large maple.

154

After another ten yards or so, the woods cleared, and gave way to Alfaro's neatly trimmed back yard. The house stood about twenty yards away.

Plastic chairs, a table, and an umbrella occupied the slab of concrete that served as the patio. A sliding glass patio door led to the kitchen, but the view beyond was obscured by a set of vertical blinds, the long slats only partially open.

There was another window at the back of the house. The blinds were partly open, a ghostly glow coming from the room.

He raised the binoculars to his eyes. The night vision display was a luminous green, and significantly improved his view of the house's interior. Beyond the patio door, through the vertical blinds, there was a kitchen.

It appeared to be empty.

He scanned to the room from which the glow emanated. From his vantage point, he didn't get a full view, but he saw the edge of a computer monitor, desk, and chair. No people, though.

He lowered the binoculars. Valdez looked at him expectantly.

"I don't see anyone inside," he said.

"Thorne and wife is gone?"

"That's what we'll have to find out. Let's move."

Moving low and fast, he led Valdez across the lawn, to the patio. There was no house yet built on the left, and the home on the right was under construction, no nosy neighbors presenting a threat, and the entire neighborhood was quiet, the only sounds the plinking of rain, and water trickling through gutters.

It took Valdez less than ten seconds to quietly spring the lock on the sliding patio door. She was so skilled that he almost asked, as a joke, if she had been a burglar prior to joining their organization, but he doubted she would appreciate his attempt at humor. Women were so mysterious, so easy to offend, that he had to be careful.

The door vanquished, they slipped inside the house as silently as ghosts.

32

When the Jesus freaks arrived, Mike had been in the unfinished house next door for about half an hour, camped beside a first-floor window in a dark, dusty space that would one day be someone's bedroom. He had no intention of waiting for the loonies to ambush him in his own home. He'd found himself a perfect fighting hole and hunkered down to wait.

He had a Winchester 1200 pump-action shotgun, a Taurus .44 magnum, plenty of ammo, binoculars, a pillow to cushion his backside, and a canteen of cold water. Using the binoculars, he kept a vigil on the wooded rear perimeter of his property, as he was certain that was the direction from which they would approach.

He wasn't disappointed. Sometime past three in the morning, two black-clad figures stealthily scrambled across the back yard, easily defeated the lock on the patio door (it was cheap anyway), and entered his house. They moved with the swift efficiency of highly trained professionals, and both of them were armed.

He'd had them in his sights. Had the Winchester loaded and ready to blow. Only one thing had stopped him from spraying them with buckshot before they'd breached his home, and he was almost ashamed to admit it to himself.

It was the woman. She was absolutely stunning. Latina, long midnight-black hair woven in a ponytail, jewel-like dark eyes, and though it was difficult to tell from the tracksuit she wore, looked like she had a hard body, too.

He'd always had a weakness for beautiful women. That was why he hadn't settled down yet, in spite of his family's endless chiding about when he was going to give them grandkids. There were too many hot women out there for him to turn in his bachelor card and miss out on all the fun.

What he told people was that he would settle down only when he found The One. The perfect woman, the lady of his dreams, someone gorgeous yet tough. He'd yet to find her, though a few had come close, and he was convinced that if he settled on someone else, just to get married and shut everyone up, *then* Miss Right would appear, and he'd feel like a fool for not having waited for her.

There was no way the woman in the tracksuit could be The One—she was a member of that fruitcake religious organization, for starters—but he'd be damned if she didn't look the part.

Just figured. He sees a woman that looked as if she could be The One, but she happens to be a nut job. Life was crazy like that.

He wouldn't have minded popping her partner, though, the short, stout dude with the pale face and boulder head who'd talked all that crazy shit on the phone, but there was no point. They weren't going to find anything in the house. Anthony and Lisa had left over an hour ago, and there was nothing inside that would tell these freaks where they had gone.

He hoped Anthony would contact him soon. Shortly after they'd left, he'd uncovered some interesting stuff on Kelley Marrow. He'd e-mailed it to Anthony's account on Jarhead, as he had asked, but was antsy to talk to him about it.

Binoculars pressed to his eyes, he watched his house. He hadn't drawn the blinds on one of the windows facing him—it was a window to his master bedroom—and he saw the woman flick on the ceiling light and step inside, gun drawn. She quickly swept around the room, ponytail swaying.

He licked his suddenly-dry lips.

He felt like a Peeping Tom—one watching his own house. How nuts was that?

She peered inside the closet, the master bath. He was glad that he'd maintained his Marine discipline of keeping his living space totally squared away. You could have eaten a meal off those tile floors in the bathroom and bounced a quarter off the tightly drawn bed sheets.

Concluding her search, she switched off the light and left.

He sighed, lowered the binoculars. After this, he could use a cold shower.

Perhaps twenty minutes later, the intruders left the house via the patio door. They were empty-handed. They blended into the forest like shadows, and were gone.

He wondered if he would see the woman again. He hoped that he would, and face-to-face next time. He had to know if she really believed all the crap her partner had been saying. Just out of curiosity.

He waited a few more minutes, and then he took his guns and entered his house through the rear door.

Nothing appeared to be out of place. Except one thing—the lid on the trashcan bulged, as though packed to capacity, and he saw something gleaming underneath.

Bomb?

Carefully, he lifted the lid with the barrel of the shotgun.

"What the hell?"

The can was full of empty beer bottles—every bottle of the twelve-pack he'd been keeping in the refrigerator, looked like. Underneath the bottles, he glimpsed squashed cans of soda, and a brand-new, unopened bag of potato chips.

At the sink, a residue of beer foam clung to the basin.

Automatically, he knew the short, nutty guy had been responsible. Probably thought beer, chips, and soda were sinful. Freak must've been dropped on his head at birth.

He was going to look through the rest of the house, when he noticed one other thing out of place, too.

All of the rental property keys that had been hanging on the rack in the kitchen were gone.

33

The house featured a living room with large curtained windows that overlooked the front yard, so Anthony and Lisa bunked in there. Lisa curled up on a cream-colored fabric sofa, while Anthony reclined on a matching armchair that he moved nearer the windows, to keep a close watch on Mike's property a few doors down.

A Glock 19 and a Colt .45, both loaded, lay on the glass cocktail table, and he had the Beretta 9mm on a lamp stand beside his chair. He did not expect that he would need to use the guns while they occupied the house, but keeping firepower close at hand had become a matter of necessity that night.

Funny how his long-time obsession with hardware was paying off, at least in giving them greater peace of mind.

He'd plugged the new cell phone into an AC outlet to charge the battery. Although he'd wanted to call Mike to give him the number and let him know they'd gotten settled in okay, cellular service was not yet activated. According to the instructions, it could take up to an hour for the phone to be ready for use.

Lisa had quickly tumbled asleep. Sneakers on and using an extra jacket as a blanket, she slept clutching a throw pillow, legs drawn up to her chest, mussed hair covering her face. She was as beautiful in repose as she was awake—even after they'd spent the last several hours on the run.

Silently, he promised her that he would get her through this ordeal alive and unharmed.

The only sounds were the rhythmic patter of rain, and Lisa's hushed breaths. He wanted to sleep, too, but he could not close his eyes without hearing the fanatic's choir-boy voice.

We represent the truth. We shine a light in the darkness. We are subduing the earth to prepare it for the King's arrival. Dominion will be ours . . .

From his military experience in the Middle East, he'd learned that the worst part about facing an enemy insanely committed to a wacky cause was that he would never back down. He did not believe in negotiation or compromise; annihilation of those who opposed his will was the only acceptable conclusion. Death in the service of the mission was welcomed as the path to martyrdom, whether that meant the undying love of seventy heavenly virgins or some other absurd prize.

How many of these cultists were out there? Hadn't Bob said they were everywhere?

The thought made him shudder.

He decided to occupy his restless mind by skimming Bishop Prince's book. A floor lamp provided soft light for him to read by.

The Keys to the Kingdom was comprised of ten chapters. The chapters had titles organized by "keys," such as, "Key # 1: God Wants You to Be Happy," "Key# 2: How to Ask God for What You Want," "Key # 3: You Reap What You Sow," "Key # 4: Let Go, and Let God," "Key # 5: Fortify Your Temple," and so on.

It was a slim volume, barely two hundred pages, written in plain language that could have been digested by a fourth-grader. It was heavy on New-Age style, personal fulfillment jargon, and oddly short on nuts-and-bolts theology for a book written by an ordained pastor.

In the chapter, "God Wants You to Be Happy," the bishop explained that God was committed to giving you the desires of your heart, no matter how minor they might be. It was appropriate to petition God for blessings such as a plum parking spot at the local supermarket, the best table at a posh restaurant, or that pair of designer shoes you wanted. The key to receiving these benefits was to "believe you are highly favored by God." Do that, and God would shower you with treasures, as if God were little more than a super-duper ATM that dispensed gifts to those who punched in the correct PIN.

In another chapter, tithing to your church—"sowing a seed for the Kingdom," in the bishop's phraseology—was declared a required practice of all godly people. Anthony understood that churches relied on donations in order to fund their operations, and he took no issue with that—but instead of the average ten percent, the bishop stated that a *twenty-five percent* portion of a believer's gross income was the only acceptable tithe in the eyes of God, because God, according to the bishop, "expects and deserves better than an average contribution."

In the same chapter, the bishop made his case for why pastors, "the shepherds of the flocks," deserved to be supported in grand fashion by their congregations: housed in mansions, dressed in tailored Italian suits, decked out in fine jewelry, driven in luxury cars, and flown in private jets. The historical Jesus, in the bishop's worldview, had been a wealthy man—apparently, carpenters had been high rollers back in Biblical times—and had therefore set an example for shepherds and their flocks to follow. Tithing twenty-five percent to your church would not only allow your pastor to live the ostentatious lifestyle he deserved, *you* would also reap the harvest of the "seeds" you sowed, too, which often manifested as a job promotion, an unexpected windfall, a new car, maybe even a new house.

Throughout the text, cleverly interwoven with testimony, devotions, and simple "believe God loves you and you'll be happy" success lessons, were the bishop's strident views about "the Kingdom of God." The Kingdom, he argued, was not some heavenly destination in the hereafter. It was the present world, and it was the responsibility of "God's Army" to subdue the earth to God's will, a task which, when completed, would herald a new golden age.

Governments, schools, economic systems, mass media, and all other aspects of society should possess a "Kingdom Agenda." The Kingdom Agenda meant no separation of church and state: laws should be written, executed, and adjudicated based exclusively on Biblical principles. The practice of "false religions" should be a felonious crime. Science textbooks used in schools should be revised to reflect the "Biblical interpretation" of nature and science, and the teaching of opposing theories and doctrines should be banned. Any sexual practices deemed "perverse" should be punishable as a crime, even if practiced in the privacy of one's home between consenting adults. Popular culture should be cleansed of "demonic influence" and reshaped to fit wholesome standards.

As Bishop Prince wrote:

Secular society celebrates the wicked, the immoral, the perverse. When will we, the righteous inheritors of the kingdom, the chosen of God, rise up to claim that which is ours? When will we march with God to

161

*cleanse the Kingdom of depravity, sin, and evil?
When will we seize dominion of the Earth, which the
Lord charged us with in Genesis? When? I'll tell you
when, my friend—we will arise now!*

In the closing chapter, Bishop Prince extended an invitation for the reader to visit one of his New Kingdom Churches, to learn the joys of becoming a "servant of the Kingdom." A listing of the church's locations was included. The church's headquarters, the "Kingdom Campus," was based in Austell, Georgia; they had an additional twenty-two satellite churches across the United States, and eleven churches overseas. Total worldwide membership was said to be two hundred and eighty thousand souls.

When Anthony closed the book, the needle of his intuition was vibrating like a dowsing rod above an underground well. He placed the book on the cocktail table, hands trembling.

On the sofa, Lisa sat up. Her eyes were open and alert.

"I thought you were asleep," he said.

"I was." She shook her head. "Bad dreams."

"I haven't slept at all. I've been reading."

"Oh?" She glanced at the book on the table. "Any thoughts?"

"Bishop Prince is our guy. I was suspicious when you told me about his church printing the Bible . . . but now I know for sure." He tapped the book cover.

She shifted on the cushions, folding her legs underneath her. "Do tell."

"First, a little background on his Santa Claus god philosophy." He picked up the book again, cracked it open. "According to the bishop, if I pray for a good parking spot the next time we go to the store, and if I'm living the life of a loyal, favored servant, then I'll get the primo spot."

"A parking spot?" She frowned. "That's a tad bit trivial."

"My thoughts, too. I thought if God was inclined to grant prayers, it would be for something a little more significant than giving someone a parking space near the front door. But what do I know? I'm not a bishop."

"What else does he say?"

"That Jesus was rich, and because of that, pastors deserve to live like hip hop moguls. Mansions, tailored suits, Bentleys, the whole nine. At the congregation's expense, of course. Oh, and if you

Brandon Massey

tithe twenty-five percent of your gross earnings and pray every day, you'll get that Benz you've been wanting."

"Typical prosperity preaching," she said, lips curled as if she had tasted something sour. "That's been popular ever since Reverend Ike rolled up to his pulpit in a mink-lined Rolls-Royce."

"Reverend who?"

"Ike. It's not important—he's only one of many who teach a prosperity doctrine. By telling people that Jesus was rich they justify their own desire to accumulate money and material possessions."

"My memory of the Bible might be failing me, but wasn't it Jesus who said it was easier for a camel to go through the eye of a needle than for a rich man to get into heaven? Didn't he say the meek shall inherit the earth—not those *wearing* minks?"

"That's exactly what he said in the Gospels, yeah. Bishop Prince and a lot of others like him manage to put their own twist on the scriptures, though, to suit their ends."

"Why do people fall for that?"

She shrugged. "He taps into something people want to hear, I guess. Don't forget, I've seen this guy in action, Tony—he's very persuasive. He knows how to push your buttons and make you open your wallet."

"Let's move on to the important stuff," he said. "In the midst of all that prosperity nonsense, he talks about 'the kingdom,' taking dominion of the earth, and placing the 'servants of God' over everything. Government, schools, media, law enforcement—you name it, sweetheart, they want to control it. I'm a little rusty on my grasp of forms of government, but it sounds like he wants to set up a theocracy"

"A government run by the church," she said.

"Specifically, *his* church."

"He says that in the book?"

"It's all there—conveniently sandwiched between his lessons on how to make God give you your dream home."

She was nodding. "Feed the masses what they want to hear, meanwhile, you're inserting ideas related to your true intentions."

"Demagogues, dictators—that's how they tend to work," he said. "They don't rise to power on a platform of stripping away personal freedoms and liberties. No one would support them if they did. They entice people with promises of wealth, security, abundance, happiness, divine blessings."

"They appeal to our basic human needs," she said.

163

"Including our need to believe we have opposition, an enemy. In the bishop's case, the enemy is anyone who doesn't believe in his agenda—the 'unrepentant sinners' who are ruining the world for the true believers. His definition of unrepentant sinners is pretty broad, too: most mainstream scientists and media, anyone who doesn't go to church every Sunday or who practices a different faith . . . writers like me who aren't creating 'wholesome' entertainment."

"How nuts," she said, scratching her head. "Can we say, for sure, that Bishop Prince's followers are the ones we've been running from?"

"The fanatic who called us uses a lot of the same jargon as Bishop Prince," he said. "He spoke about subduing the earth, taking dominion, all that crap. And let's not forget that New Kingdom Church printed the Bible that Bob gave me."

"All of which is suggestive, though not totally conclusive," she said. "For the time being, though, Bishop Prince is the only suspect we've got."

"I'm trying to figure out how my dad could've been involved with him and his church. What else do you know about them?"

"Only what I've already told you. If we could go online, we could do some research."

"I can't connect my laptop to the Web here—there's no wireless network for me to tap into," he said. "Come morning, we can drive around, maybe find a connection at a coffee shop."

"In the meantime, we're back to square one," she said. "The Bible that Bob gave us. Up for any more transcription?"

"I'm too wiped out to look at that or anything else."

Yawning, he dropped the bishop's back onto the table. He avoided looking at the man's face. He was no closer to understanding why the photo haunted him, and thinking about it served to only deepen his fatigue.

"We ought to try to get some sleep," she said. "Both of us are exhausted. A few hours' rest will do us some good."

"What about your bad dreams?"

She smiled wearily. "If you hold me, maybe you can keep them away."

34

They lay together on the sofa, Lisa curled atop him, head resting against his chest. The floor lamp burned on the other side of the room, leaving them submerged in shadow.

Outside, a fresh storm brewed. Rain attacked the roof and windows with growing violence, and he heard, faintly, a crack of thunder that sounded like distant rifle fire.

Drawing deep breaths, he gazed at the dark ceiling, trying to ignore the turbulence outdoors and surrender to sleep. He was stuck in a maddening state between sleep-like-a-stone fatigue, and nerves frayed just badly enough to keep him suspended on the thin edge of wakefulness.

Apparently plagued by her own brand of insomnia, Lisa said, "We never did resume our conversation from lunch."

"What was it about? So much has happened since then it feels like we were at lunch a week ago."

"We were talking about having a baby."

"Oh, yeah, that."

She laughed. "Yeah, that."

He stroked her hair. Although both of them were exhausted, he sensed that she had brought up the subject to try to recapture some semblance of normality, a sense of how their lives had been before chaos had come crashing in. Perhaps it would ease the transition to sleep and keep the nightmares at bay.

"I haven't changed my mind," he said. "I still don't want kids right now."

"You said, 'right now.' That means you may want them later. This is progress."

Covenant

"I feel the same. I wouldn't want to bring a child into this world."

"Yeah, yeah, you've said that before. But you'd make a wonderful father."

"How do you know?"

"You appreciate the value of a father."

Her words pierced his heart like a needle. He was silent for a moment, the drumming rain filling the void in conversation.

"My dad was the best," he said. "Funny, smart. Generous to a fault. Loved his family to death—you never, ever, had any doubts about his priorities. I wanted to be just like him when I grew up."

"I wish I'd gotten to meet him. And your mom, too."

"You would've loved them." He smiled wistfully. "They'd have gone nuts over you, too."

"You think so?"

"I know so."

"I don't know how you do it, going on after losing both of them when you were so young," she said. "I can't imagine what it would life would be like without my folks."

"Not a day goes by when I don't think of them," he said tightly, emotion constricting his chest. "Sometimes when we're out to dinner or somewhere, I see older couples together, looking happy, and I think to myself, 'those could be my parents.' They could still be here, happy, our entire family together, none of this fucked up shit going on with me, Danielle, or Reuben." He blew out a heavy breath. "But that's life, huh?"

Quiet, she lifted her head off his chest. Her eyes were full of understanding, love. She kissed him softly, and then snuggled against him again.

"No matter how good of a father I might be, I couldn't protect a child from life," he said.

"Life?"

"You know, life these days. So much senseless, unpredictable violence. Kids at home doing their homework getting hit by stray bullets. Kids getting gunned down at school by a psychotic classmate. Kids being snatched by some pedophile when they're walking home."

"It's not like it was when we were kids."

"If any of those things happened to our child, I would snap. I would go on a rampage."

"Like Ghost?"

166

"Yeah. As Ghost likes to say, 'the world ain't your damn friend. The world is a mad dog and you've gotta keep it on a short leash.'"

"*You* said that, not Ghost. You created him, remember?"

"Sometimes I forget."

"But you know, as much as we try, we can't protect children from everything. Getting bumps and bruises, coping with tragedy . . . that's always been part of life. It makes a child strong. Look how strong it's made you."

"I'd never want our kid to be like me. I'd want him or her to be like you."

She gazed at him. "And how am I?"

"You have peace." He closed his eyes, and as sleep tugged at him, the words floated up from some well of thought and feeling deep in his soul. "You see . . . goodness in people. You can bow your head to pray . . . and have faith that God hears, and cares."

"God hears everyone. He cares about everyone. That's what I believe."

"I used to."

"Maybe you will again some day."

Silence overtook them. Their breaths deepened, became synchronized in a slow, steady rhythm. He began to drift away.

"So," she said suddenly, "if all of this stuff works out for us, if you find out who's behind what happened to your dad, and if you get justice—whatever form it takes—do you think you'll feel differently then about having children?"

Blinking heavily, he said, "Don't know . . . maybe. I don't know how I'll feel about anything . . . if that happens. What happened to my dad . . . been sitting on my shoulders like a lead weight for fifteen years. I don't know how it feels to have peace . . . 'cept when I'm with you."

"Tony, that's the sweetest thing anyone's ever said to me in my life."

"Don't tell anyone. Wouldn't want to damage my macho image."

She laughed softly, and one of her hands found his. "Even if we never have kids, so long as we're together, I'll be happy."

"I'll remember . . . you . . . said that."

Wrapped in a cocoon of shared body heat, they fell asleep in each other's arms, while outside, the thunderstorm gathered force, like an army preparing to strike.

167

35

As Valdez wheeled away from the subdivision, Cutty used Genesis to pull up a report of Alfaro's real estate holdings. Alfaro was an industrious fellow. Under the name of his company, Alfaro Enterprises LLC, he owned eleven properties, including his home in Duluth.

On what Cutty considered a Holy Spirit-inspired hunch, he had pocketed all of the keys they'd found in Alfaro's kitchen. Comparing the address labels on the keys to the report, he determined which one was missing: it belonged to a house in Roswell.

"Intriguing," he said. "The missing key is for a house in Roswell. How much do you want to bet that's where Thorne has gone?"

Valdez nodded, adulation shining in her lovely eyes. "What is address?"

"Not so fast, my fair lady." He wagged his finger at her. "Let's not forget that Thorne abandoned his vehicle at Alfaro's. According to the DMV, Alfaro owns a motorcycle and a late-model Jeep Grand Cherokee. The motorcycle was there, but the Jeep was not."

"Ah, si. Thorne is driving."

"Time is of the essence. Before we set off on another pursuit, let's be certain of the sinner's whereabouts."

With a few quick keystrokes, he opened the vehicle tracking module that Genesis offered. The capabilities were quite impressive. By entering a license plate number or VIN, you could locate a vehicle via a complex, GPS mapping scheme. The majority of automobiles currently rolling off assembly lines had factory-installed GPS navigation systems, satellite radio receivers with a unique ID code registered to the driver, and, in other cases, after-market theft deterrent transponders that purportedly only activated if the vehicle were stolen and the police notified. All of the devices fed data to remote servers that Genesis could secretly access and use to process an exact location.

He entered the license plates information he had pulled from the DMV. About a minute later, a color street map appeared on the computer display. The location of Alfaro's jeep was indicated by a pulsing red dot, and a white balloon caption above the marker gave the address.

"Now this is truly intriguing," he said. "Alfaro's jeep is only a few doors away from his Roswell property. What do you make of that?"

"Eh?" She glanced away from the road, frowned. "That is strange, si?"

"Si." He inputted the address for Alfaro's Roswell home into the navigation panel. "Let's check 'em out."

Gaze sharpening, Valdez pushed the big SUV along the rain-slick road. In spite of the late hour, she looked fresh. Unlike his last partner, a stodgy old warrior who'd always seemed on the verge of falling asleep, Valdez seemed tireless.

It was a trait they shared. He had not slept in over twenty-four hours, and might not close his eyes for many more. The devil was busy toiling to destroy the Kingdom, and God's warriors had to be ever-vigilant, always striving to beat back the darkness. As a matter of necessity, he'd learned to grab micro-naps, fifteen minutes here and there, just enough to keep him on point.

On those rare occasions where he was without a mission to engage his energies, he still practiced remaining awake for long stretches; alert wakefulness was like a muscle that needed to be exercised daily. At such times, he would occupy himself by holing up in his small bedroom and transcribing certain passages from the Bible, and would get so engrossed in the activity that he would lose all sense of time and place. After one particularly long session, he snapped out of his trance to discover that he had copied a favorite verse from Romans, *The wages of sin is death,* over twenty-four hundred times.

Oddly enough, Father had often used Bible-verse transcription as a means of punishing his children. A cramped, enclosed room in their cellar had held only a hard cot, a toilet, a jug of water, a Bible, and a notepad and pencils. Father had banished him to the room many times, with the command to repeatedly write a verse that best described his sin, until Father decided he had made sufficient penance. He had spent as many as three consecutive days locked in the room, famished, yet scribbling with swollen fingers.

As often happened, what had once been punishment for him as a child had become his joy as an adult, sustenance for his spirit.

He glanced at Valdez. He wondered what she did to rejuvenate her spirit and stay refreshed.

He wondered, too, how she looked whenever she relaxed, loosened her hair out of the ponytail, and let it flow over her shoulders. He wondered how her face appeared when she was sleeping.

He wondered what she wore to bed. Or if she wore anything at all . . . .

As he visualized how she might appear nude, he experienced a hot charge of almost excruciating lust.

These are sinful thoughts. Cast them out. Out!

He blotted his palms on his lap. They were clammy with perspiration.

To protect against further spirit-damaging thoughts, he switched on the radio. The Suburban, like all vehicles in their fleet, was equipped with a special radio attuned to a digital signal owned by the church: Kingdom Radio. Around the clock, Kingdom Radio broadcast The Prophet's sermons and life-enhancing affirmations, wholesome music produced by the Kingdom Choir, scripture readings (on the hour, every hour), relevant news, and talk-show programs hosted by various elders on subjects of interest to faithful servants.

There was also Kingdom Television, which offered similar 24/7 content. Currently, Kingdom Radio was available only through specially equipped radio systems, and likewise, their television station was available exclusively via a closed-circuit network in the residences located on the Kingdom Campus.

When they had completed their mission to seize dominion, however, their television and radio programming would be the only selections offered to the public. The airwaves were full of corruption and wickedness that rotted mind, body, soul, and spirit. The Prophet had an ambitious plan to cleanse the flocks, keep them fit for the Kingdom.

On the radio that night, the Prophet happened to be delivering a fiery sermon on the sins of carnality.

The flesh is weak, my friends! Yes, it is. If you are not careful, if you don't keep your spirit immersed in God's word, your flesh can be an instrument of sin! You know I'm telling the truth! At this very minute, someone is listening to this message, but he isn't really hearing it, because his sinful flesh is blocking it out with fantasies of carnal pleasures . . .

Cutty's face burned. It was as if the Prophet knew the depravity that lurked in his heart, and had intended this rebuke especially for him.

He had heard stories that sometimes the Prophet did, in fact, personally deliver admonishments. Servants had reported entering their homes to discover the Prophet waiting for them, ready with a scolding word. Others had received phone calls from him in the middle of the night. Some had even gotten text messages on their cell phones, charging them with sin and demanding repentance.

What was done in the dark would come to light. There was no concealment of sin from the Prophet. God revealed all to his anointed shepherd, for the health of the flock.

As he listened to the Prophet's resounding voice, he accepted the sermon as a warning to bring his lust under control. The Prophet had promised him the desires of his heart once he completed the mission, but he would grant blessings only to one with a *clean* heart.

"A powerful message," he said to Valdez. "It's a blessing to hear him teach."

"Si," Valdez said.

She seemed unaware of the turbulence in his spirit, and he took that as a blessing, too. He was being given an opportunity to deal with his sin in private.

Outside, the rain was coming down in sheets. Lightning stabbed the horizon, and thunder rolled across the low sky.

Driving carefully, Valdez turned onto the block where Alfaro's rental property was located. Cutty scanned the addresses with his night-vision binoculars.

"Alfaro's house is ahead, on the right," he said. "The address where Alfaro's jeep is being kept is three doors down from the property, on the left."

"Drive by?" Valdez asked.

"Yes, but cut the headlights, and don't slow down. The rain should give us cover."

She doused the headlights, and the road ahead fell dark but for a nearby streetlamp. Rainfall tinted the color of copper hammered the pavement. They passed through the pool of light, and neared Alfaro's home.

It was a modest split-level with a detached garage. A lamp burned in a room upstairs.

Next, he scanned the house on the left, a ranch. Light also glowed in the front window. The jeep was not parked in the driveway, but it could have been stored in the garage.

Valdez halted at the Stop sign at the end of the block. She looked at him, eyebrows raised.

"Okay," he said, "here's the plan . . ."

36

As if God were clapping a set of giant cymbals, a clash of thunder jarred Anthony out of sleep.

He'd been dreaming about being on a bass boat with his father. The front of his dad's checkered shirt was saturated with glistening blood, and the fabric was ripped as if by a rifle round. Horror froze Anthony speechless in his seat—but his dad was speaking to him in his familiar amiable way, utterly oblivious to his gruesome wound. *I've been waiting on you, son,* he said, absentmindedly adjusting the fishing rod. *Your mom and I both have been waiting on you to get to the bottom of things. How much longer are you gonna keep us hanging, huh? I thought you had my I'll Show You Gene. How long's it gonna take for you to show those folks some real justice . . .*

Suddenly awake, he bolted upright on the sofa, automatically grasping the Beretta he'd left in reach on the carpet. He chambered a round and paused, breath bottled in his chest.

Disturbed by his abrupt movement, Lisa stirred awake, too. Her eyes were wide.

"What's going on?" she asked.

"Wait." He raised his finger. Listened.

Rain marched across the roof and machine-gunned the windows. A boom of thunder rattled the walls and floor.

But the inside of the house was silent, and felt as empty as the vacated place that it was.

He checked his watch, squinting to read the hands in the gloom. Five minutes past four. They'd been asleep for less than an hour.

"Well?" Lisa asked.

"It's nothing," he said. "The storm woke me, that's all."

"Okay." She closed her eyes and lay against him again. But he gently moved from underneath her.

"Sorry," he said. "I can't sleep any more."

"Can I?" She kept her eyes closed.

"Sure. I'll wake you if I need something."

Perhaps it was due only to the dissonant music of the storm, but his nerves were as taut as guitar strings. He approached the front window, peeled back the curtains, and looked toward Mike's rental house.

A spectral flicker of lightning temporarily obscured the view. When the brightness faded, he saw that the light he'd left burning in the second-floor bedroom was off. Blackness shrouded the property.

While the floor lamp still glowed in their hideout, the thunderstorm could have prompted a power outage that had killed the light in the rental if the homes drew electricity from different lines. It was a plausible explanation.

But he didn't like it.

Gun drawn, he swiftly searched the entire house and garage. They were alone, and the jeep was as they'd left it. There were no signs of an intruder.

But he wasn't satisfied.

Back in the living room, he pulled on a baseball cap—and then shrugged into his concealable body armor vest. He strapped a nylon utility pouch around his waist and filled it with two magazines of 9mm ammo and a speed-loader of ammo for the .45.

As he prepared, Lisa came awake again. "What're you doing?"

"I was about to wake you up. I need you to stay alert for a little while."

"For what?"

He hung his night-vision binoculars around his neck.

"I'm going to go outside and look around."

"What? Why? Is there something wrong?"

"It's probably due to a power outage, but the light I left on at Mike's house is off. I'm going to look into it. I want you to stay here while I'm gone."

Fear brightened her eyes. "You think they found Mike's place?"

"I didn't say that."

"But you're thinking it. I know you—it's all over your face."

174

After three years of marriage, she could read him as easily as a book.

"Let me come with you," she said. "I don't want to be alone."

He shook his head. "Like I said, it's probably nothing, just me being paranoid. No point in you going out there and getting your hair wet. I know how fussy you can be about your 'do."

"Very funny. I still want to go."

He holstered the Beretta, and grabbed the Colt revolver.

"I'll be back in fifteen minutes," he said. "You got your piece?"

She unzipped her purse and showed him the gun.

"Keep it close," he said. "Stay away from the windows, too."

"But—"

"Please, Lisa. I need you to wait here."

"You're in one of your stubborn moods, I see." She placed the purse on the sofa cushion beside her. "But you better come back soon, or I'm coming out there to get you."

"Fair enough."

He kissed her, and quickly moved through the house to the back door. He stepped through the doorway and closed the door behind him.

Cold rain immediately drenched him, bounced off the bill of his cap. He wished he had thought to bring a rain jacket. But he had fought in worse conditions.

He clasped the .45, muzzle pointed to the ground. Moving low and fast, sloshing through muddy puddles, he rounded the rear corner of the house. All clear. Keeping close to the wall, he moved along the western face, crept around the big AC condensing unit, and neared the front corner, where a downspout dispensed a gurgling river of rainwater into the grass.

Rumbling thunder shook the earth beneath his feet. A crack of lightning briefly brightened the night.

He inched around the corner, the house shielding half his torso. He placed the binoculars to his eyes and swept the lenses across the rental.

The green display revealed nothing of concern.

But his intuition was buzzing. He was certain the fanatics had somehow found the house and cut the light. He didn't know why they would have done that—perhaps they wanted to toss the place in darkness—but he felt them out there as surely as he felt the cold rainwater dripping down his neck.

It was time to turn the tables, go on the offensive, and force them to give him some answers.

Crouched, he moved away from the house, across the grass, toward the street. Thunder rocked, lightning flared, and the .45 suddenly leapt out of his grasp with a *ping!*, spinning away into the rain in a burst of orange sparks.

Rifle fire. Shit!

Muffled by the storm, the shot had originated from the area of Mike's rental. The sniper must've been concealed in the shrubs, waiting—and he'd known exactly where to expect Anthony to appear.

These people somehow knew he and Lisa had been hiding in the house. But how could they know that? Did they know everything?

Figure it out later.

He ran for cover.

37

Cutty had fooled Thorne.

He'd instructed Valdez to park the SUV around the corner, and they'd returned to Alfaro's property on foot, entering via the back door to stay out of sight of the house where Alfaro's jeep was garaged. When they'd entered the home and determined it was empty, in spite of the burning lamp in the bedroom, he suddenly realized the game Thorne was playing.

The cunning ploy would have deceived a lesser man.

He had turned off the light. Then he'd hunkered down in a dense block of holly ferns at the front of the property, hood drawn over his head, the Remington balanced on a collapsible bipod.

Like a mouse catching the scent of cheese, within twenty minutes, Thorne had emerged from around the home where Alfaro's jeep was stored. He moved right into Cutty's telescopic sight.

It should have been a textbook case—one head shot, one kill. But the turbulent storm had conspired to throw off the bullet's intended trajectory. He'd succeeded only in blasting Thorne's gun out of his hands.

"Shit, shit, shit," he said, and was thankful that Valdez was not near. He had ordered her to remain in the house until he radioed her. The use of foul language was sinful, but he would seek penance later.

As he prepared for another shot, Thorne fled to the street and took cover behind a sedan parked at the curb.

Rain pounding onto him, Cutty placed his eye to the scope, and waited. Sooner or later, Thorne would have to move—and next time, he would not miss him.

"The devil can't protect you from me," he whispered, face pressed against the cool, adjustable cheek piece of the rifle stock. "God is delivering you into my hands."

A barrage of thunder sounded as if it would split the earth in half. Whips of lightning lashed the night.

Cutty shivered. God's awesome power, channeled through the intense storm, charged him with such a holy fervor that he felt as if he could take hold of the next thunderbolt God delivered and hurl it like a spear toward Thorne, blowing him apart and plunging him straight to hell.

A van grumbled down the street, coming in Cutty's direction, tires spewing water. As the vehicle passed by, obstructing his line of sight, he shifted aim to the left, anticipating Thorne using the van's passage to make a run back to the house in which he and his Jezebel had taken refuge.

Instead, Thorne broke across the street, fleet-footed as a cheetah, and by the time Cutty pivoted the rifle in his direction, he vanished around a tree, taking himself beyond Cutty's range.

To get Thorne in his cross-hairs again, he would have to move.

"Fuck!" He knocked away the rifle.

Valdez's voice crackled in his earpiece: "Is okay?"

He realized that he hadn't shut off his radio. She had heard his numerous obscenities. He was setting an exceptionally poor example of proper Christian behavior throughout this mission, and if he continued, might give Valdez cause to doubt the purity of his heart and reject his imminent proposal.

"I'm sorry for the language I used—but Thorne broke away from the house," he said. "I can't see him. I think he's coming our way."

"Need help?"

"No." He withdrew his Glock from the holster. "Sit tight. I'll handle him on my own."

38

Using the van for cover, Anthony dashed across the street, splashing through puddles, and ran into the front yard of a darkened home, where a maple provided shelter from the rain and the gunman. He pressed his back against the slick trunk, a drift of mud sucking at his shoes.

Across the street, the .45 lay in the rain-battered grass. He had the Beretta as a back-up—keeping a back-up piece had been hard-wired into his brain since boot camp—but was thinking that if the shooter's aim had been adjusted upward, *he* might have been lying on that grass. Lisa would have been left to fend for herself, and his vow to get justice for his family would have been forever unfulfilled.

But luck had been on his side again. This was the second brush with death he'd experienced that night, the first being when the sniper had sent a smoking round through the windows of their SUV. He didn't want to give the guy a third crack at him. The fanatic seemed to be a skilled marksman, and he probably would not miss again.

He slipped the Beretta from the holster and racked the slide to chamber a round.

He took off into the backyard of the property. A slide-and-swing set stood in the middle of the lawn, swings rocking in the rain. Pulses of lightning threw the playground apparatus into such stark relief that it resembled the animated bones of some ancient, lumbering dinosaur.

He looked to the right, where Mike's place stood, four houses away. None of the properties were separated by fences, and he didn't see any dog kennels. He saw only a couple of utility sheds, a flower garden, and an old pick-up on cement blocks. Every house had patio furniture and barbecue grills.

He ran across a couple of back lawns, weaving around patios, keeping close to the homes. He didn't see the rifle-toting zealot. But that didn't mean he wasn't prowling the night.

And where was his partner, the Latina woman? She had to be in the proximity, too. Had to watch for her.

He crept alongside the attached garage of the next home, angling toward the street again. He worried the guy was anticipating him making a rear approach, because that was what he would have thought if their roles had been reversed. The man was crazy, but he had keen instincts.

He reached the front of the house and surveyed Mike's place next door. Clear.

He ran to the row of shrubs along the front. Examining the holly ferns, he found snapped branches and tamped down leaves. The guy had been concealed there with his rifle.

He glanced at the front door, and, on a hunch, approached it. The door opened when he twisted the knob.

He waited for a bellow of thunder, to give covering noise if the hinges creaked, and went inside.

The house was quiet. The interior was dark but for a dim light above the range in the kitchen. It had not been on during his prior visit.

Cloaked in shadow, a slim, feminine figure stood posted at a kitchen window that overlooked the back yard. The partner.

She did not give any indication that she had detected his entrance.

Grateful for the carpeting to mute the sound of his wet shoes, he tipped across the living room.

Thunder shook the walls. Rain beat a frenzied tune on the roof.

His clothes were completely soaked through, but inside, he was on fire. Adrenaline had burned away the night's fatigue, superheated his muscles, ignited his fighting instincts.

He paused at the edge of the kitchen, which was floored in linoleum that would squeak underneath his rubber soles and give him away.

When thunder grumbled again, he charged forward.

The woman began to whirl around, but he had the pistol pressed to the back of her head before she could complete her turn. She let out a thin squeal of surprise, and froze.

"Don't scream," he said quietly. "Put your hands in the air."

Silently, she did as he commanded.

"Move against the wall, to the left," he said. "Keep your hands up, and spread your legs."

Hands in the air, she pivoted to face the wall near the oven, and widened her stance. She glanced at him over her shoulder. Her dark eyes were as placid as a pond, completely submissive.

"Okay?" she asked, in heavily accented English.

"Yeah, okay," he said. "I've gotta ask you—how the hell did someone like you get tied up with a bunch of religious maniacs? You don't look crazy."

She blinked at his question, and steel surfaced in her eyes. He saw that same steel in his own gaze when he looked in the mirror— steel forged from experience with death and other terrible things.

Although he aimed the gun at her back, now that her attitude was on display, she didn't appear to be afraid of him. Her lips curved in a faint smile, as if she possessed some damning secret.

"What's so funny?" he asked.

"Eh?"

He looked her over. She wore a hooded rain jacket, and underneath, a black tracksuit. He patted down her jacket, discovered that she had a belt holster hiding a Smith & Wesson .38.

"I'll be taking this." He took the revolver and stashed it in his waistband. "Where's your partner?"

"Is outside, he look for you. Please, do not hurt me."

"Listen, answer my questions and you'll be fine. What's your name?"

"Maria Valdez," she said slowly.

"What's your partner's name?"

"Is Noah Cutty. Si."

Cutty and Valdez. Finally, he had names to attach to these people. Although the names might've been aliases, they lent an extra weight of plausibility to the night's surreal events.

"What organization sent you to kill me and my wife?" he asked.

She frowned, gaze bewildered. Either she truly did not understand him, or she was playing dumb.

"Which church are you from?" he asked.

"We are loyal servants of the kingdom." She spoke in a flat monotone, as if she'd been programmed to speak the words.

"That sounds like the same nonsense your partner was telling me."

"Is no nonsense."

He scanned her up and down again. He remembered that her partner also wore a solid black tracksuit.

"You and your partner, you're dressed alike," he said. "Is that some kind of uniform?"

"Eh?"

"Just turn around," he said. "Slowly."

She did as he asked. Holding the gun on her, he peeled away part of the rain jacket, to reveal the tracksuit top. There was a small golden emblem embroidered on the breast pocket.

"I've seen that badge before," he said.

Releasing a sharp cry, the woman seized his wrist, brought it to her mouth, and bit down savagely.

He shouted—the pain was so intense that he almost dropped the gun. As he tore his arm away from her teeth, blood spraying, she delivered a slashing chop to his throat.

Gasping, he lurched backward, throat feeling as if he'd swallowed a hot coal.

With the fluid speed of a trained martial artist, she dipped, took hold of the front of his shirt, and slammed her foot hard enough into his abdomen to knock the breath out of him. Screeching, she jerked him forward, leveraging his own momentum to catapult him through the air over her. He crashed onto the floor on the other side of the kitchen, inadvertently biting his tongue and tasting salty blood, his pistol clattering out of his fingers and spinning under a table, out of reach.

He coughed, spluttered, shook his head as if clearing away dust. He felt blood seeping from his bitten wrist, pain burning around the wound. His stomach ached from when she plunged her foot into it, even though he was wearing the body armor vest under his shirt.

He'd gotten basic martial arts training in the Corps, but it had been years since he'd used the techniques. Unfortunately, this woman moved like she *lived* in a dojo.

Behind him, she bounded to her feet as agilely as a cat.

Better remember your lessons fast, or she's gonna finish you off, man.

Breathing raggedly, he spat out a mouthful of blood and began to rise. As he got up, she stalked toward him. She was grinning maniacally. Enjoying this.

No way I'm going down, not here, not now.

He lunged at her. Evading him easily, she kicked him in the ribs, her foot a dark, deadly blur. He grunted, knees wobbly. He turned back to face her.

Just in time to catch another slashing kick, this one to his midsection. The blow sent him reeling drunkenly against a table, chairs toppling to the floor.

His eyes watered. Jesus. She kicked with such velocity and power that in spite of the body armor he wore, he was sure she was leaving behind nasty bruises.

Maybe trying to fight this girl head up was a bad idea, he thought, dimly.

Spinning like a ballerina, she kicked him again, a perfectly placed blow against his chest that made his heart clutch. He stumbled against the refrigerator, knocking it backward. He groped for the handle to keep from losing his balance and spilling onto the floor.

Dancing around him, light on her feet, she kicked him in the ribs yet again, drawing a hiss of pain from him and hurtling him back against the table.

He bent over, groaned. His body ached in what felt like a hundred places. He wasn't cut out for this kind of combat, and was clearly overmatched against this female Bruce Lee.

As she circled him, the woman's dark eyes were amused. She was *toying* with him, he realized, as if he were little more than a lame sparring partner that she could put down at her leisure whenever she got bored with knocking him around the room.

That idea pissed him off more than anything else, and he felt a fresh surge of adrenaline coming on.

She whirled to kick him again. He anticipated this one, blocked the kick, but she was so damn fast, she spun like a dervish and punched him in the face, a sharp snapping blow to his jaw, and his legs bowed, almost gave way. She hammered him twice more with that machine-gun fist, and he felt himself going down then, all of the fight gone out of him, chopped down by one of the most unlikely opponents . . .

No . . .

A reserve of strength came from somewhere. He got his legs under him before he toppled over. Then he seized her by that tracksuit, lifted, and swung her with all his might.

She flew across the room, screaming with what sounded like surprise.

She slammed against a bank of cabinets. Groaning, she sank to the floor. She curled into fetal position, her body a dusky shape in the dimness.

"Didn't want to do that . . . senorita," he said, throat raw and aching. "I was taught . . . never to raise my hand to a woman. But you had that shit coming."

She unfolded her body and rose into a crouch. She pointed a silver-plated pistol at him, the gun glinting in the faint light.

While she had been contorted into a ball, legs drawn to her chest, she must have retrieved the weapon from a concealed spot, probably an ankle holster. It looked like a .22—a smaller caliber, but it could nonetheless do some damage if you hit the right spot.

Although he had the .38 stashed against his waist and wore the vest, he raised his hands in the air. No point in pushing his luck a third time in one night. The look in her eyes dared him to go for it.

"Only wanted to . . . talk," he said, and took a step backward. He lowered his hands, and one of them brushed across the back of a chair. "You were . . . one who drew first blood—literally."

"I do not want to kill you, senor Thorne."

"Good, 'cause I don't want to die."

The door at the front of the house banged open. A man yelled: "Valdez!"

That would be her partner, Cutty.

Valdez moved forward, gun honed on him. He backed up another step. Clutched the wooden back of the chair.

Cutty stormed around the corner. He was short, perhaps five-two, but as stout as a bull, and looked about as angry as one.

He had already drawn his gun, a large semi-automatic glistening with raindrops.

Anthony heaved the chair at him, and fled down the hallway.

39

Lisa had long known that Anthony was stubborn about doing things his way. It was one of the traits of his that she loved, though sometimes it drove her nuts. He was a man of purpose and action and let nothing deter him from what he thought was right.

But she was stubborn, too. He hadn't married some docile little wifey. Like it or not, she had a mind of her own and a willingness to use it.

For maybe ten minutes after he ventured out into the storm, she waited on the sofa, purse clasped at her side, top unzipped to give quick access to the gun. Then, she couldn't tolerate sitting still any longer. She got up and went to the front windows.

Stay away from the windows . . .

She peeked through the curtains. Outside, the storm raged as if a colossal battle were taking place in the firmament, rivulets of rain hitting the glass like expended shells.

She didn't see Anthony, but the light was still off in Mike's rental house. Anthony had lamely tried to convince her that he believed it was due to a mere power outage. As if she had a big "G" tattooed on her forehead that stood for "Gullible."

Both of them knew that, somehow, the church crazies had found them. If they had learned about Mike's rental—and God knows she didn't want to speculate how—then why couldn't they discover that she and Anthony were hiding in this place, too?

Her lips drawing into a taut line, she spun away from the window. Quickly, she gathered all of their things. She hurried into the garage and loaded everything into the jeep.

Although she worried about how long they'd have to live this paranoid, nomadic lifestyle, it no longer felt as disconcerting as it had earlier. When your survival hung in the balance, you could adapt to anything.

But being on the run, constantly looking over their shoulders, would make it difficult to go back to the comfortable world of live, work, and play, make it hard to immerse herself in the minutiae of mundane affairs, and make it impossible to believe that life was as simple and orderly as she had once thought. She finally understood how delicate the fabric of their world really was, how one unexpected event could rip out a patch that forever altered your existence.

Most of all, she finally understood, at a heart-deep level, how Anthony had become the man that he was. This descent into strangeness and terror might result in them actually becoming closer than ever.

Gun at her side, she hit the button to open the garage door. The door clambered up, and the thunderstorm charged in.

She moved to the edge of the doorway and looked toward Mike's rental again. What she saw robbed the breath from her lungs.

The troll-like crazy man, wearing a rain slicker, was going inside the house.

Anthony's in there. I can feel it. The nut is going in after him.

She hustled behind the wheel, fired up the engine, and reversed out of the garage. Rain crashed onto the truck so violently she felt as if she were inside a steel drum being pelted by gunfire.

She hadn't intended to close the garage door—she wanted Anthony to know that she had gone—but when she saw a metallic object in the grass that looked suspiciously like one of his revolvers, she halted in the driveway and hopped out of the truck.

Instantly, she was drenched. She raced across the lawn, almost lost her balance on the slick grass, plucked the handgun off the ground, and scrambled back to the dry comfort of the jeep. She placed the revolver on the seat beside her.

He had armed himself with two firearms before leaving, but he wouldn't have dropped the revolver in the grass and left it there unless he'd had no choice, unless he'd been on the run.

She glanced at the rental house.

Now what? How could she help Anthony if he were in a tight spot? What if he didn't make it out of the house alive?

No, he will *make it. Don't you dare to think otherwise.*

An idea came to her. She whispered a prayer, and pulled out of the driveway.

40

Running down the hall, the fanatics at his heels, Anthony dashed into the first bedroom, on the left. He slammed the door, found the lock and twisted it, for all the little good that would do.

The bedroom was furnished with functional pieces: double bed, dresser, desk, lamp. It looked like a standard-issue hotel room, which was probably the point in a pre-furnished home.

The dresser was near the doorway. Quickly, he gripped the edges of it and hauled it across the door.

The door erupted open, but smashed against the obstructing dresser. Cutty roared in rage. He charged the door again, and the wood buckled and the dresser rocked.

Backing away, Anthony drew the .38 he had taken from Valdez out of his waistband. He swung out the cylinder.

"Shit."

The gun had no ammo. Not one round. Unfortunately, the spare .45 ammo that he'd stored in his pouch wouldn't fit the weapon, either.

He had no choice but to run.

There was a curtained window on the other side of the room, lightning flickering outside the glass. He slapped the locks open, lifted the window, and kicked out the screen. It winged away like a kite into the rainy night.

Across the room, Cutty hit the door again, hard as a juggernaut, and finally tipped over the dresser. It crashed to the carpet with a thunderous boom.

Anthony squirmed out of the window and, as he dropped to the grass below, heard Cutty's semi-automatic chopping the air above him, and the man's infuriated cursing.

Anthony landed on the ground, the impact rattling his shins and knees. He stumbled against the house.

He wasn't in shape for this kind of stuff any more. His lungs ached, his throat felt packed with glass shards, his wrist felt as if it had been gnawed on by a rabid dog, his entire torso hummed with pain from the savage kicks the deadly woman had delivered, and his face was swelling from the punches he'd endured.

But he kept moving.

Sliding against the back wall placed him out of Cutty's range, but Valdez might be coming to head him off outside. He sure as hell didn't want to tangle with her again.

As he rounded the corner, a bullet zinged past his shoulder and struck a plastic trash bin that stood against the home next door. Anthony ducked, kept running. Without needing to look, he knew Cutty was leaning out the bedroom window taking a desperate shot.

In the front now. No sign of Valdez. Maybe he'd lost her, maybe she'd gone to retrieve their vehicle to run him down. No matter. He had to scramble.

He sprinted across the front lawns of the next two homes, zigzagged around the third, raced through the backyard, cut left at the perimeter to go between that house and another, and finally saw the home where he had left Lisa, directly ahead on the other side of the road.

The garage door was open. But the jeep was gone.

What the hell was going on? He'd asked her to wait inside. Had she gotten spooked and taken off?

Using what felt like his final reserves of strength, he ran to the right. At the four-way intersection, he looked both ways, squinting against the slanting rain.

About twenty yards down the road on the right, the jeep idled at the curb, taillights glowing.

He realized, then, what Lisa was doing: she was saving his ass.

He rushed to the truck, hammered his fist against the passenger side window. She unlocked the door, and he climbed inside, dripping water onto the leather upholstery.

"Go," he said in a garbled voice.

Without a word, she punched the gas.

41

The windshield wipers swept across the glass at a frenetic rate, and angel wings of water flapped from the tires as the SUV soared down the dark street.

Checking over his shoulder to confirm no one followed—yet—Anthony drew deep breaths, and finally slowed his racing pulse. He picked up the .45 off the seat, and examined the weapon; it was in usable condition, with only a nick on the barrel from the rifle round.

"I found it in the front yard," Lisa said. "I thought you might want it."

Rain had plastered her hair against her face and soaked through her velour suit, giving her the appearance of a survivor from a shipwreck. But she had never looked more beautiful to him.

"All I have to say is, I married well," he said.

She gave a brief smile. "I felt nervous waiting in the house. Not long after you left, I loaded the jeep with our stuff."

He glanced in the backseat, saw their belongings. "When did you leave?"

"After I packed up, I kept an eye on Mike's rental. I saw that nut go inside, the guy, and I had a feeling that you were in there. I thought we might need to get away from them again when you came out, so I decided to take some initiative and park around the corner, where he couldn't take aim at us again with his sniper rifle."

"For a second there, you lost me."

"But you figured it out fast. Married folks' telepathy."

"I heard that."

They were on a residential road flanked with rain-battered elms and maples. Several blocks ahead, he spotted a traffic light, and vehicles traveling back and forth. The prospect of entering a populated area promised no security, however—the fanatics clearly cared nothing for laws and public safety.

"Is that blood on your wrist?" she asked.

"I was bitten."

"Bitten? By a dog?"

"Sure felt like it." He reached behind him and grabbed the strap of his duffel bag. "The woman who mistook me for a steak—her name is Maria Valdez, by the way. Her partner's name is Noah Cutty."

"How'd you find that out?"

"She was in the house. I stole up on her and put a gun to her head. That tends to make people talk—and bite back."

"Jesus."

"It was necessary. I needed answers."

"How did she end up biting you?"

"She was one tough bitch," he said. He massaged his battered face. "I'm lucky she didn't kill me."

"We'll have to get the wound disinfected. The human mouth carries a lot of bacteria."

"We'll get to that later." He dragged the duffel onto his lap, dug through it. "Where's the cell phone?"

She handed him her purse. He unzipped it and found the phone buried beneath the gun and the Bible. He powered it on, and the display brightened.

"Finally, we've got service," he said.

"Are you going to call Mike and make sure he's okay?" Lines of worry threaded her face.

"That's exactly what I'm going to do." He punched in the number for Mike's cell phone.

On the first ring, Mike answered. He sounded wide awake.

"Yo, man, where the hell are you?" Mike asked. "I've been going nuts here!"

Anthony nodded at Lisa to let her know Mike was fine, and then said, "We're on the move again. The goons found your rental house, and some way, knew we'd holed up in that new crib a few doors down that you'd put a contract on."

"You went there? Smart."

"I thought so, too, until the loony rifleman almost sniped me when I came around the corner," Anthony said. "Where are you?"

"I'm at home, man. They came here—I watched 'em from next door. They tossed the place a bit, but took the keys to all my properties."

"And the key to the Roswell house was the only one missing, wasn't it?"

"Sure was. Why?"

"They must've pulled up a listing of the houses you own. That's how they tracked us—part of it, anyway."

"This is freakin' crazy," Mike said. "You know who these goons are working for yet?"

"New Kingdom Church, in Austell," Anthony said. "I'm about ninety-nine percent certain of it."

"That's the church with the big time pastor? Prince or something?"

"Bishop Prince. You've heard of him?"

"He's on TV all the time. I see him when I'm channel surfin' late at night."

"I guess I need to watch more TV," Anthony said.

"You get a good look at the lady goon? She looked like a dime piece."

"I got more than a good look at her—I almost got an ass-kicking from her. She'd chew you up and spit you out, Mike, seriously."

"No shit?" He sounded awestruck.

"Hey, she's playing for the wrong team, remember?"

"Right." Mike cleared his throat. "Anyway, I sent you an e-mail on Jarhead. About Kelley Marrow. You need to check it out."

"It might be a while before I can get online. Anything earth-shattering?"

"It's an obituary," Mike said. "From about a month ago. She was a teenager, looks like. Pretty sad."

"How'd she die?"

"No idea. It didn't say."

"Thanks for doing the legwork. As soon as we get somewhere I can log on, I'll check it out."

"Where you headed to next?" Mike asked.

"Not sure yet. They're tracking us and I can't figure out how. Do you have GPS on this bucket? Or a Lo-jack, or any other kind of satellite hook-up?"

"All I got on there is satellite radio."

Anthony glanced at the radio console, which was currently turned off.

"Okay," he said. "We've gotta shake these assholes. I'll call you later—you need anything in the meantime, this is our new cell phone number."

"Got it. Be safe."

Anthony ended the call. Lisa had steered onto a brightly lit, four-lane thoroughfare, the road lined with shuttered restaurants, gas stations, and strip malls that seemed to be dissolving in the rainfall, like images of a dream.

"We've gotta ditch this ride," he said.

"How can they be tracking us in this? It doesn't have GPS, does it?"

"No, but they knew which house we were in." He tapped the radio interface. "I think it has something to do with this."

"The satellite radio? Can they do that?"

"I've never heard of it, but why not? The receiver in here gets signals from a satellite and decodes them into music or whatever. I remember when we got your Beemer with satellite radio, and in order for them to bill us for the monthly subscription, they had to use some kind of ID code in the receiver."

"I remember." She was shaking her head. "Does it ever end?"

"Maybe they've gotta sync up the signals with other GPS satellites to make it happen. I don't know. But they knew *exactly* where we'd gone, Lisa, and I'm sure that so long as we're driving this ride, they're gonna keep following us."

"So why not just remove the radio? Why do we have to find another car?"

"They already know what we're driving. Ripping out the radio would buy us only a little time. We need something clean."

She braked for a red light. White signs pointing toward entrance ramps for Georgia Highway 400 North and South were posted ahead.

He looked in the side mirror. There was one pair of headlights behind them, and they belonged to a compact-size vehicle, not a Suburban.

Not yet.

"Where to, then?" she asked.

"South," he said.

"South to where?"

"Somewhere we can get another car."

42

Cutty stood alone in the garage in which, only a short while ago, Thorne had parked the jeep. Beyond the open door, the storm punished the night, as if God were venting his displeasure at Cutty's repeated failures to eliminate the man.

He'd come *so close* to nailing Thorne that it could only be Satan keeping him out of harm's way. Overhearing on his radio that Thorne was in the house with Valdez after Thorne had miraculously evaded him outdoors, Cutty had rushed inside and gotten a crack at him—and Thorne had given him the slip again.

A perfunctory search of the residence in which they had taken refuge had turned up no clues as to their ultimate destination, other accomplices, or strategy. Thorne and his Jezebel had left behind no trace of themselves, as if they were not physical beings at all, but only visiting spirits. They'd proven so elusive that the notion that they were phantoms seemed almost plausible.

This had become more than an opportunity for him to curry favor with the Prophet, more than a chance to win Valdez's hand, more than a shot to earn a promotion in the division.

This had become a trial of faith.

At such times, weaker men crumbled into a state of despair and cursed God's name, while the strong called on the Lord for support and offered praise.

He lowered himself to his knees on the concrete floor, bowed his head, closed his eyes, and submitted a prayer requesting the deliverance of his enemy into his hands. He praised God's goodness and mercy. He thanked God for the Prophet, the divine mouthpiece, and this opportunity to serve them both.

As he prayed, he removed the silver crucifix from around his neck and clasped it in his palm, gripping it so tightly that the metal edge punctured his skin and drew blood.

He continued to pray, oblivious to the pain, lost in communion with the spirit.

When he emerged from his prayer trance and looked up, Valdez had parked the Suburban in front of the driveway. He straightened, ran outdoors, and climbed in on the passenger side, stowing his rifle in a steel rack on the dashboard.

Valdez had pulled away her rain-jacket hood. Drops of water glistened like jewels in her lush hair.

"Ready?" she asked.

"One thing before we get going," he said. He paused, carefully choosing his next words. "I wanted to ask you: are you okay?"

She nodded.

"You sure?" he asked.

"I am okay. Si." A slight frown crinkled the edges of her features.

"I was only concerned because of your encounter with Thorne. Did he uh . . . touch you?"

Her frown deepened. "Touch me?"

"On the radio, I overheard your scuffle. Did he touch you in any uh . . . inappropriate areas?"

Crimson flushed her cheeks. She shook her head angrily.

"I handle myself, senor Cutty."

Once again, he had violated one of those invisible boundaries that separated men from women.

"Of course," he said. "You're a servant in our division. You're highly capable and trained. I was only . . . never mind."

Jaw rigid, she turned away, clenching the steering wheel. "Where to go now?"

He was grateful for the change in subject. Besides, it was time to get moving.

"Gen's tracking their vehicle," he said. "Let's see where they're headed."

He opened the map on the MDT display. Currently, Thorne was traveling south on Georgia 400, a highway that extended from the northern reaches of metro Atlanta all the way south to Buckhead, where it merged with Interstate 85.

He estimated that Thorne had a ten-minute lead on them.

"Get to 400 south," he said. Unfamiliar with the neighborhood, he inputted the highway into the navigation system.

She roared away from the curb, windshield wipers flinging away the persistent downpour.

He studied the dot inching down the map. Where was Thorne going? Had he learned how they had pinpointed his precise location at the house? If Thorne was wise to them—and at this late stage, Cutty couldn't risk underestimating the man any more—he would have figured out that satellite tracking had betrayed him, and would be planning to ditch the vehicle and find alternate transportation.

In metro Atlanta, the most popular alternate transportation was MARTA, the metro rail and bus system. At that early morning hour, taxis could be hailed only within downtown Atlanta, or at the airport. Or, Thorne could be plotting to steal a car.

He entered a command to access a listing of area MARTA stations and shopping malls, a popular place to find parked vehicles to steal. In a few seconds, he received several results.

He looked at the map again.

"I think I know where Thorne is going," he said.

43

At Anthony's direction, Lisa exited the highway at Abernathy Road, in Sandy Springs. She braked for a traffic light at the bottom of the exit ramp.

"My old stomping grounds," she said. "Why are we coming over here?"

Before they had married and moved to Grant Park, she had lived in a condo in Sandy Springs. At least three times a week, he would make the long trek from Decatur to pick her up for dates. Over time, he'd learned the area well. Perimeter Mall, a popular metro shopping destination, was in the vicinity, and a large MARTA station was nearby.

It was the perfect setting for the strategy he had in mind.

"I want to go to your old condo," he said. "We're going to leave the jeep in the garage."

"Ah, gotcha. Good idea."

When the light turned green, she made a left. They took an underpass beneath the highway they had exited. Corporate parks bordered the road on either side, dark, glassy, modernist buildings pointing like stakes toward the swollen sky.

Farther ahead, corporations gave way to retail: strip malls full of chain businesses and restaurants, all of them still closed. She turned right, and after a quarter mile or so, Heritage Condominiums rose into view on the left, the community fronted by tall elms and pines. Entering the parking lot, they rolled down a blacktopped slope toward the entrance for the underground parking garage.

The wide door hung open.

"They still haven't fixed this door," she said. "All that damn money I paid to the homeowner's association the years I lived here, you'd think they would've used some of it to repair the door."

"I was sort of counting on them not having fixed it yet," he said. "Nothing as trustworthy as good ole' bureaucracy."

The garage was a cavernous, dimly lighted space, perhaps three-quarters occupied. Spaces were assigned to residents by numbers painted on each spot.

She cruised slowly down the aisle. "Any preference for where I park?"

"See if you can find a spot in the back. Why make it easy for them?"

At the far end of the garage, in the corner, there was a vacant slot between the cinderblock wall and a black Harley motorcycle adorned with orange flames. She parked, cut off the engine.

He had already placed his duffel and their suitcase on his lap, and stashed the .45 in his waist-band holster.

She grabbed her purse, and they got out of the truck. The slamming doors echoed through the garage.

"Now what?" she asked. "Are we going to steal a car here?"

He shook his head. "That might take too long. I don't know how much of a lead we have, and I don't want them to catch us while I'm trying to boost a ride. First, we need to drop off their radar and put some distance between us."

"We're going to the MARTA station," she said.

"Married folks' telepathy is for real, isn't it?" He glanced at his wristwatch; it was twenty minutes to five. "When do trains start running on Saturday?"

"They start around five am, every day. I remember that well. When I was working at the firm downtown I'd catch the first train every morning."

"Then let's go. I want to be on that five o'clock."

They hurried to a stairwell in the middle of the garage. He motioned for her to hang back. He pushed open the door, hand resting on the butt of the revolver.

The stairs were deserted, the only noise the patter of rain. They ascended the steps to the first level, the courtyard. An awning sheltered them from the elements.

"Is there a back door out of here?" he asked. "I don't like the idea of walking out through the front gate."

"There's a rear entrance. Follow me."

They threaded past condo units, patios full of plants and furniture, stairwells, and around a large swimming pool, the rippling surface reflecting the sky. As they prowled through the complex, they saw not a single resident. It reminded him of being in a war zone, where locals stayed indoors for fear of encountering enemy soldiers.

At the fence at the back of the courtyard, there was a lever-activated gate. They went through, and descended steps to asphalt and the rear entryway. Unlike the front, this vehicle entrance was secured by a white cross arm that lifted whenever a resident swiped a card through the reader.

He edged in front of Lisa and stepped around the arm. The adjacent road was draped in tall trees that overhung the pavement and shed droplets of falling rain like tears. Across the street, woodlands dominated.

"This is mostly a service road for some stores and restaurants around here," she said. "If we go left, it'll take us toward the MARTA station. It's only a few blocks away."

He checked his watch. "It's a quarter to five. We'd better double-time it."

They started off down the road at a jog, keeping close to the curb. No vehicles passed by. A streetlamp ahead was the only relief from the darkness.

"When this is all over, I'm going to sleep for three days," she said, breathing deeply of the cool air. "I know I'm tired, but I've stopped feeling tired, and that must be bad."

"You've crossed the threshold," he said. "When the crash comes later, it's gonna hit you hard."

"Do you think these people chasing us ever sleep?"

"They didn't seem tired at all to me. My guess is that they do this sort of thing all the time, probably at night, mostly. Also, they might have a backup team to relieve them."

"So the longer this drags on, the better it is for them. They can wear us down."

"In theory," he said. "But I don't plan on slowing down at all until we've found the truth."

The cover of trees began to thin. They paused in the shelter of an oak.

He surveyed the area. To the left, several hundred yards away, there was a strip mall with a gigantic parking lot. Beyond that, the MARTA station stood, a multi-level parking garage attached to the building.

A few vehicles traveled back and forth through the area, headlamps aglow, but none of them were Suburbans. There were a handful of vehicles parked around the strip mall, but none of them were the fanatics' vehicle, either.

But that didn't mean they weren't conducting surveillance from afar. What if Cutty had set up his rifle somewhere nearby and was waiting for them to emerge in the open? He remembered how close the guy had come earlier to nailing him.

"I don't like this scene," he said. "We'll be too exposed walking to the station. This was a mistake on my part."

"We don't have time to go back. We don't know how much of a lead we have on them, like you said. We've gotta walk by faith."

He rolled his eyes. "Come on, Lisa, faith doesn't have anything to do with this."

"You're wrong—faith has *everything* to do with it. Why did you go talk to Bob in the first place?"

"That was different."

"Was it?"

With that, she started running toward the strip mall. He caught up with her and tried to grab her arm, but she increased her speed, eluding him.

"Dammit, Lisa! Stop! This is crazy!"

She ran on, purse knocking against her ribcage. Slowed by the duffel and suitcase, weighted down by his body armor vest, firearm, and ammo, he struggled to keep up with her.

Legs pumping, they sprinted across the parking lot, shoes clapping on the blacktop and sloshing through puddles. They cut around the strip mall, plowed across a sward of grass, ran under the boughs of a line of trees, and neared the road that fronted the MARTA station.

Close by, tires squealed. The Suburban careened around the corner, headlights glaring.

Lisa had run across the street and reached the revolving doors of the station. She waited for him.

"Get inside!" he shouted.

Seeing the Suburban drawing near, she pushed through the doors. Half a block away, the SUV shrieked to a stop. The passenger door sprang open, and Cutty leapt outside, hand underneath his jacket, undoubtedly caressing a pistol.

Heart in his throat, Anthony raced up the stairs and shoved through the revolving doors so fast he almost fell down. When he hit the other side, Lisa beamed at him.

"We made it," she said. "They won't follow us in here. We're safe."

But Anthony was looking over his shoulder.

"Not over yet," he said, gasping for air. "He's coming in."

44

Only a smattering of people filtered through the MARTA station, most of them burdened with suitcases and dressed in t-shirts, halters, shorts, and sandals, like travelers bound for trips. With the high price of gasoline, taking the train to the airport south of the city was an increasingly popular choice.

A couple of burly policemen wandered the lobby, but they gave Lisa and Anthony only a casual glance. Anthony realized that with the bags they carried, they looked like airport-bound people, too. But they were toting firearms and ammo in their luggage.

He pulled Lisa around a corner. There were men's and women's restrooms nearby, and farther ahead, a stairwell that led to the boarding platform, and the trains.

He handed her the suitcase. "Go downstairs and wait for me. I'll be there in a minute."

Nodding, she took the luggage and scurried down the steps. He looked around the corner, into the main corridor of the lobby.

Cutty had pushed through the revolving doors at the front of the building. He had his hand inside his jacket. He attempted to appear non-threatening, but his eyes were deadly blue points as he scanned the station.

Anthony ducked inside the men's restroom. Vacant. Above the trashcan, there was a red emergency phone mounted on the wall, used to summon MARTA security.

He quickly ran down his options. He had plenty of firepower, and might be able to win a gunfight with Cutty, but a shootout in a public place would put the lives of innocents at risk. No good. Do something else.

He picked up the handset and pressed "o," according to the posted instructions.

After two rings, a tired-sounding woman answered. "Good morning, MARTA security. How may I help you?"

"A man just entered the Sandy Springs station," Anthony said. "Blonde, short, wearing a dark raincoat and a black tracksuit. He's armed with a gun and plans to board a train."

"Sir, can you please—"

He hung up. Gaze on his watch, he waited, one hand underneath his shirt and resting on the butt of the revolver.

After two uneventful minutes, he stepped outside the restroom. The MARTA police officers were escorting Cutty out of the station. Cutty was protesting furiously, face tomato-red.

Anthony scrambled down the steps to the boarding area. He found Lisa beside a MARTA BREEZE card vending machine, rocking nervously on her heels, suitcase beside her.

When she saw him, relief passed over her face.

"I saw that guy, Cutty," she said. "As soon as he came down the steps, two cops stopped him. Did you have something to do with that?"

"I told them he had a gun. Boarding a train with a firearm is a big no-no these days."

"But we've got guns, too."

"They don't know that, though, do they?"

Shaking her head and smiling, she swiped a BREEZE card through the turnstile, passed it back to him, and he slid it through. They dashed across the concrete platform to the southbound train, and boarded the passenger car at the end. He wanted to see every person who walked onto the platform.

Lisa sat on one of the seats facing forward, but he remained standing, gripping a hand strap for support. Watching.

"We're safe now, baby," she said. "You can relax."

"Not yet."

A young husband and wife dressed for a tropical vacation boarded, laden with luggage. Anthony glanced at Lisa, and read the same thought in her eyes: they both wished they were heading to the airport to fly to some far-flung, relaxing destination.

He returned his attention to the platform. Even after the doors whooshed closed, and the releasing brakes sighed, and the train began to crawl forward, he still watched.

"We're safe," Lisa said.

The train pulled out of the station.

"Sit." She grasped his hand, tugged him. He finally sat next to her, placing the duffel between his feet.

"There's no way they can find us now," she said. "We're off the radar."

He nodded. But when he noticed the surveillance camera mounted in the upper corner of the compartment, his gut tightened.

45

Cutty slammed the Suburban's door so hard the entire vehicle shuddered.

"Goddamn cops!" he said. "They wouldn't let me get near the fucking train 'cause someone told them I had a gun! I know it was that goddamn Thorne! Shit!"

"Si," Valdez said in a calm tone. "No can carry guns on train. Is law."

"It's not God's law! *We* answer only to God—not a couple of prick cops! I should've killed them both!"

He punched the dashboard, bruising his thick knuckles against the console, and nevertheless bashed it again, and again. Valdez watched him quietly, as if he were a child throwing a temper tantrum and she was the responsible adult. That condescending look of hers put the lid on his rage. She was the rookie here; he was the veteran warrior. He needed to act like it.

After all, God was always watching, always judging, and would not approve of his childish behavior and foul language. He would need to seek forgiveness for these transgressions.

But this mission was testing him. He'd flashed his U.S. Marshal badge at the dolts, a fake that looked as credible as the genuine article, and the assholes had insisted that he wait in their office until they confirmed his identity. He'd given them the number to call to validate his ID—a number that would be answered by a member of their organization—and the dickheads had said they would follow their own confirmation procedures, thank you very much, sir, come with us, please, at which point he had stormed out.

The cocksuckers. They were supposed to obey without question. They were supposed to be on *his* side.

Although he'd come close to blowing the cops away, in hindsight, killing them would have caused more trouble than it was worth. Their organization had high-ranking servants and powerful contacts in law enforcement, making the police agencies invaluable allies. Gunning down two officers in cold blood would have damaged those relationships and raised the ire of the Director, who would have been responsible for cleaning up the mess. The Director had ordered him to eliminate Thorne and anyone who stood in his way, but that command didn't include a license to murder honest cops.

His throbbing knuckles were bright red. He gently massaged them.

"Okay?" Valdez asked softly.

"I know I've said this before, Valdez, but I get so fired up with holy passion, so caught up in doing God's will, that I lose my head. I'm not making excuses for my behavior, and I will seek penance later for my angry words . . . but my Lord, I'm positively *obsessed* with God's thirst for justice. That's the kind of man I am. You understand?"

"Si. Is okay."

"It is?"

"Si."

Her eyes were so warm, so empathetic. He had the sudden and almost irresistible urge to kiss her. It was only by the grace of God that he resisted. When one was at a moment of weakness, Satan offered the temptations of the flesh.

But a film of cold sweat had beaded on his forehead. He used a handkerchief to wipe it away.

"We've got to get on Thorne's trail again," he said.

"They go south, to city?"

"Probably. Let's see what I can dig up on Gen."

He dragged the keyboard onto his lap and accessed the MARTA rail schedules and routes. The southbound train would make over a dozen stops, the last one being the airport, south of Atlanta. But there were also trains running east and west, and north.

Too many possibilities. He had to dig deeper.

He instructed Gen to tap into the rail security network. Like most mass transit systems across the country and throughout the world, MARTA utilized surveillance cameras on their trains, and in the stations, too. Gen could invade the network by stealth, slip into those cameras, and show him what they were recording.

Covenant

At five o'clock in the morning, there were only a limited number of trains running across the metro area. He first checked surveillance video on the southbound line.

Each passenger car was equipped with a camera. He toggled views from one car to the next.

"Got 'em," he said. "Get on 400 South, right now."

Valdez rocketed away from the curb.

The camera was located in the upper corner of the car, and transmitted images in black-and-white, in real-time. He clearly saw Thorne and his wife sitting together near the back of the compartment, talking. He would've liked to pick up audio, too, but that wasn't a component of the system.

Thorne suddenly glanced up at the lens, as if he sensed Cutty observing them.

Thorne's awareness of the camera was proof that he worried Cutty might be watching. He obviously was discovering the awesome powers of the Kingdom that he'd dared to defy, and perhaps he was beginning to realize that he'd aligned himself with the wrong side.

Cutty pressed a button to split the screen into two equal-size panes, shifting the passenger car view to the left-hand side of the display. On the right half, he scrolled through a list of available surveillance cameras posted at the stations along the train's route.

As soon as Thorne and his wife disembarked, he would get a visual of the boarding platform they would have to walk to leave the station. They didn't have a vehicle to facilitate their escape, and few cabs and buses were operating at that hour.

They would, at last, have nowhere to run, and nowhere to hide.

46

As the train blasted south along the elevated rail tracks that cut through the middle of Georgia 400, Anthony continually glanced at the surveillance camera.

Lisa followed his gaze. "You keep looking at the camera. You think they can watch us?"

"The camera is linked to a network. Networks can be hacked."

"Why did I ask?" She ran her hands through her hair. "Do we have to take a space shuttle to the moon to escape these people?"

"Come on." He grabbed their bags. "Let's move to another car."

In the next compartment, there were only two passengers, both college-age guys. One was asleep, head tilted back and mouth lolling open. The guy sitting beside him listened to loud rock on an iPod and bobbed his shaggy-haired head almost violently. He looked at them without interest.

A surveillance camera monitored them in there, too.

"Must be surveillance in every car." He turned to Lisa. "You have some lipstick? A dark shade?"

"Lemme see." She dug in her purse and handed a stick to him. "This is the darkest color I have. It's called merlot."

"That'll work."

He climbed onto the seat underneath the camera. Using broad strokes, he painted a thick coat of lipstick over the lens.

The rock fan passenger was watching him. He grinned and gave Anthony the thumbs-up sign. "Fucking A, dude. Big Brother sucks."

Anthony returned the thumbs-up, and settled onto a seat with Lisa.

Covenant

"Now we've got a little bit of privacy," he said. "My guess is that they'll have cameras in each station, too, but maybe we can throw them off long enough for us to get away."

"Where do you want to go?"

"To Buckhead, maybe. Somewhere we can find a car to boost. Unless you have another idea?"

"Hmm." She pursed her lips. "I was thinking—my baby sister's in Houston visiting her boyfriend until Sunday night. She left her car at her apartment, and I've got a key to her place."

"Isn't it near a station?"

"It's about two or three blocks from the Midtown stop."

"We'll go there then."

While Lisa closed her eyes to doze, he rummaged in his duffel and found Bishop Prince's book. He stared at the cover photo.

The bishop's face still troubled him, for reasons that continued to elude him. But there was another element of the picture that made sense.

On the lapel of his suit, Bishop Prince wore the same golden badge that he had seen on the breast pocket of Valdez's tracksuit. Although the picture did not provide close-up detail of the emblem's intricate embroidery—he could make out images of a bird of some kind, a sword, and a cross—the capital letters "NKC," in a bold, elegant typeface, were easily readable.

NKC. *New Kingdom Church.*

He pointed out the badge to Lisa and explained what he'd seen on the woman's jacket.

"That sounds conclusive to me," she said. "At this point, the accumulated evidence is impossible to deny."

"I only wish I knew how my dad got involved with these people." He gazed out the window, the urban landscape fleeing past in a dark blur. Sighing, he examined the bishop's face again. "I feel like we're missing something obvious."

"Like what?"

He shrugged. "Something. Maybe in that Bible. Maybe in this book."

"Well, we're both tired. Soon as we can get settled somewhere safe, get some rest, and clear our heads, things will start to fall into place."

"But for now, we definitely know one thing for sure."

"Which is?"

He tapped the book, finger stabbing the bishop's beguiling smile.

"The face of our enemy."

47

By the time the train pulled into the Midtown station, the two college kids had disembarked at a previous stop and left Anthony and Lisa alone in the car.   They got to their feet as the locomotive slowed, Anthony craning his neck to find the camera that would be watching the area, while Lisa searched for it, too.

"There it is," she said, face pressed to the glass. "It's in the middle, above that trash can. It moves left to right. See it?"

He saw it. Suspended from the rafters by a steel arm veined with black cables, the small camera was one of a bundled pair that scanned the area. The other one was angled in the opposite direction, to monitor activity on a separate train line.

"I see it," he said. "Stand by till I give the word."

Counting under his breath, he began to clock the speed of the camera's arc.

With a screech of brakes, the train drew to a halt.   The passenger doors rattled open.

Lisa hung back from the doors. Anthony waited until the camera had ratcheted away from the train, and said to her, "Now. We'll go across the platform and stand by that trash can. We've got about five seconds before the camera swings back our way."

Lugging their bags, they hurried off the car and onto the platform. There were only a few passengers boarding or leaving the rails at that hour, and those that wandered past ignored them in that familiar way that urbanites did, immersed in their own little bubbles.

Standing close together beside the wastebasket, almost directly beneath the camera, they waited. The lens pivoted to the left, sweeping over the train they had exited, and moved its cyclopean gaze to the stairwell beyond the platform.

When it had reached the limit of its leftward scan and resumed the rightward rotation, he nudged Lisa.

"Now."

They took off at a jog. They reached the stairwell and pounded up the steps.

Halfway up the stairs, he grabbed Lisa's arm.

"Wait. Step down. There's another one at the top."

She turned away, descended a step. A young woman brusquely rushed by them

He waited until the swiveling camera had raked past. "Go."

They streaked up the staircase and cut right, to the doors. Finally, no more cameras.

They ran outside into damp air, a cool drizzle, and the drone of the city. The vaulted sky had yet to release sunshine; dawn was an hour away yet.

A few vehicles grumbled past on Tenth Street, but none of them were black Suburbans. That didn't inspire a sense of security, however—an urban environment offered countless hiding places.

"Where's your sister's apartment?" he asked.

"Not far." She took his hand, and they crossed the street.

They were in the heart of Midtown. High-rise condos and apartments. Skyscrapers housing corporate headquarters. Fashionable boutiques. Trendy restaurants. Yesterday afternoon, he and Lisa had met for lunch at a brewpub only a few blocks away. Their lives had changed so much in the past twelve hours they might have been in a different universe.

But if this nerve-shredding ordeal ended with the justice his family deserved, it would have been well worth the pain, stress, and exhaustion. Worth everything. A day or two of sheer hell could never compare to the past fifteen years of misery—or the prospect of a future without closure.

They traveled two blocks south down a wide, glistening sidewalk, and stopped at a towering condominium called, "The Summit." An awning protected against the rain. Beyond the dual set of glass doors, there was a small vestibule; one needed a keycard to gain entry to the lobby, or you had to be buzzed in by a resident or doorman.

As Lisa combed through her purse for the keys, Anthony looked around. Most of the storefronts were dark. A weekend athlete in an orange rain-licker jogged along the other side of the street, a black Labrador keeping pace with him.

Also across the street, fixed atop a lamp post, he noticed a camera.

Midtown was under surveillance, too.

"Shit." He spun away to hide his face.

"What's wrong?" She had the key and accompanying keycard in her fingers.

"This neighborhood is being monitored by security cameras."

"Are you serious?"

"They're supposed to keep you safe from the bad guys. Other cities have a similar set-up, I've read. The problem is when the bad guys are the ones watching the cameras."

They stepped inside the vestibule, and she swiped the keycard through the reader. They entered an air-conditioned lobby with polished stone tile, soft lighting, and potted ferns. Ansel Adams prints, probably reproductions, hung on the walls.

A black man with jug-ears and snow-white hair sat behind a crescent-shaped granite desk, bifocals balanced on his nose, a book resting near a folded newspaper.

"Morning, folks," he said. "It's a mess out there, ain't it?"

"Sure is," Anthony said, and Lisa muttered agreement. They headed toward the bank of stainless steel elevators.

"You look familiar, young lady," the doorman said. "You got kinfolk here?"

"My baby sister lives on the ninth floor."

"Knew I wasn't blind yet." He cackled. "Y'all have a blessed day now."

As the elevator transported them to the upper floors, Anthony said, "Did you notice the old head's book?"

She shook her head. "What was it?"

"Another book by Bishop Prince."

"He's everywhere, Tony, like I said earlier. You've only lately begun to notice."

"The old head seemed like a sweet guy, sort of reminded me of my granddad. I wonder if that's what it's like when dictators take over countries—ordinary people blindly following tyrants."

"That's a disturbing thought. And probably all-too accurate."

The elevator arrived at the ninth floor. Lisa led him to the door of her sister's unit and unlocked it.

"Let's make this quick," he said, thinking about the camera that had spied them entering the high-rise. "I don't know how much time we've got before they track us here."

48

Cutty had lost his visual on Thorne and his wife on board the train—they had entered another compartment and cleverly painted over the camera lens—but it was not going to save them. Traveling into the thick of the city, there was no way Thorne could avoid the Kingdom's omnipresent eyes.

Valdez pushed the SUV down GA 400 South at eighty-five miles an hour, the tires churning up rain from the pavement. Based on the camera images transmitted to his MDT, Cutty knew the train had a lead on them. It had already passed down the highway and pulled into the Buckhead station, near Lenox Square Mall.

They sped through a toll plaza without slowing, the Cruise Card scanners reading the transponder mounted on the windshield. Ahead, there were exits for Peachtree and Piedmont roads, major arteries that ran through the heart of Buckhead, one of the biggest commercial and residential districts in the city.

"Get off on Peachtree here," he said, "and stay on it. We'll keep pace with the train and catch them when they leave the station."

Nodding, she veered off the highway.

He watched the screen, following the action at the Buckhead station. The range of vision shifted as the surveillance camera pivoted. A handful of passengers disembarked from the train, but not Thorne.

"Keep going south," he said.

They rumbled down Peachtree, the typically busy thoroughfare virtually deserted at that early morning hour. They blasted past Lenox Square Mall, and a row of swanky restaurants and hotels.

The train stopped next at the Lindberg Center. On the camera, he watched one person disembark, and it was neither Thorne, nor his wife.

Next, the Arts Center station. Two young men left the train.

He toggled to the Midtown station. The train had about a five-minute lead on them, but Valdez was closing the gap, skillfully navigating the wet roads and cautiously running through red traffic lights.

At Midtown Station, three passengers disembarked. But he saw something that sent him bolting upright in the seat.

Two shadowy shapes waited inside a passenger car, staring out the window. The camera continued its revolution to the right, and the figures slid out of view. But when the camera panned to the left again, the silhouettes had vanished.

Son-of-a-bitch.

"They got off at the Midtown station," he said. "Peachtree and Tenth Street. Go!"

Mashing the accelerator, Valdez ran a red light at Seventeenth Street.

Cutty shoved the keyboard off his lap. He withdrew the Glock from the holster, and chambered a round.

They bumped and swerved along Peachtree. The road was not a straight thoroughfare—it had a series of curves that prevented Valdez from reaching a high speed, lest she throw the big SUV into a tailspin.

He rolled down the passenger-side window. Cold raindrops trickled down his face, but he was so focused on his intent that he barely registered the wetness.

He was thinking about cutting Thorne down, drive-by style.

They swung onto Tenth Street and thundered toward the Midtown station. He didn't see Thorne or his woman in the vicinity, but if they had gotten off the train only five minutes ago, they could not have traveled far.

Valdez braked at a light. "Where go now?"

"Circle the area. A hunch tells me they're on foot. They've got to be within a six-block radius of the station."

"Si."

"Meanwhile, I'll check surveillance video. This entire section of town is saturated with cameras."

49

The apartment was a tidy one-bedroom decorated in warm, earthy colors, furniture with smooth lines, and lots of photos of family and friends. A floor-to-ceiling window in the living room granted a jaw-dropping view of the Midtown skyline.

"Car keys," Lisa said from the kitchen, and tossed Anthony a set of keys. "As soon as I powder my nose, we can go."

While she headed down the short hallway to the bathroom, he approached the living room window, and looked to the road below.

Passing through a pool of light cast by a streetlamp, a large black SUV crawled south along the road at a deliberate pace, like a lurking spider. It crept by the condominium, rolled to the corner, made a right, and disappeared from view.

A charge of adrenaline leapt through his heart. He ran to the bathroom and pounded the door.

"Lisa, we've gotta go *now*. I think they've found us."

"I'm coming!" The toilet flushed, and the water turned on.

He raced to the coat closet in the foyer. Inside, he found a red silk scarf, and snatched it out.

He returned to the living-room window. The SUV had doubled back and was drawing toward the condominium again.

This time, it would stop.

Lisa came out of the bathroom. He handed her the scarf, and the car keys.

"Wear this," he said. "You're going to drive."

50

Cutty instructed Valdez to park in front of a high-rise condominium called The Summit. A surveillance camera posted across the street had observed Thorne and his wife entering the building only ten minutes ago.

He didn't know why they'd come there—perhaps an accomplice of theirs resided in the place—but it was irrelevant. He would eliminate them, and anyone who dared to assist them.

"Circle to the other side of the block and keep an eye on the parking garage exit," he said. "They try to run out, drive away, whatever, you stop them."

"Okay," she said.

Holstering his gun, he climbed out of the truck, and Valdez pulled away.

In the vestibule, a keycard reader restricted entry. He removed a laminated card with a special magnetic strip from his wallet, and slipped it through the device.

The system flashed a green light, and he was inside.

Knock, and it shall be opened to you. God rewarded his loyal servants with the keys to the Kingdom.

"Good morning, mister," an elderly doorman said from behind a desk. His name tag read Jim.

Cutty gave the guy and his desk a quick, appraising glance, and saw the book lying at the man's elbow.

"Great book, isn't it, Jim?" Cutty asked. "I've read that one eight times, and all his others more than ten."

"Is that so?" The man's eyes danced. "Bishop Prince is the prophet, he sure is. I been serving the kingdom six years now, myself. Best years of my life."

216

"I've been serving for twelve wonderful years. Praise God."

"He's worthy to be praised, ain't he? Deserves all the glory."

Cutty had been prepared to show his fake U.S. Marshall badge, but it would not be necessary here in the company of a fellow kingdom servant.

"A young man and woman entered about ten minutes ago," Cutty said. "Did you see them?"

"Sure did. Didn't catch their names, but the young lady, she's a sister of one of our residents." He grinned. "Pretty young thangs, both of 'em is."

"Which unit does the sister occupy?"

"Lemme look here." Jim pushed up his bifocals on his nose, licked his finger, and paged through a three-ring binder. "All right, here it is. Nine oh-seven. Ninth floor, that is."

"God bless you, sir." Cutty hurried to the elevators and punched the button to summon a car.

Jim shut the binder, dark eyes troubled. "Mister, is you some kind of police officer?"

"A police officer? Yes, of a sort." Cutty smiled. "Better to consider me a faithful servant like yourself, humbly doing the Lord's work."

Leaving the old guy with a befuddled expression, Cutty boarded the elevator, and got off on the ninth floor. He checked both ways along the corridor, and then stalked toward unit 907.

He kicked in the door. It flew away, smacked the wall.

He charged inside, crouched low, sweeping the gun around the shadows, finger tingling on the trigger.

The unit was quiet, and felt empty.

Nevertheless, he checked every area, switching on lights: kitchen, living room, bathroom, bedroom, closets.

Thorne and his wife were gone. They'd departed so recently that he could still *smell* them.

"Fuck, fuck, fuck!" he shouted.

His cell phone vibrated. He read the number: it was division headquarters.

Fuck.

"Cutty speaking," he said.

The Director's gravelly voice greeted him.

"We need to talk."

51

The silver Volkswagen sedan that belonged to Lisa's sister was stored in the parking garage on the building's third level. Lisa wrapped her head in the scarf Anthony had given her, put on a pair of sunglasses, and got behind the wheel.

In the back of the car, knees pressed to the floor, Anthony kept his torso as flat as a sheet of wood across the seats. He'd covered himself with a windbreaker jacket that had been lying on the leather cushions.

"Does your sister have GPS, Lojack, satellite radio, or anything like that on this ride?" he asked.

"Not to my knowledge."

"Then let's get the hell out of here."

She pulled out of the parking spot and began to drive, tires humming across concrete. He pressed his head against the seats, one hand clenching a Glock, the other gripping the .45.

If they were stopped, he was prepared to pop up like a jack-in-the-box and start firing.

"The Suburban's parked outside the garage," she said in a soft voice, as if worried the fanatics had eavesdropping technology, too. "I can't tell who's inside. The windows are tinted."

Probably, the woman, Valdez, was in the SUV on watch. Cutty would have gone inside the building to get them. The guy would not have forfeited a chance to spill blood.

"Keep driving," he said. "Don't slow or deviate at all. Act normal."

"Okay."

Sweat drenched his brow, trickled onto the leather against which his face lay.

Although he was well-hidden, he felt as vulnerable as if he were lying on the hood of the car.

A few seconds later, he was jostled in the seat as the car kissed the street outside the garage. The tires sang against the wet pavement.

"We're clear," she said. "They're not following us."

Underneath the jacket, he closed his eyes and released a sigh that seemed to come from the bottom of his soul.

Finally, they were free.

He hoped.

52

Once they had driven north of the Atlanta city limits and entered suburbia, Anthony rose in the seat and asked Lisa to pull off the highway.

In the parking lot of an apartment complex in Marietta, they found an old Buick sitting on a flat, but the car had a valid license plate. He used his Swiss Army Knife to remove the plate, and put it on the Volkswagen, trusting that it would be a day or so before the owner of the Buick noticed the missing tag.

It was reasonable to assume that since the lunatics had learned they were at the condo in Midtown, they would discover Lisa's sister lived there, and might soon begin searching for her vehicle. With no GPS, satellite radio, or other high-tech snares on the car to aid their hunt, they would turn to auto tags.

To stay ahead of these people, he and Lisa would have to continue to out-think them.

"We're all set," he said, easing into the front passenger seat. "Now, we need to find a hotel where we can lie low for a while, and think."

"And sleep," she said, eyes red with fatigue.

There were numerous hotels off I-75 in Cobb County. They decided on a budget-priced chain hotel that advertised free Internet access, and that offered quick passage to the highway. He used a moist toilette to clean the grime and crusted blood off his wrist, and then went inside, alone, to book a room.

At the front desk, he paid cash for a room for one night, adding a couple hundred dollars as a deposit for incidentals. He claimed that he didn't have his driver's license, gave his name as Mark Justice, the pseudonym of a local thriller writer that no one would be likely to connect to him, and supplied a fake Atlanta address and phone number.

He requested a second-floor room on the western side of the hotel, which would provide him a view of any vehicle that entered the parking lot, and access to a side exit.

In the gift shop, he purchased a pack of Band-Aids, disinfectant ointment, pain reliever pills, and bottles of water.

Finally, he and Lisa entered their room with all of their bags in tow. They stripped out of their soggy, soiled clothes, and showered together.

There was nothing sexual or romantic about their shower. It was an opportunity for them to decompress, together. He washed her back; she washed his; and for several minutes afterward, they held each other, letting the warm water cascade over them.

As they clung to each other, neither of them spoke. Words would have failed to convey the closeness he felt toward her. The sense of partnership. They were in this together, to the end. Her commitment to him—twelve hours ago, it would have been so easy for her to demand that he drop her off at her parents' while he went at this alone—inspired a quiet sense of awe. He had a few buddies who were married, some longer than he had been, and they spoke disgustfully of how their wives failed to support them, how they had drifted apart and lived in separate words linked together solely by children, or a house, or plain old habit. Commitment was not embodied in the mere exchange of vows; it was best exemplified in action, and Lisa had gone far above and beyond anything he ever could have expected, or asked.

"I wouldn't want to be anywhere else," she said suddenly, head against his chest, as in sync with his thoughts as ever. "This is where I'm supposed to be. Doing this with you."

He kissed her wet forehead. "Thank you. I hope it's not all for nothing."

"It's not. There's always a purpose, a plan. Even if we don't immediately understand what it might be. Over time . . . it all becomes clear."

"You really believe that?"

"If I didn't, what would be the point of anything? Life would be meaningless."

He closed his eyes and let the water bead against his face, her words ricocheting around his mind.

After they toweled off and dressed in underclothes, she cleaned and bandaged his wrist wound, and he swallowed two pain reliever capsules. Then, she pulled the curtains over the windows and adjusted the air conditioner, while he hung a "Do Not Disturb" sign on the door and set the bedside alarm clock for ten o'clock in the morning.

"We'll get about three hours of shut-eye," he said. "After that, it's back to work."

"Wow, three whole hours." She stretched out across the king-size bed. "I'm joking, but with the way I feel right now, the idea's as tempting as a full night's sleep."

With the curtains drawn, shadows gathered in the room. Although none of the pockets of darkness were deep enough to hide an intruder, he imagined faces floating in them, shining fanatical eyes watching, plotting.

You're safe, he told himself. *Relax.*

Nevertheless, he buried a handgun underneath his pillow. He put another piece on the nightstand, beside the clock, and Lisa had placed her .357 on the table on her side of the bed.

He closed his eyes and, after a short while, drifted asleep.

He dreamed, again, about his father. They were on the lake, fishing rods dipped into the silver water. Blood glistened on his dad's shirt, of which he again seemed unaware.

Something jerked the end of Anthony's line, and he pulled it out to discover that it was a not a fish, but a rifle, and he reeled it in and dropped it onto the floor of the boat, and his dad picked it up and thrust it into his hands, saying, *"Now you take this gun and you go get them suckers, son, go get justice for me, dammit, 'cause it's time for war . . ."*

53

At dawn, Bishop Emmanuel Prince typically would offer his morning prayers on the eastward-facing balcony of his hilltop mansion as the sun's rising face kissed the Kingdom Campus. It was a ritual he'd performed daily for decades except under the most extreme circumstances, and served to ensure that he began each day in alignment with the Holy Spirit.

Although he was on the balcony that morning to greet the sun, fully dressed in his normal clothing—two-piece suit, silk tie, Italian loafers—he did not kneel. He did not bow his head. And he did not pray.

What he did was survey the Kingdom Campus—as if he were seeing it for the last time.

The vast, highly ordered complex of buildings and green space was arrayed before him in its entire splendor, like a finely crafted model train set lying at a child's feet on Christmas morning.

For forty years, his father, and then, he, had labored to bring their divinely-inspired vision of a kingdom on earth to fruition. From his father's birthing the church in an elementary school basement in southwest Atlanta, to the glorious, twenty-four hundred acre wonder they enjoyed today, it was the blessed fruit of forty years of faithful service to God.

They had accomplished much, but there was so much work left to do. The King would not return to earth until his servants had established dominion in every nation. Their ministry had touched and influenced millions—but the world contained *billions* of souls that needed to be saved . . . or condemned if they turned away from God's gentle, loving hand.

Sometimes, he was stunned by the audacity of the vision God had given him. Humbled by the ambitious, holy mission with which he had been charged. Although he was a preacher's son, he had never expected that God would call on him to lead his people into glory. When he'd received the Call, he'd been a junior in high school and a star player on the varsity basketball team, with dreams of going to college on an athletic scholarship.

He'd also been—and he shared this point openly in his sermons—a fornicator, and a frequent abuser of alcohol and marijuana.

One night after a playoff game in which he'd scored twenty-seven points and his team had emerged victorious, he'd gone with some teammates to a party. There were horny high school girls there, weed, and kegs of beer. He eagerly indulged his taste for all three vices, and had been so intoxicated that by the time he and his buddies piled into a van to go home, he neither realized, nor cared, that the designated driver was drunk, too.

On a winding, dark country road, the driver swerved to avoid hitting a massive buck, and not only swiped the animal, but slammed into an oak tree at seventy miles per hour. The van crumpled like a soda can in a trash compactor, and the passengers, none of whom were wearing seat belts, perished instantly in the wreck.

Except for Bishop Prince.

Limbs horribly twisted, ribs broken, blood gushing from a deep gash in his forehead, he'd been certain that he was going to die, and cried out for God to save him from Hell, which was the fate he surely deserved for the sinful life he'd led. He promised God that he would serve him, in any capacity demanded, if only his life were spared.

Crying and pleading, he suddenly realized that a man stood on the shoulder of the road, at the edge of the wreckage. He was as tall as a tree. His face was luminous. His flowing robe glowed white as the stars.

An angel of the Lord. He fell into a stunned silence.

The ethereal visitor approached the van and stuck his gigantic hand through the ruptured windshield. He touched Bishop Prince's forehead, a sensation like static electricity dancing on the bishop's flesh, and he heard a booming voice in his mind as resonant as thunder.

God has heard your cry, and he forgives you. Serve him for the rest of your days and order your life as a testament to his enduring goodness and mercy.

There was a blinding blaze of light . . . and when it faded, he was standing in the high school locker room, minutes after the night's playoff game had ended, still dressed in his sweaty basketball jersey and sneakers.

He was awestruck. And knew in his soul that God had found him worthy of a second chance.

When the teammate who'd driven the doomed van dropped by his locker a minute later and ask if he wanted to come to a party, he told him firmly that he was going home to study the Bible with his father. His response drew a strange look from his friend, but he didn't care. He quit the basketball team the next day and announced to his family that he planned to attend a theological college.

The path of his destiny had been revealed, and there was no turning back. God had important work for him to do. He'd been chosen.

Now, decades later, one minion of the devil threatened to destroy it all.

During his ministry, Bishop Prince had conquered hundreds of Anthony Thornes, godless men with grudges to bear over some wrongly perceived sin of his or the church. Few of them were credible threats. All of them were summarily eliminated.

Touch not mine anointed, and do my prophets no harm, the Lord had declared in the book of Psalm. God granted special protections to those engaged in the important work of Kingdom building.

Thorne, however, was proving to be a special case. Their intelligence indicated that he'd received assistance from a high-ranking, former church official, but they had been unable to determine the precise nature of the information that the Judas had passed to Thorne. They had in their arsenal some of the most powerful technological equipment known to man, unprecedented access to databases, surveillance covering *every square foot* of the Kingdom Campus and much of the outside world—yet they did not know what the Judas had given Thorne.

But considering the Judas' extensive knowledge of the Kingdom's global operations, and his wicked motives, it was certain to be utterly devastating.

Footsteps approached from behind: boot soles against marble in a familiar marching cadence. The Director of the Armor of God appeared at his side on the balcony.

Although the Director was much shorter than Bishop Prince— the bishop stood six feet seven, while the Director was barely six feet—the Director was one of the few people in the world who did not behave as though he felt miniaturized by the bishop's presence. Bishop Prince respected that about him. A man should fear only God, not other men.

He couldn't say as much about other so-called men, including the President of the United States.

The Director's face was all hard angles, his thin lips a slash, his dark eyes like darts. He was clean shaven, his steel gray hair trimmed in a precise crew cut. He was dressed that morning in a white shirt and dark wool slacks with creases so bladelike they could have sliced paper, and his black leather boots had a mirror shine.

For a long moment, neither of the men talked. They watched the rays of the rising sun bleed across the land before them.

Bishop Prince wondered if the Director also pondered the precarious position of their organization. Over the years, he had given nearly as much to the church as had Bishop Prince and his father, single-handedly building the Armor of God from a fledging outfit that employed a handful of fellow, God-fearing ex-Army Rangers into a formidable, highly trained, well-equipped, instantly deployable armed force that numbered in the hundreds. He had saved the Kingdom from catastrophic scandals many times, often taking it upon himself to fire the sniper rifle that silenced the Satan-inspired voices of dissent.

The Director cleared his throat. "I've ordered Cutty to return to the Kingdom Campus. He and I will convene at oh-nine hundred hours."

"I see. So Thorne is still alive?"

"Affirmative, sir."

"You've spoken very highly of your agent, this Noah Cutty."

"He's fully capable, one hundred perfect faithful," the Director said.

"But Thorne lives."

"Thorne is an extraordinary target, your grace. He's got considerable military training."

"Our agents are highly trained as well, yes?"

226

"They're the best," the Director said with obvious pride. "Our man Thorne happens to have a vendetta he's willing to die for."

" 'A life is not worth living until you have something to die for,' " Bishop Prince said. "Dr. Martin Luther King Junior once spoke those words. Thorne has allowed Satan to mislead him, but he believes fully in his purpose, as we've witnessed. That makes him most dangerous."

"But not invincible," the Director said. "Cutty has never failed us. He will succeed, sir, at whatever we command him to do."

Bishop Prince turned to regard his old friend.

"I want to ensure that he does," he said.

54

At the sound of rapping on a door, Anthony snapped out of sleep as quickly as if he were casting off a blanket. He grabbed the revolver from underneath the pillow and panned it around the shadowed room.

Beside him, Lisa had awakened, too, and had her hands on her gun.

A closer listen revealed that the knocking was at the door of a nearby room. A woman called out, *"Housekeeping,"* in Spanish-inflected English.

He pushed out a heavy breath, lowered the gun.

"Aren't we quite the pair?" Lisa said.

He glanced at her. "You woke up fast."

"I guess you've rubbed off on me."

The clock's green numerals read a quarter to nine. They had slumbered only about two hours, and the alarm wasn't scheduled to sound until ten. But the compressed period of sleep had rejuvenated him—some of his old military habits had finally returned.

"I've slept enough," he said. "How're you feeling?"

"Like getting to work."

"Then let's get to it." He switched on the lamp, cut off the alarm, and pushed out of bed. "I'll get us up and running online."

"It doesn't look like they have room service," she said, paging through a hotel guest guide and tossing it back onto the nightstand. "Just in-room coffee. I'll brew a pot—it should hold us over until we have a chance to grab some food."

He clicked on the desk lamp. A laminated placard with instructions for how to access the Web via the hotel's wireless

228

network stood on the corner of the desk. He powered on his laptop, followed the directions, and soon was online.

Lisa placed a mug of steaming coffee at his elbow, and pulled up a chair to sit beside him at the desk. Crossing her legs Indian-style, she took a sip of her own coffee.

"What's the plan?" she asked.

"The first thing I want to do is check out the message Mike sent me about Kelley Marrow," he said. "Based on whatever that tells us, we can go from there."

He logged onto his Jarhead account and found a private e-mail waiting for him from Mike, screen name, IronMike707, which had been sent at 2:13 in the morning. The subject line read, "Kelley Marrow."

> *Yo AT,*
> *Been Googling Kelley Marrow. I found an obituary from this past March that I think might be hers. The link's below. Check it out.*
> *Peace,*
> *Mikey*

Anthony clicked on the link at the bottom of the message. Another web browser opened, transporting him to a page on an obituary-archival Web site called "GeorgiaLegacy.com."

He and Lisa leaned forward in their chairs, reading. There was no photo of the deceased, only a single paragraph of text.

> *Kelley Ann Marrow, age 13, of Kennesaw was called home to the Lord on March 19. An honor-roll student, Kelly loved singing in the church choir, spending time with family and friends, horseback riding, and playing with her family's two dogs. She is survived by her loving mother, Susan Marrow, an older brother, Tommy, and a host of extended family. Funeral services will be held 11am, Saturday, at Covenant Funeral Home, Kennesaw.*

Lisa was shaking her head. "Thirteen years old. So young. Her family must've been devastated."

"I wonder what happened to her," he said.

"Could've been an illness. Or an accident."

"And her name happens to be in the Bible that Bob gave me? I'm not thinking she died by accident or illness, Lisa. That's a tad bit too random to me."

"Maybe." Her gaze narrowed; he could see the gears in her mind working toward the same conclusion he had drawn. "But we don't know for sure that we're talking about the same person."

"Then let's be sure."

He turned to the laptop again. He entered the Web address for a site called Omega Search.

Unlike Google, which was a search engine for finding virtually everything known to man, Omega Search was a free search engine exclusively for finding people. It pulled data from public records and government sources: court documents, county and state property records, and so forth. In the Information Age, nothing was private anymore.

He'd become aware of Omega Search and similar sites when conducting research for his suspense novels. Ghost was a savage fighter, skilled with firearms and old-fashioned fisticuffs, but what made him so deadly effective was that he was equally adept at using technology to locate clues. To write credibly about such a character, Anthony had needed to educate himself on the capabilities of the information-gathering world.

In the name entry field at the top of the Web page, he typed "Susan Marrow" and specified the city and state as "Kennesaw, Georgia."

Within seconds, the site returned an address and phone number for Marrow—including a date of birth that revealed she was thirty-seven years old.

"Bam," he said.

"Wow," Lisa said. "That was so easy it's scary."

"Easy to find her, but the next step might not be so easy."

"Which is?" Then she blinked, gave him a knowing look. "Wait. Are you thinking what I'm thinking?"

"You know I am. We've got to convince her to talk to us."

55

As the morning sun burned off the last traces of the night's storm clouds, Cutty piloted the Suburban along the smoothly paved roads of the New Kingdom Church Campus. He had a nine o'clock meeting with the Director, and he didn't dare arrive late.

Hours earlier, he had dropped off Valdez at the women-only servant dormitories. Their parting had been awkward. After a night of frenzied searching for Thorne and his wife, Cutty regarded the summons back to the campus, his mission incomplete, as profoundly humiliating.

Valdez's eyes had been full of pity for him, not the admiration to which he had grown accustomed. He wondered if she would request a re-assignment with a more capable partner.

With time to spare, he'd sought refuge in his studio apartment in the men-only barracks reserved for church security agents. Confining himself to the tiny closet with a flashlight, pen, paper, and Bible, he copied a verse repeatedly that best expressed his ignominy, Psalm 69:7. *Because for thy sake I have borne reproach; shame hath covered my face.*

He might have continued his transcription ritual until nightfall if his wristwatch alarm had not beeped, signaling that it was time for him to depart for the meeting.

As he drove, Valdez's sweet fragrance lingered in the SUV, mocking him with the fantasy of sensual pleasures he would never know. The Prophet would not grant blessings to one who had failed him. Although the Director had not communicated the purpose of their imminent discussion, and though he'd assumed the Director had given him until 0800 that morning to eliminate Thorne, apparently the Director—never known for his patience—had grown

231

frustrated with waiting for results, and would be taking disciplinary action.

To soothe his spirits, Cutty took enjoyment in observing the ordered grace and wholesomeness of the Kingdom Campus.

Red crepe myrtle trees in full bloom lined the road, blossoms rustling in a soft breeze. People jogged or walked on the sidewalks, alone, accompanied by canine companions, or in small groups. All wore proper Kingdom attire. There were no women in low-cut shorts or revealing shirts, no bare-chested men, nothing that would offend one with a sense of decency. Everyone was smiling and bright-eyed and energetic, too, happy to be among God's chosen people.

A shuttle bus passed by in the opposite direction, transporting servants to the Kingdom Market, a store so massive and comprehensive it would have made Wal-Mart look like a convenience store. Loud speakers posted on a series of poles broadcast godly music from Kingdom Radio.

On a great hill in the distance, overlooking the land, loomed the Prophet's mansion, like a castle floating in the clouds.

The Kingdom Campus had been conceived by the Prophet as a self-sustaining city, the seat of the empire that would soon envelope the entire earth. Cutty knew servants who had not ventured off the grounds in years. There was no reason to leave, as everything one could possibly need and desire was provided there.

If it had not been for his servant's calling, he doubted he would have ever wandered beyond the Kingdom walls, either. When he'd lived on the commune with his family, he'd never left, and not only because Father had forbid it. Simply put, living among God's people was more fulfilling than interacting with the immoral, filthy secular world.

The Armory, the headquarters of the Armor of God, stood on the western boundaries of the campus. A low slung, battle-ship gray, windowless, concrete building that covered several acres, the Armory resembled a top-secret military command post. True to the spirit of the structures it recalled, the majority of the work done there took place underground, in a vast warren of corridors and rooms so heavily reinforced they could have withstood a nuclear assault.

After going through a sentry-manned gate, he plunged into an underground parking garage that ran seven levels deep. Their fleet of custom-equipped vehicles—sedans, SUVs, vans, sports cars, motorcycles, even a few RVs—occupied many of the parking spaces.

When speedier travel was required, they had the use of an airstrip, hangar, two Gulfstream jets, and several Bell helicopters, all located on their private airport.

He parked at the garage's bottom level and strode toward the glass double doors at the far end. An intricately detailed seal, the same emblem stitched on their uniform jackets, was emblazoned on the doors in shimmering gold, black, and white paint; the motto beneath was, "Defending God's Kingdom."

He laid his thumb on the fingerprint scanner station, and the doors swung open, admitting him into a brightly lit lobby. A long, wide, stone-tiled corridor stretched ahead, ranked with doors without windows. Each level of the complex was named after a book of the Old Testament, and small signs beside each room bore labels based on that naming convention.

A couple of agents ahead crossed the hallway and entered a chamber. Neither of them paid attention to him. He approached a bank of elevators near the entrance; they carried one deeper into the bowels of the division, or to the higher levels above.

He took the elevator down another three levels, and entered a more dimly lit, shorter corridor than the one above. There were three doors—one on the right, two on the left.

He approached the door on the right, where the sign read "Exodus A."

Before going inside, he checked his watch. It was exactly nine o'clock. The Director could not berate him for tardiness.

He bowed his head, uttered a short prayer asking for divine mercy, and opened the door.

But he did not find the Director waiting for him at the oak conference table.

He found the Prophet, Bishop Emmanuel Prince.

56

Susan Marrow lived in Kennesaw, a suburb on the northern rim of metro Atlanta. All Anthony knew about the town was that a Civil War battle had once been waged near Kennesaw Mountain—and that a local ordinance required all heads of household to possess a registered firearm.

Marrow's home was in an established neighborhood of bungalows and ranches with verdant, well-tended lawns. Anthony cruised along the tree-lined street in the Volkswagen, while Lisa, riding in the passenger seat, searched for the address they'd found on Omega Search.

The morning sunshine was bright, the sky a clear turquoise canvas. It gave him a more optimistic mood than he had any logical reason to have considering their circumstances. On a balmy June day such as that one it was easy to believe that everything would work out in their favor.

Lisa pointed to a home coming up on the right. "There it is."

The Marrow residence was a quaint bungalow with white clapboard siding, blue shutters, a veranda, and a detached garage. The small yard was a lush green, neatly maintained, and a bed of hydrangeas basked in the sun.

A white Honda Pilot was parked in the driveway.

"Looks like someone's home," he said. He slowed to a stop and parked alongside the curb in front of the house.

Lisa turned to him. "How do you want to do this?"

Although the record on Omega Search had included a telephone number, they hadn't called ahead. They doubted that Marrow, if she were inclined to speak at all about her daughter, would have done so over the phone with a stranger.

"Let's play it straight," he said.

"And tell her we're on the run from a group of church assassins? She might think we're nuts. I would."

"Or she might believe us."

Carrying the Bible that Bob had given him, he climbed out of the car. They took a flagstone walkway to the front door.

Two ornately carved stone angels stood opposite each other on the veranda steps, faces tilted to heaven. A virtual greenhouse of potted plants and flowers thrived on the pine-floored porch, suffusing the air with a medley of scents, and a wicker bistro set sat amidst the greenery, a circle of tea candles on the table.

The weathered door was burnished oak, featuring a stained glass window at the top that depicted a winged angel in flight. A peephole was set at eye level.

Before he pressed the doorbell, a chorus of high-pitched barking erupted. After he pushed the bell, the dogs' barking got even louder.

"Two dogs," Lisa said, recalling the obituary.

As they waited, he suddenly had the distinct sense that someone was on the other side of the door, examining them through the lens.

He wasn't confident they would pass a visual inspection. Although they had changed into fresh clothes—he wore a polo shirt and jeans, Lisa wore jeans and a blouse—with their reddened eyes and fatigue-lined faces, they had the look of a couple of drifters living on the edge.

"Miss Susan Marrow?" he called out, lips close to the door. "My name is Anthony Thorne, and this is my wife, Lisa. We'd like to speak to you about your daughter, Kelley."

He held up the Bible to the peephole.

"Someone named Bob gave this Bible to me, and your daughter's name is written in it."

A few seconds later, the dogs quieted. The door opened.

A petite blonde with delicate features stood on the threshold. She wore a white blouse half-covered by a denim gardening apron smudged with soil, jeans, and sneakers. A silver cross hung around her neck.

She had striking green eyes. With them, she closely appraised both him and Lisa.

Behind her, an identical pair of Pomeranians sat obediently on their haunches, watching them with interest.

"I'm Susie Marrow," she finally said. She had a melodic voice and a syrupy Georgia accent. "What can I do for you folks?"

"Bob gave me this." Anthony handed her the Bible. "Check out the front page."

"It's a very long story," Lisa said. "Rather incredible, too."

Susie opened the book and read the inscription on the front page. She frowned, gave the book back to Anthony.

"Come on in, please," she said. "Don't mind the dogs. They're friendly."

The dogs sniffing at their heels, they followed her down a hallway with a hardwood floor. Photos crowded the walls. He noticed several pictures of a pretty girl who had inherited her mother's blonde hair and green eyes: one shot showed her astride a dark mare, in full equestrian gear; another was a recent-looking graduation portrait; others were taken when she was a much younger child. She was smiling in almost every picture, a fun-loving child whose life had been cut far too short.

Anthony's curiosity about the cause of her death sharpened.

Susie led them into a small but fastidiously neat living room furnished with cloth armchairs and matching sofa, a glass coffee table, more photos, and lots of live plants. The walls were the color of eggnog, edged with ornate crown molding. A large window framed by sage-green curtains overlooked a vibrant flower garden in the back yard.

Strains of music drifted to them from another room in the house. It sounded like big band, swing era stuff, music for dancing and good times.

Because her daughter had died three months ago, Anthony had expected a bereaved woman, someone still in the throes of grief and reluctant to accept visitors, with a home and yard in disarray. But Susie Marrow seemed to be in high spirits, and her home was in excellent condition. He wondered what helped her get by.

Susie untied her apron from around her waist. "I was working in my garden, but please, make yourselves comfortable. Can I get y'all some iced tea? I brewed a fresh pitcher this morning."

"Sweet tea?" Anthony asked.

"Of course. This is Georgia, honey."

"We'd love some, thanks," Lisa said.

When Susie left the room, both dogs trailing her, they sat together on the sofa. Anthony looked around, hoping that something would jar loose a revelation, a clue.

"Nice house," Lisa said after a few minutes had passed. She clasped her hands in her lap, crossed her legs. "Very cozy."

"I wonder where she keeps the gun she's required to have by law," he said. "Hopefully not in the kitchen."

"Stop it." She gently punched his arm. "She seems really sweet. I wonder what we said that made her invite us in?"

"I think Bob's name was the magic word." He indicated a photo on a side table that had caught his eye. It was a shot of Bob—sans horn-rimmed glasses—Kelley, a dark-haired teenage boy a few years older than the girl, and their mother, at an outdoor celebration of some kind. "The old guy in the picture is Bob."

"That's him?" She stared at the photo.

"You seem surprised. Like you thought he was a figment of my imagination."

"It's not that. I had a different image of him in my mind, I guess. I was thinking he'd look like some kind of super spy. He looks like a grandfather."

"That's 'cause he is." Susie returned with a silver tray that held a glass pitcher of iced tea and three tall glasses. She placed the tray on the cocktail table and poured tea. "He's my daddy. Kelley's grandpa."

"We're very sorry for your loss," Anthony and Lisa said, almost simultaneously.

Anthony caught a flash of grief in the woman's gaze that was so searing that he had to look away.

"My baby's in a better place now," she said softly.

Anthony wanted to ask how Kelley had died, but a direct question would have seemed rude. Instead, he took a sip of the sweet tea, which was delicious, and told Susie so.

"I second that," Lisa said, raising her glass. Then, in a somber tone: "Thirteen years old. So young. She's with the Lord indeed."

"I believe that with all my soul," Susie said. She sat on an armchair across from them, sipped her tea. The Pomeranians flanked her legs protectively. "There are some folks who'd say God sent her to a much different place if they found out what happened . . . but that's the beauty of our country. We're free to believe whatever we like."

Not if Bishop Prince gets his way, Anthony thought.

"Kelley loved to sing in the church choir, I read," Lisa said. "Which church do you attend?"

"I used to attend New Kingdom, in Austell. We all did."

"You, your children, and Bob," Anthony said.

"Bob." She smiled wistfully. "Only people in the family call Daddy that name. He must really trust you."

He let the remark pass. If Bob trusted him so much, why hadn't he given him all his damning evidence against New Kingdom from the beginning and spared him all this trouble?

"How long did you attend New Kingdom?" Lisa asked.

"Nine years," she said precisely. "I know that 'cause the kids and I started going to the church after my husband died—he was a firefighter here in Kennesaw. Died rescuing a child from an apartment blaze." She sighed and swirled her glass absently, clinking together the ice cubes. "My husband and baby are together now in heaven, waiting on me and my son to join them one day."

In spite of the multiple tragedies that had struck her, she spoke of her family's final reunion in heaven with complete conviction. He wondered about that. When he thought of his own parents, he didn't envision a heavenly gathering with them someday, though he had once entertained such fantasies.

He thought of just . . . nothing. And at certain times, as it did then, it left him feeling cold and empty, as if nothing really mattered at all.

57

"Daddy invited me to bring the kids to the church," Susie continued. "He'd been working at New Kingdom for a while by then. Growing up, I'd never much been into church. But after my husband died, I needed to believe there was something more than living and dying."

"And you found it there?" Anthony asked.

"Let me tell you, honey—the minute I set foot in that sanctuary and said I was a visitor, I was just overwhelmed with attention. Folks 'bout fell over themselves to introduce themselves to me and my kids. Everyone was so darn nice, so eager to be a friend and make sure I knew that yeah, there was a whole lot more to life, and I could find it right there with them. Next thing I knew, I'd joined up, and I was going to in-home Bible study and reporting to a servant leader."

"What's a servant leader?" Lisa asked.

"Sort of like a coach or a mentor, I guess you'd say. Your servant leader heads up your Bible study group and checks in with you a lot, prays with you, makes sure you're growing in your faith and being accountable to the Lord and the church—not being a backslider, as they like to say."

"Sliding back to your old life," Anthony said.

"Back to your sinful ways, uh-huh. And some of everything is considered sin. Like missing Sunday service or Bible study. Doubting what you're being taught. Not paying your tithes. Questioning the Prophet's authority or ideas."

"Bishop Prince, you mean," Anthony said.

"We were supposed to call him the Prophet." Crimson burned her cheeks. "What a joke."

239

"But you liked him at one time, or else you wouldn't have joined," Lisa said.

"Liked him?" Susie laughed bitterly. "I used to believe everything the Prophet—excuse me, *Bishop Prince*—taught. From God's mouth, to his ear, is how he said he 'received' his sermons. He had an anointing on him like I've never seen, or so I'd thought. It was something to see."

"I've seen him in action on TV," Lisa said. "He's quite charismatic."

"We devoted our lives to the church, and we were happy to do it," Susie said. "Soon as we got settled in good with the church, we got busy doing Kingdom building."

"Kingdom building?" Anthony asked.

"Each and every servant doing his or her part to make the world a better place," Susie said. "A *cleaner* place. Spiritually cleaner, I mean. The secular world celebrates sex outside of marriage, gratuitous violence in entertainment, air-headed celebrities, morally bankrupt values. Everyone knows it, everyone complains about it, but no one does anything. Well, Kingdom building is all about doing something concrete, making your contribution."

"What would you do?" Lisa asked.

"I work for the county as an acquisitions librarian," she said. "That means I have a lot of say over the books we purchase for our collection. I would campaign against acquiring any books that were morally questionable—like your books, Mr. Thorne. That violent, vigilante fiction you write?" Disgust twisted her face. "Hmph. Let me tell you, I made sure that it wasn't on the shelves of *my* library, no matter how much the patrons fussed about it."

Anthony looked at Lisa, and the shock on her face mirrored his own. This woman knew exactly who he was.

Perhaps that was another reason why she had invited them inside her home.

"Shouldn't a library patron have the right to decide what he or she wants to read?" Anthony asked. "What you're describing is a form of censorship."

Susie laughed hoarsely. " 'Course it is. That's what Kingdom building was all about. Limiting choices and restricting freedoms. 'Giving people what they need,' as Bishop Prince calls it—which isn't the same thing as giving them what they want."

"Giving them material approved by the church, in other words," Lisa said.

"I was awfully misguided, but I didn't see it that way at the time," Susie said. "Outside of my work at the library, I was in a church group, too. Mothers Against Violence In Entertainment—MAVIE. MAVIE would send protest letters to television networks, record companies, book publishers, video game creators, film studios. A couple of years back, we organized a demonstration on the set of a big-budget action movie filming right here in Atlanta. Let me tell you, we splattered ourselves with red dye, carried around fake severed body parts, really whooped it up, put on a good ole' show."

"I remember that," Anthony said. "It made the news."

"Uh-huh. National news, too. Those Hollywood folks were so mortified they left town with their tails between their legs and filmed their trash in Canada instead. I thought that was a shining moment for the Lord."

"Sounds like you were very zealous," Lisa said.

"More like very dumb. Now look, I *still* despise gratuitous violence in media and think it glorifies the worst in human nature, but my personal beliefs don't give me the right to keep other folks from watching it or reading it—even if I think they're rotting their brains by doing so." "So you no longer attend New Kingdom, I gather," Lisa said.

Susie looked at them as if Lisa's comment were the most absurd statement ever made.

"After what happened to my baby? After what that terrible man who calls himself a prophet did to her?"

Embarrassment seared Lisa's face, and she stammered.

"We're sorry," Anthony said. "It's just that Bob never went into any details with me about Kelley. He didn't tell me much about his family at all, actually."

"And I apologize if I offended you," Lisa said. "We're in the dark here, honestly."

Susie gazed out the window for a long moment, a faraway look in her eyes.

"Before Daddy went away, he told me you might come calling, Mr. Thorne." She turned to him, and her eyes seemed to be aglow. "He didn't tell me what was going on between you two, and to be honest, I don't want to know—but he said I should help y'all with whatever you ask. He said you were going to get justice for all of us."

"Bob has a high opinion of me," Anthony said.

"Shouldn't he?" Susie asked, her gaze direct.

"I'll take you up on your offer for help." He picked up the Bible, opened it to one of the pages full of highlighted passages, and showed it to her. "What do you think of this?"

Susie took the book, and scowled as she had when holding it the first time. "I was going to tell you this. This isn't my daughter's Bible, even though it says here that it is."

The bottom fell out of Anthony's stomach. "That's not Kelley's Bible?"

"No. I have her Bible. It's still in her room . . . I haven't moved anything in there." She dabbed at her eyes, looked away from them.

"All this time, we thought it belonged to her," Lisa said.

"Could be that's what Daddy wanted the servants to think if they got hold of it," Susie said. "He knows how they tick better than anybody."

"We've been through maybe ten percent of the highlighted verses," Anthony said. "We haven't been able to make sense of them, but we were thinking they were some kind of coded messages."

"I doubt I could figure them out, either." She riffled through pages. Shrugging, she passed the Bible to Lisa. "But your thinking about a code is right on the nose, dear. Daddy loves crossword puzzles, brain teasers, word games, that sort of thing. Lives for it, bless his heart."

"Where is Bob?" Anthony asked. "Maybe I can call him and clear this up."

She shook her head. "I got no idea where he is. He's gone, and I don't have a number for him. He called me late last night, and I had a funny feeling that he'd gone out the country, or was planning to soon."

"Great," Anthony said. "We're back to square one."

Susie rose. "I'm sorry. I wish I could be more helpful to y'all."

"Thanks anyway for taking the time to speak to us," Lisa said. "We appreciate the hospitality."

At the front door, Anthony paused. "One more thing."

"Sure." She had picked up one of the Pomeranians, and cuddled the dog in her arms.

"After becoming so disillusioned with the church, and after what happened to your daughter, what helps you cope? You seem so . . . together."

Lips buttoned in thought, Susie hesitated, absently stroking the small dog behind the ears.

"I'll tell you what, some days are much harder than others," she said. "But my gardening helps me a lot. The past couple of months, it's been my passion, my escape, I guess. Like it's all that shocking if you look 'round the house."

"Gardening, huh? That's the key?"

"The key?" She frowned. "Well, if you wanna put it like that . . . the key's been my faith."

"But after your experience at the church . . ."

"Mr. Thorne, what does having faith got to do with anybody's church?"

He considered her question for a moment, and couldn't think of an answer. Awkwardly, he thanked her again for her time and walked away from the house to join Lisa on the sidewalk, Susie Marrow's question still echoing in the chambers of his mind, summoning thoughts that he wasn't prepared to consider.

58

Cutty had never been blessed with a personal audience with the Prophet. In his stunned mind, he thought the experience of being in the same space with the holy man was perhaps the equivalent of what Moses had felt when confronted with the presence of God in the burning bush.

He dropped to his knees and bowed his head.

Although the Prophet sat in a high-backed chair on the other side of the chamber, Cutty felt the man's aura radiating from him like waves of intense heat, as if some sort of spiritual sun blazed in the man's soul. Fat beads of sweat appeared on Cutty's forehead, and his palms, pressed flat against the cold tile floor, became clammy.

"I am not worthy of this," Cutty whispered, trembling. "Am I in the correct place, your holiness? I was ordered to meet the Director here."

The Prophet answered in the booming voice that had captivated millions across the world.

"You are in the right place, indeed, Noah Cutty—exactly where God wants you to be. I informed the Director that I wished to speak with you myself."

Words failed Cutty. Mute, he kept his head lowered to the tiles, drops of sweat coursing off his brow and plopping against the floor.

But questions stormed through his mind. Did the Prophet wish to personally rebuke him for his failure to eliminate Thorne? Was he going to cast him out of the ranks of the Armor of God and relegate him to a lowly role in the Kingdom? Was he going to condemn him to hell for his ineptitude?

Please, have mercy on my soul, Lord, he prayed, feverishly. *Please ask your prophet to deal gently with me.*

Cutty heard the Prophet push his chair away from the table, heard the thud of footsteps as the Prophet approached, and caught a hint of the anointed one's scent—he *smelled* like divine power made manifest.

The Prophet touched Cutty's shoulder. Cutty flinched as a sensation like electricity buzzed through his muscles.

"On your feet, Kingdom servant. We will speak to each another as men of God."

Cutty inclined his head, and stood on wobbly knees.

The Prophet was six feet seven inches tall, which gave him nearly a foot and a half height advantage over Cutty. His awesome aura served to make him seem even larger, impossibly huge, giant-like.

Before him, Cutty he felt no bigger than a ground-hugging insect.

Cutty was dimly aware that they were not the only ones present in the softly-lighted chamber. A trio of others lurked in the shadows, well-built men clad in white tracksuits, Armor of God agents assigned to the Prophet's private security detail. Although they worked in the same division, if Cutty had made a threatening move to draw a weapon or somehow harm the Prophet, they would not have hesitated to chop him down—Cutty understood this without needing to be told, for he would have done the same thing.

With a long finger, the Prophet directed Cutty toward a leather chair. "Sit."

One of the agents pulled out the chair for Cutty, and Cutty did as he was told, thankful to relieve his watery knees. Another agent handled the chair across the table for the Prophet.

The Prophet folded his long, slender hands on the polished tabletop and gazed directly at Cutty. Cutty wanted to look away—looking into the Prophet's dark eyes was like looking at your own terrible fate if you disobeyed God—but an unseen force held his head still, as if his skull had been placed in a vise.

"You have been a loyal servant of the kingdom for twelve years," the Prophet said. "For the past eight, you have served as a soldier for God, in whatever capacity has been asked of you. Yes?"

"Yes." His voice was ragged, and he cleared his throat and said in a clearer tone, "Yes. That is true, your grace."

"Faithful servants such as you are the foundation of the Kingdom. The sturdy stones on which the Kingdom stands. Without your service, our Kingdom would be doomed to crumble and wash away as readily as a child's sand castle underneath the breaking waves of the ocean."

Listening to the Prophet's mesmerizing voice, Cutty's lips parted slightly, and he found himself tilting forward, entranced.

If the Prophet had ordered him to place his Glock to his own head and pull the trigger, he would have done so without hesitation.

"Will you continue to serve our God as you have done thus far?" the Prophet asked.

"Absolutely. Nothing means more to me than serving the Lord. I'll do anything required, I'll die for God, for you."

The Prophet smiled. He leaned back in his chair, slender fingers tented.

"God speaks to me daily," the Prophet said. "He gives me messages to deliver to the flock, in my sermons, in my books. Have you read my most recent book?"

"*The Keys to the Kingdom?* Yes, I've read it—ten times."

A nod of approval. "What did you think of it?"

"You shed light on many things that had sometimes perplexed me. It was a blessing on my life."

"Thank you. As I was saying, God speaks to me daily, and I share these messages in sermons, in written materials, and in other forms. But those are messages intended for our global flock. Occasionally, our Lord will give me a message that I am charged to personally deliver to only *one* servant."

Cutty remembered the stories of the Prophet appearing in a servant's home, or servants receiving phone calls or e-mails from the Prophet. Although he had known such things occurred, he had never imagined that he might one day be the recipient of such a communication.

The Prophet leveled his gaze on him.

"This morning, God gave me a message to deliver to you, Noah Cutty."

"Me?"

"Do you wish to receive it?"

"Yes!"

"You are to bring Anthony Thorne Junior here, to the Armory, alive and unharmed."

Cutty frowned. "You want Thorne alive? But the Director said earlier that I was to eliminate—"

The Prophet raised his finger, and Cutty's words faltered in his throat as he realized the terrible sin he had committed.

He bowed his head and clasped his hands together in his lap. He trembled as if expecting a bolt of lightning to crackle through the ceiling and strike him down where he sat.

The Prophet said, "When God commanded Abraham to take Isaac, his only son, to a mountain top in the land of Moriah and present him as a burnt offering to the Lord, did Abraham ask God why?"

"No, your grace," he said, unable to meet the Prophet's penetrating gaze. "Abraham obeyed God without question. Questioning God's authority is a sin. I beg your forgiveness for my trespass."

The Prophet rose from his chair and strolled around the table. He placed his hand on Cutty's shoulder as if they were brothers. Cutty's shoulder tingled from the contact.

"Do what God commands, Noah Cutty," he said. "Serve him, and you will be blessed with the desires of your heart. There is one servant, Maria Valdez, your partner, for whom your heart longs, yes?"

Cutty's lips quivered. The Prophet knew of his feelings for Valdez? He'd told no one about his growing affection for her.

But the Prophet was God's messenger. He knew everything.

"Yes," Cutty said. "I'm very fond of her."

The Prophet chuckled softly. "It is not good for man to be alone. The man who finds a wife finds a good thing, for a good wife is the crown of her husband."

"I will serve God," Cutty said. "Please, forgive my doubts—Satan tried to lead me astray."

"The Adversary is busy at work, indeed, even within Kingdom walls," the Prophet said. "Rise now."

When he rose, the Prophet folded him into a warm, brotherly hug.

"God and I love you, Noah Cutty," the Prophet said. "We forgive you."

Cutty held onto him like a child embracing a father. Warm tears slid down his cheeks.

This was the most memorable day of his life—the day that God's Prophet had personally called upon him to serve and bring the

Kingdom glory. If only Father could have seen him then. He would have been so proud.

The Prophet gently nudged Cutty away.

"Go now," the Prophet said. "Be the warrior for the Lord that you were born to be. God and I will be with you."

"I will not fail you."

Cutty almost ran out of the conference room.

59

"Kelley Marrow committed suicide," Lisa said.

Pulling away from Susie Marrow's home, Anthony came out of his near-trance, and glanced at her. "Yeah. That's what I was thinking, too. I didn't dare say it to her mom, but that was what my gut told me."

"Along with Susie's reluctance to share any details about the girl's death, her remark that some people would dispute that her daughter is in a better place because of how she died—what she really meant that some Christians believe that by committing suicide, you earn a first-class ticket to Hell."

"As if they would know," he said under his breath. "What could Bishop Prince have done to the girl that would make her commit suicide?"

"I don't know." She was shaking her head. "Something so terrible her mother didn't want to discuss it."

"Neither did Bob, because he sure didn't bring it up with me."

Lisa opened the Bible to the front page. She traced the letters of the girl's name as if reading Braille.

"You're thinking about the code Bob might have used," he said. "I almost forgot—you're into brain teasers and word games, too."

"As often as I've spanked you at Scrabble, I don't know how you could forget that."

"Okay, whatever, I'll give you your props."

"Can we find a coffee shop around here?" She closed the book. "I've got to be somewhere I can think, and besides that, I'm famished."

Fifteen minutes later, they found a Starbucks on Barrett Parkway, Kennesaw's main commercial drag, a riot of restaurants, shopping malls, bowling alleys, and movie theaters. Lisa found a table in a quiet corner of the café, and Anthony went to the counter and purchased bagels, cream cheese, espresso, and a pass to use the shop's Wi-Fi network.

Back at the table, as he took a sip of espresso and felt the caffeine blast through his nervous system, Lisa slathered cream cheese on a bagel, bit into it, and chewed hungrily.

"This stuff is way outside my diet, but I don't care," she said. "I need major brain fuel before I can crack Bob's puzzle."

"Since you're the puzzle queen, you can work on that, while I do research on the church," he said.

Swallowing a mouthful, Lisa nodded.

He booted up his laptop and used his pass to access the network. He began his research by visiting the most logical of places.

The New Kingdom Church International Web site.

60

The site's Introduction page looked as if it might have been designed to herald a major Hollywood film. A flock of white doves swooped across the screen, and dramatic orchestral music burst from the computer's speakers, prompting Anthony to lower the volume. Meanwhile, shots of Bishop Prince in action behind the pulpit cascaded across the display, his voice rising above the music like thunder: *"The kingdom is not in heaven! The kingdom is here on earth! Will you be worthy? God wants you there right now!"*

The intro passed, and took him to the home page. The site appeared incredibly well designed, with striking, fast-loading graphics, easy to read text, and intuitive navigation. The Web sites of many major corporations paled by comparison.

A "Sow a Seed" button shimmered prominently in the navigation bar. Clicking on it carried him to a page where a video clip of a smiling Bishop Prince immediately began to play. He was dressed in a tan suit and sat in a gold-trimmed chair that resembled a throne.

"God loves a cheerful giver," the Bishop said in a genial voice that nonetheless carried authority. "We are exhorted to sow seeds for his kingdom, for which we will surely reap a bountiful harvest. Sow your seed for the kingdom and get ready for the blessings in store for you, my friend."

The video ended, and the site automatically transported Anthony to an encrypted payment page. The church accepted donations online via credit or debit card, and electronic check. You also could set up an automatic bank draft to pay your tithes, and there was a link to the Kingdom Credit Union site, though only church members could join.

"They have their own credit union," Anthony said.

Lisa looked up from a notepad, where she was scribbling with a pen.

"That's becoming common these days, Tony," she said. "Even our church has joined up with other smaller churches to form a credit union. It can be a good thing, if the organization is on the up and up."

"Maybe. But the thought of these people having access to my money creeps me out."

He visited a page that enabled you to submit a prayer request. For a small donation, the church's team of "prayer warriors" would petition God on your behalf, and rest assured that it would be effective, as "God hears the prayers of the righteous."

Not even prayer was free at New Kingdom.

A link offered a guided visual tour of the New Kingdom Church Campus. He selected it. It was like taking a virtual journey of Disney World. Covering over two thousand acres, worthy of its own zip code, the campus was meticulously planned, populated with aesthetically pleasing buildings, lush landscaping, walking trails, lakes, and environmentally-friendly shuttle buses that transported residents throughout the complex, from the sanctuary to the Kingdom Market.

"This is unreal," he said. "They have their own warehouse store, Lisa. It looks bigger than a Navy Exchange."

"Their own store, their own schools, even their own medical clinics and housing. When I went there for my friend's wedding, I was totally blown away. You'd never have to leave the campus for anything."

"Incredible." He stared at the screen. "They have an entertainment complex with bowling alleys, miniature golfing, movie theaters, restaurants."

"The sanctuary seats around twenty-five thousand, I've heard," she said.

The camera swept over the sanctuary, a massive structure capped with a gold, geodesic dome. A view of the building's interior showed seemingly endless rows of pews, plush seats designed to keep the faithful comfortable during their worship experience. The main stage, book-ended by giant video screens, was large enough to accommodate a rock concert.

The tour then visited the businesses that the church operated. The enterprises included a publishing company, a food service vendor, real estate management, a television studio, a radio station, and many, many others. They employed a workforce of "over two thousand loyal servants."

Next was a sweeping front view of the bishop's home, a palatial structure built of white stucco and stone in the style of a French Country chateau. The sprawling residence sat atop a steep hill overlooking the campus.

The bishop lived in a house fit for a king. Literally.

The tour ended. He chose a page that contained the bishop's bio.

Bishop Emmanuel Prince was the seventh child of his family, the offspring of an interracial marriage—black mother, white father. His father, deceased, had founded the church forty years ago in the basement of an Atlanta elementary school. Prince had assumed the senior pastor duties about twenty-one years ago, and had led an explosive growth in membership, from eight thousand members to the two hundred and eighty thousand members worldwide the church currently boasted.

He was married to a gorgeous, fair-skinned black woman at least fifteen years younger than him, and had four, school-age children. A video titled, "The Bishop and The First Lady at Home" showed the family interacting at the dinner table, in their mansion, everyone smiling, as if every day of their lives defined harmony and perfection. Prince spoke of "sowing kingdom seeds" daily, and how he and his family had reaped the blessings that came with obedience to kingdom mandates.

Anthony finally clicked away. The site was nothing more than a PR tool designed to fill the church's coffers.

On Google, he entered "Bishop Emmanuel Prince" in the search field. The engine returned over five million pages of results, the number of hits one might have found for an A-list movie star.

He visited the first few sites. They amounted to blatant, excessively flattering portrayals of Prince and his ministry. "The Prophet saved my life," one person wrote, and recounted a story of how he had begun to "sow kingdom seeds," even though he was unemployed and living on meager savings, and how he'd eventually found a new, better-paying job, thanks to the Prophet's teachings.

Oddly, he found similar testimonials on many of the other sites. The names of the devotees were changed, but the stories were basically identical—someone's life had been in shambles, but when they began to "sow seeds," their fortunes magically turned around.

Each personal testimony concluded with a link that went directly to the "Sow a Seed" page on the New Kingdom Web site.

He changed the search to include the bishop's name, and the phrase, "sow a seed." He received over one million hits. Although all of the pages might not have been enticements to donate to the church, it seemed likely that a large number of them were.

How much income did the church generate annually from online donations? The sum was probably staggering.

He modified his search to include the bishop's name, and the word, "controversy."

The search returned only a couple dozen pages. The first search result bore the title, "Bishop Emmanuel Prince Exposed!" He chose the link.

The site was down.

He clicked back to Google, and looked for the "Cached" page link—a snapshot of the page the last time Google had crawled it. But there was none.

He visited the next site in the results list. The page was up. The text read: *"Bishop Emmanuel Prince knows he risks controversy when he declares that sowing a seed for the kingdom will reap blessings, but he is an anointed leader who is moved by God to speak truth to power."*

Other sites in the list either were unavailable, or contained more content praising Prince. None of the inaccessible sites had cached pages.

He altered his searches to include the name of the church, and other words such as "corrupt," "immoral," "fraudulent," "crime," "felony," and "murder." Although many sites appeared for the various searches, the ones he could access did not include any negative statements, and all of the others were down.

They monitor the web, Bob had told him.

It was unbelievable . . . but New Kingdom had apparently scrubbed the Internet of all damaging material. The resources that would have been necessary to ensure that a sanitized image of the church and its leader was presented at all times were surely formidable—about as formidable as the assets that had enabled the fanatics to track them across the city as easily as if they were mice in a maze.

If he launched a blog and posted negative remarks about the bishop, he wondered how long it would take for the church to shut it down. Days? Hours? Did they utilize software that constantly scanned the Web in search of slander? Did they dispatch viruses to infect the servers and disable the sites?

It was an egregious violation of freedom of speech. But he suspected that they cared little for the Bill of Rights.

His imagination, stimulated by the discoveries, kicked into higher gear. What if they had the capability to even learn *who* was seeking proof of corruption—and could trace the user to the physical address where the user's computer resided?

There's no way they can do that, he thought. *You're letting your imagination get the better of you.*

But a shudder passed through him. He looked around the café, gazed through the windows to the parking lot. He noticed nothing out of the ordinary, but . . .

Just to be safe, he closed the browser windows, and logged off the network.

Across the table, Lisa was busy at work. Several small squares of paper, torn from a notepad, lay scattered before her. A letter was written on each square in black ink. It looked like a homemade Scrabble set.

"What're you working on?" he asked.

She glanced up at him, blinked as if surfacing from a trance.

"Following a hunch," she said. "I think Bob created an anagram using Kelley's name, and I'm going to solve it."

61

A snow-white, chauffeur-driven Mercedes Maybach transported Bishop Prince and the Director across the Kingdom Campus. They were escorted front and rear by black SUVs bearing Armor of God agents, forming a three-vehicle motorcade.

The Maybach was an exemplary machine, ultra luxurious. It featured double-quilted, diamond-stitched leather seats. Hand crafted wood trim fringed with twenty-four carat gold. Utterly unique, custom details such as the Kingdom's emblem embroidered in the headrests—and bullet-proof windows and reinforced steel panels that could have repelled a machine-gun ambush.

He owned another similarly equipped Maybach, that one as black as night. He also counted among his personal fleet a Rolls-Royce Phantom, an Aston Martin, a Ferrari, two Bentleys, and more Mercedes and BMWs than he cared to enumerate.

He had long reveled in the accouterments of wealth. Wealth was a sign of God's favor. God had smiled on King Solomon, the legendary monarch of Biblical times, blessing him with great wealth, wisdom, and a reign of peace.

He often envisioned himself as a King Solomon for a new age. But the Kingdom he was building was still new, still expanding.

Still warding off threats.

He reclined in the seat, customized to accommodate his elongated frame, and gazed out the one-way window. It was a sunny morning, and Kingdom servants were out in multitudes, walking, jogging, playing sports, and conducting daily business.

Many of them waved at the passing convoy. Ordinarily, he would have lowered the glass and returned the greetings of his loyal flock, but he kept the window sealed, quietly ruminating on how blissfully ignorant they were of the tenuous position in which their Kingdom found itself.

He turned to the Director. The military man was seated next to him, brow furrowed in thought.

"Noah Cutty was indeed zealous, as you promised he was," Bishop Prince said. "I pray that he's competent as well."

"Cutty should have no major issues collecting Thorne, sir. I expect we'll have Thorne in our custody before nightfall."

The Director's original plan had been to simply eliminate Thorne, but that morning, the chief technology servant had contacted them with the disturbing news that the Judas' treachery ran deeper than they had thought. According to recent investigative traces of their database, the Judas had plundered their most confidential data sources and copied volumes of highly combustible data onto a storage device of some kind—including explicit details about their most classified project, Revelation.

Revelation. The intricately layered, holy vision that had come to Bishop Prince in a dream several years ago, the execution of which he and the Director had been toiling and scheming ever since. If the plans leaked into the wrong hands, there was no telling the havoc Satan could wreak on the Kingdom.

Common sense suggested that the Judas had given the storage device to Thorne. Eliminating Thorne would prove of no consequence if he had passed his information to others. A thorough interrogation was in order—and though Bishop Prince had never participated in such affairs in the past, the threat they faced was so acute that he might question Thorne himself.

"You understand my concerns, yes?" Bishop Prince said. "The Judas could expose our work."

"He wouldn't have transferred the data to Thorne at their meeting," the Director said. "That would've been too risky, for both of them. He'll be leading Thorne to it. That's how he operates—that's how he was *trained.*"

"By you," Bishop Prince said.

The Director accepted the rebuke with a shrug. He was the only man on earth who could have gotten away with a response like that in the bishop's presence, and he knew it.

"We should assign more men to this mission," Bishop Prince said. "We have a force of hundreds. Why are we entrusting a task of this magnitude to one agent and his female partner when we could dispatch an entire team to capture Thorne right now?"

The Director's eyes hardened. "As you should be aware, sir, we've always used two-agent teams for domestic missions. It gives us a measure of anonymity. A squad of say, five of our vehicles boxing in Thorne somewhere and attempting to apprehend him could be a public relations disaster. Thorne isn't an average civilian—the man's a Marine, not long out of service, heavily armed, and you hit him with lots of firepower, he's going to hit back." The Director smacked his fist against the palm of his hand, causing Bishop Prince to flinch slightly. "You want some snot-nosed brat with a camera phone recording video of a major shootout between him and our agents, and posting it online for the whole world to see? Or perhaps you'd like to see those vultures in the TV news crews coptering over the scene and talking up every eyewitness within five miles? Best of all, how about we mistakenly kill a few innocent civilians in the process, create some nice collateral damage? Too many variables can go haywire with deploying a large unit—and that's why I don't allow it."

"We have monitoring capabilities online, and contacts in the media. We could shut down any story before it spread, clean up any fallout."

"I will handle this my way." The Director's mouth was a sharp line. "You preach your sermons—I keep your ass safe. That affirmative with you? *Sir?*"

Bishop Prince paused. "I don't appreciate your tone, Director. Remember your place."

The Director's fists had been clenched, his jaw tight. He blew out a hiss of air.

"I'm sorry, your grace," the Director said. "This is a tough spot for all of us. I ask only that you trust me as you have in the past, and relax. We've dealt with breaches like this before. We must remember, God is on our side, and no weapon used against us will hurt us."

He smiled at the Director's paraphrased scripture. The Director was not known for his Biblical erudition. Bishop Prince wondered if the man ever cracked open the book at all.

"God can speak through the most unlikely mouths, I see," Bishop Prince said.

The Director shrugged, offered a rare smile.

The motorcade arrived at the tall wrought-iron gates of his mansion. The agents at the guard booth waved them through, and the vehicles entered the long, wide, curving driveway.

"Do you wish for me to remain on the premises, sir?" the Director asked.

"That won't be necessary. Contact me with any updates you receive."

Bishop Prince glanced at his Piaget watch. The Swiss timepiece featured an eighteen-carat white gold case and bracelet set with baguette and trapeze-cut diamonds, a dial with trapeze and brilliant-cut diamonds, and a winding crown set with round brilliants. Priced at over a quarter of a million dollars, the watch had been a present from a European financier who wanted Bishop Prince to guarantee that his soul would be conveyed to heaven after his death—a destination the bishop had assured him was his upon receiving the gift. He who gives greatly to the man of God shall receive greatly from God, too.

It was eleven o'clock.

He just remembered: he had a date with an angel.

62

"An anagram," Anthony said. "You mean a word that, if you switch the letters around, can form another word, right?"

"Exactly. A single word, a phrase—any of them can be used to create an anagram."

He slid his chair beside hers and studied the small letters arrayed on the table.

ELELMRWOAYKR

"Each letter comes from the name 'Kelley Marrow,' " she said. "We've found out that this Bible never actually belonged to the girl, so Bob must've meant to use her name as a code to shed light on these highlighted scriptures."

"Do we have to use all of the letters?"

"That's usually how it works. You have to use every letter in the original word or phrase, and you can use the letter only once in the new word. For example, 'parental' and 'paternal' is an anagram. So is 'eleven plus two' and 'twelve plus one.' "

"Now I know why I asked you to handle this stuff."

"Come on, you ought to be better at this than I am, baby. You're the writer. Words are your stock in trade."

"Stories are my stock in trade. The words are only a method to communicate my meaning."

"Just like Bob's anagram."

She began to move the squares around the table. He picked up the Bible and paged through it.

There were hundreds of verses highlighted in several colors. Which, when strung together sequentially, made no coherent sense,

260

as they'd learned from their tedious efforts to transcribe some of them last night.

Think, dammit. What is Bob trying to tell us?

He swung the laptop toward him and powered it on. Lisa ignored him; she was submerged in concentration, hands flying as she arranged and re-arranged letters.

He restored the Internet connection. On Google, he entered the search term: *anagram*.

Over a million results popped up. He selected a site that featured something called an anagram server.

He skimmed the Web site. The anagram server would create an anagram from the word of your choice, or assist in decoding one, for free.

In the Decode field, he typed: KELLEY MARROW.

Within a few seconds, the server returned a list of thirty-seven possible results. He read the list.

"Well, I'll be damned," he said.

"What is it?" Lisa asked. She looked up. She was grinning.

"I think we've got our answer. What're you smiling about?"

"Why don't we compare?"

He read the letters she had configured. Her solution was the same answer the anagram server had placed at the top of the list.

YELLOW MARKER

"That's the one I found online," he said. "I used an anagram generator Web site."

"I used this." She tapped her head. "Good old-fashioned brain power. No computer can compare."

"I think it was Einstein who said that he didn't know the answer for everything, he just knew where to go to find it." He opened the Bible and sped through the pages. "If I ever see Bob again, I'm gonna give him a gold medal for cleverness. Marking up all these passages in different colors, making it look like some studious teenager's Bible—that was a stroke of genius."

"What's the first verse highlighted in yellow?" she asked.

"Just a minute." He turned a page so frantically that he tore the corner.

He located the first passage outlined in yellow marker. It was Genesis 34:1-2. He read it aloud:

And Dinah the daughter of Leah, which she bare unto Jacob, went out to see the daughters of the land. And when Shechem the son of Hamor the Hivite, prince of the country, saw her, he took her, and lay with her, and defiled her.

They had read the same verse last night, and it had meant nothing to him. But reviewing it this morning brought gooseflesh to his arms.

Lisa chewed her bottom lip. "I don't get it. Do you?"

But he hardly heard Lisa—Susie Marrow's words were whispering through his thoughts: *After what happened to my baby? After what that terrible man who calls himself a prophet did to her?*

He dug Bishop Prince's book out of his satchel. He stared at that face. That disturbingly familiar face.

. . . he took her, and lay with her, and defiled her.

And he realized, at last, the terrible truth.

Hands trembling, he fumbled out his cell phone.

"What is it?" Lisa asked. "Who're you calling?"

"The one who can give us the answers we've been looking for," he said. "My sister."

63

On the fourth ring, Reuben answered the phone at the house in Decatur. Hip-hop boomed in the background.

"Reuben, it's your Uncle Tony. Turn down that music, will you?"

"My bad." The music's volume dropped several decibels. "Wassup, Unc? I been working on that press release blaster thing for you since the crack of dawn, man. Be done soon, today prob'ly."

Anthony had to concentrate for a moment to remember what the hell the kid was talking about. The press release blaster. The program he'd asked Reuben to create, to help promote his books. It was as if he'd the conversation about it with his nephew in a previous life.

"Thanks, Reuben. I appreciate it. Listen, is your mom around?"

"Nah. She spent the night with some dude. She got her celly with her, though."

"She never answers when I call her cell."

"Just keep blowing her phone up. I gotta do that sometimes to get her."

"That's what I'll do then."

"You got a new number or something, Unc? I never seen the number you're calling from."

"What's your mom's cell number?" he asked, ignoring the question. "I don't have it memorized."

Reuben gave him the number. Anthony scribbled the digits on a notepad.

"You all right, man?" Reuben asked. "You sound kinda uptight or something."

263

"I can't get into it right now." A troubling thought occurred to him. "Hey, why don't you go to a friend's place for the rest of the day? Somewhere you can chill out."

"Huh?"

"Reuben, I don't have time to explain. Just do it."

"But I'm working on this code, man. Can I stay another hour?"

"Fine, one more hour. Then go. And be careful. Call me at this number when you're settled."

He terminated the call and punched in Danielle's number. After five rings, voice mail picked up. He hung up and called again, fingers drumming the table, Lisa watching him with a befuddled expression.

On the third attempt, Danielle finally answered in a scratchy voice. "Who the hell keeps calling me?"

"It's me, Tony. We've gotta talk. Right away, and in person. Where are you?"

"Boy, you done lost your goddamn mind? You having some kinda war flashback or what?"

"We're coming to pick you up. Give me an address. Please, Danny, it's important."

She muttered something under her breath about his rudeness, but she gave him an address in Stone Mountain, which he jotted down.

"What's this all about, anyway?" she asked. "You talkin' crazy, Junior."

"We'll be there within an hour." He hung up before she could ask more questions.

"Now, will you please tell me what's going on?" Lisa asked.

"I'll tell you on the way," he said, gathering their things. "Let's move out."

64

Sitting in the SUV in the bowels of the Armory's underground garage, re-reading Thorne's file for perhaps the tenth time and wracking his brains for a strategy to apprehend the man, Cutty suddenly received an emergency notification from Genesis.

There was a possible hit on Thorne.

After they had lost Thorne and his harlot at the Midtown condominium, Cutty had directed Genesis to place wiretaps on the telephone lines of Thorne's family and friends. At a quarter past eleven o'clock that morning, an unidentified cell phone had called the home in Decatur at which Thorne's sister and nephew resided.

The mystery phone could have belonged to anyone. But he remembered that Thorne had ditched his cell in a restaurant trash bin in Duluth. Most likely, Thorne had purchased one of those pre-paid gadgets that didn't require ID or credit authorization—and which would show up as "caller unknown" on a wiretap.

In a revelatory flash that could have only been divinely inspired, a plan instantly formed in his mind.

"The Lord and Prophet are my shepherds," he whispered, reciting a variation on Psalm 23 that he'd learned during Kingdom Bible study. "They guide me on the path of righteousness for the sake of the Kingdom."

He called Valdez. At the sound of her soft voice, a shiver trickled down his spine, and he thought of the Prophet's promise. *A man who finds a wife finds a good thing.*

"I'll collect you in five minutes," he said. "We have a new mission, and the spirit has revealed to me the perfect means to fulfill it."

65

In light, late-morning traffic that metro Atlanta enjoyed only on weekends, Lisa drove to the address in Stone Mountain, a forty-five minute trip from Kennesaw. Anthony sat in the passenger seat, the Bible open on his lap, and explained to her his theory about Bob's intended message to them based on the verse in Genesis.

"God, I hope you're wrong," she said when he finished. "But it's such an awful possibility it has to be right. It explains so much."

"Including, maybe, why they killed my dad." His gut was as tight as a drum; the prospect of learning the truth at last had virtually given him a stomach ache of anticipation. "It's not going to be an easy conversation with Danny. But it's long overdue."

He also searched out the other scriptures marked in yellow. As he located each one, he folded back the top corner of the page, for quick reference afterward, and read the passage aloud to Lisa.

"After the verse in Genesis, the next one is from second Samuel, chapter four, verse seven," he said. "It says, *'For when they came into the house, he lay on his bed in his bedchamber, and they smote him, and slew him, and beheaded him, and took his head, and gat them away through the plain all night.'*"

"What the heck does that mean?" She glanced away from the road with a frown.

"Don't know. But it's damn violent. Like something I would've written."

"We'll have to chew on that one for a while."

He licked his finger, flipped forward in the book. "The next one is from Nehemiah, ninth chapter, thirty-fifth verse. *'For they have not served thee in their kingdom, and in thy great goodness*

266

that thou gavest them, and in the large and fat land which thou gavest before them, neither turned they from their wicked works.' "

"That reads like an accusation directed at New Kingdom," she said. "They have great resources, but do wicked works."

"Power corrupts," he said. "According to what Bob told me, they've committed every crime under the sun."

"Any more?" she asked.

"Let's see." He searched, found another passage. "Jeremiah, twenty-third chapter, fourteenth verse. *'I have seen also in the prophets of Jerusalem an horrible thing: they commit adultery, and walk in lies: they strengthen also the hands of evildoers, that none doth return from his wickedness; they are all of them unto me as Sodom, and the inhabitants thereof as Gomorrah.' "*

"Sounds like a reference to Bishop Prince," she said.

"The self-proclaimed prophet? Who walks in lies and encourages evildoers?"

"And commits adultery," she said, with a disgusted grimace.

Thinking of the interpretation at which they'd arrived about the bishop, Anthony felt a little ill, too.

"Next is Micah, chapter two, verse one," he said. "*'Woe to them that devise iniquity, and work evil upon their beds! When the morning is light, they practice it, because it is in the power of their hand.' "*

"Could be a generalized indictment of evil people," she said.

"Very generalized. Too generalized for Bob to have included it, unless he wants us to interpret it some other way."

"Let's table that one for further consideration." She slowed the car as they approached a traffic light. "Is this our turn?"

"Yeah, make a right," he said, and lowered his head to the book again. He flipped through pages. "Okay, found another one. John, chapter eight, verse thirty-two. *'And ye shall know the truth, and the truth shall make you free.' "*

"When you find the truth, you'll be free, baby," she said. "You'll be free of the weight you've carried on your shoulders all these years. You'll have closure."

"I want justice," he said. "It's not enough to simply know the truth. I have to do something about it."

"We will," she said. "Is that the last one? It sounded like a closing statement."

"Hang on." He riffled through more text. "Wait. Galatians, chapter four, verse sixteen. *'Am I therefore become your enemy, because I tell you the truth?'* "

"I don't understand that," she said. "Bob is your enemy?"

"It's the last verse marked in yellow." He closed the Bible, clasped it in his lap. "I've gotta think on it."

"That gives us three scriptures we'll have to review later," she said. "The rest are clear, relatively speaking."

"The others we think are puzzling might actually be clear, too. Bob's plan is too important—he couldn't risk us drawing the wrong conclusions. I'm thinking we've got to take a step back and view the scriptures in the context of what we've learned. Much easier said than done, though."

"He couldn't have picked a better book for hiding a message, that's for sure," she said. "Show a Bible passage to ten different theologians and ask them what they think it means, and you'll get ten different interpretations."

"That's why I hated Sunday school," he said. "My take on things was usually different than the teacher's, but they would say I was misinterpreting the text."

"It's not like math," she said. "There are no definitive answers."

"I sure could use a definitive answer right now. We think we know what the bishop has done, but we still don't know where Bob has hidden all his damning evidence. Or if he really has any."

"He does," she said. "We'll figure it out."

He looked up at the road. "Hey, our street's coming up. Make a left."

66

They turned onto a twisting road that wound through an older neighborhood of split levels and ranches with big, sloping yards. Anthony indicated the house nearing on the left.

It was a brick ranch that had seen better days. Peeling white trim. Rain gutters clogged with leaves. A sheet of plywood covering one of the front windows like a pirate's eye patch. Two old, rusty cars were parked in the muddy driveway, one of them sitting on cinder blocks, and random pieces of junk—old tires, hubcaps, and other assorted auto parts—littered the weed-choked lawn.

Danielle's Ford Explorer was parked at the end of the driveway. Lisa inched in behind the vehicle.

"This boyfriend of hers must be a real winner," she said. "This place reminds me of *Sanford and Son*."

"Please, no smart-ass comments to her. She's going to be pissed that you're here at all."

"I promise to keep my mouth shut."

He reached over Lisa and tapped the horn three times.

"If she's high like usual, she won't bother to come to the door," Lisa said.

"She's expecting me."

Lisa looked doubtful. After about five minutes and several more honks, Danielle still hadn't come out.

"She must be puffing on some good stuff," Lisa said.

"I'll be back." Grabbing the bishop's book, Anthony got out of the car and approached the house, weaving around the discarded auto parts.

The door bell was broken. He rapped on the scarred front door with his fist.

269

"Danielle! It's your brother! Open up!"

Another minute passed, and the door finally opened. Danielle stood on the threshold, blinking sleepily and rubbing her puffy eyes.

Anthony's physical features were a balanced blend of traits he'd inherited from his mom and dad, but Danielle had taken almost entirely after their father. She had his mocha complexion, thick eyebrows, penny-brown eyes, high cheekbones. She was slim like Dad, too, and stood only a couple inches shorter than their father's five-ten.

She wore her normal everyday gear of long, wrinkled t-shirt, and faded loose-fitting jeans. Her dry hair was tied up in a blue scarf.

The familiar scents of marijuana and cigarettes wafted from inside.

"Damn, it ain't been an hour yet, Junior," she said in her raspy smoker's voice. "I was sleepin'. Shit."

Although she was only twenty-nine, she looked and sounded older. Her eyes were smudged with dark circles. Her complexion had a bleached-out quality, like wood left out too long in the sun.

For a long time, he'd wondered where the sister he remembered from his childhood had gone. The adorable, bright-eyed girl who'd race on bicycles with him up and down the street, who'd had the guts to ride all the roller coasters with him at amusement parks, who'd liked to capture butterflies. That happy girl had grown up into this bitter woman who rarely had anything nice to say about anyone, who cared only about satisfying her own pathetic addictions.

But he thought he finally knew what had happened.

"I said I'd be here *within* an hour," he said. "Anyway, let's go. You're riding with us."

"Where we going?"

"I'm taking you to get some breakfast. How's Waffle House sound?"

At the mention of breakfast, her eyes brightened. "What you wanna talk about?"

"I'll tell you when we get to the restaurant."

"Nah, Junior. I wanna know what you wanna talk about right now—or else I might not go to the damn restaurant."

He paused. "I want to talk about the people who killed Dad."

A shadow passed over her eyes.

"I ain't all that hungry," she said. "I'm taking my ass back to bed. Later."

She tried to close the door. He stuck his foot between the door and the jamb.

Her lips tightened. "Step back."

"I know who was behind it, Danny," he said.

"You don't know shit, Junior, and you need to let it go. Now step back, I mean it."

"Does this man look familiar?" He showed her the cover of Bishop Prince's book.

She gaped at the bishop's photo, lips parted.

His gut clenched. He knew, then, that his theory was right.

"I finally figured out what's been bothering me about this guy," he said. "Isn't there a strong resemblance between this man and Reuben? A *father and son* resemblance?"

She pulled her gaze away from the photograph, looked at him. And then, she started to cry.

67

They went to a nearby Waffle House on Memorial Drive. Sitting in a corner booth apart from the other diners, they ordered coffee, and Danielle lit a Newport and began to talk.

"It all started with this girl I was going to school with, freshman year," she said. "Yvette Taylor. We had a few classes together, so we became cool, eventually. She was real sweet and smart—good people. She spent the night at our house a couple times, for slumber parties. You remember her, Junior? She had a lil' crush on you."

"Is that right?" Lisa asked, and gave Anthony an inquiring look.

He shrugged. "I don't remember her. But at that point, you and I were sort of in our own little teenage worlds. I was playing three sports, and you were hanging out with these girls who you seemed to spend every waking hour with on the telephone."

"Anyway, Yvette and her family went to this church in Austell," Danielle said. "New Kingdom. Her folks lived in Decatur, like us, but they would get up early every Sunday to make that long-ass drive all the way across town to Austell. Yvette said it was the most amazing place—it was really big, and you'd go there feeling broken down and walk out blessed. It was worth the long drive to them.

"She'd talk about it so much that I started to get really curious. I liked going to our family church, but we'd grown up going there, and it was small. I wanted to see something different. So Yvette had a slumber party one Saturday night, with me and two of our other girlfriends. The next morning, all of us got up and went to New Kingdom with Yvette's family."

"Did Mom and Dad know about this?" he asked.

"Of course they did. They thought it was fine, since I was with Yvette's family. They'd met her folks and thought they were cool. They didn't have a problem with me going to a different church, broadening my horizons.

"Well, the church about blew me away. It wasn't anywhere as big as it is now, and they didn't have the entire campus all built up, but it was still something incredible to me. It was so organized, and the people were all like Yvette and her family, really nice and friendly. They made me feel at home.

"That first service I went to, Bishop Prince gave the sermon. He was . . . the only word I can think of is 'electrifying.' I actually cried listening to him preach the word, and I never did that."

"He's a very charismatic speaker, no doubt about it," Lisa said.

"And I thought he was the finest man I'd ever seen in my life," Danielle said. She blew out a ring of cigarette smoke and shook her head. "So tall, with this chiseled face and killer smile. He just looked . . . *perfect*. Like the ideal man, if that makes any sense. He must've been about thirty-five then, way older than me, but I didn't care. Before the service was over I was praying to God to send me a man like him to marry one day.

"So after the services, he would go in the lobby and meet everyone in the congregation, right? I was too nervous to meet him, but Yvette insisted that I go talk to him. She said he was down to earth, not intimidating. She convinced me to get in line to shake his hand.

"We must've waited in line for like ten minutes. We finally get up to him, and I was about to hit the floor, I was so anxious. He was so huge. But his eyes were mesmerizing. He actually knew Yvette's name—she said he knew the name of every single member. He shook my hand, asked me my name, and thanked me for coming. He said he hoped he would see me at their Youth Conference, the following weekend. I babbled something about promising to go."

"Did you go?" Anthony asked.

"Shit, you kidding?" Laughing bitterly, Danielle tapped ashes into a tray, sipped her coffee. "Mom and Daddy couldn't have kept me from going. I ran my mouth about Bishop Prince all week, and by the weekend I think they were happy to let me go just so I would get out of the damn house and they wouldn't have to hear me say his name any more."

"Did you tell me?" he asked. "I don't remember hearing anything about him."

"I'm sure I did. But you were all into your stupid sports, remember, you didn't pay me any mind."

"Typical of the eldest sibling," Lisa said to Anthony. "I'm the oldest of three sisters—I've been there, honey."

"So Yvette and I went to the Youth Conference that Saturday morning," Danielle said. "Workshops, games, seminars, that kind of stuff. Bishop Prince made the opening remarks, and I swear, sometimes when he would look around the room, he would look right at me. It gave me chills." Although her hand was curled around a hot cup of coffee, she shuddered, remembering.

"After his talk, some of us went outside to the field to play games. Some kind of fellowship building thing, I don't remember what exactly. But after a little bit, I had to go to the ladies' room. Yvette stayed outside, she was flirting with some boy, so I went inside the church building alone to find the restrooms.

"On my way out of the ladies' room, I see the bishop strolling down the hallway, coming in my direction. Alone. I was so nervous I literally froze in place. But he smiled at me, and started to talk, and he actually remembered my name. I couldn't believe it. He said he was glad that I'd kept my promise to come to the conference. 'God makes promises to us, just like that, and he keeps his word, too,' he told me. Or something like that. I was so dazed just by talking to him I barely heard what he was saying.

"The next thing I know, a few minutes later, we ended up in his private office."

Danielle took a pull on her Newport, exhaled a raft of smoke, and looked out the window, eyes glassy.

Anthony knotted his hands in his lap. He had a sudden, irrational urge to break things, to turn over the table, to strike out at . . . something. Bishop Prince would have been an acceptable target for what he was feeling.

Sitting beside him, Lisa touched his knee, as if sensing his rage and cautioning him to keep it at bay. He blew out a deep breath and drank some coffee, but barely tasted it.

"You know what's sad?" Danielle smiled, but it was a melancholy expression, full of old hurts. "I *wanted* it to happen. All week, I'd dreamed about being with him, even prayed for it. I remember thinking, when I was with him in his office, that God had answered my prayer. How fucked up is that?"

274

"It wasn't your fault," Anthony said. "You were only fourteen, Danny, a child. The sick sonofabitch took advantage of you."

Danielle sniffled, wiped her watering eyes with the back of her hand. Lisa pulled tissues out of her purse and handed them to her, and she accepted them gratefully.

"He said it would be between us, and God, our little secret," Danielle said in a fragile voice. "He said God was going to bless me for accepting his divine seed."

"His divine seed?" Anthony clenched his hands into fists. "Are you kidding me?"

"That's so disgusting," Lisa said.

Danielle blotted her eyes. "I didn't tell anybody what happened. But the next day, Sunday, I went to church with Yvette again. After service, when I met the bishop in the receiving line, I thought he would give me special attention, but all he said was, 'Good morning, Danielle, thank you for visiting today, be blessed.' Or some lame shit like that. Like . . . like nothing had ever happened between us. He was the first person I'd ever been with. I gave him . . . something special . . . something I'll never get back. And that was all he could say? Thank you for visiting, be blessed?"

Almost angrily, Danielle dried her eyes with a tissue. She lifted her cup, found it empty, and snapped at the waitress for a refill.

"Sorry, she's had a difficult time," Anthony said to the waitress, by way of apology for Danielle's outburst. The waitress shrugged, as if such rude behavior were normal, and refreshed their mugs.

When the woman had left, Danielle said, "Anyway, after he gave me the cold shoulder, I was really depressed. I thought there was something wrong with me, that I wasn't good enough for him or something. I remember Mom knowing something was going on with me, but I wouldn't tell her what it was. A couple weeks later, though, I missed my period."

Lisa reached across the table and found Danielle's hand, and Danielle clasped it tight.

"Did you tell anyone then?" Anthony asked.

She shook her head. "I guess some part of me was still thinking about what Bishop Prince had said about his divine seed, and how I was carrying it inside of me. In spite of how he'd dissed me, it made me feel special, like I had a little piece of him growing in me. I know how dumb that sounds, but . . ." Her words trailed off. She ground out her cigarette in an ashtray, and lit another.

"Anything you felt back then is understandable," Lisa said. "You were so young, so innocent."

"Hmph. I wasn't innocent enough to be up front with my parents. When I started showing, I started wearing my clothes extra baggy, and I made up some shit to keep from having to go to gym at school, 'cause I didn't want other girls to see me. The baby was my secret."

Anthony tried to recollect what his sister had looked like back then, and couldn't. He remembered little about Danielle during that period other than the fact that she spent so much time with her giggly girlfriends.

"When did Mom and Dad find out?" he asked.

"When I was about four months along."

"Four months?" Lisa asked.

"I might've hidden it even longer, but I was in the bathroom one morning, taking a shower, and Mom walked in to get something out of the cabinet. She took one look at my belly, and . . ."

"She lost it," Anthony said, remembering how emotional his mother had tended to get.

"For real. She made me tell her how it happened. Then she told Daddy. Daddy called the church, told someone there what had happened, and demanded a meeting with the bishop, or else he was going to the police." Her eyes dimmed. "Bad move."

"What did they do?" Lisa asked.

"Let me guess," Anthony said. "They warned him to keep quiet."

"In so many words, yeah," Danielle said. "The church security people, whoever they are, they didn't threaten to hurt us, exactly, but they basically said that if we went to the police, it would be a bad move on our part, that they had contacts in the police department, judges in their pocket and a team of top lawyers, and they'd drag us through the mud, totally mess up our lives."

"I can't believe all of this was going on in the house, and I was totally unaware of it," Anthony said.

"I *asked* Mom and Daddy not to tell you—shit, not to tell anyone," Danielle said. "When I saw Mom and Daddy so upset, it finally started to sink in how wrong it was, how sick Bishop Prince was. I was embarrassed. I mean, why would I want the whole world to know that some pedophile pastor had gotten me pregnant? Why would I want you to know, Junior? Hell, what could you have done, anyway?"

Silent, Anthony dragged his hand down his face, wiped away a film of stale sweat.

"A few days after Daddy called the church, he said someone came up to him after work and gave him a briefcase full of money," Danielle said. "Something like twenty-five grand."

"Hush money," Lisa said.

"But Dad didn't take it," Anthony said.

"You and him, you're a lot alike," Danielle said. "You get something in your head about doing things a certain way, doing the right thing, and you won't let go. Daddy turned the money down and started trying to dig up dirt on the bishop. You know he worked at the newspaper. I guess he figured to write an investigative report, an expose or something."

Anthony recalled his father's mood that fateful morning on the lake. Dad had been withdrawn and contemplative, unusually so.

Finally, he knew why.

"We all know what happened later," Danielle said. "The church warned Daddy to quit what he was doing. He wouldn't. So they *made* him quit—and then they made it look like an accident."

Anthony closed his eyes and pressed his fingers firmly against the lids, to hold back the tears that wanted to flow. A few escaped anyway.

"Maybe a month after the funeral, Mom took me out of school," Danielle said. "I was really starting to show by then, couldn't hide it any more, and we didn't want to deal with the questions from everyone."

"I vaguely recall when Mom told me you were pregnant," Anthony said softly. "I don't remember having much of a reaction at all. After I saw Dad die . . . I was like a zombie for a while."

"We made up a story, told people some boy from school had gotten me pregnant." Tears glistened in her eyes again. "I love my child with all my heart, but Lord help me, sometimes I feel like he's here to punish me. To remind me every day of what I did . . . and how I let my daddy get taken away."

"No," Anthony said. "No, you can't blame yourself, Danny."

"But it's all my fault." Tears coursed down Danielle's cheeks, and she grasped Lisa's hand as if Lisa were her only anchor to sanity. "*I* wanted to go to the church in the first place . . . *I* flirted with the bishop . . . *I* got Daddy killed . . ."

277

No wonder she had given up on life to float on an endless series of marijuana highs, he realized. It was probably the only way she thought she could cope with the guilt.

"That's not true, Danny," Anthony said gently.

"You were the victim, sweetheart," Lisa said, rubbing Danielle's hand.

"Mom and I, we were too scared to tell anyone the truth," Danielle said. "Going to the cops was out of the question—the church people talked like they owned the damn cops. We just never talked about it any more. Ever. And I think the pain of it all, of losing Daddy, cut at least thirty years off Mom's life. She was never the same." She looked at Anthony. "None of us were."

A hush fell over them. Beyond their booth, diners were talking, laughing, eating. Anthony felt completely isolated from them, as if he were enclosed inside an impermeable bubble that separated him and his family from the rest of the world, hermetically sealed inside a private universe of sorrow and angst.

Earlier, he had wanted to break something. Now, he wanted to scream. He fought back the urge by reminding himself that screaming would do nothing. Had it helped him that morning on the lake, as he'd screamed and screamed while stuck in a boat with his dad's dead body in his arms?

He buried his face in his hands. His lungs burned, as if he's swallowed molten lead.

The waitress stopped by and asked them something. He looked up at her, blinked fuzzily.

"You know, food," the waitress said. "Want to order some?"

"We're fine, thanks," Lisa said. She shifted to Danielle. "Does Reuben know who his father is?"

"Hell, no," Danielle said. She shook her head fervently. "Until you came to me this morning, Junior, I wouldn't so much as speak that evil man's name."

"But does Reuben ever ask about his father?" Anthony asked. "Because he asked me, once, and I told him that I didn't know anything about his father—because I didn't."

"He used to ask. I'd tell him that his father lived somewhere far away, and I didn't know how to reach him." She shrugged. "Maybe three years ago, he stopped asking. It's just better that way, him not knowing and all—even though he looks more like his father every day."

278

Anthony glanced at Lisa, and read in her eyes that she was thinking the same thing as he. He went on.

"Reuben's going to find out the truth," he said. "I've been working to bring the bishop and his whole church to its knees, to expose everything they've done over the years, including what they did to Dad. We're going to get justice."

"You sound just like Daddy," Danielle said with a sad, broken grin. She stubbed out her cigarette in the ashtray. "Always got to do the right thing."

"It's what Dad would want," he said. "Mom, too."

"I know," she said, a faraway look in her eyes. Then she blinked, fixed him with a stern glare. "I wanted to ask you: how the hell did you find out about all this? We never told anyone."

"Someone on the inside of the church clued me in and has been feeding me info. We're close to a major break."

"I hope you bring 'em down," she said. "*Him*, especially. I know I can't be the only one that sick bastard's touched."

Anthony thought about Kelley Marrow. How many more Kelley Marrows and Danielles were out there, suffering the consequences of Bishop Prince's perverse desires? How many promising young lives had been cut short, or wrecked? How many families destroyed?

"I'm going to bring this to an end," he said. "I promise."

68

Once Cutty was inside the house, he drew his pistol.

Music thundered from upstairs, making the floor, walls, and windows vibrate. The devil's music.

He swept through the first level. The house was dusty and cluttered, decorated with old upholstered furniture and soiled carpeting spotted with cigarette burns. It reeked of cigarette smoke, and faintly of marijuana, too.

This home was an incubator of iniquity, a womb of the wicked.

Little wonder that Thorne had grown up there.

After proving the first floor vacant, he ascended the staircase, raking his glance over the framed photographs assembled along the wall. Hell-bound sinners, all of them. No one who feared God would live in such a spiritually vapid house.

Upstairs, all of the doors were ajar, except the one at the end. The satanic music came from behind the door.

The knob turned when he twisted it. He didn't worry about the occupant detecting the sound of his entry. The music of the damned was so explosively loud it would have prevented one from hearing the Judgment Day trumpets.

Inside, a thin teenager sat at a desktop computer, hammering away on the keyboard, his back to the door. He didn't even hear Cutty crossing the trash-strewn room.

But the kid certainly felt the gun that Cutty placed at the back of his head.

Part Three

The Kingdom

69

They returned to the home of Danielle's boyfriend so Danielle could retrieve her car. Until his work was done, Anthony had advised her to pick up Reuben and hide out at a friend's house. Although he hadn't been worried earlier that the zealots would harm his sister and nephew, as they'd seem concerned solely with him, with his newfound knowledge of the importance of their roles he considered them potential targets, and he would not relax until they were safely sequestered.

As the three of them stood in the driveway beside their vehicles, he peeled several hundred dollars out of his money clip and offered the bills to Danielle.

"This is for anything you need in the interim," he said. "But I hope I don't have to tell you—"

"I'm not going to smoke it up, Junior, all right?" She folded the money into her purse. "I don't even feel like doing that shit right now. I wanna keep my head clear—shit, I need to keep it clear to talk to my baby about everything I gotta tell him, you know?"

He pulled her into his arms and hugged her, and when he let her go, Lisa stepped forward and embraced her, too. In the past hour, the two women had found an unexpected kinship.

"Hurry up and get out of here, Danny," he said.

As Danielle walked to the house, his cell phone rang. The display didn't give the number, which immediately stirred the hairs at the nape of his neck.

In spite of his reluctance, he answered—and heard the voice that he expected.

"Found you again, Thorne," Cutty said. "Did I not tell you that God would lead you to me? Seek, and ye shall find."

How had they gotten his cell number? Anthony spun around in a circle in the driveway, half-expecting to find the fanatics hidden in the shrubbery. He'd been so meticulous . . .

"Is it them?" Lisa whispered.

He covered the phone, nodded.

Near the front door, Danielle had paused, somehow sensing the changed mood.

"What the hell do you want?" Anthony said into the phone.

"I have someone who wants to speak to you," Cutty said. "Say hello to your nephew."

Anthony's breath stopped.

"Uncle Tony," Reuben said. His voice was tight as he struggled not to cry. "Man, come get me, okay, please? They . . . they said they're gonna . . . gonna k-k-kill me if you don't listen to them . . ."

Reuben's voice snapped, and a sob escaped him. The sound tore like a serrated blade at Anthony's heart.

"Reuben, listen to me, everything's going to be fine," Anthony said, striving to keep his own tone calm. "I promise you that. I need you to stay strong, okay?"

"O-okay . . ."

"I'm not going to let anyone hurt you. You hang tight, keep your head up."

"All . . . all right." Reuben sucked in a shaky breath.

"Where are you?" Anthony asked.

"I-I don't know. They . . . they got a blindfold on me . . ."

"Did they snatch you from the house?"

"Y-yeah. I'm . . . sorry . . . I know you told me to leave . . ."

He realized they'd placed a wiretap on his family's house. When he'd called earlier that morning searching for Danielle and had spoken briefly to Reuben, they must have traced his call, which gave them his cell phone number—and probably the idea to snatch his nephew, too.

In hindsight, he should've seen it coming.

"Don't worry about it," Anthony said. "It was my fault. You just stay strong while I work on bringing you home safe, all right?"

"How inspiring," Cutty said, on the line once more. "Everything's going to be fine now that Uncle Tony is on the job."

"You keep your goddamn hands off him."

As if summoned by maternal instinct, Danielle raced across the driveway, back to them. Lisa moved forward to intercept her.

Cutty said, "I've told you before how profanity offends me, Thorne. Would you like me to vent my displeasure with your language on your nephew?"

"Don't touch him, Cutty," Anthony said. "Please. He's innocent."

"I beg to differ. When I collected him from your family home, this young sinner was listening to music so obscene that I'm rather surprised my ears didn't bleed. He's on the same wicked path that you've been walking, a journey that'll take both of you straight to hellfire and eternal damnation."

"He's only a kid. Leave him out of this. This is between you and me."

"Indeed it is," Cutty said. "You've led me on quite a chase. It is clear that the devil highly values your service, as he continues to aid you. But my God is far greater than your fallen angel."

Anthony ground his teeth. Cutty had him by the balls, and he knew it, and the wacked-out asshole was going to prolong the agony.

Lisa and Danielle huddled next to each other, faces tight with trepidation. He wanted to assure them that everything would be okay, but he had only a fuzzy notion of the play Cutty was going to make, and it was not comforting.

"You've obviously snatched my nephew because you wanted leverage," Anthony said. "Well, now you've got it. You've got the ace. What're you going to do with it?"

"I've always held the ace, Thorne. My God is always in control. He's the architect of my destiny, the captain of my fate."

"God's been leading you all along, huh? That's why we kept giving you the slip."

"Trials and tribulations are placed before us to strengthen our faith."

"You have an answer for everything."

"Those who serve God have access to his infinite wisdom, Thorne."

Anthony wanted to pull his hair out. It was impossible to hold a reasonable conversation with the guy. He was utterly committed to his delusional beliefs, and there was nothing more frightening than a man who never doubted himself, who never questioned his actions.

"What do you want from me?" Anthony asked.

"Sir."

"What?"

"What are your orders, *sir*. Say it like you were taught to do in the Marine Corps, with enthusiasm."

"You want me to sound off?" Anthony almost laughed. "I'm not going to dishonor the Corps by sounding off to a piece of shit like you."

"We have the ace, Thorne. Don't test the Lord."

"Whatever." Anthony exhaled through clenched teeth. "What's your big plan?"

"We're going to make a trade. I turn over your nephew, and you come with me."

"Come with you where?"

"Wherever God decides you must go."

"I thought you wanted to kill me."

"I am only a loyal servant of the Kingdom, Thorne. I obey a power greater than myself."

"Bishop Prince, you mean," Anthony said. "The so-called prophet."

"*The* Prophet. God's mouthpiece. The Anointed One. Don't you dare speak disparagingly of him—you're hardly fit to serve as his footstool."

Anthony hesitated. Presumably, once he gave himself up to Cutty, he would be transported somewhere, and interrogated.

They must've believed that he'd learned something so damaging to their organization that they couldn't take any risk on him passing along the information. They wanted to get him in a cold room, put the screws to him, and force him to confess whatever he knew, and to whom he'd told it—and *then* they would kill him. It was the classic interrogation scenario, and once he was in their custody, there would be no bargaining for his freedom, no opportunity to escape.

It would be over.

Telling them that he hadn't managed to fully decipher Bob's messages would prove fruitless, too. They believed that he possessed the evidence that could harm them, and they weren't exactly open to debate.

He needed time to conceive some kind of counter action, but time was something he simply didn't have.

"I don't know," Anthony said, stalling for time.

"Pardon me?"

"I've gotta think about this. You're asking me to give up my freedom."

"I'm not asking you, Thorne—I'm *commanding* you. Disobey, and your nephew suffers. Is that what you would like?"

"Then we make the trade in a public place," Anthony said quickly. "We can do it at South Dekalb Mall, it's in Decatur."

Cutty laughed. "You've no leverage here. We're doing this my way."

Anthony swore under his breath.

"We will make the exchange at a church on Hidden Creek Road," Cutty said. "It is called Mount Moriah Baptist. The building is abandoned, concealed within dense foliage, and has a large parking lot in the rear that abuts a forest."

"I think I know where it is."

"You'll come alone. You'll be unarmed."

"Fine."

"Listen to me very carefully, Thorne. If you attempt any heroics, I *will* kill your nephew."

Anthony glanced at Lisa and Danielle, nodded grimly. "Understood."

"You'll be there in forty-five minutes. That's precisely one-thirty. Not a minute later."

Cutty terminated the call. Anthony looked at the phone as if it were a snake, and turned to the women.

"There's been a change of plans," he said.

70

His angel had arrived.

A bank of twelve televisions covered a wall of Bishop Prince's master suite, the displays broadcasting video from surveillance cameras placed throughout the estate. Although he normally dressed in a chamber designated for that purpose, as he donned another custom-tailored Armani suit he could barely keep his attention away from one of the screens.

His angel was bathing in a guest bathroom. The camera, concealed in a light fixture, offered a side-view of her lounging in the frothy Jacuzzi.

As he watched, she lifted a slender leg out of the water, stretched it in the air before her with the easy limberness of a ballerina, and caressed the smooth skin with a bar of soap. It was such a sensuous act that he was convinced she knew he was secretly observing her, and was teasing him.

With effort, he turned away to fetch his shoes.

On an ordinary day, one of his personal assistants would have brought all of his clothing to him, and attended to him as he dressed. He had given the house staff and his assistants the day off, as he did at least once a week. The Lord had rested the seventh day, so surely he could grant those in his employ a day of rest.

The only individuals laboring for him that day were his Armor of God security detail. There were two agents stationed at the estate gates, and three more distributed throughout the property. As Satan never ceased his attempts to sow discord and wickedness, those who served as God's warriors must be ever vigilant.

The Kingdom had to be advanced, at all costs. There was much work yet to be done, and unlike Moses, he intended to be present to lead God's people into the Promised Land—an era of total Kingdom rule over the earth.

Other fundamentalist leaders had sought to restore God's sovereign control over society through political maneuvering: backing candidates sympathetic to their causes, lobbying those in power, and attempting to sway the faithful masses to vote for change. While of noble intentions, their failure was the result of ill-conceived strategy. The average American was a slothful, unrepentant heathen and could not be relied upon to cast the proper votes at the ballot box, or even to vote at all, and politicians were notoriously corrupt, peddling their influence to the highest bidder.

No, Kingdom rule had to be installed by more forcible means. Had not Joshua, Moses' successor, led an army into the land of milk and honey?

Enter Project Revelation, his divinely-inspired vision to return God to his rightful place as the head of society, with God's anointed servants executing his will.

In the dressing chambers, he eased onto the gold-trimmed bench, and slipped on a pair of Italian loafers. The room, like every other space in the mansion, was spacious, and lavishly appointed with antique furniture, much of it from the Louis XVI era.

The home covered fifteen thousand square feet and included seven bedrooms, but he lived there, alone. His wife and their four children resided in a much smaller home on campus, and received him for visits perhaps once a week, sometimes less often.

The estate had been built solely for his pleasure, and the pleasure of those he entertained.

After inspecting his appearance in the mirrors, he left the suite and entered the main hallway on the second floor, an eighty-foot long corridor with marble flooring. The marble tiles were so highly polished they reflected his face almost as clearly as a pool of water. The cathedral ceiling was well above his head, with a panel of skylights that admitted sunshine by day, and moon glow at night.

Several doors led off the hall. He stopped at a closed door on the right, twisted the knob.

It was a huge bedroom, decorated entirely in white: white walls and ceiling, white carpeting, white wooden furniture. The white, queen-size, hand-carved poster bed was draped in a white duvet. The bedside clock was white. Even the doorknobs were white.

He crossed the room to the bathroom door, which was slightly ajar, and pushed it open.

Like the adjoining room, the large bathroom was also entirely white.

The only thing inside that was not white, in fact, was the thirteen-year-old girl in the bathtub. She was of bi-racial heritage—Korean mother, black American father—with flawless, honey-brown skin and a ripened physique that belied her tender age.

Her name was Chastity.

For the past several months, her mother, a longtime servant of the Kingdom, had allowed her to stay with him whenever he requested her company, in return for divine blessings that he spoke into their lives. There were, after all, many ways to sow seeds and reap a bountiful harvest.

Soaping her body languorously, her back to him, Chastity did not notice that he stood at the door. She was softly singing one of his favorite hymns, "Blessed Assurance."

As he looked upon her, pleasant warmth spread through him.

His father, the late Dr. Theodore Prince, had spoken often to him of his "thorn in his flesh," a reference to Paul's letter to the Corinthians. But his father had talked of it in vague terms, declining to provide details when pressed, and Bishop Prince had begun to believe that his father suffered from some debilitating, mysterious ailment.

Matters became clear when, as a seminary student, he entered his father's church office one day to find an adolescent girl sitting on his father's lap, his trousers gathered around his ankles and his eyes squeezed shut in rapture. The girl let out a startled screech, but his father had only looked at him and said, *So, you've discovered my thorn.*

Bishop Prince had backed out of the room, face burning. Ashamed of his father, but more ashamed of himself.

Unexpectedly, the shocking scene had excited him.

Later that day, his father had pulled him aside. *Whatever you may be feeling about what you witnessed, son, remember what the Lord said to Paul: I will not take away your thorn, for my grace is sufficient for you, and my strength is made perfect in your weakness.*

He had expressed gratitude to his father for the insight. His father had always been such a wise man, strong in the Lord. Bishop Prince was proud to be his son and to have inherited the mantle of the Kingdom . . . even though he'd inherited his father's weaknesses of the flesh, too.

Chastity suddenly caught sight of him in a mirror. She looked at him over one suds-capped shoulder, and grinned.

"You were listening to me singing," she said.

"With pleasure," he said. "You sing like the seraphim."

She giggled. "I guess I'm okay."

He approached the tub. She kept her gaze on him, almond-shaped eyes sparkling, adoring.

The look in her eyes said she would do anything he asked of her, *anything*, and he found the prospect exhilarating. It was the same look he saw in the eyes of the Kingdom servants. Deep admiration. Complete submission. Total acceptance of his status as the appointed instrument of God, and as such, the understanding that he, and he alone, could lead them to a more fulfilled life than they could ever achieve on their own. They needed him, they craved him, because without him, their lives were meaningless . . . like rudderless ships adrift at sea.

"You look really nice," she said.

"I wore this suit for you."

She giggled again. She was so adorable, so innocent.

"Finished with your bath?" he asked.

She nodded, and a coquettish smile curved across her fine features. "Will you towel me dry?"

So innocent . . . yet she sometimes displayed a surprisingly mature flirtatious streak, as if she were developing a growing awareness of his weakness. He could speak to a roomful of heads of state without experiencing a trace of anxiety, could grin confidently into television cameras that beamed his face to millions of homes across the globe—but her asking him merely to towel her dry made his knees rubbery.

My grace is sufficient for you. My strength is made perfect in your weakness.

He reached for a fluffy white cotton towel, stored on a nearby rack, unfolded it, and knelt to receive her.

"Ready when you are, my angel."

71

Driving Danielle's Explorer, Anthony traveled along a two-lane road that cleaved through a densely wooded area. Pines and maples overhung the roadway, painting the ground in alternating patterns of light and dark.

To an onlooker, he would have appeared to be alone. Lisa and Danielle—Danielle on the verge of hysterics; Lisa struggling to keep her together—had gone to the family house, to await the outcome.

But he had a special passenger.

Concealed under blankets in the cargo area, Mike said, "Yo, AT, can you crack open a window or crank up the AC? It's hot as hell back here, dog."

After his call with Cutty, Anthony had used the cell phone of Danielle's boyfriend to ring Mike; he'd wanted to avoid setting off the church's wiretapping system again. Mike had sped to the area on his motorcycle and met him in the parking lot of a nearby gas station.

As Anthony had expected, Mike was armed and hungry for action. Anthony had quickly filled him in on the pertinent details of the situation.

"You think we're on our way to the spa?" Anthony asked. He switched on the air-conditioner. "That why you asking to be driven in comfort?"

"Yeah, I'm looking forward to my facial and back massage."

"I could use a manicure myself."

"You think that hot chick's gonna be there at the handoff?"

"Probably. Crazy as a wood lizard, mean as a rattlesnake, and armed to the teeth."

Mike chuckled. "Just how I like 'em."

"Get set. The spot's coming up on my left."

Flanked by pines, Mount Moriah Baptist Church came into view, marked by a crumbling brick sign posted near the road that listed service times for bygone days. The church itself was a small, squat, one-story structure constructed of faded bricks. Slats of plywood covered the windows. The tall white cross standing atop the roof was missing an arm.

A "For Sale" sign leaned in a patch of overgrown grass near the boarded-up entrance, listing a phone number in faded black print.

"If you're ever in the market to buy church property, Mike, you ought to check this place out," Anthony said.

"I'll keep it in mind."

Anthony slowed the SUV and eased into the driveway. Broken tree branches and pine cones littered the asphalt, weeds sprouting between cracks in the pavement. The driveway led around the side of the building and emptied into a large parking area.

In the far corner of the lot, he saw his nephew, and Cutty.

"I see them," Anthony said.

They sat at a wooden picnic table underneath a row of trees, Reuben sitting on one bench, Cutty on the opposite bench, positioned behind him. Reuben looked unharmed, just scared. The Suburban was parked nearby, front end facing Anthony.

There were no other vehicles in the area, no people, and the property abutted a shadowy forest that appeared to go on forever.

At Anthony's arrival, Cutty stood. He'd changed from his black tracksuit uniform into a white one. One hand was shoved in his jacket pocket.

Valdez, also clad in white, climbed out of the Suburban.

"Your girl's here," Anthony said to Mike.

"How's she lookin'?"

"Like an angel of death."

Valdez walked to Reuben and placed her hand on his shoulder. Reuben stiffened at her touch.

The kid so strongly resembled his father that Anthony wondered why it had taken him so long to make the connection.

He backed the truck into a parking spot about ten yards away, and cut the engine.

He got out.

As they had discussed beforehand, Mike would remain hidden in the vehicle until the fanatics prepared to drive away with Anthony as their prisoner. To stay in touch during the exchange, Anthony had called Mike's phone using the cell belonging to Danielle's friend, and had then clipped the cell to his belt. They kept the lines open on both their phones, creating a crude two-way radio system.

At the right moment, Anthony would speak a code phrase, signaling Mike to launch an ambush . . . and they would keep their fingers crossed that it would work.

Hands at his sides, Anthony moved in front of the Explorer. The area was silent, the chirpings of birds distant and soft. A cool breeze carried the pungent scent of the woods, damp from last night's storm.

Anthony nodded at his nephew. "How you doing, Reuben?"

"I'm . . . I'm okay," Reuben said, but he trembled like a leaf in the wind.

"Hang tight, kid. This'll be over soon."

Anthony started to advance. Cutty raised his hand.

"Hold it right there," Cutty said. Cutty peered around him. "You come alone?"

"My wife stayed home. She wanted to tag along, but I told her that she'd be bored by you."

"Shut up." Cutty's face reddened. He looked at Valdez. "Go check him out."

Valdez approached Anthony, the breeze plastering strands of her hair against her rosy cheek, a smirk on her face as if she were privy to some secret.

"You again," Anthony said.

"Turn to car," she said, and when he turned, she shoved him hard against the hood.

"Looks like we've switched places this time." He raised his arms and spread his legs. "I still think you're on the wrong team."

"I am a loyal servant of kingdom," she said.

"You've said that before. Is that the church servant slogan or something?"

Ignoring his remark, she searched him and found the .45 he'd deposited in his holster underneath his jacket.

"I told you to come unarmed, Thorne," Cutty said. "Are you incapable of obeying directions?"

"I was worried someone might car-jack me on my way over here."

"You're despicable," Cutty said. "Valdez, restrain him, please."

"What about my nephew?" Anthony asked.

"We'll let him go after we've secured you," Cutty said. "Now drop your hands, asshole."

"Asshole? I thought profanity offended you, Cutty."

"Just do it, dammit!"

Anthony lowered his hands. Valdez drew his arms behind him. He heard the jingle of metal chain, and then felt the cold steel rings close around his wrists.

He pulled against the cuffs, found them tight and unyielding.

"Bring him to the truck," Cutty said.

Valdez grabbed his arm. Together, they shuffled across the parking lot.

Reuben rose shakily. A fresh wave of tears streamed from his already-reddened eyes.

"Hey, man, don't let these people see you cry," Anthony said, but his own voice was fragile. He was praying Mike wouldn't let him down. "Everything's going to turn out fine."

"It certainly is," Cutty said. "God is good."

Reuben swallowed, wiped his eyes with the back of his hand. They arrived at the back of the Suburban, where the tailgate doors hung open. A cleared-out space, roomy enough to store a grown man, awaited.

"Sit." Valdez nudged him down.

Anthony sat on the lip of the bumper. "All right, you've got me. Now let him go."

"Go ahead," Cutty said to Reuben. "Get out of here, you little sinner. Remember what I said about calling the police—we *own* the police."

Slowly, Reuben backed away, his tearful gaze fixated on Anthony.

"Uncle Tony . . ."

"Go home, Reuben," Anthony said. "Your mother's waiting there for you. She needs to know you're okay. Hurry now."

As Reuben hesitantly retreated, Cutty rounded the picnic table. Madness, or delight—Anthony wasn't sure which, perhaps a measure of both—gleamed in his cold blue eyes.

"God delivered you to me," Cutty said. "Where is your devil god now, Thorne? Why don't you call on him to save you?"

Anthony finally uttered the code phrase that he and Mike had decided upon.

"Can't we all just get along?" he asked.

Sneering, Cutty punched him in the face. Anthony rocked sideways and nearly tumbled off the bumper. Jaw numb, he spat out a thin stream of blood.

"Dear God." Cutty massaged his knuckles. "That felt so good."

"Not as good as this is going to feel to me, asshole," Valdez said.

The woman had drawn a semi-automatic pistol. She leveled the gun at Cutty.

What the hell?

"Valdez?" Cutty said, in a quavering voice. "What . . . what are you doing?"

"I'm with the FBI, you prick." She chambered a round in the gun. "Put your hands in the air. *Now.*"

Anthony's mind reeled. The FBI?

Drawing backward a step, Cutty slowly raised his hands.

Then, in an eerily calm voice, he said, "No weapon formed against me shall prosper," and fled into the woods.

72

Valdez fired several rounds at Cutty, but the guy, crouched low and scrambling in an erratic, zigzag path through the trees and undergrowth, nimbly escaped gunfire. His white tracksuit faded in the shadowy distance.

"Dammit!" Valdez lowered her smoking pistol. "We lost him."

"You're really FBI?" Anthony asked. Thanks to his aching jaw, the words were like stones in his mouth.

"On your feet," she said. "Turn around."

He did as she asked. She unlocked the handcuffs and clipped them to her utility belt.

He rubbed his chafed wrists. Circumstances had taken such a dramatic, unexpected turn that he felt dizzy. Why was the FBI involved? Had Bob known about it, and if so, why hadn't he told him?

Although Valdez had gotten him out of a jam, until he had a better handle on what was going on, he had to be careful. Cops, whether of the local or the federal variety, always harbored an agenda—and it might not be the same as yours.

"I work out of the Atlanta field office," Valdez said. "I've been undercover at New Kingdom for three months."

"You speak English like a native."

"That's 'cause I am a native. Born and raised in Spanish Harlem."

"I thought I'd just caught that New Yorker accent."

"The poor grasp of English, that was part of the act, kept that sack of shit Cutty from taking me too seriously." She looked toward the woods, lips twisted in disgust. "That guy is freakin' *loco*, about drove me outta my damn mind. I shoulda popped him while I had him point blank."

"You saved my ass. I owe you."

"You bet your ass you do." She gave him a tight smile. "You're gonna return the favor before we're all done."

"Hey!" Mike rounded the corner of the Suburban, Reuben at his side. "Got the signal, AT, then I heard what went down. Sorry I missed the party."

Hands on her gun, eyes sharp as daggers, Valdez looked from Mike, to Anthony.

"Who is this clown, Thorne?" she asked. "Friend of yours?"

Anthony said, "Maria Valdez, meet Mike Alfaro. Mike, meet Valdez."

"The pleasure's all mine." Mike grinned at her. "You were in my bedroom last night, senorita."

"I remember you now," she said. "You own the dump in Duluth."

"Dump? My place is no dump."

"Freakin' pig sty."

"What're you talking about? My house is totally squared away, spotless."

Watching everything, Reuben shook his head. "Uncle Tony, what's the deal? This is like, crazy, man."

"Everything will make sense soon," Anthony said. "Come here. Let me take a look at you."

He put his hands on Reuben's narrow shoulders and checked him for injury. The kid appeared to be fine, only shaken up a bit, but Anthony found it difficult to look at his nephew without seeing his father.

"You okay?" Anthony asked.

"I'll be all right."

"We need to get you home," Anthony said. To Valdez, he said: "What if Cutty notifies your bosses at the church about what happened here? Your cover's blown."

"If you help me do my job, it won't matter," she said. "I saved your ass, you save mine."

"You don't need my help," Anthony said. "You're with the FBI. I'm just working solo."

"You got me, AT," Mike said. "We're a dynamic duo."

"You guys are trying to be funny, right?" Valdez said. "An informant in New Kingdom was helping you, Thorne. I know that for a fact, 'cause he got me in."

"You mean Bob?"

"That's not his name."

"His family calls him Bob."

"Whatever. Bob, Bozo, who gives a damn. He gave you something, and I want it."

Now things were starting to clarify.

"We can talk on the way to my family's place." Anthony tapped the side of the Suburban. "We should disable this ride in case Cutty comes back."

Casually raising her pistol, Valdez blew out the SUV's two rear tires.

"You're really something else," Mike said.

She glared at him as she holstered the gun. "I got one round left in the clip, asshole—don't make me use it."

Mike winked at Anthony.

The four of them piled into the Explorer. Anthony slid behind the wheel, Valdez hopped into the passenger seat, and Reuben and Mike climbed in the back.

Before starting the engine, Anthony called Danielle. He told her that everyone was fine, and that they would be returning shortly with a special guest. He hung up before she could ask him anything else.

He twisted the key in the ignition, glanced at Valdez. "By the way, can you give me back my piece?"

She withdrew the revolver from her jacket and handed it to him.

"You've got my .38, too, mister," she said. "You took it from me last night. Before I beat your ass like a pinata."

Heat warmed Anthony's face. "Well . . ."

"Damn, you gonna take that off her, AT?" Mike said.

"Ah, she got lucky, Mike."

"Lucky?" Her lips puckered sourly. "I spent six years in the Army before I joined the Bureau, and before that, I earned a black belt in karate—second degree. We can step outside the truck right now and see if luck has anything to do with me resuming last night's ass kicking."

The look in her eyes was dead serious. Anthony didn't know what to say.

"Shit," Mike said. He sounded awed. "You've got a helluva chip on your shoulder, senorita."

"If I didn't have attitude, men would treat me like I was only a dumb piece of eye candy. I've thrashed men tougher than both of you, so I suggest you act accordingly."

"We get your point, Valdez, take a chill pill." Anthony shifted into Drive. "Anyway, the gun is in my bag at the house. Wasn't loaded, though."

"I never packed live ammo while I was working the field with these dirt bags. The gun was for show. Cutty was plenty happy to do all the wet work anyway."

"How many has the nut job wasted?" Mike asked.

"Too many to count." She stared at Anthony. "You give me your info, Thorne, and we can bring down the whole organization."

"We're back to that again." He exited the parking lot and swerved onto the adjacent road. "But I'm sitting here trying to figure out that if Bob got you inside, like you say, then why didn't he give you everything you needed to make your case. Why involve me?"

"Beats me. You'll have to ask your Bob if you ever see him again."

"But you infiltrated the church months ago," he said. "Don't you have enough dirt on them from your own investigation to shut them down? You've witnessed murders, and I can only imagine what else."

"I've got plenty, yeah. But I need it all. You don't want to go in half-assed against these people."

"They have big cheese contacts, says AT," Mike said.

"At the very highest levels," Valdez said. "If we don't hit them with everything we've got, they'll shut us down, smear the reps of everyone involved so badly I wouldn't even be able to get a job guarding rug rats at Disney World."

"You think Bob gave me the whole enchilada, then?" Anthony asked.

"Didn't he?" She glared at him.

Shrugging, Anthony glanced at Reuben in the rearview mirror. The kid, following their conversation quietly yet intently, still looked a little shell-shocked.

He was going to feel much worse after he learned the truth of his paternity.

"All of this will make sense to you later, Reuben," Anthony said. "Your mom will explain."

"Hey, I'm just listening, Unc," Reuben said with a shrug.

"Speaking of which." Valdez turned around in the seat and fixed Reuben with a penetrating stare. "You can't repeat anything you've overheard here to your friends. This is a federal investigation. We clear, kid?"

"Yes, ma'am." Reuben nodded vigorously.

"If you run your mouth, she'll beat your ass like a pinata like she did your uncle," Mike said.

Valdez flipped Mike the bird, and he laughed.

"I need to know, Thorne," she said. "Are you going to help me out? Yes, or no?"

"I'll help you," Anthony said. "Under one condition."

"Name it."

"You've got to help me, too."

73

Lisa answered the door. When she saw Valdez standing between Anthony and Mike, she screamed.

"It's cool, sweetheart," Anthony said. "Valdez is with the FBI. She's been working undercover at the church."

"Oh." Lisa put her hand against her chest as if to calm her heart. "You're serious?"

"We'll get you up to speed," Valdez said.

They filed inside. A tearful Danielle let out a squeal of joy at their entrance, pulled Reuben into her arms, kissed him, and asked him over and over again if he were okay. True to his age, Reuben acted as if he were embarrassed by his mother's lavish attention.

Anthony drew Mike aside from the others.

"What's up?" Mike asked.

"I need to talk to Lisa, alone," he said. "Think you can keep Valdez occupied for a few minutes?"

"You kiddin me?" Mike's eyes danced. "I've met my future wife, AT, for real."

"All right now." Anthony laughed. "Slow down, tiger."

"What are you two knuckleheads jawing about?" Valdez asked, charging between them. Lisa trailed behind her, looking thoroughly perplexed.

"The old married folks need some alone time," Mike said. He took Valdez by the arm and guided her away. "Meanwhile, senorita, let's talk about some of your favorite action movies . . ."

Anthony asked Lisa to grab the Bible, and then he led her into his father's study and shut the door. The air was heavy with dust, so he opened a window. Afternoon sunlight and a cool wind poured into the room.

Lisa waited beside the desk, arms crossed over her bosom. "What's going on, Tony? I've got so many questions I feel as if my brain's about to blow a few blood vessels."

Quickly, he summarized what had happened.

"That crazy guy, Cutty, or whatever he's called—he got away?" she asked. "That makes me very nervous."

"We shot out a couple of tires on his truck, so he shouldn't be able to follow us," he said. "Honestly, I think he'll be more concerned with telling his bosses about Valdez's betrayal."

"But you don't completely trust her, either."

"She's a cop, so no, I don't trust her. If we tell her what we've learned, she'll call the Bureau, and they'll bring in back-up and push us out of the picture."

"Is that so bad? We all want the same thing. We want to bring down Bishop Prince."

He shook his head firmly. "I'm doing this my way. I think that's why Bob entrusted his info to me. He didn't want to follow normal legal channels."

"Because the church might raise roadblocks."

"They have connections everywhere, Lisa. We've seen proof of that. Bob couldn't risk going to the cops. He needed someone like me."

"Someone with a personal stake in getting justice." She chewed her bottom lip. "What next, then?"

"We don't tell Valdez everything. But we get her to take us to the church."

"The Kingdom Campus?" Her eyes got huge. "Why? That's like going into the lion's den."

"Based on the scriptures we've read, I think that's where we have to go. I'm certain of it, actually. Look here."

He opened the Bible and found the two yellow-marked passages that supported his theory. He read them to her, and explained his interpretation.

"The idea's been bouncing around in my head like a pinball ever since I read those verses this morning," he said. "Bob hid his evidence in a place where virtually no one would ever expect to find it."

"But what you're proposing is incredibly risky, Tony. If you're wrong—"

"I'm not wrong."

She held his eyes for a long, quiet moment. "How can you be so sure?"

He turned away from her and swept his gaze across the photos on the desk, the sports memorabilia and the journalism award plaques on the shelves. The relics of his father's life. Looking at the items, as it usually did, caused his breath to catch in his chest.

But his father's legacy wasn't defined by dust-filmed objects sitting on shelves and desks in a forgotten room.

"One thing my dad taught me that I'll always remember is that I should trust my instincts," he said. "To believe in myself and do what I think is right, no matter who doubts me or says I can't do it. That's why I'm so sure."

She gave him a measured look, and then nodded.

"So let's do it," she said.

He deposited the Bible in his pocket, and they left the study. They found Mike and Valdez sitting in the living room. Mike was running off at the mouth about movies, gesturing wildly. Valdez, half-listening, yawned.

"Hey, there they are," Mike said, and rose off the sofa.

Valdez shot to her feet, too. "Where the hell were you? I have a job to do here, Thorne, and not a lotta time to do it."

"It's just a job for you. But it's my life, my family." He pointed to a portrait of his father that hung on the wall. "See him? That's my dad? He's dead, and guess who's responsible?"

"I'm sorry," she said in a softer tone. "*Dios mio*, you've lost so much."

"So you'll excuse me then if your job isn't my top priority."

"Okay, guys." Lisa stepped between them. "How about we continue this conversation in the car?"

"Where do you want to go?" Valdez asked.

"I think you can guess the answer to that question, too," Anthony said.

Valdez's dark eyes glimmered. She withdrew a cell phone from her jacket.

"In that case, we're gonna need a search warrant," she said.

74

Danielle and Reuben stayed behind at the house. Danielle promised Anthony that she would tell Reuben everything about his true paternity, though she confessed that she had no idea how to navigate such a difficult conversation. "I wish I could tell you how to break it to him, but I can't," Anthony said. "All I can say is that he deserves to know the truth, and you're the only one who can give it to him." She said she would do her best.

They took the Explorer, bringing along Anthony's duffel bag containing their weapons, lots of extra ammo, and other equipment, including his notebook computer. Valdez drove, while Anthony rode shotgun and Mike and Lisa occupied the backseat. The New Kingdom Church campus was in Austell, about a forty-minute trip from Decatur, which gave them an opportunity to talk.

"This morning, I was online searching for dirt on New Kingdom," Anthony said to Valdez, "and I couldn't find anything. When I'd try to pull up a site that promised something juicy, it would mysteriously be offline."

"Mysteriously, huh?" Valdez smirked. "Let me tell you, guys-- most of New Kingdom's operating budget goes into two buckets: technology and security. I've seen the reports. You wouldn't believe how much they spend."

"You and Cutty were able to find us almost anywhere we went, dig up anything about us," Anthony said. "So yeah, I'd believe it."

"Genesis was behind that," Valdez said. "That's what they call their records management and surveillance network."

"Genesis, huh?" Mike laughed. "Like from the Bible?"

"Laugh all you want, but it's linked into pretty much everything," she said. "What *is* funny is that Bishop Prince personally hates the Internet. Says it allows unrepentant sinners to 'congregate in virtual dens of iniquity.' His exact words."

"Well, the Internet enables individual expression," Lisa said. "Anyone can publish a blog, or a Web site, or a Facebook profile, and rant about any topic they want. I'd imagine that a free flow of information poses a threat to the control he wants to establish."

"But they've cracked down on the Web pretty hard, like you found, Thorne," Valdez said. "The tech division's created spidering programs that crawl the Net constantly, searching for heretical content."

Anthony scowled. "Heretical content? What is this, the Spanish Inquisition?"

Valdez shrugged. "That's what they call it. Anyway, when they find something on a page that triggers an alert, they'll move fast to delete the content, or shut it down. They'll send a virus or whatever, screw up the server. If you posted something nasty on a blog today about the church, or the bishop, it would be wiped out by tomorrow morning."

"Like I was thinking," Anthony said.

"What if you were online looking for so-called heretical content on the church?" Lisa asked. "Could they find you?"

"If you entered in a high number of searches, yeah," Valdez said. "I don't know the technology behind how they do it, but they've traced people like that."

"That's, like, nuts, man," Mike said. He didn't laugh that time.

"As much as Bishop Price hates the Web, that hasn't stopped him from using it to solicit donations," Anthony said. "I found thousands of testimonials about sowing seeds for the kingdom, and every one linked back to the church's donation page."

"They bring in a fortune from online donations," Valdez said. "Bishop Prince may despise the Web, but he's better than anyone else at exploiting it."

Anthony stroked his chin. "How much do they bring in annually from all of their activities and businesses? Rough figure?"

"All of them?" Valdez blew out a chestful of air, drummed the steering wheel with her thumbs. "Three billion, I'd say."

Anthony jerked upright. He felt as if the floor had dropped from underneath him.

"Did you say three *billion*?" Lisa asked.

"You got it, girlfriend."

"Holy shit," Mike said. "That sounds like a Fortune 500 company."

Anthony was shaking his head. "How do they do it? I've read about some of their business interests, but still, there are major companies who don't haul in that much every year."

"You've only read about the businesses they make public," Valdez said. "They have a private holding company, a conglomerate I guess you'd call it, that owns huge amounts of stock in some very profitable companies in a wide range of industries: pharmaceuticals, oil, insurance, real estate, manufacturing, whole lotta stuff."

"But they operate as a tax-exempt religious organization," Lisa said. "Are they paying taxes on all that money?"

"Their holding company is a for-profit business, so they pay their taxes to Uncle Sam. Thing is, most of what's left over after taxes gets funneled back to the church." She threw Anthony a look. "Now you know how they can afford to do what they do."

"It still sounds shady to me," Anthony said.

"Almost like money laundering," Lisa said.

"We've got our contacts in the IRS checking into it," Valdez said. "If we can nail them on tax fraud, that'd be fine with me, whatever works."

"Hey, it brought down Capone," Mike said.

Quiet, Anthony gazed out the window. Winning justice for his dad's murder was one thing. But taking on a multi-billion dollar organization? He never could have imagined this, and wondered if he would have wanted to even try if he'd known from the beginning what he was up against.

He suspected that was why Bob had been so vague at their meeting.

He turned to Valdez. "What was your Bureau assignment at New Kingdom?"

"I infiltrated the Armor of God—that's their defense division— to investigate domestic terrorism."

"You're shittin' me," Mike said. "This is from a church?"

Valdez said, "When people think about terrorism, they think about some international sect of Muslim extremists planting bombs in the subway or flying planes into buildings. That's the stuff that grabs the headlines, but it's a lot more than that. We've got threats right here on American soil, from homegrown groups that don't have squat to do with radical Islam."

307

"Remember Oklahoma City, guys?" Lisa said. "Plotted and executed by good ole' American citizens."

Valdez nodded. "White supremacist organizations, anti-government militia movements, animal rights extremism, eco-terrorism—we investigate all of them under the umbrella of domestic terrorism. Most of them are small-time operations, with objectives that would have a relatively minor impact on the nation as a whole. Not New Kingdom's."

Dread grabbed the pit of Anthony's stomach. "What are they doing?"

"I don't have the full picture yet," she said. "But I know the name of the project. It's called Revelation."

"That's a book in the Bible, too," Mike said. "I remember it from Catholic school. Got all kinds of weird symbolism about Armageddon."

"Which is what they've got in mind," Valdez said. "From what I've been able to dig up so far, they're planning attacks on some very high-profile national targets—landmarks, transit systems, *and* people."

To Anthony, the wave of anxiety that rippled through all of them was almost palpable.

"To what end?" Lisa asked.

"Scare tactics," Valdez said. "Think about what happened to us after September 11. That sense we had as a nation of being invincible? After that, it was gone. We were scared as hell, so when the government revamped flight security and made it a major pain in the ass to fly anywhere, and when they passed legislation that made it easier for them to do surveillance on private citizens, we were all for it, weren't we? Whatever measures they told us would protect us from the bad guys, we were down with them--even if we had to give up some freedoms and conveniences that we'd used to take for granted."

Anthony sensed where this was heading, and he shifted uneasily in the seat.

"You guys already know the church has cronies in the government," Valdez said. "But you don't know how highly placed they really are. I'm talking big shot senators, okay? I'm talking about people who, if certain individuals were eliminated, would move into the Oval Office."

"No way," Mike said, but the tremor in his voice made it clear that he believed every word.

"Now you think about a country," Valdez continued, "under siege by mysterious terrorists destroying national symbols of pride, detonating explosives in mass transit systems and killing thousands of innocent people, and you see our most valued leaders get knocked off—and you tell me then how willing the scared-shitless American people would be to accept a new set of rigid laws designed to supposedly restore order and keep us safe."

"Bishop Prince's Kingdom agenda would become a reality," Anthony said softly.

Everyone fell silent.

75

For several minutes, the only sounds in the SUV were the purring engine, and the hum of the tires spinning against the highway.

Valdez was on I-20 by then, traveling westbound. Downtown Atlanta passed by on the right, skyscrapers poking at a thickening dome of gray clouds.

Anthony wondered if the church planned to destroy any of those tall buildings. When he spotted a MARTA train speeding along tracks, he wondered if the rail system were a target, too.

Think about how people would freak out if that happened. It would be pandemonium.

It was almost too frightening to imagine, like a plot twist pulled out of a doomsday novel. Unfortunately, considering the staggering resources the church commanded, it was entirely plausible.

"Tell us about the Armor of God," Anthony said.

"It's a paramilitary force, approximately seven hundred men strong," Valdez said. "They serve as Bishop Prince's personal bodyguards, provide security on the Kingdom campus, and handle other missions, as ordered by the Director. Most of them are ex-law enforcement or military."

"Is that how that Bob guy got you in, 'cause you served in the Army?" Mike asked.

"That helped. They want experienced people, and they're smart enough to know that they have to go outside the church to get 'em."

"Do you have to be a believer in the church's doctrines to work for them?" Lisa asked.

"When you're selected, they put you through a nine-week training program on a wilderness retreat they own in Montana," Valdez said. "It was a lot like boot camp, physically demanding, except with an extreme focus on New Kingdom dogma. You're memorizing Bible passages, chanting church slogans, and listening to Bishop Prince's sermons constantly. Totally brain-numbing, but that's the point."

"Like some radical Islamic terror cell training camp," Anthony said.

"Good analogy. Super fanatical, group-think environment. If you don't believe in New Kingdom's teachings when you go in, by the time camp's over, you sure do—or you learn pretty damn well how to fake it, like I did."

"How'd you keep from being brainwashed?" Lisa asked.

"Soon as I got out of camp, I slipped away and met with a Bureau shrink. She put me through some deprogramming sessions, cleaned all of that crap out of my head. But I can fake it when I need to."

"Cutty sure wasn't faking the funk," Anthony said.

"Cutty?" Disgust curled Valdez's lips, as if the man's name tasted foul in her mouth. "The word on him was that he was always a freakin' psycho—he set a fire in his house when he was something like sixteen, torched his entire family."

Lisa shuddered. "Are you for real?"

"What the hell do you think?" Valdez said, steel in her voice, but her anger seemed directed at Cutty, not Lisa. "His family was in a survivalist cult, raised him on a commune out in the boondocks. They'd make him sleep in a closet if he broke some stupid rule, beat him for breathing too hard, that kind of craziness. After he snapped and burned up the house, he was locked up in a psych ward until someone at New Kingdom doing ministry outreach there discovered him. Like they say, it was a marriage made in heaven."

"Good thing he's gone, huh, guys?" Mike said.

"We hope he is," Anthony said.

"There are others as dangerous as him," Valdez said. "Look, the pay for an agent in the Armor of God isn't all that great. People get into it because they believe Bishop Prince is chosen by God."

"Anointed," Anthony said, echoing what he had heard earlier.

"Even though he's a pedophile," Lisa said. Her voice was thick with scorn.

Valdez glanced away from the highway, eyebrows arched. "You know about that?"

"The bishop raped my sister when she was fourteen," Anthony said. "My nephew, Reuben . . . well, do you notice a resemblance?"

"I knew there was something about that kid!" Valdez put her hand to her mouth. "That's awful."

"My dad found out about it, tried to do the right thing—"

"You don't have to finish—I can put the pieces together." She touched his arm. "I'm so sorry."

"It's taken me fifteen years to get to the truth," Anthony said. "If Bob hadn't gotten in touch with me, I'd still be wandering in the dark."

"Yeah, good old Bob," Valdez said. "Would've been nice of him to help me out, too, before he split. He's our damn informant."

"What did this Bob dude do at the church anyway?" Mike asked.

"Top administrative brass, and before that, he was the Deputy Director in the Armor of God," Valdez said. She turned a probing glare on Anthony. "He knew everything—which I'm assuming he passed on to you."

Anthony shrugged. "You know what they say about assumptions."

"Let's get back to the bishop," Lisa said. "Have you heard about him hurting other girls?"

"I've heard rumors," Valdez said. "It's on the *low-low* down-low—passing that kind of gossip around the Kingdom can get you flat-lined. But I have it from a good source that Bishop Prince doesn't even live with his wife and kids in that mansion of his, 'cause he entertains his angels there."

Anthony's stomach did a sickening flip flop. "His angels?"

"That's what he calls them," Valdez said. "The story is that some of the servant families who live on campus supply their daughters to Bishop Prince, to use whenever he wants, in return for some blessing or whatever."

Lisa made a sound of revulsion in her throat. "That's got to be the most disgusting thing I've ever heard in my life."

"Before I went undercover, I researched cults," Valdez said. "It's fairly common for the cult leaders—almost always a man, of course—to have total sexual access to everyone in the group, children included. David Koresh, remember that guy?"

"Waco, Texas," Mike said.

Valdez said, "Koresh convinced his followers that he was a descendant of King David and his seed was divine, and since it was, he was the only man in the sect allowed to get laid. And he could get some from anyone, whenever."

"Pedophile Prince told my sister something like that, too," Anthony said. "He told her she should be honored to accept his 'divine seed.'"

"He's unbelievable," Valdez said. "But even though he's the scum of the earth, his ministry, if you want to call it that, has tapped into something that lots of people respond to very passionately."

"The prosperity preaching," Lisa said.

"That's part of it, but more than that, it's his kingdom theology," Valdez said. "When he talks about the erosion in morals and values in modern society, how popular culture is so shallow and freakin' screwed up, and hits you with how if we embrace a kingdom agenda, people will start acting like they've got some decency because it'll be the law of the land . . . listen, when he gets going on that, the servants go nuts, they're ready to do anything to make it happen.."

"A lot of people are fed up with the state of the world," Anthony said. "He's a demagogue, using people's emotions to manipulate them for his own purposes."

"But he believes in it," Valdez said. "He's not a cynic feeding the masses whatever *mierda* they want to eat. He's convinced God is telling him to do this stuff."

"That makes him super dangerous," Mike said.

"You said it." Valdez glanced at Mike in the rearview mirror. "Right now, according to the Director of the Bureau—and he'd never say this publicly 'cause the church's supporters would have his balls for breakfast—Bishop Prince is the most dangerous man in America."

76

As Six Flags Over Georgia floated into view on the left of the highway, roller coasters stretching for the clouds, Valdez exited the interstate and made a right off the ramp, onto a busy strip lined with chain hotels, gas stations, and fast food joints. She swerved into the parking lot of a Texaco, stopped near an air pump/vacuum machine, let go of the wheel, and whirled in the seat to face Anthony.

"Okay, the Kingdom Campus is about a half-mile ahead," she said. "But we need to talk strategy before we get there. Bob told you where you could find the goods, correct? Did he put the data on a flash drive, a disc, or what?"

Mike and Lisa looked to Anthony, too. Anthony shrugged.

"I don't know," he said.

Valdez's eyes dwindled to dark points. "Don't screw with me, Thorne."

"I'm being straight with you. The info could be on a disc, or a flash drive, or some other storage device. Bob didn't tell me."

"What the hell did he tell you then?"

"I know the info is on the campus. But I'm not sure where, exactly."

"You're lying." Her gaze skewered him. "You don't trust me."

"I don't trust anyone."

He met her hot glare. She didn't blink. She looked ready, in fact, to punch him in the face.

"How's the security on campus, senorita?" Mike asked, breaking the tension.

Valdez sighed, tucked a lock of hair behind her ear. "Tighter than a drum. They've got complete surveillance of every area, foot patrols, cruisers, choppers. Every agent wears Kevlar vests and carries pepper spray, stun batons, and 9mm Glocks."

"They sound like cops," Lisa said.

"They're more dangerous than cops," Valdez said. "They don't bother to read you Miranda rights."

"Response time to an incident?" Anthony asked.

"Depending upon where the threat originates? Three minutes, max."

"Not much time." Anthony cracked his knuckles. "We'll have to move like lightning, then."

"We'll have the advantage of surprise," Mike said. He swatted Anthony's shoulder. "We can do this, AT. Piece of cake."

"To hell with that crap, we're calling back-up." Valdez flipped out her cell phone. "I need them to bring me that search warrant, and we can use the extra firepower."

"Hold on, I'm not going to storm in there with the feds," Anthony said. "You call them, and our partnership ends here."

"We can't do this on our own," Valdez said. "We're way outnumbered. They'll shoot to kill."

"So will we," Mike said.

Valdez gnashed her teeth. "Freakin' stubborn jarheads."

Anthony only smiled at her.

"All right," Valdez said. "I'll tell my team to get set, but I'll hold 'em off till we get to Bob's drop."

"Fair enough," Anthony said.

Phone in hand, she started to get out of the SUV. Anthony stopped her.

"Make the call in front of us," he said.

"You're paranoid, you know that?" But she remained in her seat and punched in a number. She had a terse conversation with her contact, and put away the phone.

"They've got the warrant. They'll stage about a mile from campus." She read her watch. "Should be in place in thirty minutes."

"That gives me time to figure out where we need to go," Anthony said. "Let's head on in and cruise around."

"Didn't you hear me?" Valdez said. "I told you I can't take anything out of there without a warrant. I'm not working for the church any more. I've gotta follow the law now."

"You're not going to take anything. You're only going to drive around so I can find Bob's drop. Right, guys?"

"Just a look-see," Mike said, nodding.

"Never hurt anything," Lisa said. Her gaze connected with Anthony's, and he thought about married folk telepathy.

Muttering under her breath in Spanish, Valdez slammed the Explorer into gear.

77

The front gates of the church campus were so massive and ornate Anthony felt as if they were entering a beachfront luxury resort. Opened wide enough to permit four lanes of traffic, the gates were at least ten-feet high, painted snow-white, with intricate gold and silver scrollwork of angels and doves. A gigantic electronic billboard in front flashed the time and the temperature, and featured a digitized image of a smiling Bishop Prince, with a slogan that proclaimed: *Serving God's Kingdom.*

Serving God's kingdom? It made Anthony sick.

About a hundred yards past the gates, the road diverged into six lanes: three going in, three going out. Large yellow signs hung above each entryway, bringing to mind a toll-road plaza. They were marked "Staff," "Members," and "Visitors." Each entrance included a guard booth manned by broad-shouldered men clad in white tracksuits and aviator sunglasses.

"No one can simply drive on in, huh?" Anthony said.

"You got it." Valdez nosed the Explorer into the Staff lane and produced a laminated photo ID card from her jacket.

"When I came here for my friend's wedding, they slapped a visitor sticker on my car," Lisa said. "They made me give my name and city of residence, too."

"All visitors are logged," Valdez said.

"What if you object to giving your personal info?" Anthony asked.

"Then you don't get in," Valdez said.

"Damn, is it a church, or a base?" Mike asked.

317

Valdez lowered the window and showed her ID to a guard. He nodded curtly, said, "May God bless you," in an artificially cheerful voice, and the white gate arm lifted.

There was a Welcome Center ahead, an Art Deco style brick building with lots of windows, fronted by a huge water fountain. A colorful sign at the main intersection bore arrows pointing the way to various destinations such as the Sanctuary, Kingdom Market, Medical Center, and Kingdom Academy.

"Where to?" Valdez asked.

"Just drive around," Anthony said.

Grumbling, she hung a right.

The property was meticulously landscaped, with lush trees, abundant beds of flowers, and swaths of trimmed grass that reminded Anthony of the putting greens on a golf course. The assortment of brick buildings—housing such amenities as the medical clinic, fitness center, and post office—looked brand new.

Armor of God soldiers were out in full force, too. They whisked across the wide sidewalks on Segways, their ivory cycling helmets matching their uniforms, weapons bristling from their utility belts. Others cruised in black Dodge Chargers with "NKC Security" splashed on the door in bold white letters.

But there were also signs of ordinary life in progress. Many people were out walking or riding bicycles. A group of teenagers played touch-football in a field, a woman jogged on a paved path with her dog alongside her, and families were having picnics in a park area.

"I hate what Bishop Prince stands for," Anthony said, "but on the flip side, so many of the people living here look perfectly happy."

"It's 'cause they don't know what goes on behind the curtain," Valdez said with a nonchalant shrug. "Most of these people don't wanna know the price they pay to live like this."

"Ignorance is bliss," Lisa said. "Give us bread and circuses, and we'll support anything."

"I wonder what they'll do when they find out the real deal," Mike said.

"They'll get over it," Valdez said. "People adapt. They always do. Till the next crackpot comes along, then they'll be standing in line to be brainwashed again."

Anthony winked at Lisa. "I think we've finally met someone who's more cynical than I am."

"That's what I was thinking," Lisa said.

"I call it as I see it, guys," Valdez said.

She braked at a four-way intersection. A shuttle bus filled to capacity rumbled past, an electronic signboard above the windshield announcing that it was bound for the Kingdom Megaplex. Anthony saw a gold geodesic dome on the horizon, which he knew from his online tour was part of the church's main sanctuary.

On their right, in the hazy distance, the bishop's mansion floated like a heavenly castle in the hills.

"Got any idea where we need to go yet?" Valdez said.

"Make a right," Anthony said as he stared at the mansion, thoughts churning.

Valdez followed his gaze. "The bishop's estate?"

"I want to see it up close. I'm curious."

"Curious, my ass," Valdez said, but she made a sharp right turn.

The road was divided by a grass median lined with red crepe myrtles, flowers waving in the breeze. They cruised past the Kingdom Academy, which accommodated grades kindergarten through twelve, a baseball field, a football stadium, and a preschool center, Kingdom Kids. Like the other buildings, all of the facilities appeared new, and were as well-designed as schools one might find in a moneyed suburb, the better to influence the children, fertile young servant minds, to feel proud of their education.

"The bishop lives near the schools," Anthony said.

"He visits them weekly," Valdez said. "Lets him keep tabs on the angels-in-waiting."

"Disgusting," Lisa said.

Once beyond the schools, woodlands bordered the road on both sides, dense with oak, elm, maple, pine. The street converged to two lanes, growing steeper as it wound through the hills, and the sidewalks vanished, too.

There was no traffic. But after about a quarter of a mile, the forest began to thin, and there was a rightward bend in the road marked by a twenty-foot-high column of stacked stone. A sign in front of the rock warned: PRIVATE PROPERTY - NO TRESPASSING.

Valdez brought the SUV to a stop before they emerged from the canopy of trees.

"This is as far as we go," she said. "Around that bend is the gate to his mansion."

"Guards?" Anthony asked.

Her gaze lacerated him. "Why do you want to know?"

"Indulge me, please," Anthony said.

"At least two at the gate," she said. "If the bishop is home, there'll be another three inside the house. His personal security detail."

"Anyone else in there?" Mike asked. "Like a maid or butler or something?"

"He's got a house staff, but they're ordinary civilians, harmless."

"So five goons," Anthony said. "Not great odds, but not impossible to handle."

"We can take 'em," Mike said.

Anthony bent to unzip his duffel bag at his feet. He removed two handguns, his Glock and his Colt revolver, to complement the Beretta he already wore in his waistband holster, and he fished out extra ammo, too.

"Whoa, you guys aren't going in there," Valdez said. She took out her cell phone. "I'm calling my team—and *we're* going in with our search warrant."

"You wait for your search warrant—we don't need one." Anthony finished holstering his guns and pocketing the extra ammo in his pouch. He turned to Lisa in the backseat. "We'll be right back, sweetheart. Keep the engine warm."

"Be careful," Lisa said. She clasped one of his hands, her eyes glistening with a mixture of worry and cautious hope. "I'll be waiting for you."

"Ready?" Anthony asked Mike. Mike had two guns slotted in his shoulder holsters, body armor protecting his chest, and a waist pouch that held plenty of ammo.

"Let's do it," Mike said.

They climbed out of the truck.

"Both of you assholes, stand down!" Valdez charged out of the SUV, phone pressed to her ear. "I'm not gonna let you screw up my investigation!"

Ignoring her, they marched in step along the side of the road. Anthony inhaled deeply of the pine-scented air. Calmness had settled over him like a coat—his heart beat at a moderate rate, his muscles were loose and relaxed, and the guns on his person felt like natural extensions of his own body.

"Hey!" Valdez shouted.

"She's plenty pissed," Mike said to Anthony. "Makes her even hotter."

"I wouldn't say that to her right now if I were you," Anthony said. "She might beat your ass like a pinata around the road."

Cursing in English and Spanish, Valdez caught up to them.

"Look, my team's on their way," she said. "ETA sixteen minutes."

"Great," Anthony said. "They'll be just in time to clean up after us."

"Jesus, Thorne." Her cheeks bloomed red. "Why are you so goddamn stubborn?"

"You must've been talking to my wife. She asks me that every day."

"Fine." She planted her fists on her waist, squinted as she surveyed the road ahead. "If you two clowns are determined to go in there, then you better let me help you."

78

Marching at a brisk pace, they neared the giant stone formation at the curve in the road. Valdez edged in front of them.

"I'm wearing the Armor of God uniform," she said. "You guys hang back and I'll take them by surprise. Be ready."

"I was born ready," Mike said.

"Never been more prepared," Anthony said, and meant it. Adrenaline buzzed through his blood, but that sense of calm remained with him, that feeling of implacable purpose. As if all his training, all the fights he'd endured, all the grief his family had suffered, had been to prepare him for this day, this moment.

"On my right-hand signal," Valdez said.

She rushed around the stone pillar. Mike and Anthony peered around the corner, watching.

"Look at her, man," Mike whispered. "I'll be damned if I don't ask her to marry me."

"Maybe you should ask her to dinner first, do things in logical order. Just a thought."

"Don't rain on the parade, AT."

Ponytail swinging, Valdez sprinted down a long, steep driveway flanked on both sides by sheer rock walls. At the end of the drive, there was a set of wide, wrought iron-gates. The entrance was fronted by a guard booth stationed atop a squat stone foundation.

Beyond the gates, nestled behind oaks and pines, the mansion stood on a sloped crest of grassy land.

At Valdez's approach, a guard in a white tracksuit emerged from the booth. He called out a greeting that Anthony could not hear. Valdez raised her right hand, as if waving.

Game time.

Anthony exploded from hiding, the wind at his back like the urging of an avenging angel. Mike brought up the rear.

Spotting them, the guard shouted, "Halt!" and started to draw his pistol, but Valdez swung her upraised hand like a hatchet and chopped it against the guy's throat. He let out a garbled scream. Whirling like a dust devil, she nailed him with a brutal roundhouse kick to his temple, and he dropped to the ground.

Another guard bounded out of the station, pistol drawn. But Anthony had been expecting him, already had his gun chambered, and squeezed off a shot. The round punched the guard in the chest and plunged him backward into the doorway almost comically, as if he were a drunk who had fallen on his butt while trying to make his way outside.

Valdez had flipped over the first guard onto his stomach and was slapping a pair of handcuffs on him. The guy's eyes were dazed, and he breathed in ragged bursts.

Anthony charged into the booth. The agent was rising on wobbly legs. Although Anthony's hollow-point round had hit him in the chest, the agents wore Kevlar vests, so the round had not penetrated his tissue, only knocked him down and temporarily stunned him.

Anthony rapped the butt of his pistol against the man's head, and the blow sent him spilling back to the floor, unconscious. He grabbed the guard's ankles and dragged him out onto the driveway, turned him face-down.

Mike used the guard's own restraints to cuff his wrists.

As they finished securing the sentry, Valdez scrambled into the booth.

"You've got about two, three minutes to get inside," she said. "After that, this area is gonna be swamped with reinforcements. We sacked these dirt bags here, but on the surveillance cameras the others will have seen what went down."

"You're staying out here?" Anthony asked.

She mashed a button on a control panel, and the motor-operated gates began to whir open.

"I've risked my job by going this far, Thorne," she said. "I've gotta hold them off here and wait for my team and our warrant. But this is only my job—it's your life, like you said."

"Thanks for everything, Valdez."

"*De nada.* Here, take one of these."

323

There were two tactical rifles stored in racks on the booth's interior wall. She strapped one over her shoulder, and offered the other one to him.

Anthony passed the gun to Mike.

"Watch my flank," Anthony said.

Mike flipped the strap over his shoulder and checked the rifle's chamber to confirm that it was loaded.

"We're good," Mike said. He blew a kiss to Valdez, turned to Anthony. "Lead on."

79

After enjoying quality time with his angel, Bishop Prince left her to shower in his private quarters. The girl was reluctant to see him go, but he counseled her that selfishness was sin, and patience was a virtue. With that, he promised to return to her soon.

The angel, of course, was still a virgin, still ripening on the vine of womanhood. He was waiting for the perfect time, enjoying the delicious heightening of intimacy, and when release arrived at last, it would be all the sweeter for his having waited.

Sometimes, he didn't wait. There were instances when his urges overwhelmed him, and he immediately took advantage of an opportunity. The thorn in his flesh resisted total control, or else it would not have been a thorn; it would have been sinful perversion, and he would have been doomed to hellfire.

But God had better things in store for his prophet. *My grace is sufficient . . .*

In his master bathroom suite, in a marble-tiled shower enclosure with twenty-four-carat gold taps, he showered. He showered after each visit with his angels, even if he hadn't removed any of his clothing during the encounter. It was, he admitted, compulsive behavior, as if he believed on some level that frequent purification could wash away the stain of what his flesh had done, as if mere bathing could dislodge the thorn.

He hummed an old Negro spiritual as he lathered soap across his lean physique. The song was a favorite of his maternal grandmother's, a knobby-knuckled woman who had picked cotton in Mississippi: *We shall overcome . . . we shall overcome . . . we shall overcome, someday . . .* When he reflected on overcoming, however, he thought about Kingdom rule vanquishing secular society once and for all.

He was in the enviable position of having the entire day to do with as he wished. Tomorrow was Sunday, and he was scheduled to give a sermon to his congregation, but he never prepared sermons in advance, and indeed, would not know the message he was to deliver until he arrived at the podium and gazed into the hungry eyes of the devoted. When you were God's sanctified instrument, you didn't require notes or planning; you needed only to listen. As the King had taught: *He that hath ears to hear, let him hear . . .*

Later that day—after another visit with Chastity—he might even see his wife and children. He hadn't seen them in over a week and was overdue for a visit, though his wife, the First Lady of the Kingdom, annoyed him with her petty gossip about the wives of church officials. His four children, who ranged between the ages of eight and seventeen, were barely tolerable, too, whiny and hopelessly spoiled by their mother.

Upon reconsideration, perhaps he wouldn't see them. He didn't want to spoil his buoyant mood.

Finished showering, he toweled dry and dressed in another suit, a custom-tailored, charcoal gray Brioni. It was a new suit. He never wore the same garments twice, and once he'd worn one, he would ship it to a star forward in the NBA, a loyal servant who tithed fifteen percent of his hefty salary to New Kingdom and believed that donning clothing worn by his bishop guaranteed his success on the basketball court.

As he was knotting his tie, someone knocked urgently at the suite's outer door.

"Yes?" he asked. Though he was in the dressing room, his baritone resonated throughout the entire master wing.

One of his bodyguards—he was loathe to think of them in those terms, but that was what they were—rushed into the dressing room, chest heaving.

"A threat has breached the front gates, sir."

"For the love of God, relax, my friend. A threat has breached the front gates of the campus?"

"The front gates of the *estate*, your holiness."

Something clutched Bishop Prince's heart. He would not dishonor himself by labeling it as fear.

"Then take care of it," Bishop Prince said. "No weapon formed against you shall prosper. Godspeed."

"Please remain confined to your suite until we've eliminated the threat, sir."

Grunting, Bishop Prince dismissed the servant with a wave. The man fled the room, barking into a hand-held radio.

Although Bishop Prince received death threats frequently, the agents of evil had never infiltrated his private residence. He had a lurking suspicion of who the adversary might be.

He went to the wall of closed-circuit televisions and jabbed a button on a remote control. The screens flickered on.

The cameras showed close-up views of the back of the house, the front, the sides, and various rooms within, including the angel's guest room. Dressed in a white leotard and tights, the girl sat on the bed, supple legs crossed Indian-style. She brushed her long, dark hair with slow strokes, a gentle smile on her face, as though she were thinking of him.

It was difficult to pull his gaze away from her. Sighing, he pressed a button on the remote to receive a different set of camera views.

More rooms were shown, but he also got a look at the property from a more distant vantage point. The camera, he recalled, was concealed in a tree near the gates.

Two men were stalking across the driveway to the house. Both had guns.

As he'd suspected, one of the men was Anthony Thorne.

His grip tightened on the remote control.

Thorne's appearance meant Noah Cutty had failed. He looked forward to reprimanding the Director for the ineptitude of his allegedly most capable soldier.

But why had Thorne come to the estate? What was he seeking? Was this an assassination attempt, or did Thorne have another purpose?

He didn't know. Although they had wanted to capture Thorne and interrogate him to learn what the Judas had given him, Thorne was proving such a formidable adversary that perhaps eliminating him immediately was the only viable alternative. Elimination was the course of action that his security detail would pursue, unless he directed them otherwise.

He decided that he would let his servants do their jobs.

"God and I tried to have mercy on you, Thorne," he said to the monitor. "But you've forced our hand."

He left the displays and went to prepare. God had promised that no weapon formed against the faithful would prosper. But God did not suffer fools lightly, either.

80

As Anthony and Mike ran across the vast front yard, keeping to the cover of the trees, someone fired several shots at them. The gunfire had the distinctive crack of a high-velocity rifle, and it originated from the house.

Anthony crouched behind an oak tree. Mike hunkered behind a pine on Anthony's left.

Anthony's heart continued to beat at a moderate pace. No reason to panic. Of course these people were going to fight back.

Lying flat on the ground, shoulder pressed against rough bark, he peered around the tree.

Seen up close, the bishop's residence was even more impressive. A majestic facade with stucco and stone accents, and limestone and fieldstone moldings and veneer. Wide covered porch marked by graceful arches supported by stone columns. Lots of dormer windows. A small turret set high on the right, domed with metal. It looked as if someone had extracted a nobleman's chateau out of the French countryside and deposited it on this hill in metro Atlanta.

The turret in particular caught his attention. The window was halfway open. The elevation and angle would have made it a perfect fighting port for a sniper.

In the infantry, they'd been trained to clear a house from the top down, to avoid using doors and windows and to create a mouse hole for your own entry with demolitions, after which you methodically worked your way down to the lower levels, always keeping the high ground above the enemy. But they lacked the manpower, resources, and time to do this one by the book.

Anthony glanced over his shoulder at Mike, and with a hand signal, indicated the gunman's probable position. Mike lifted the rifle to his shoulder, and waited.

Here we go.

Anthony broke cover and sprinted to the house. Rifle fire shattered the day, twice from the turret, once from Mike, and then the day was still.

Anthony leaped over a bed of azaleas and reached a set of long windows on the far left of the front door. He hugged the wall beside the window frame, breath whooshing through his lungs.

He hated windows. Sometimes they were booby-trapped, or at the least, your enemy had them covered and was waiting to blast you if you dared to enter through them. A cooked off hand grenade to clear the interior would have been useful right about then.

But he reminded himself that there might be innocent people inside. The bishop's servants. Had to be careful.

Mike dashed across the yard and took cover behind one of the veranda's stone columns. No one fired on him, which meant the turret sniper either had taken up another position, or been knocked out of the game entirely.

Anthony hoped for the latter. Then, the odds would be even, two-on-two.

He and Mike exchanged a quick look. Turning, Anthony fired his pistol near the bottom of the window, blowing out glass shards that clattered to the veranda floor. Keeping his head out of view from inside, he stuck his arm through the ragged hole in the pane, grabbed the bottom of the window, and raised it.

While Mike provided supporting fire, Anthony climbed inside through the window. He snatched a satiny curtain out of his face, and scanned his gun across the room.

The theme of unbridled opulence continued inside the house. It appeared to be a formal living room, huge, full of shadows. There was a vaulted ceiling, stone and plaster details, intricate crown molding, elegant arches and columns, rich marble floor. One wall featured a stone-detailed, baroque-style fireplace over twenty-feet high. All of the furniture looked to be antique.

No guards or servants were in sight. Anthony called out to Mike, "Clear," and Mike scrambled inside, the rifle hanging from his shoulder.

"Quite a crib he's got here," Mike whispered, looking around appreciatively. "I ought to pastor a church."

Presumably, with two agents left, one would probably on the lower level somewhere, and the third would surely be keeping close tabs on the bishop. The house was foreign territory, so enormous it could take time to find the room he wanted, and time was a luxury that was steadily dwindling. The FBI would be on site soon.

Anthony advanced across the living room, weaving around furniture, boots whispering across the marble. The shadowed house was as silent as a lurking beast.

On the right, an archway led to the foyer and a grand staircase. They avoided it—going there would place them in the line of fire from numerous vantage points. Instead, he traveled to the far end of the living room, where another archway beckoned into a gigantic, elliptical dining area.

The mahogany dining room table was long enough to accommodate thirty people. A crystal chandelier depended from the coffered ceiling, softly reflecting the gray daylight. Another broad archway connected the dining room to the main corridor, and ahead, a smaller doorway gave access to a butler's pantry.

Mike grabbed the back of a chair. Swinging it around, he heaved it through the archway, into the hall.

A shot rang out while the chair was in midair, puncturing the seat cushion, and giving away the gunman's position as somewhere toward the far end of the corridor. The chair slammed against the wall, splinters and cotton stuffing flying.

By then, Anthony was already on the move.

He hustled across the rest of the dining room, crossed into the butler's pantry, and rounded the corner into the kitchen. A black-haired guard was crouched behind a large granite island. He whirled at Anthony's entrance, raising a pistol, but Anthony got off a shot first. The round drilled into the man's chest, lifted him off his feet and threw him against a wooden stool.

Anthony cornered the island. The guy lay on the marble tile, a stupefied expression on his face. Not dead. Body armor had saved him, too.

Anthony pressed his boot against the man's throat. The guy blinked, gasped.

"Where's the bishop's bedroom?" Anthony asked.

Confusion swam in the guard's eyes. Anthony leveled the gun at his head. The guard's gaze honed in on the muzzle—and instantly clarified.

"You heard me loud and clear, asshole," Anthony said. "The bishop's bedroom—where is it?"

"We ain't got all day," Mike said.

The guard swallowed, made pointing motions with a trembling finger. "Up . . . upstairs."

"Where upstairs?" Anthony asked.

"E—east . . . side."

"Where's the third goon?" Mike said.

"Upstairs . . . by . . . stair . . . staircase."

"Any house servants in here?" Anthony asked.

"N-no . . ."

Anthony glanced at Mike. "KO this guy."

Mike slammed the butt of the rifle against the guard's temple, knocking him unconscious. They cuffed him and left him on the floor.

From the kitchen archway, he surveyed the main hall. Numerous doors led off the wide corridor. The grand spiral staircase was near the middle, a luxurious blend of carved stone and wrought iron.

Keeping to the far edge of the hall, they moved toward the staircase. In a cased niche on the right, Anthony spotted a portrait of Bishop Prince. Posed alone, clad in priestly vestments, the man wore a haughty expression, as if he were a conquering king.

In an alcove to the left of the stairs, there was an elevator with brushed steel doors and gold trim.

"An elevator," Mike said. "Damn, this guy's ballin' like Jay-Z."

"Some struggling single mother who believes in his ministry paid for this," Anthony said.

"And a grandmother living on a fixed income."

A hot column of anger surged up Anthony's throat, and he choked it down. He'd save his rage for the bishop.

On the panel, there were arrows to go up, or down. Anthony pressed the Up button.

The elevator chimed, a sound that would have been heard upstairs, too, and the doors slid open. He leaned inside the car and selected the button for the second level.

Machinery humming, the car began to ascend.

Mike in the lead this time, they quick-stepped to the staircase and began to ascend, too, keeping to the edge of the risers, where they would make the least amount of noise.

Anthony not only hated windows in combat situations—he hated stairs, too. It was easy to get pinned down on a staircase, easy to be surprised by the enemy, easy to get killed.

He hoped the elevator trick worked.

A few steps above Anthony, Mike rounded the corner at the same moment the elevator chimes sang, signaling the car's arrival on the second floor.

"Oh, shit . . ." Mike started, and his words were cut off by the unmistakable sound of a fierce blow, and a grunt of pain.

Anthony's heart clutched. Legs pumping, he hurried around the corner.

The elevator diversion had failed—the third bodyguard had been waiting for them. The guy, perhaps in his mid-twenties, bald-headed, well over six feet tall, so wide and muscle-bound he could've played the role of Goliath in a Biblical story re-enactment, had grabbed Mike and flung him across the floor. Mike was on his knees, spitting up blood, and the guard stood over him, about to twist the rifle strap around Mike's throat and snap his neck.

Anthony raised his gun to fire, and the agent dropped Mike and rushed him. He was snarling like a beast, absolutely fearless, and Anthony remembered what Valdez had said about Cutty, that he wasn't the only lunatic in their division. Here was another one.

Anthony shot the guy in the leg. It didn't even slow him—he was so high on adrenaline it was as though he were immune to pain. He smashed into Anthony head-on, hauled Anthony off his feet and slammed him against the wall, and Anthony's skull banged against the plaster, broke away big chips and sent stars wheeling through his vision.

"Fear the Lord!" the man bellowed, bright blood spreading across the thigh of his white tracksuit. His breath smelled, crazily, of spearmint bubble gum, and his eyes shone with manic glee. "Fear him!"

Anthony slumped to the floor on watery knees. His gun had dropped out of his hand.

The agent grabbed Anthony by the collar of his shirt and snatched him upright as easily as if Anthony were a child. He swung Anthony around and lifted him up high, above his head, like a pro wrestler posing for a promotional photo, and then he viciously body slammed Anthony onto the hard marble floor.

Anthony felt the crushing impact in the deepest core of his bone marrow. His vision wavered, head pounding.

"Praise God!" the giant zealot shouted. "He is a mighty God indeed, worthy to be praised!"

Somewhere behind him, as if from a great distance, he heard Mike shout, a familiar sound of rage. Then there was a loud smacking sound, and Mike's battle cry dropped into a gurgle of pain.

"I am the lion of the Lord!" the giant declared.

By then Anthony had regained some of his bearings. So when the Goliath bent over him, his nostrils flaring and sweat glistening on his crazed face, Anthony sprang upward and lunged for his eyes. He dug his thumbnails deep into the guy's sockets.

The guard roared in agony.

Moving fast, Anthony seized one of the guy's tree-trunk legs and drove him back toward the staircase railing. Mike had staggered upright by then, and he grabbed the guy's other leg. Together, they shoved, like buddies trying to push a car out of a ditch.

Howling, off balance, blood leaking from his injured eyes, the agent hammered them with his big fists, but they grunted, lowered their heads, and forced the man over the railing. He plunged to the marble twenty feet below, crashing against it with a wall-jarring boom. He lay lifeless on the floor like a broken doll.

Silence settled over the house again.

The back of Anthony's head throbbed painfully. He massaged the swelling knot, winced.

"You all right?" he asked Mike.

"I'm solid." Hunched over, Mike spat out a mouthful of blood. "Damn, that was one tough sonofabitch."

"Three down, one more to go." Anthony retrieved his pistol off the floor, looked toward the second-level hallway beyond the landing. "I want to handle this one alone. You understand."

"Figured you would." Mike chambered a round in his semi-auto. "I'll hold it down here."

Anthony started toward the eastern wing of the house, where he hoped to bring this to an end at last.

81

Bishop Prince did not fear Thorne. He feared no man. Only God was worthy of fear.

But, fear or not, he was prepared for Thorne.

Upon the breach of the gates, Bishop Prince had retrieved two things: his sweet angel. And a .357.

As gunfire rang out across the grounds, he'd found the girl hidden in the closet in her room, shuddering, tears glistening on her cheeks. Crooning to her, he'd picked her up and carried her out of there as easily as if she were a kitten, her arms slung around his neck, head snuggled against his chest.

He'd kissed her on her tear-damp forehead and taken her to his safe room.

The door to the chamber was concealed behind a blast-proof panel of one-way glass in the master suite. From the outside, it appeared to be a simple full-length mirror, but a corner of the bronzed frame flipped away to reveal a fingerprint scan panel. Once the mirror-door swung open, a carpeted staircase ahead descended deep beneath the ground floor of the house.

A holy man of God, the Lord's anointed prophet, had to protect himself against the machinations of Satan's minions. In the event of a kidnapping attempt, bombing, or assassination plot, the safe room would serve as a refuge against the wicked, an oasis from the damned.

The area resembled a penthouse apartment, and was as lavishly furnished as the other areas of the mansion. A back-up power generator kept the lights, closed-circuit security monitors, cable-equipped television, and appliances running. There was enough food in the pantry and freezer to sustain him for several weeks, a buried phone line to facilitate contact with the outside world, wall-panels reinforced with Kevlar—and a weapons arsenal in a steel cabinet.

From the cabinet, he'd retrieved the Smith & Wesson .357 and loaded it with frangible ammo. He returned to the top of the staircase, clasping the angel's hand, pulling her along with him.

At the threshold of the door, he stared through the window at his bedroom beyond, and waited.

Weeping softly, the girl wrapped her slender arms around his waist, clutching him as if he were the only stable anchor in the world. He stroked her silken hair.

"Hush, my angel," he said. "You are in God's unchanging hands. You are safe."

The chamber was sound-proof; there was no danger that Thorne would hear them. But her crying perturbed him, for it implied doubt in God's promise of deliverance for his servants, and such doubt was sin.

He did not harbor any doubt whatsoever. God had not appointed him as the leader of the Kingdom only to revoke the position before the work was done. The Kingdom was young yet, and he was its crown prince.

Greatness was his destiny, glory his reward.

82

. Gun drawn, Anthony moved across the long, wide, marble-tiled corridor. From outside, he heard commotion, someone barking into a megaphone.

A window was ahead, dark silky curtains admitting only a thin slice of grayish daylight. He peeled back the curtains and peered through the glass.

The FBI had arrived at the estate gates, two black Bureau utility vans and four unmarked sedans blocking the driveway. About a dozen agents were busy rounding up several Armor of God soldiers. Valdez, wearing a vest that read FBI across the back in yellow letters, was shouting orders into the megaphone.

In a few short minutes, the feds would trample inside to demand the evidence they believed he was going to find for them. He dropped the curtain, kept moving.

Past the window, a door ajar on the left claimed his attention. He nudged it open with the toe of his boot. Swept the gun from left to right. All clear.

It looked to be a girl's bedroom. Everything was white—walls, carpeting, furniture. The effect was almost blinding.

He moved inside. Across the room, the door to a walk-in closet door hung open. He went toward it.

Inside, he found schoolgirl uniforms, leotards, spandex, string bikinis. All the pieces of clothing were in sizes fit for a teenage girl.

On a shelf atop the hangers, there were jars of lubricant and bottles of scented oils.

His stomach lurched. This must have been a room in which Bishop Prince lodged his so-called angels.

Never in his life had Anthony wanted to get his hands on someone so badly. To think of what the bishop had done to his sister, to so many other young girls . . . Anthony was intoxicated with rage, could feel it blowing through him like a hot summer wind.

He backed out of the room. Around a bend in the corridor, he found a set of ornate double doors with glimmering gold hardware. The lever gave at his touch.

If Bishop Prince had been hiding in his bedroom, he would have locked the doors. He must have gone to ground in another area of the house. Such a luxuriously appointed home probably included a panic room.

Anthony pushed open the doors and scanned left to right. Clear.

The master suite was enormous, and as opulently decorated as the rest of the house. The vaulted ceiling was at least twelve feet high, and there were lots of windows, yet all of them were darkened with blinds and heavy curtains. Another set of doors led to a covered balcony.

The massive bed, a four-poster model carved from mahogany, panels inlaid with gold and diamonds, sat on a raised platform. It was larger than the ordinary king-size, to accommodate the bishop's great height, and so wide it could have comfortably slept three average-size adults. It was draped in a silk, burgundy-and-gold duvet.

As he regarded the bed, the two Bible scriptures that had led him to this room reverberated through his mind. He had mulled over them so often that he had memorized them both.

The first was from 2 Samuel, 4:7: *For when they came into the house, he lay on his bed in his bedchamber, and they smote him, and slew him, and beheaded him, and took his head, and gat them away through the plain all night.*

The second was Micah 2:1: *Woe to them that devise iniquity, and work evil upon their beds! When the morning is light, they practice it, because it is in the power of their hand.*

It was the reference to a "bed" in each respective passage that hatched the idea that had brought him there. Bishop Prince's bed. Where he devised evil works.

Where one could behead him.

Bob had selected perhaps the only location on the campus where no one would ever think to look for the evidence that could destroy the church: the place where the great man slept.

It was such an audacious plan that it *had* to be true.

Anthony approached the bed. His knees trembled so badly that he tripped on the platform steps, just managed to keep from falling. He caught a glimpse of himself in a full-length mirror across the room, and almost laughed at his clumsiness.

Sweat drenching his brow, he deliberated for a moment. Where to begin? Where could you conceal something on a bed so that even the man who slept on it every night would be unaware of its existence?

Under the mattress seemed too obvious. But how about under the bed frame . . .

He holstered his gun, and got to his knees. Starting at the footboard, he began to trace his fingers underneath the frame. The wood was smooth and cool. He moved from the footboard and over to the left side, sliding his hands all the way up to the headboard.

Come on. Please. I know you're under here.

At the headboard, he lay flat on his stomach, so he could run his fingers underneath the complete length of it. Near the center of the headboard, his right arm extended so far that his entire shoulder was wedged between the bottom panel of the frame and the marble tile, his fingertips brushed across a slight ridge.

Heart knocking, he tried to pull it away. It didn't come, so he scraped along the edges of the object. Felt like plastic. Or maybe tape.

He found the end of the strip, and carefully, peeled it off.

A small, lightweight object dropped into the palm of his hand. It felt like a flash drive.

He clenched his fingers around the item and extracted his arm from underneath the bed.

The room was full of murky shadows, but his tactile impression proved correct: it was a USB flash drive, swaddled in masking tape.

"Thank you, God," Anthony whispered.

He placed the device in his waist pouch with his extra ammo, and zipped it closed.

"So that's where the Judas concealed his betrayal," a stentorian voice boomed behind him.

Anthony spun, reaching for the gun on his hip.

Bishop Prince shot him.

83

Thorne lay sprawled and motionless beside the bed.

The revolver held loosely in his hand, Bishop Prince emerged from the doorway of the safe room.

"I ought to thank you, Thorne," he said. "You've succeeded where all of my other servants have failed."

Thorne did not respond. His eyes were shut, but it was difficult to tell if he were still breathing.

After the chest shot, he had should have expired and gone to hell where he belonged.

Beside Bishop Prince, the girl was crying again. She gripped his free hand so tightly that the blood had drained from his fingers. The violence had frightened her. Such an innocent one, she was.

He spoke a command to activate the room's recessed lights. Pulling the girl along, he advanced toward Thorne's prone body.

In the light, he saw, quite clearly, that the man wasn't breathing.

"You died as I hear your father died," Bishop Prince said. "One bullet to the chest, and his fate in hell was sealed."

Bending, Bishop Prince reached for the nylon pouch around the dead man's waist, where the sinner had pocketed the flash drive.

Like Lazarus, Thorne snapped awake.

84

Bolting upright like a coiled spring, Anthony swung his fist at Bishop Prince and connected solidly with the man's jaw. The crunch of shattering cartilage and bone was the most satisfying sound he'd ever heard in his life.

The bishop tumbled backward. An exotic-looking teenage girl at his side released a shrill scream.

Getting to his feet on wobbly legs, Anthony drew his gun.

The bishop crawled backward, gasping for air, a .357 in his grasp. His eyes were stunned, as if he'd witnessed Anthony climbing out of a grave.

"Body armor, man." Anthony tapped his chest. "You think I'm crazy?"

The bishop sneered. He hugged the girl to his side.

Then, he put the gun's muzzle against her head. She let out a thin mewl of terror.

"Take . . . care," the bishop said, words slurred by his injured jaw. "You wouldn't want me to . . . harm this sweet . . . angel."

"You wouldn't hurt her. She's one of your prized girls."

"What do I . . . care?" Bishop Prince grinned smugly. "I have hundreds . . . like . . . her."

Anthony did not lower his gun. "You're sick."

"Great men . . . of God have . . . great appetites. But . . . what would you know of that? Little men like you, weak in faith . . . nursing foolish vendettas." Bishop Prince spat blood at Anthony's feet. "You envy the rewards . . . bestowed on the anointed."

"If you're the anointed, I wouldn't want anything to do with God."

341

"God doesn't want you, either, Thorne. Neither did he want your father. Your father . . . he's burning in the hottest furnace of hell."

Anthony shot the man in the shoulder. The round knocked Bishop Prince flat onto the floor. Shrieking, the girl scrambled out of his arms.

"Leave," Anthony said to her, and nodded toward the doorway. "My friend is outside, and help is on the way. They'll take care of you. Go."

Hugging herself, sniveling, she fled out of the room. Bishop Prince called after her in a blood-choked gurgle that was a hollow imitation of his normally resonant voice, but the girl didn't look back.

Bishop Prince turned his glare on Anthony. Although his shoulder bled from the gunshot wound, defiance seethed in his eyes.

"Strike me down, Thorne," he said. "Dare to touch God's prophet, and see—"

Anthony kicked him in the ribs, cutting off his lunatic rant. The bishop winced and curled into fetal position. He coughed up blood.

Anthony placed his boot at the base of the bishop's long neck and pressed down. Wheezing for air, the bishop squirmed like an insect nailed to a board.

Millions followed this vile man. He would not have been fit to serve as the spiritual leader for a congregation of cold-blooded killers. Anthony would have taken pure pleasure from placing a bullet in his brain.

But there was something he had to know.

"Who killed my father?" Anthony asked. "You were behind it, but I want to know who pulled the trigger. I want to know who I saw at the lake."

In spite of his agony, Bishop Prince managed a cruel smile. "You . . . don't know?"

"Tell me who did it, asshole."

Malicious pleasure brightened the bishop's eyes.

"A loyal . . . servant of the kingdom."

"Tell me!"

"It could have been any . . . of my faithful servants. I command . . . legions."

"You *know* who did it." Hot tears streamed down Anthony's cheeks. "You know!"

Bishop Prince grinned, though half his face was red and swollen and blood wetted his lips.

Anthony dropped to his knees and drove the muzzle of the gun into the bishop's mouth, jammed it in so deep the bishop gagged on the steel, hands batting futilely at Anthony.

Anthony screamed at him: *"Talk, motherfucker, tell me who killed my dad, you fuckin' tell me, I'm gonna kill you, I'm gonna fuckin' kill you, you sick fuck!"*

The bishop's skin had begun to turn blue. Yet his eyes, full of secret knowledge, were mocking.

Anthony curled his finger around the trigger. Although the bishop's face was beneath him, he saw the shadowy figure darting away from the banks of the lake, and felt a rifle, not a pistol, in his own hands, felt his finger around the trigger, saw the mystery man in his sights, and all he had to do was pull the trigger and avenge his father, avenge him, do it for his family, kill him now . . .

A stern command broke through the haze: "Back off, Thorne. Hands in the air."

Anthony blinked through his tears, sucked in a hitching breath. His vision swam into focus.

Valdez was at the threshold of the suite. She was backed by several armed FBI agents. All of them aimed guns at him.

"Back off," Valdez said in a softer, yet authoritative tone. "It's over, Thorne."

Mike edged around the agents. "We did it, AT. Right?"

Anthony let go of the gun, the pistol still lodged in the bishop's throat, and raised his hands.

Face bluish, Bishop Prince snatched the gun out of his mouth. He clawed at his neck, choking and gagging, his suit jacket soggy with blood.

Anthony rose and backed away a few steps. He was aware of the balcony doors behind him.

"Arrest . . . this . . . trespasser," Bishop Prince said, spluttering. "Assaulted . . . me . . ."

Valdez glanced at the bishop as if he were pure slime. "We're arresting *you*. We've got paramedics outside who'll attend to your injuries."

"It's only a flesh wound," Anthony said. "He deserved a lot worse."

Valdez barked out a command to her team, and two square-jawed agents came forward, grabbed the bishop under the arms, and hauled him to his feet. They began to recite his Miranda rights.

"What? You can't . . . arrest *me*," Bishop Prince said. "You have no . . . evidence of anything."

"There's a white room down the hall," Anthony said. "That's where he kept 'his angels.' You guys can start searching in there—one of the victims ran out of here a few minutes ago."

"We found her downstairs," Valdez said. "We'll take good care of her and sweep every inch of this hellhole, see what else we can find."

"God will protect me from the snares of the wicked," Bishop Prince said, on the verge of babbling as agents escorted him out of the room. "He will deliver me from the hand of my oppressor. I am his anointed prophet!"

"Shut your snot-catcher," Valdez said.

"When I speak to God, I'll ask him to go easy on you unrepentant sinners," Bishop Prince said with a leer, before they led him out.

"What a freak," Mike said.

"All right, Thorne." Valdez scrutinized Anthony. "You get the goods?"

He nodded. "It was taped underneath the bed frame. A flash drive."

"Of all the freakin' places." Valdez rolled her eyes. "Well, great work. Hand it over. We'll take care of things from here."

Anthony looked from her, to Mike. Mike glanced at the balcony doors, and inclined his head almost imperceptibly.

Anthony took off running. The other agents raised their guns.

"Hold your fire!" Valdez yelled at her team. "We'll nab him at home."

Anthony kicked open the doors and raced to the edge of the covered balcony.

Outside, the clouds were breaking up, and the sun was coming out again.

85

Anthony climbed over the balcony and dropped to the ground below.

Ahead, FBI agents and an ambulance crowded the mansion's driveway. Although the agents looked at Anthony curiously as he approached, none attempted to stop him.

Valdez had granted him leave, but it would not be long before she would come calling.

Beyond the driveway, around the stone pillar, Lisa waited in the Explorer. He got inside and kissed her lustily.

"Nice to see you, too," she said. "All in one piece."

"Let's get out of here, sweetheart."

She started to twist the key in the ignition, paused. "Did you get it?"

"We'll see in a minute."

"What about Mike?"

"I'm sure he'll be hitching a ride with Valdez."

As she made a U-turn and sped away from the estate, he grabbed his notebook computer out of the duffel and powered it on. He plugged the flash drive into the USB port.

The drive contained over thirty PDF files, each titled by year; another group of files was named, "Revelation Phase 1," Revelation Phase 2" and so forth, seven phases in total.

He selected a file at random. The document was over a hundred pages long. He read the first page.

Missions Executed by the Armor of God in the Year of
Our Lord, 2009

345

Summary: 2009 saw a broad range of threats to the Kingdom, most related to our interests in new Kingdom territories across the United States. In total, 47 threats were identified, and eliminated . . .

"Well?" Lisa asked.

He skimmed a bit more. A pleasant chill skipped down his spine.

"We've got it," he said. "My God, we've got it all."

86

Back at the family home, they found Danielle on the sofa in the living room, smoking a Newport and watching television. A box of Kleenex sat on the coffee table, wads of tissue scattered around.

At their arrival, she mashed out her cigarette and stood. "What happened? You end it?"

"Lisa will tell you everything," Anthony said. He looked to the staircase. "Reuben upstairs?"

"In his room."

"Did you tell him, Danny?"

"I said I would." Sighing, she eased onto the sofa again, and lit another cigarette.

Anthony went upstairs and knocked on Reuben's door. Unlike every other time that Anthony had visited his nephew, no music pounded from inside.

"It's open," Reuben said.

Reuben lay on his back on the bed, gazing at the shadowed ceiling, hands crossed behind his head. The only light in the room issued from the computer monitor. The web browser displayed the New Kingdom Church Web site; Bishop Prince's bio filled the screen.

Anthony felt so sorry for the kid that he didn't know what to say. He pulled the desk chair over near the bed, and sat.

For a couple of minutes, neither of them spoke.

"Your mother told you about your father," Anthony finally said.

Reuben didn't look at him. "He ain't my father, man. He's just some dude who got her pregnant."

Count on a youth to get straight to the point, no chaser.

"How do you feel about it?" Anthony asked.

"The guy's a twisted motherfucker. Getting with girls younger than me? That's sick, man."

"Your mom loves you, Reuben, in spite of what happened. I love you, too. I love you like a son."

Reuben shifted to face him. He looked so much like his father that it was disconcerting, their eyes the same shade of gray. But the souls reflected within those eyes were vastly different—Reuben was a kid, and he had a good heart.

"It's kinda weird that you called that dude my father," Reuben said. " 'Cause you know, I've always sorta looked at you like you were my father, know what I mean?"

"You have?"

"Yeah, man," he said, as if the truth were obvious. "Who else I got? You've always been there for me and Mom."

"Thanks, Reuben. I needed to hear that." Anthony clapped his nephew's shoulder.

"Yo, you wanna sleep here?" Reuben sat up, examining Anthony's face. "You look like you need to crash, for real."

"In a while. I've still got some work to do. Did you finish that press release blaster?"

"Man, I was putting the finishing touches on it when that crazy dude jacked me this morning. But we could use it now, for sure. You got something you need to send out?"

Anthony held up the flash drive.

"There're some files on here that I'm going to upload to my author web site," he said. "I drafted a press release on my way here. I want to direct the media to a page on my site where they can find all the files."

"Aw, that's easy." Reuben grabbed another chair from the corner of the room and dragged it in front of the computer. "Let's do this."

87

Using the program Reuben created, Anthony sent a one-page press release to over ten thousand news and media outlets across the Internet, from CNN.com to MSNBC.com, from Reuters to The Associated Press, from *The New York Times* and *The Huffington Post* to *The Times* in London.

Although New Kingdom dispatched web crawlers that canvassed the Internet and identified damaging content, the breadth and sheer number of media sources that Anthony contacted ensured maximum damage, in minimal time. By the time the church shut down his server—if the crush of media-generated traffic didn't manage to do so—it would be too late.

"Now we need to get out of town." Anthony pushed away from the computer. "I don't think we want to be around when the reporters come. It'll be a zoo."

"Where we gonna go?" Reuben asked.

"I'm not sure. Let's go talk to the ladies of the family."

Reuben followed him downstairs. Lisa and Danielle were in the living room, Lisa relating what had happened.

Anthony started to tell them, *It's done,* when he glanced down the hallway and noticed that the door to his father's study was open.

No one ever left that door open.

Dread gathering in him, he moved down the hallway. A cool draft drifted from inside the room.

Lisa called after him, but he ignored her. He pushed open the door all the way. When he and Lisa had spoken privately in there earlier that day, he'd opened the window on the other side of the study, to let air circulate.

But he hadn't removed the screen, too. He stepped into the room.

Someone pressed a cold muzzle to the side of his head.

"Guess who?" Cutty said from the shadows behind the door.

Anthony held his breath. He didn't have any of his guns, and had taken off his body armor, too.

In his peripheral vision, it looked as if Cutty bore a silencer-equipped nine millimeter.

"Did you think I'd abandoned my mission, Thorne?" Cutty said. "I am a loyal servant of the Kingdom until the day God calls me home to glory."

"You should have run away," Anthony said quietly. "It's all over now. You'll go to prison."

"Wrong," Cutty said, and pulled the trigger.

The bullet ripped across Anthony's left shoulder, spinning him around. He crashed against his father's desk. Pens and pencils clattered onto the desktop, fell to the floor.

Never should have let my guard down, Anthony thought. *I knew this nut was still on the loose . . .*

Pain swelled across his shoulder, the bloodstain on his shirt steadily growing. He had been shot before, but those prior injuries had been only flesh wounds, and he'd recovered quickly.

This time, he wasn't sure if he'd been so lucky.

None of his family came running. The silencer had done exactly what it was designed to do.

"Heaven," Cutty said was saying. "I am going to *heaven.* You and your family are going to hell—now get up and *move.*"

Keeping the gun trained on him, Cutty grabbed his arm. His short, strong fingers dug like meat hooks into Anthony's flesh. Anthony struggled to his feet, dizziness tipping through him.

After all he had been through, fifteen agonizing years of hoping for justice, it couldn't possibly end like this, with him slaughtered in his family's home on the very day of his redemption.

Cutty pushed him through the doorway, and into the hall.

"Go to the living room," Cutty said. "I'm going to shoot your family members one at a time, and you're going to watch, and you're going to pray to God to forgive you for all the wicked acts you've done, and when I'm done with them, I'm going to finish you off."

He poked the gun against the back of Anthony's head, and Anthony began to shuffle down the carpeted hallway. Blood trickled from his fingers and dripped onto the floor as he walked past the photos of his family and the time-faded pictures of his beloved father.

No. It couldn't end like this. Not after they had suffered so much.

But he was out of options.

Reuben and Danielle were sitting together on the sofa, talking. They stopped in mid-sentence and gasped.

"Not one word or move from any of you," Cutty said. "You disobey, Thorne dies."

Both of them froze.

Where is Lisa? Anthony wondered, wildly. *Where the hell is she?*

Her purse, which had been sitting on the coffee table, was missing.

"Go sit across from your family, Thorne," Cutty said. "You'll have the front row seat as I bring God's vengeance to you heathens."

Anthony crossed the room, lowered himself slowly into the chair. Searching in the corners of his eyes for weapons, but finding nothing, dammit.

"Where is your harlot, Thorne?" Cutty asked. "I was certain that she was present."

"I am," Lisa said, from somewhere behind Cutty. "And I'm no harlot, you crazy sonofabitch."

As Cutty whirled to face her, gunfire boomed. Cutty's head snapped backward. He bounced against a wall and collapsed to the carpet in a dead heap, a bloody hole drilled through the center of his forehead.

Danielle screamed, clutched Reuben to her.

Still aiming the pistol at the fallen zealot, Lisa emerged from the shadows of the hallway. She slowly lowered the gun, staring at the man she had killed.

Anthony realized that when he had entered the study, she must have followed, suspicious, and waited in the powder room off the hall when she knew he was in trouble, waited for her shot.

He went to her. She was shaking. He carefully removed the gun from her clammy fingers.

"It's okay, baby," he said. "Everything's fine, it's over."

"He shot you," she said softly, gaping at the blood on his shirt. "Oh, my God . . ."

"I'll be okay, I think," he said. "Can someone get me a towel?"

As Reuben raced to find one, the doorbell rang.

"That'll be the FBI," Anthony said.

88

Valdez hustled inside, two agents flanking her. Mike was behind the three of them, beaming like a kid on Christmas morning, but his eyes widened when he saw Anthony pressing a blood-stained towel against his shoulder.

"Hand it over, Thorne," Valdez said, ignoring his injury. "Or else you're facing charges on all the carnage you guys left behind on the church's property."

"No need to make threats." He gave her the flash drive. He'd let her find out later that every piece of damning evidence it held had already been leaked to the media. He doubted it would hurt her case, and might even speed the process along.

She gave the device to one of her agents. He plugged it into a PDA, watched the handheld's screen for a few seconds, nodded at Valdez. "We're good."

"You guys are clear," Valdez said. "We'll clean up the collateral damage."

"Got one more piece of collateral damage waiting for you in the living room," he said. "Your old partner."

"You're shittin' me." Her eyes sharpened. "Cutty came here?"

"Who the hell do you think shot me?" Anthony said.

"Hey, sorry. We'll call our crew, get this squared away ASAP."

Anthony stepped aside, and Valdez and her agents entered the house. Reuben directed them to Cutty's corpse, which Danielle had covered with a blanket.

Mike came inside, too. He checked out Anthony's wound. "How serious is this one?"

"I think my luck's still good," he said. "It's feeling like another flesh wound."

"You better get it checked out."

Anthony nodded. "We're planning to make ourselves scarce shortly, get away for a while. You wanna come with?"

"You kiddin'?" Mike winked. "I'm hanging around—I got a date tomorrow with the senorita. We're going to the firing range."

"Lucky you," Anthony said. "Make sure I get an invite to the wedding."

"You'll get more than an invite, AT. You're gonna be the best man."

89

That evening, the media frenzy began. The expose on Bishop Prince and New Kingdom Church was leading news on all the major television and cable networks.

By then, Anthony and his family had left town. On the way, he sought medical attention at an urgent care clinic and had his gunshot wound attended to, and it was a minor injury, as he'd hoped.

Later, using an alias, they checked into a beachfront hotel in Panama City, Florida.

The staggering influx of Internet traffic shut down the server that hosted his Web site, but hundreds of news sites and blogs already had downloaded the documents and posted them on their own servers. The evidence would circulate through cyberspace indefinitely, outpacing the church's capacity—and soon, ability—to squash it.

Over the next two weeks, Bishop Emmanuel Prince was charged with several hundred counts of various federal crimes, including but not limited to extortion, blackmail, solicitation to murder, conspiracy to commit murder, conspiracy to commit terrorist acts, embezzlement, mail fraud, racketeering, child pornography, and child sexual abuse.

Several members of the bishop's inner circle stepped forward to negotiate plea deals, including the Director of the Armor of God.

Even a high-ranking Senator, a favorite for the White House in the next Presidential election, went down in flames, damned by his close association with the bishop. Numerous federal and state judges and law-enforcement officials either resigned, or tried to disavow their church ties.

The Kingdom Campus was shut down, and residents were given time to secure alternate housing, and schooling for their children. To Anthony, the sight on television of families leaving the church grounds after having invested so much of their lives in the organization was perhaps the saddest spectacle of the whole affair.

Through it all, Bishop Prince confessed to nothing and refused to cooperate. "God will deliver me from the snares of the wicked," was his consistent response to the charges. Legal pundits predicted that he would serve a life sentence at a federal prison, with no possibility of parole.

Late one night, lying in bed in their hotel room with an ocean view, Anthony said to Lisa, "You awake?"

She murmured, turned over, her face a dark oval in the blackness.

He stroked her cheek with the back of his finger. "I've been doing a lot of thinking."

"About?"

"You know. What we did."

"And?"

"I've changed my mind about something."

She traced a gentle circle across his chest. "Go on."

"I'm ready to be a father, if you're ready to be a mother," he said.

"Really?"

"I'm sorry it took me so long to come to this decision. I guess I . . . I had to go through some things first."

"What about what you'd said before, about not being able to protect a child from the world?"

"Well . . . we can't spend our lives worrying about what the world might do to us. We'll take life one day at a time—and when we have to, we'll fight." He kissed the tip of her nose. "You ready to be a mother?"

She took his hand in hers and slid it down her stomach, and lower still, to her warm center.

"I'll take that as a 'yes,' " he said, and kissed her again.

90

One weekday morning a month later, Anthony was at home, writing in his office, when a text message arrived on his new cell phone. It came from an unknown phone number—but when Anthony read the message, he immediately knew the sender's identity.

Want to chat? Come to front porch

He went upstairs and removed two ice-cold cans of Coke from the refrigerator. He took them to the veranda.

He also brought his Beretta, wearing it in a hip holster for all to see.

Bob sat in a rocking chair on the porch, legs crossed, a smart phone resting in his lap. He wore aviator sunglasses, a University of Georgia baseball cap, cargo shorts, blue flip flops, and a rumpled Hawaiian shirt. Like a professor on summer vacation.

There was no car parked in front of the house. Anthony suspected that Bob had taken care to conceal his vehicle.

Anthony settled into the chair next to him and offered him the cola. Bob took it, popped the tab, and enjoyed a long sip.

Anthony tilted his soda toward Bob's pale legs. "You need to work on your tan."

"Where I'm going, I'll have plenty of opportunity to do that." Bob grinned.

"I don't expect you'll tell me where you're going."

"Somewhere with lots of sun."

Anthony took a sip of the Coke, gazed out at the sun-splashed day.

"I'm sorry about your granddaughter, Kelley," Anthony said.

356

"I never expected it to happen." Bob's voice was bitter. "I was a fool. I thought the man understood boundaries, would never violate the blood relative of his closest associates."

"He's evil," Anthony said.

"Many of his victims went with him willingly. With others, he applied force. Kelley was one of those latter ones."

"Again, I'm sorry."

Bob stared at the soda can in his hand as if wondering how it had gotten there. "Afterward, Anthony, she couldn't handle the shame. She got her mother's prescription sleeping pills and painkillers . . ." He pushed out a ragged breath. "The church kept it out of the media, as we were expert in doing. But I wasn't the same after that."

"It finally became personal for you," Anthony said.

"After twenty years," Bob said. "I finally found myself with a conscience."

"Clever tactic, to build the coded message around her name with the anagram."

"I had to guard against the possibility that the Bible would fall into the wrong hands. If one of the Armor of God soldiers had somehow gotten it, they would have found out who Kelley was and dismissed the book as meaningless, a teenage girl marking up her study Bible."

"Why not go to the media yourself with the expose?"

"I would have been incriminating myself, Anthony. You've read the files? My name is all over them."

"You could have sent it to the media anonymously."

"That would not have been satisfactory. My point was not only to expose the bishop and the church. I wanted a shot at redemption, and I thought I could get it by letting someone else expose them—someone who's lost so much because of what I did."

Bob removed his sunglasses. He noted the gun on Anthony's hip, and anxiety glinted in his eyes.

"Galatians, chapter four, verse sixteen," Anthony said. " 'Am I therefore become your enemy, because I tell you the truth?' I figured out what you meant by that—even though in the file from fifteen years ago, you still omitted your own name as the one who killed my father."

"But you knew," he whispered.

"In the back of my mind, I think I knew from the moment you contacted me." Anthony grunted. "That didn't stop me from trying to beat the answer out of the bishop."

"I thought you might kill him. In fact, I actually hoped you would. You write those violent thrillers about that vigilante, Ghost."

"Ghost is a fictional character, Bob. Killing the bishop would've given him the easy way out. There are punishments worse than death."

"No truer words." Bob finished the cola and placed the can on the small table between the chairs. "So?"

"So, what?"

Bob glanced at the Beretta again. "What're you going to do about me?"

"I'd long vowed that when I finally came face to face with the man who killed my dad, I was going to put a bullet in his head."

Anthony drew the pistol out of the holster, and chambered a round. Bob tensed, looked ready to bolt from the porch.

For a few seconds, neither of them spoke.

"But I've since changed my mind," Anthony said.

"Thank God." Bob sighed, visibly relieved.

"I've been reading the Bible a bit lately," Anthony said. "That surprises me, really. After all the terrible things I've seen in this world, I never thought that old book had much to tell me about anything. I'm not saying I plan to start attending church anytime soon—though my wife would love that—but I've been reflecting on some things."

Bob said nothing. Waited.

"I'm going to leave you with a scripture to consider, for a change," Anthony said. "After I give it to you, I don't ever want to see you again."

Bob was quiet.

"Isaiah, chapter fifty-five, verse seven," Anthony said. " 'Let the wicked forsake his way, and the unrighteous man his thoughts: and let him return unto the Lord, and he will have mercy upon him; and to our God, for he will abundantly pardon.' "

Bob bowed his head, hands clasped as if in prayer. "I'd like to believe that, Anthony. I really would."

"Good-bye, Bob."

Bob slid on his sunglasses, and descended the veranda steps. He pushed through the front gate and ambled down the sidewalk, hands in his pockets, and soon disappeared around the corner.

Anthony sat outside for a few more minutes, sipping cola and enjoying the sunshine.

Then, he went inside and called his nephew. He had promised to take the kid fishing one day, and he intended to keep his word.

Sign up for Brandon Massey's e-Newsletter

Readers of Brandon Massey now can sign up for his free email newsletter by visiting his web site at www.brandonmassey.com. Members receive a free short story, a monthly issue, opportunities to win prizes in exclusive contests, and advance information about forthcoming books. Go online today to www.brandonmassey.com and sign up. Membership is free!

About Brandon Massey

Brandon Massey was born June 9, 1973 and grew up in Zion, Illinois. He lives with his family in Atlanta, Georgia, where he is at work on his next thriller. Visit his web site at www.brandonmassey.com for the latest news on his upcoming books.

Made in the USA
Lexington, KY
05 October 2015